Alaska Adventure Romance Collection

A Single Year In The Bush

A Summer Nanny In Fairbanks

The River Home

Homer: End Of The Road

Together In The Wild

Renee Hart

LARGE PRINT EDITION

Impassioned Romance Books

ISBN-13: 978-1537010328

ISBN-10: 1537010328

Table of Contents

A Single Year In The Bush

Description: Lauren has her dream job in Boston as a journalist with a loyal following. When she's confronted by her boyfriend's secret lover at a company party at the magazine she works at, Lauren swears off men for at least a year, maybe two or three.

Her cousin Amber invites her to share in a wilderness adventure in Alaska. She has some friends that need someone to house sit for them at their "off the grid" homestead.

Lauren decides that getting away might help her get over her broken heart. But the peace and quiet her cousin promises doesn't work out quite the way they planned.

Chapter 1

Lauren flipped through the pictures on her cell phone hitting delete time and again as old memories washed over her. She knew this was a cheesy way of rubbing salt into her wounds and that it wasn't actually helping. Tears pressed against the back of her eyelids, but she refused to give in to the emotional release of crying again. Her stuffy nose and red-rimmed eyes needed a rest anyway.

Working her way backwards over the last five years only reminded her of how much she'd invested in her dream of 'happily ever after' with Dylan. She thought it was a dream that they both shared, and had no reason to think otherwise. For goodness sake, they'd even gone out and bought some furniture together and had been looking at real estate ads for a couple of years.

The only thing that had been missing was a formal proposal, a ring to seal the deal and a date to firm up the commitment. There'd always been some rational sounding reason to put off that 'next step' in their relationship. Of course, now she was forced to admit that those reasons usually came from Dylan and she'd always gone along with his explanations. Now she wondered why that didn't send up a red flag.

A classic picture of the whole Conrad family gathered for her Grandmother's 87th birthday, with Dylan standing

right in the middle of the group, forced her to pause. She noticed her mother on the other side of him holding on to his arm with a big smile on her face as if she'd reeled in the biggest fish ever. Even her normally skeptical father had been taken in by
Dylan's well-bred mannerisms and smooth demeanor. She'd feared their reaction to Dylan's betrayal almost more than her own emotional storm.

Pictures like these couldn't simply be deleted and her photo editing skills weren't really up to the task of making him disappear. She sighed and tossed the phone off to the side. Maybe it was time for a new phone and a new laptop, a new apartment AND a new job where no one remembered the beautiful flowers that came to her desk on every romantic occasion.

Worst of all was the shame of finding out just how deep the treachery of Dylan's deception went when it was revealed in all of its gory details at an office holiday party. She knew the next 'scandal of the month' would eventually erase her infamous scene as she was confronted by the 'other woman' living in the shadows of Dylan's life, but she would always bear the scars. Conversations at the water cooler still stopped suddenly when she walked into sight and her imagination was quick to explain the reason why.

She got up and walked into the kitchen hoping to find some way to distract herself. As she scanned the empty shelves of the refrigerator, she knew it was going to take more than food to fill this void. She needed a major change in surroundings, at least for a while. Just going out to their favorite grocery store or calling for take-out was fraught with enough memory potholes to bring her down.

Lauren Conrad's lifelong dream was to write the 'great American novel', but working as a journalist allowed her to satisfy the urge to express her thoughts on a daily basis. She loved her job at the magazine and was well along the way to reaching the top of her field. She had her own by-line and a string of faithful readers that kept up with her articles in every issue.

Most of the people she'd gone to college with had given up on finding their own niche in the publishing world. It was a tough field with a lot of competition. She was happy with her small success, well, at least she had been, up until now.

The sudden ringing of her cell phone caused her to freeze in mid-step. Suspended in the short distance from the kitchen and the living room, her mind raced with a dozen reasons for a call at this late hour. Concern for her family finally overcame all other thoughts and she hurried to dig the phone out from between the couch cushions. The sight of her cousin's goofy face under a pair of moose antlers almost brought a smile to her face as she scrambled to answer before it slipped to voice mail.

Amber's voice burst out of the speaker with all of her usual energy and enthusiasm and Lauren barely managed a mumbled 'hello' before she was overwhelmed with a surge of information. Amber talked for three minutes before she stopped long enough to even check if she had an audience.

"Lauren, Lauren. Are you there? Are you listening to me?"

"Yes, darling, I'm here, but you are aware that it's two o'clock in the morning here?" Lauren asked with a half-smile in her voice.

Amber paused for a moment to consider the time before she launched into another burst of chatter that ran together into an indecipherable mess to Lauren's sleep-deprived brain. She managed another three or four minutes of ongoing dialogue before stopping to ask a question. Lauren's mind drifted as her cousin talked about her latest scheme, something about friends that needed help with something.

Amber was Lauren's younger cousin by only three months. The two of them had spent their summers together at their grandparent's farm. When their grandfather's death forced their grandmother to give up the farm, she'd moved closer to Lauren's parents in the city. The two girls continued to spend their summers with her there until they both went to college and eventually in their own separate ways.

Amber was currently living out her latest adventure in Alaska and every phone call was a riveting tale of close encounters with wild animals and other harrowing exploits. Lauren envied her cousin's free-spirit and often wondered if she'd somehow missed out by jumping into her career right out of college. She'd forgone adventures for a chance to get on that first rung of the corporate ladder.

Amber didn't have the pile of worries that came with maintaining a full-time job and the other responsibilities that were included in having that kind of life. She lived season to season and adapted to whatever challenges came her way with a carefree attitude. The men in her life seemed to change with the seasons and moving on never seemed to bother her. It was just part of her adventure.

'She also doesn't have a broken heart or broken dreams', Lauren thought with a sigh. Her thoughts were interrupted by Amber's sudden silence as she waited for an answer to her question.

"I'm sorry, Amber. What was your question?" Lauren asked.

"I wanted to know, what do you think about my idea?" Amber huffed impatiently. "Are you ready to take some time off and have an adventure of your own yet, or not?"

Lauren's mind reeled at the thought that perhaps this call was the answer to her prayers and maybe this was the fork in the road that she desperately needed. She had absolutely no idea what Amber had proposed or even what it would require of her if she said yes, but the desire to say yes was far stronger than anything resembling her usual common sense.

Later she would attribute this lapse in judgment to a lack of chocolate or simply sleep deprivation, but right now, she was seeing a life line being extended to her. Everything in her shouted out to grab hold and hang on. She knew Amber would never put her into danger or compromise her safety in any way and letting go of her fears might get her back on track in her own life. Casting aside every consideration, she said the one word that would change everything.... "Yes".

Chapter 2

The next few weeks kept Lauren too busy to consider the magnitude of the commitment she'd made to Amber. Moving to Alaska from Boston was quite a task, even if it was only for a year. The list of things she needed to do was long enough, but she relished the distraction of it all.

Once she got over the shock of what she'd agreed to, her one saving thought was that somehow, some 'thing' would cause everything to fall apart and she wouldn't have to actually follow through on her word.

Arranging a leave of absence from her job went smoothly enough, much to her surprise. Her editor was very supportive about her writers taking sabbaticals to refresh their creativity.

Lauren's request was met with a level of enthusiasm that shook her confidence a bit. When she asked her boss for the time off she answered "Why absolutely! Take all the time you need."

She figured it was common enough to consider oneself to be irreplaceable, but the truth is that no one really carries that much weight. Her 'loyal' readers would simply move on and find another 'favorite' when she was gone.

Subletting her apartment for a year was another hurdle to be faced. She didn't want to totally give it up. She'd stumbled into this place right out of college and her memories here went back pre-Dylan by more than a few years. It would be nearly impossible to find another apartment in this city with the right location and rent control.

She posted a notice about wanting to sublet on the bulletin board at work and within an hour, she had three interested parties vying for her place. She quickly made a choice and worked out the details.

Packing up her personal belongings and putting them into storage took a while longer, but she used it as an opportunity to purge everything that tied back to 'that man'. Hauling it all to the nearest thrift shop and donating it for a 'good cause' gave her satisfaction. It felt good to erase those traces of his presence from her life.

Wiping the dust from her hands as she turned in the last box, she vowed to swear off men for at least a year, maybe two or three.

Her wilderness adventure far from the dating scene, would give her time to reassess her expectations and hopes for love and marriage.

If she'd understood her cousin's description of their location for the next year, there was little chance of romance with their nearest neighbors being bear, moose and wolves. She could focus on her writing and hone her survival skills at the same time, if she had any survival skills beyond finding the best latte in town.

Her final loose end was breaking the news to her

parents. She'd managed to bring them down gently in regards to her breakup with Dylan, but put off telling them about Alaska for as long as possible.

Family gatherings usually included talk about Amber's gypsy lifestyle and lack of direction. Her parents were always pointing out to her how proud they were of her accomplishments at the magazine. She was sure they wouldn't approve of her pulling up roots and running off to the wilderness to join her cousin.

She decided to call her grandmother to enlist support for her plan.

"Grandma, guess what? I'm going on an adventure with Amber. We'll be house sitting for some friends of hers who have a farm in the Alaskan bush. I'll be gone for a whole year."

"Wonderful, dear. I'll miss you, but you girls will have the time of your life. I'm thrilled to hear you're breaking out of your routine to spend time in nature. It sounds like something I would have loved to do when I was your age."

Her grandmother was a strong, independent woman that had chosen her own path in life. She'd been a powerful influence for Lauren and Amber. She'd always encouraged them to find their own way.

"Have you told your parents yet?" she asked.

"No, not yet. I'd like you to come to dinner when I break the news to them. If you're there to support me, maybe they won't freak out quite as much."

"Of course dear. I'm always happy to be your buffer," her grandmother joked.

***

Now it was time to face her parents and tell them the news. She arranged a nice, quiet dinner for the four of them at a nearby restaurant. She knew it was a bit cheap to use public decorum as a way of avoiding an emotional scene, but her mother was prone to histrionics when things weren't to her liking. Her father was much more circumspect in his responses so she wasn't worried about his reaction.

Their salads were on the table and Lauren was in the middle of taking a deep breath to begin her speech when her mother interrupted.

"So, Sweetheart, are you going to tell us what this is all about, or do we have to wait until after dessert? The suspense is killing me," her mother quipped with a smile.

Lauren tried to cover up her nervousness with a big gulp of water, but only succeeded in watering down the front of her blouse. As everyone scrambled for napkins, Lauren snuck a look at her grandmother who was calmly cutting up her salad, seemingly unaware of the sudden tension at the table. Clearly, the ball was in Lauren's court.

"Well, Mom, Dad....," Lauren stammered, suddenly at a loss for words.

Her mind frantically sorted through all of the opening lines she'd rehearsed, but nothing was working. As a writer, words were her talent, but dialogue had never been her strong suit. She cast a look around the restaurant hoping for some other distraction, but the waiter was busy at another table and there was no help to be found.

"So, when are you leaving for Alaska?" her grandmother asked with a big grin.

The sudden silence at their table was broken only by the sound of her grandmother taking a large bite of her salad and chewing it loudly. Lauren's parents were both staring at their daughter in amazement. It couldn't have been more startling if she'd announced that she'd been selected to go to the moon as the first journalist ever.

Her father reached over and picked up his fork and began eating his own salad. His wife looked at him in astonishment and then turned back to her daughter.

"Just what does she mean, 'when are you leaving for Alaska?'," her mother asked tersely. Her lower lip trembled, but she managed to stay calm.

Lauren figured there wasn't much point in dragging this out or trying to soften the blow so she quickly laid out Amber's plan for the next year.

"We'll be house sitting and taking care of some animals for Amber's friends." she explained. "I need to get away from Boston for a while after what happened with Dylan," she tried to plead her case while heading off any drama

Renee Hart

about her decision. "I've always wanted time to write my novel, and this'll be the perfect opportunity."

Her father and grandmother kept nodding in all the right places while her mother sat there as if frozen in her chair.

Lauren couldn't read the look on her face, nor anticipate her next response. She was completely unprepared when it came.

"That sounds like a wonderful plan, Sweetheart," her mother began. "I'm so happy that you're finally going to have an adventure or two of your very own."

That said, she picked up her fork and began to eat, leaving Lauren with a look of complete astonishment. She didn't even blink when her grandmother snuck her a look and gave her a wink and a grin. It appeared that all of the hurdles were behind her and Alaska lay ahead.

Chapter 3

Lauren's plane landed in Anchorage with a bump and a bang as an overhead bin sprang open dumping its contents into the empty seat below. Fortunately, all of the surrounding passengers escaped injury and everyone had a laugh at the relief of finally being back on the ground. This was the not the final leg in Lauren's journey, but it was the last leg she'd travel in a 'real' airplane. From here on, she would be relying on the wilderness honed skills of 'bush' pilots, according to her cousin, Amber.

Lauren didn't want to think about that as flying had never been one of her favorite modes of transportation. She was happy to gather her things and get off of this plane alive. The creaks and groans of the aging plane had given her fits all the way from Seattle. She was sure it was going to fall apart and drop them in a fiery death spiral at any given moment.

Lauren wasn't too surprised to find the modern airport in Anchorage rivaled the ones she was used to on the East coast. Although it was barely spring, the arrival gates were bustling with the early seasonal workers and a few tourists hoping to get ahead of the summer influx.

Lauren felt a little bit smug that she was more than a tourist in the largest state in the nation. She was actually going to live here for an entire year. Just the thought of it gave her the shivers from excitement.

"Lauren, over here!" The shout of joy broke into her thoughts as she recognized her cousin's voice calling to her from across the way. Amber had never cared about making a scene in public. Lauren smiled as she spotted her cousin running towards her waving her hands in the air. Dropping her bags, she steeled herself to be overwhelmed. Amber didn't disappoint her, turning their reunion into a full-on event.

"I can't believe it's been ten years since I've seen you!" Lauren said, staring at the beautiful woman standing before her. Gone were the two young girls that had grown up together, and gone were the college students that had shared a dorm room. Their twenties had been spent a continent apart with a smattering of e-mails and phone calls holding them together.

Now that they were both in their early thirties, Lauren wondered how their new relationship would reflect the missing years and life experiences between them. Amber wasted no time, grabbing the two closest bags and started to hustle her out of the airport.

"Come on. We've got to hurry. I'm double-parked outside and they can get ugly about that here," she said a little frantically.

She led the way out through a side door to a beat-up old pick-up truck waiting by the curb. Effortlessly tossing the bags into the back of the truck she ran around and jumped in the driver's side while Lauren struggled to follow her lead and heave the rest of her luggage over the rusty side of the truck without getting her clothes dirty.

Amber didn't notice her cousin's reluctance to climb up into the torn and dirty seat in her stylish skirt and white blouse. She was busy grinding the starter and looking around for the closest exit. The truck roared to life and she slammed it into gear just as Lauren managed to pull the bulky door closed. She fell back into the seat and nearly screamed as a pile of fur let out a yelp and jumped up towards her. The dog stared at her in surprise and then turned round and curled back up on the seat.

"Never mind her," she said. "Maggie wouldn't hurt a fly and she's not much of a people dog. It'll take her a while to get used to you, but she will."

Lauren breathlessly watched her cousin dodge traffic and tear around corners. Amber still drove like a teenager on a joy ride. She didn't relax her grip on the edge of the seat until they'd screeched to a halt in front of an old warehouse on the outskirts of the city.

"We're going to be staying here for a couple of days until my boss, Carson, gets back from his run. That'll give us some time to get you outfitted for winter and order some supplies," Amber said as she jumped out of the truck. "Then he'll fly us up to the homestead so we can get acclimated before the Dorman's head off to Greenland. They'll teach us everything we need to know in the next few weeks before they leave. I sure hope you're ready for this."

This last part she said with a dubious look at Lauren's high heels and fancy skirt. "I do hope you've brought some jeans..."

Lauren laughed at the look on her cousin' face. "Yes, I brought jeans. I'm so happy to be here with you!"

It was clear they had some catching up to do and she was looking forward to it. Giving her cousin a hug, she shook off her jet lag and took a deep breath of the cleanest air she'd ever breathed.

The mountains seemed close enough to touch and the wilderness seemed to press in along the edges of the airfield that ran next to the building. She half expected a moose or a bear to step out of the trees and wave hello. She was in Alaska!

Chapter 4

The next couple of days were a flurry of shopping and packing as Amber explained that her job with Carson involved scheduling his flights and deliveries for several remote homesteads on his route. She explained how she and Carson were often the only link these people had with the outside world during the long, dark winter months. They handled everything from food deliveries to transporting someone with a medical emergency, including women about to give birth.

It was through her job that this opportunity came for her and Lauren. One of Carson's clients needed someone to 'house-sit' for their very remote homestead. The couple that owned the homestead were going to spend a year in Greenland to continue their genetic study of the caribou's DNA pools and compare their findings with their research here in Alaska.

Carson wasn't happy about losing his personal secretary/receptionist/general manager, but he was resigned to her need for a change. Amber didn't explain any more than that and Lauren sensed it was better not to ask.

***

Renee Hart

As they drove to Wasilla on yet another shopping expedition, Lauren marveled at the juxtaposition of wilderness with stores and strip malls. Moose and bear walked the streets of these cities as freely as any stray dog in Boston. Wiping the sweat from the back of her neck, Lauren commented on how hot it was for Alaska. Amber laughed and said that anytime you didn't like the weather, just wait a little while. It would change and not always for the better.

Suddenly she jammed on the brakes and swung into the parking lot of a little strip mall. Lauren looked for a clue to her cousin's sudden move, but didn't see what had caught her eye. Pulling up next to a panel van with a hand-lettered sign, Amber threw the truck into park and jumped out.

"Come on! We've got to get you a pair of bunny boots," she said as she disappeared around the corner of the truck.

Sure enough, the sign on the truck said, "BUNNY BOOTS". She went to the back of the van just as the back door slid up and her cousin shoved a bulbous pair of hideous white boots at her.

"Try them on," she ordered Lauren. "Make sure you've got plenty of wiggle room for a pair of wool socks."

Lauren couldn't believe the size and weight of the boots her cousin handed her and wondered how she was even going to be able to walk in these monstrosities.

"Are you kidding?" she asked. "Will I really need

these?"

"*These* will keep your little tootsies toasty warm at 50 below and then you'll thank me for making you buy them," Amber replied with a grin.

Lauren groaned at the thought of going outside at 50 below, but figured this was one area that she'd best leave to her cousin's expertise. Shoving her feet into the boots, she pretended she was modeling a pair of fancy shoes. Her silliness made both women giggle.

The bored 'bunny boots' vendor took her $100 bill with barely a glance and closed the back of the van before disappearing around the corner. Lauren heaved her boots into the back of the pickup with a sigh. Money was flying out of her wallet a lot faster than she'd planned. She pictured herself sitting outside a shopping mall with a sign asking for donations to get home when all this was over.

The two women finished their shopping and headed back to their warehouse lodgings.
Carson was flying in the next morning with Amber's replacement and within the next couple of days, they'd be heading out into the wilderness to begin their training program.

***

The next morning, Lauren was the first one up and she made a pot of coffee before stepping outside to see what kind of day it was. She was surprised and delighted to find a mama moose with a cute little calf standing near the pick-up. She pulled out her cell phone hoping to snap a close-up to send to her grandmother.

The moose eyed her warily, but didn't seem to mind her presence. She took a couple of steps closer hoping to capture the baby's cute face. She failed to notice the mama's ears falling back and the look in her eye.

Suddenly, a strong arm came around her waist and jerked her backwards towards the door. At the same time, the mama moose lunged towards her with definite intent. Lauren gasped as she was pulled back into the building and the door was slammed shut. The thud of both hooves against the side of the door literally shook the building. Lauren was stunned by force of the blow and struggled to catch her breath and her composure.

Turning to face her rescuer, she found herself looking up into the bluest eyes she'd ever seen close up. The anger mixed with concern on the handsome face was arresting under the sleep-mussed blond hair, and Lauren didn't know whether to laugh or cry after her escape from disaster.

Carson was upset with her ignorance, but he tempered his response with a sudden awareness of her soft blue eyes and silky brown hair. He still felt her warmth against him as he'd pulled her inside. He swallowed hard to calm himself before he spoke.

"Do you have any idea how dangerous that is?" he asked through clenched teeth. "Never! Never approach a wild animal with their young. A mother moose can stomp you clear to China if you make her mad enough."

"I didn't realize…I just wanted a picture of the baby….it was so cute," Lauren faltered.

"What happened?" Amber asked as she came around the corner with a cup of coffee in her hand.

"Your 'cheechako' cousin here just tried to get a close-up of a *cute* little baby moose," Carson answered. "Didn't you explain anything to her about the local wildlife?"

Amber looked annoyed and concerned at the same time as she reached out to pull Lauren away from Carson's exasperation.

"There hasn't been any time for that. We've been running around trying to take care of your business," she retorted. "Come on, Cuz. Let's get you a fresh cup of coffee. You look like you need another cup."

Lauren realized that her first cup of coffee was soaking the leg of her jeans as she followed Amber.

She had no idea where her cup or her phone had ended up. Maybe the mama moose had stomped them to China. Somehow, she managed to keep her composure as she went to the little bedroom to change her jeans. Her thoughts kept slipping back to blue eyes and tousled blond hair. Then she came to her senses and reminded herself why she'd come to Alaska.

Chapter 5

Amber was kept busy for the next two days training her replacement on a million little details that existed only in her head. She'd been running Carson's operation for five years and documentation was the last thing that got any attention. It was a 'fly by the seat of the pants' enterprise that only worked because the need was far greater than the inept way that Carson ran his business.

Lauren busied herself with sorting through her wardrobe and taking inventory of her cosmetics and personal toiletries. There wasn't going to be any shopping for such things once they left the city and she wasn't sure what she really needed out in the wilderness.

She realized that most of her clothes would be of little use on the homestead and packed up any dresses and skirts to lighten her load.

"You can store whatever you don't need here in the warehouse. There's plenty of extra space," Amber assured her.

She'd recovered her cell phone which the moose had ignored in her haste to get her baby away Lauren's ignorant blunder. The pictures actually turned out great and her grandmother and parents enjoyed her e-mails explaining her close encounter.

Carson was away much of the time on business, but his

anger had faded that same day he'd rescued her, and he was quite charming towards her after that. She couldn't quite put her finger on it, but there was a definite tension in the air between Amber and him. She suspected there was a story, but no one was talking.

If she hadn't sworn off men, Carson might have held a little more interest to her....if.

***

The day finally arrived for the two women to travel north to the homestead. Amber had already explained that there were no roads that went to the area. The only way in or out was by plane or dogsled.

"The homestead is located between two major wildlife refuges on the migratory path of the caribou. It's Carson's last stop on his north run before he heads back here. He'll only come once a month, weather permitting," explained Amber. "Carson usually stays overnight on his runs before heading back south," she mentioned with a sly look at her cousin.

In addition to their own research, the Dorman's provided a way station with food and housing for anyone passing through the area, so the occasional visitors were to be expected. There were geologists that monitored the volcanic activity and forestry teams stopping by every now and then.

They also had a couple of neighbors they traded with for

supplies. They always relied on each other in times of trouble.

The station was off-the-grid and self-sufficient, most of the time.

"Believe me Cuz, it's not going to be boring at all," Amber assured Lauren.

Lauren listened to everything her cousin said with trepidation. Her encounter with the moose had made her painfully aware of her ignorance of wilderness life. God forbid she came face to face with a bear or a wolf.

The long, cold darkness of winter also worried her and she was starting to wonder what she'd gotten herself into. She was a city girl, 'a cheechako', the Alaskan term for someone ignorant about life on the tundra. She knew she wasn't prepared for what lay ahead.

The last thing she did before they left was to call her grandmother who always supported her.

"Grandma, we're getting ready to take off to fly to the homestead. Amber's boss is taking us there in a tiny plane. I'm a little nervous about being so far away from everything," Lauren said with a quivering voice.

"It sounds exciting, dear. Just think about all of the new experiences you're going to have. Go and enjoy your time with Amber, but please be careful dear. I'll be here, waiting to hear all about it when you get back."

Talking to her grandmother gave her some confidence to face what lay ahead.

Chapter 6

As Lauren squeezed into the tiny seat behind Carson's, she looked around the heavily laden plane with dread. Every bit of available space was packed with stuff. Her seat was the only clear area in the back and even Maggie had to squeeze in next to her as there was no room in the co-pilot's seat where Amber was sitting. The dog looked nonchalant and didn't seem to mind sharing space with Lauren.

Carson was running through his pre-flight checklist and Amber was giving last minute advice to her replacement on her cell phone. The woman sounded panicked and Lauren felt sorry for her. Two days clearly wasn't enough time to learn everything that Amber had spent years working out on her boss's behalf.

Lauren wondered who would fold first, Amber's replacement or herself. A year was starting to seem like a very long time.

Lauren wriggled into her seatbelt and felt the plane shudder as Carson fired up the engine. The rough sound soon smoothed out as the Cessna's engine warmed up, but the roar was so loud that Lauren felt sick. She knew she wasn't going to enjoy this flight at all.

As they taxied to the end of the pavement she had a strong urge to demand to be let out. The words were actually on her lips when Carson hit the throttle and the heavy plane waddled down the runway. The noise from the plane would have drowned her out anyway.

Amber turned and smiled at the look on her face and from somewhere deep inside, Lauren's courage rose up and answered the unspoken dare the two of them had always used to push each other beyond their fears.

Just then the plane lifted into the air and the tops of the trees passed underneath the wings. Lauren squeezed her eyes shut and threw up a quick prayer. This wasn't the way she wanted her life to end.

As they flew along, a break in the clouds to the east revealed Mount Denali, and Lauren gasped at the sight. The view from the Cessna was astounding.

The native Athabascan's called the mountain 'Denali', which meant 'Great One". Her cell phone camera couldn't capture the magnitude of the view so she just stared at the vista trying to imprint this image on her mind forever. All of her fears and worries melted away right then through the magic of the majestic mountain.

Their flight lasted a few hours and Lauren marveled at the passing scenery. All signs of human habitation fell away the longer they flew and soon there was nothing but untouched wilderness.

The thick forests and sparkling lakes passed underneath them, along with meandering rivers and snow-capped mountains. Lauren was impressed with Carson's knowledge and experience. It looked like a blur of wilderness to her, but he kept the plane pointed in a northeasterly direction that brought them to their destination.

As he circled the private airstrip, Lauren noticed the lack of pavement. There was only a cleared area of grassy dirt with a windsock marking one end. As she looked at the makeshift runway she understood why they're called "bush pilots". She braced herself for the landing and tried not to be nervous.

Carson landed the Cessna with barely a bounce. He was clearly a skilled bush pilot. Lauren was eager to get out of the plane as they taxied over to the side, and Maggie showed her enthusiasm by wagging her tail.

***

The Dorman's had been waiting at the end of the runway in an old pick-up truck. Lauren was surprised as she knew there were no roads into this area. There was a lot to learn about the wilderness and the people that lived in it. They found ways to accomplish things far beyond her expectations.

All of their attention was focused on unloading the plane for the next half hour. Introductions were kept to a minimum as the five of them hurried to get everything packed into the back of the pickup truck. There was far more than would fit, but the arrival of another couple from the other end of the runway on their ATV subtracted several boxes from the load.

Lauren didn't have a chance to meet the other couple, but she did notice they were native Alaskans and had very little to say to anyone. When she ventured a 'hello' to them, the woman just stared back at her and the man grunted in response. They finished their business with Carson and sped off in the direction from which they'd come without another word.

There was one final package on the plane and no room for the five of them in the pickup so she and Carson were *volunteered* to walk along the path back to the house. Amber cast a worried look before she climbed into the truck with the others.

Just as the truck pulled away, an imposing man on a tall black horse rode out of the trees on the other side of the clearing. Carson didn't appear to be surprised so Lauren guessed the man had come for the package he was holding.

As the rider drew near, Lauren saw a large wolf trotting alongside the horse. Apparently it was accompanying them, as neither the horse nor the rider seemed concerned about it. She stared at the strikingly handsome man riding towards them with excitement and intrigue. Dusk had fallen and it was hard to make out his features, but he was clearly striking a primal chord in her.

As he rode up to the plane, he reined in the horse

abruptly causing it to rear slightly on its hind legs. The wolf continued on past them and disappeared into the trees. The man quickly dismounted and walked towards them. Lauren suppressed the urge to duck in behind Carson and forced herself to stand at her full height.

As the two men greeted each other, Lauren carefully took in the appearance of her new neighbor.

His dark hair and dark eyes clearly betrayed his Russian bloodline and his strong jaw and chiseled face were right out of a Tolstoy novel. He could be the leading man in any good movie. The contrast between him and Carson was especially striking and the two men were nearly opposite ends of the same spectrum of handsome.

His voice rumbled from deep in his chest and his accent prevented her from comprehending anything he was saying, so she just stared in fascination. Amber was going to be sorry she'd taken that ride in the truck.

Quickly concluding their business, the man turned to get back on his horse without even acknowledging her presence. She wanted to be offended, but as he gathered the reins and began to turn away, he paused ever so briefly and stared right at her. She felt his look go through her skin and somehow she felt like he had looked right into her soul and knew everything about her. She felt her knees going weak as he broke off his gaze and gave a shrill whistle. The horse almost seemed to leap forward with an eagerness to be off, and the wolf was at their side in an instant. The three of them disappeared into the trees before she realized that she'd been holding her breath.

She turned to find Carson watching her with an amused look on his face. She blushed to the roots of her hair and beyond. He reached out his hand and gently touched her cheek with his thumb. Everything in her wanted to be touched as she felt overwhelmed by longing.

"Be careful, Cheechako. Some things up here aren't meant to be tamed."

Carson broke the spell with a laugh as he turned to secure his firearm into his shoulder holster and, in that instant, she felt young and foolish and lost in a world that she knew nothing about. Trying to cover her embarrassment, she quickly gathered up her things and waited for him to finish his tasks.

"So, are you going to tell me," she asked hesitantly. "Who was that?"

"That was Sergei Jameson, your closest neighbor," Carson stated with a hint of his usual sarcasm. "Son of an American soldier and a Russian bride and a mystery beyond those facts. The only other thing I know about him is that he raises some of the best sled dogs in Alaska and has a team that runs the Iditarod every year and always seems to finish somewhere in the middle of the pack. You'll be seeing him again. He's also in charge of maintenance for the Dorman's."

Lauren listened to this information with great interest.

It was clear that her resolve to avoid men for at least a year was facing some unexpected challenges. So much for a wilderness inhabited by bears, wolves and moose. There were clearly even greater dangers lying in wait out here.

The two of them headed down the path towards the homestead without another word. As the trees closed in around them, Lauren edged a bit closer to Carson. She wasn't sure what was lurking in the thick underbrush. Her ears strained to catch the sound of anything moving, but the silence was complete.

Carson walked along as if he was taking a stroll through a city park. He didn't seem to fear anything as far as Lauren could see. She raised her chin and marched along behind him towards her new home, well, at least for the next year.

Renee Hart

Chapter 7

The next few weeks passed in a blur of activity as the Dorman's tried to teach the two women everything they'd need to know to make it through the winter so far out in the bush. The buildings were heated with a complex system powered by geothermal energy. It didn't require much from them and Sergei handled the more technical details, but there were still things for them to learn.

The electrical power was provided by a combination of solar panels and a wind turbine with battery back-up. The solar wouldn't provide much energy during the long, dark days of winter, but the wind was pretty constant. The Dorman's assured them that there would be enough to meet their needs if they were careful to match their peak usage to the times of maximum production. Sergei was also the expert in maintaining these systems.

Lauren was the first to catch on to how all of this worked, so she took the lead in managing the household. There was bread to be baked and meals to be prepared, both for themselves and the occasional visitors.

The greenhouse and garden area were already in production and provided an abundant crop of a surprising variety of salad greens, squash, potatoes and other vegetables throughout the summer. Winter vegetables were stored in a root cellar under the main house.

Amber found her niche out in the barn as she learned how to care for the chickens and the goats. Eggs had to be collected daily and the goats were milked in the morning and the evening. There was an abundance of both and the excess was traded for meat and other items.

Mrs. Dorman showed them how to make goat cheese and soap for trade also. There was always a demand for good homemade soap.

Two dogs kept watch over the homestead and easily kept the larger animals away from the house. They were Anatolian Shepherds bred for protecting herds and well-used to the extremely cold weather. Their thick creamy colored coats and imposing size made them a sharp contrast to Maggie's ragtag fur bag look but it only took a few sniffs for the three dogs to become fast friends. It was amusing to see the three of them running across the clearing, as Maggie was clearly no match for her new friends.

Both women fell in love with the three horses that roamed the homestead as freely as if they were pets. When anyone would step outside, at least one horse would meander over to investigate and say hello. Everyone carried sugar cubes or carrot sticks in their pockets for such occasions and the horses were quick to claim their treats. The Dorman's explained how the horses came from Sergei's breeding stock and that one of the mares was the dam to the black horse that he usually rode. When they'd gotten too old to continue breeding, he liked to retire them to homesteads where they had an easier life.

The Percheron's were used to hauling logs or the hay wagon and didn't mind being ridden. Even Lauren learned to saddle them up for a quick ride around the clearing or out to the airstrip. She rarely ventured beyond these areas. These two horses were named Daisy and Petunia. Daisy was Lauren's personal favorite.

Amber was a lot more adventurous and had learned the paths leading to all of their neighbors and to the hot springs just to the south of their place. She liked to ride Petunia, and the two of them soon became good friends. It wasn't long before Amber didn't even need a saddle or a bridle for a quick ride. She'd just hop up on Petunia's back and the two of them would stroll off.

"Be careful not to go farther out into the wilderness on the Percheron's without a gun and a clear idea of where you're going. A bear can overtake a horse on a short run," Mr. Dorman told Amber and Lauren. His words convinced Lauren to stay close to the homestead.

The third horse was far more suited for longer jaunts into the wilderness. His name was Trace and he was younger and stronger than the Percheron's. He had a special talent that the Percheron's didn't have. The Russian Draft horse was the only one that could get someone back home in the dark or a snowstorm on his own. The only catch was that you had to put your trust in him completely.

Lauren snickered when Mr. Dorman told them that.

It's going to be a long time before I put my trust in another male, horse or man, she thought.

***

It was time for the Dorman's to head off on their own adventure as it was almost summer.

"Don't worry about a thing," Amber said to calm them. "We're both ready to take care of the homestead, and we've always got the neighbors to call on if anything happens."

The Dorman's hoped for the best as they faced their own challenges in Greenland.

As they waited for Carson's return, last minute instructions and wilderness wisdom flew around the dinner table. The one thing that wasn't mentioned as often was winter when everything would change. When the subject came up, the Dorman's often passed a worried look between themselves.

Amber was already used to the harshness of an Alaskan winter, but nothing they could say would prepare Lauren for what was coming.

***

Carson arrived mid-afternoon and the four of them

piled into the pick-up where the Dorman's belongings were already packed. He wasn't going to be staying overnight as there was more than enough daylight to make the return trip. They reached the airstrip at the same time as their neighbors and everyone converged on the plane.

Lauren caught the look on her cousin's face as she got her first glimpse of Sergei riding his tall black horse. He looked just as imposing as the first time, but today, he appeared more relaxed as he literally danced his horse across the clearing.

The magnificent black stallion tossed his head playfully as Sergei urged him through a series of moves fit for a parade. The two of them were in sync both in mind and body, and horse and rider moved as if they were one being. Everyone stopped to watch their display of horsemanship.

Lauren was surprised to see that besides Carson there were two men standing next to the plane. They didn't know that they were to have visitors this early in the season, but it was to be expected as communications were minimal out here. The three men were watching the equestrian show, but turned to them as they piled out of the pickup.

The Dorman's made introductions all around as their neighbors gathered around the plane. Kuzih and Nasnan TwoRivers, the Athabascan couple, brought gifts for the Dorman's to take with them on their trip. Lauren and Amber were presented to them as the caretakers of the homestead during the Dorman's absence. They shyly welcomed the two women and offered their support over the long winter. Lauren realized that her first impression of them was wrong as their shyness was evident and their English was clear.

The two men were geologists from the university in Anchorage. It was their job to monitor and report on any volcanic activity in the area. They would be infrequent visitors throughout the long winter. Grady was the senior member while Riley, his junior colleague, was only here for the summer. They planned to stay at the homestead for the next couple of days and then head out for a survey.

Sergei was deep in conversation with Carson about his latest order when it was his turn to be introduced. Everyone stood looking at the two men in expectation as they waited to finish the introductions. The sudden silence caught their attention and both of them turned to the group.

Lauren and Amber suddenly felt their own shyness as Sergei turned his dark eyes towards them and stepped forward. As Mrs. Dorman introduced each woman, Sergei reached out his hand to take theirs in an old world manner and lifted it up almost as if to kiss it, but he stopped mid-way and bowed his head slightly. The effect was utterly charming and both women felt their insides flutter as if he'd actually put his lips to the back of their hands. Their introductions only took a moment and Mrs. Dorman quickly moved on to introduce Grady and Riley to Sergei, but Lauren and Amber were struck speechless.

Carson managed to break the spell once again as he started unloading the plane and tossing packages into different piles. The TwoRivers quickly gathered up their mail and a couple of packages and loaded them into their packs. Kuzih told Amber they'd be over in a day or two to trade for some eggs and to check on them as they drove off.

Mr. Dorman and Sergei had walked away from the plane to discuss some last minute concerns.

"How did you end up in Alaska?" Grady asked Lauren.

"Amber invited me to come and take care of the Dorman's homestead with her. I wanted a break from my job in Boston, so here I am."

Riley and Amber were busy helping Mrs. Dorman move stuff from the pickup to the now-empty plane so they could load their gear into the truck.

The moment had finally arrived for the Dorman's to depart. Amber appeared relaxed and confident as she focused on the tasks at hand and clearly ignored Carson.

Lauren was fighting off a wave of anxiety as she realized the Dorman's would be getting into that plane and flying far away in a very short time. Grady's small talk wasn't going to be enough of a distraction. She excused herself and walked over to take a closer look at Sergei's horse.

The stallion was munching grass at the edge of the runway and eyed her warily as she drew near, but didn't move away. She reached into her pocket to find a sugar cube at the bottom and drew it out to offer it to him. He stood much taller than the Percheron's and his breeding was evident in every line of his massive body. She took a couple of steps closer and reached out her hand.

Three things happened in a blink of an eye and none of them were what she'd expected. The stallion reared up on his hind legs looming over her. Mrs. Dorman screamed in terror thinking the young woman was going to be killed right in front of her as Sergei grabbed her and swung her around behind him. He put up his right hand in front of the horse. The stallion took two steps backwards on his hind legs and settled himself back to the ground. He calmly returned to munching grass as if nothing had happened.

Sergei spun around to check on Lauren and found her sitting on the ground with a look of shock on her face. She held out her hand to Sergei to show him the crushed sugar cube as her excuse. Ignoring the sugar, he grabbed her hand and jerked her back to her feet. She lowered her head expecting to be berated for her actions, but when he said nothing, she looked up at him again.

"Afon isn't good with strangers," he said quietly.

"I'm sorry. The Dorman's horses are so friendly and they love sugar," she ventured, "I thought he might like some...."

The others came over to see if Lauren was okay and

Renee Hart

made a fuss over her near-accident. Sergei moved away from the group and gathered his mail packets. He and Mr. Dorman finished their conversation as Mrs. Dorman assured herself that Lauren was still in one piece.

Amber and Riley completed the task of transferring the freight and were deep in conversation about the hot springs.

Carson had finished refueling the plane and stood by impatiently waiting to head back south. He couldn't resist one last teasing remark.

"Hey, 'cheechako', don't go taking pictures of any bear or moose you run into." As handsome as the man was, he was infuriating.

As the Dorman's said their goodbyes and climbed into their seats, Lauren suddenly wished that it was her flying away. She wasn't ready to live in a place where a simple mistake could result in serious injury or even death.

This wasn't Boston and she wasn't like her cousin, Amber. She was experienced in writing stories and telling tales. That wasn't going to be much use to her in this place. Even writing her novel seemed like a remote dream when most of her day was going to be spent just working towards surviving the winter.

These thoughts gathered in her mind like a storm cloud. She looked around the clearing hoping for a sign, something to let her know she was in the right place. Suddenly, her eyes met Sergei's as he stood off to one side watching her intently. She stared back at him wondering at his thoughts as he considered her. A small smile lifted the corner of his mouth and a sparkle in his eye changed everything and, in that instant, she saw the reason that she needed to stay.

Breaking the look between them and without another word, Sergei quickly mounted Afon and urged him towards home. The noise of the plane wasn't something the horse was accustomed to and he figured it was best to get him away before Carson started the engine. The Dorman's waved their last good-byes as the others climbed back into the pickup to head home.

Carson made a full circle over the homestead as a salute as the pickup drove into the woods. Lauren noted that Amber had jumped into the driver's seat, but for once she wasn't driving like her usual self. The steady stream of words out of her mouth, however, was unchanged. Her passengers were entertained with a barrage of tour guide patter fitting for a wilderness guide. Soon she had everyone laughing as they drew up to the guest cabins. The cousins were officially in charge.

Renee Hart

Chapter 8

The long summer days with the midnight sun seemed endless and Lauren sometimes forgot that she was in Alaska where the short summers are a treasured respite from winter's cold and icy grip.

Grady and Riley had stayed with the two women for a couple of days before heading out on the Percheron's to do their survey. The two men were a welcome distraction to the departure of the Dorman's and forced the women to step up to their responsibilities on the homestead immediately.

Lauren enjoyed preparing their meals and Amber clearly felt at home in the wilderness. Their daily routines were pretty simple once the men were gone and the care of the animals took up the bulk of their mornings and evenings. The rest of the day was theirs to use the time as they wanted. There was no TV to watch and the internet access was clearly sub-par, at least by Lauren's city standards. Neither woman was inclined to spend much time on-line anyway.

Occasionally, Lauren would sit down at her laptop and begin to type in random paragraphs hoping to find the starting point for her novel. This usually ended up with her writing about a tall, dark handsome man with an air of mystery that was positively intoxicating. She did manage to do some research on the Russian communities located in Alaska, but everything she learned only served to deepen the mystery.

Most of the Russians lived in closed communities and avoided intermingling with non-Russians. Carson's few facts clearly showed a breach in that policy as Sergei had an American father and he wasn't part of any community. The Dorman's had made it clear that the man lived alone and had only hinted at the tragic deaths of his parents in a horrible plane crash. Clearly, there was no one else to ask about any of this so Lauren's imagination filled in the gaps.

Occasionally, she would remind herself of her vow to avoid men and push away these idle thoughts, but they were always sneaking back into her mind when she wasn't looking. She decided it was time to find a new hobby and turned her attention to making new versions of goat cheese and soap. This was one area where there was an abundance of milk and lots of room for innovation. Soon she managed to build up quite a stock of both for trade. Now all she needed was someone to trade with and that was a problem the internet was especially suited to solve. The rest would be up to Carson and his delivery service.

***

Late one evening, the two women found themselves out on the deck with big bowls of goat milk ice cream and a hunger to catch up on the missing years between them. Amber went first and shared her wandering journey that ended up as far from her home on the east coast as she could get.

They laughed as they both remembered a little factoid from a tour guide that showed how, by longitude, Alaska is actually the easternmost AND the westernmost state in the U.S.

The details of Amber's romantic entanglements were sketchy at best and Lauren gathered there hadn't been anyone really special. She decided it wouldn't hurt to ask so she brought up Carson, but Amber brushed him aside as if she didn't want to talk about him. Lauren let it go.

Amber chose that moment to bring up Dylan as she was aware of their long term relationship, but didn't know about the messy break up. Lauren gave her the condensed version of her broken 'engagement' to the man of her dreams. She was tempted to expound on her humiliation, but it all seemed like ancient history from her new perspective.

"I have to confess," Amber began, "I was dreading the invitation to your wedding. I knew you'd want me to be your maid of honor and I also remembered that turquoise was your favorite color. I just couldn't see myself in a fancy turquoise dress, not even for you!"

Lauren burst into laughter at the thought of her cousin in a frilly dress, startling Maggie awake and nearly falling off her chair. She'd forgotten about their play weddings when they were little. The two of them had so many shared memories from their past.

"Do you remember the time we went to the county fair when we were twelve?" Lauren asked.

"Oh, yeah! We spent all our money getting our fortunes told by that hokey gypsy lady with the bad teeth. I was so mad at you! We didn't have anything left over to go on the Ferris wheel!"

"Do you remember what she told me…who I would marry?"

Amber paused for a moment searching her memory and the light suddenly dawned on her face.

"I do! She told you, you were going to marry a man named Dylan!" she cackled.

Then, realizing the magnitude of what she'd just said, she frowned and turned to look at Lauren.

"Oh, no…oh, no! That's not why you stayed with him for five years, is it," Amber's voice trailed off into silence. "I told you it was a stupid idea to get our fortunes told," she finally muttered.

They both sat there quietly letting their surroundings soak into them as they finished their ice cream. As they watched, a bear slipped along the far edge of the trees and disappeared from sight. Its appearance was so brief that Maggie didn't even notice, and they were left to wonder if they'd just imagined it.

Renee Hart

***

The summer passed quickly and, by the end of August, a bit of chill was in the air in the mornings and late at night. One morning, they'd woken up to a light dusting of snow, but it was gone before the coffee was ready. It was a reminder that winter was coming and they needed to get themselves ready. The woodstove in the kitchen was only used for cooking and the firewood for that was already stacked along the back wall of the kitchen. Their main heating only needed to be turned on and they'd be plenty warm enough to endure what was coming.

Sergei finished prepping the solar and wind arrays for the long winter. They would lose the solar for a couple of months in the middle of winter, but the wind turbine was designed to pick up the slack. He often came by to check on things, but Lauren rarely caught his visits as she mainly stayed close to the house. Amber would casually mention that he'd come over to do this or take care of that and Lauren was always surprised. She was left to wonder if she'd misread his half smile and the sparkle in his eye.

Maybe he was laughing at my stupidity, she thought, *and besides, no men, remember*?

***

Grady and Riley passed through a few times as they continued their study. Each time they'd stay a couple of days and the women looked forward to their visits. Riley was often seen following Amber around the barn as she completed her care of the animals.

Grady spent his free time entertaining Lauren with stories of their adventures out in the bush with wild animal encounters and raging rivers.

He wasn't a 'sourdough', a term used for Alaskans with a long string of winters under their belt, but he'd taken to the land with a passion for its pristine beauty.

"This just might be my last winter in Alaska. I feel like it's time for a change," he confessed. "It might even be time to settle down," he added with a little grin at her.

Lauren tried not to read too much into his comment. "So, just how do you explain to your boss the number of days you and Riley spend hanging out here at the homestead," she asked him with a wry grin.

"What do you mean?" Grady asked smiling. "There's nothing to explain. This is basically 'our field office'. Most of the technology here, including the satellite access for the internet and your cell phone, was installed by the university. The Dorman's have a working agreement with them."

"Oh, so you're telling me that you're just here to work?" Lauren said.

"Well, of course. There's no reason for my boss to care

that the station is currently being manned by two beautiful women. This just makes the 'field office' a lot more interesting for us," Grady concluded. "Besides, investigating the local population falls under the universities purview. We have to know who's out here if there's ever a need to evacuate this area."

This was said with a mischievous look that brought a grin to Lauren's face. She felt the attraction between them growing with each of Grady's visits. He was much more attentive than Dylan had been, and his charm was quite appealing.

***

One morning, Lauren was laying out breakfast when her cousin stumbled into the kitchen in her pajamas. She took one look at Amber's swollen face and gasped in horror. The entire right side of her jaw was swollen to nearly twice its normal size and was burning red with inflammation.

"What happened to you?" Lauren asked with fear in her voice.

"I think it's an abscessed tooth," Amber moaned, "and it hurts real bad...took some aspirin...ooohh," she groaned as she sank into her chair.

Lauren grabbed an ice pack and wrapped it in a towel for her cousin as she tried to think of what to do next.

"What do we do now?" she asked.

"See if you can get Carson on the radio," Amber mumbled as she laid her head down on the table. "If that doesn't work, try to send him a text. He's our only hope for getting me to a dentist."

Lauren hurried to try the radio first. As she checked the settings, it crackled with empty static and, after several attempts, it was clear no one was within range. She grabbed her phone to send him a text message. He responded back within the hour and told her it would take him at least two days to make his way out to them. He recommended that they try to get to Nasnan TwoRivers as she would have some home remedies that would be far more effective than aspirin.

The very idea of trying to get to the TwoRivers homestead gave Lauren the shivers. Neither of them had ever been that far on their own and she wasn't sure of the path. Amber knew the surrounding paths that led to their neighbors, but she'd never gone the entire way down any of them alone. In her condition, this wasn't the time to go out on an expedition into the wilderness.

Both women realized that Lauren would have to go and try to find the way by herself. The path they used to the airstrip on their ATV was fairly well-used and should be easy enough to follow on horseback. They had a rough map of the area the Dorman's had made for them and it seemed like the only option they had at this point.

She groaned as she realized that Daisy and Petunia were out in the bush with Grady and Riley, which meant she'd have to ride Trace. Sucking up her courage, Lauren resolved to rise to the challenge and get some help for her cousin. Amber would have taken the shotgun, but she still felt uneasy handling a firearm so she grabbed a can of bear spray and their hand drawn map. Heading out to the barn, she called for Trace and to her surprise he came running over right away.

She managed to get him saddled up and headed down the path to the airstrip. Stopping at the edge of the trees, she took a moment to sight Wolf Mountain and determine the direction of the TwoRivers' homestead in relation to where she was currently positioned.

The ATV trail was rough, but she was confident that she could follow wherever it led. Steeling herself, she moved forward into the trees. This wasn't the best time of the year to be wandering about in the woods. The bears were busy getting ready for winter and eating everything they could get their paws on. Lauren didn't want to be a part of their winter's hoard.

She followed the rough path for about half an hour before she started to see signs of human activity. She came to a clearing where wide strips of bark had been cut from the birch trees and small piles of wood chips and sawdust marked firewood cuttings. A bit further along she heard the distant sound of a chainsaw or maybe it was a boat motor.

She knew the TwoRivers homestead was near the Melozitna River. The Athabascan's used the river as their main trade route and a major source of food. Nasnan usually brought dried fish to trade for eggs or goat milk soap.

As the path widened out, she caught sight of a snug little cabin nestled in a stand of trees. A couple of dogs stood up and began to bark fiercely at her and Lauren was relieved to see Kuzih come around the corner of a shed. He looked surprised to see her riding up and hurried over to help her dismount.

"Kuzih, Amber's sick. Carson told us that Nasnan might be able to help her until he can come and take her to a doctor," Lauren blurted out.

Kuzih nodded and called out for his wife. She appeared from behind the drying racks for the fish with a bloodied knife in her hand. Nasnan's eyes widened with surprise as she took in the sight of Lauren in her front yard. She quickly stripped off her bloodied apron and wrapped it around the knife before hurrying over to see what precipitated this surprise visit.

Lauren explained about Amber's swollen face and extreme pain. Before she was finished, Kuzih pulled the tarp off the ATV and started to make preparations to head back to the Dorman's place. Nasnan listened carefully and then disappeared into their cabin. She reappeared within a few minutes with a small pack and a rifle.

Jumping onto the ATV, she motioned for Lauren to get on behind her. They would be able to travel together faster in the thick underbrush and low-hanging limbs that threatened to dislodge a rider on a tall horse. Kuzih would follow behind on Trace at a slower pace.

The two of them made good time as Nasnan pushed the ATV over the rough places and went even faster through the clearer areas. Her driving skills were equal to her husband's as she wrestled the tough little machine over the broken trail. Lauren hung on as best she could, torn between her fears and concern for her cousin.

When they could see the homestead, Lauren was surprised to see Afon munching grass at the edge of the yard with his reins trailing in the dirt. She barely had time think about it before Nasnan had parked the ATV and was headed into the lodgehouse.

Even more surprising was seeing Sergei kneeling next to the couch, holding an icepack to Amber's cheek. He had a worried look on his face and Lauren wondered if it was more than just concern. This was the first time she'd seen him inside the house, but he obviously knew his way around.

He looked relieved to see Nasnan and stepped back to give her room to assess the situation. She picked up a mug sitting on the coffee table and gave it a quick sniff. Giving Sergei a nod, she spoke to Amber to try and determine the level of her pain. Amber seemed relieved to have Nasnan there to help.

"The birch tea is good. It helps the pain and the infection," Nasnan affirmed. "The tooth will have to come out, but it's better for you to have one of your dentists for that. The tea and some herbs I brought will help you until Carson can come."

Sergei nodded in agreement with her assessment and turned to speak to Lauren.

"Amber was very concerned about you. She couldn't decide if she wanted me to help her or go after you. I told her to give you the chance to prove to yourself what you can do. You did well."

Sergei's words were followed with a sincere smile that warmed Lauren's heart all the way to her toes. He turned and left the room without saying anything else as she stood there basking in his admiration. *For that kind of attention, she'd ride to the moon and back*, she swooned inside.

When she finally came down off her cloud, she realized that he'd gone out to the barn and done the milking and collected the eggs. She'd managed to make some coffee and a pan of sweet rolls by the time he reappeared with Kuzih. Amber was safely tucked into her own bed and was sleeping soundly, thanks to the herbs Nasnan prepared for her. The four of them sat down at the table to consider what would happen next.

Renee Hart

"Carson will have to fly Amber back to the city," Sergei began. "She's going to be away for at least two weeks before she can be treated and he can bring her back. You understand..." he said looking at Lauren pointedly.

Lauren nodded, but for once her nod was sure as she basked in the glow of her success. For the first time, she was confident that she could handle everything on her own, at least for a short time.

"We won't be able to help much," Kuzih began to explain. "It's the time for the 'gathering' and our people will join together for the celebration of the harvest before winter begins. We must travel two days journey away."

Lauren hurried to assure the couple that she would be able to handle things until Amber came back. Sergei added his commitment to check on her as often as he could and the matter was settled.

Lauren divided the rest of the sweet rolls, the eggs Sergei had brought in and several bars of goat milk soap into two packs. She was proud to be able to give something back to her neighbors for their kindness. She showed Nasnan some of the different soaps she'd made and asked if there would be anyone interested in trading for them at their gathering.

"There's always an interest in trading for soap," Nasnan said. "Especially fine soap like this. I'm sure I can make some good trades for you. Is there anything in particular you'd like to trade for?"

Lauren had the presence of mind to look embarrassed before she whispered, "I'd really like some chocolate…"

Nasnan burst out laughing, which caught the attention of the two men. Her husband asked what was so funny and she answered in their native language. Sergei looked confused until Kuzih explained the joke, then he too started to laugh.

"Chocolate's a pretty rare commodity out here in the bush," he stated. "You're going to come up short on that end of the deal."

Noting Lauren's discomfort, Nasnan patted her arm.

"Don't worry. Some of our clan are coming upriver from Galena. I'll put the word out and see what I can do. We'll try and find you some chocolate."

With that said, the TwoRivers couple gathered their things and headed outside. After a quick peek into Amber's room, Sergei followed them, and Lauren was left alone to think about the events of the morning.

She'd learned a lot of new things in a very short time and her mind was struggling to process all of it. The one thing that surprised her most was the fact that she really wasn't afraid to handle things on her own for the next couple of weeks. Besides, what could go wrong…?

Chapter 9

Amber's 'mini-vacation' went smoothly. And Lauren surprised everyone by handling the homestead like an old pro.

Sergei stopped by every couple of days to check on things. She suspected that he came by more often than that, but just took a quick look around without making it known. She noticed that little things were picked up and put away, like hay forks and such that she remembered leaving here or there.

He usually appeared when she was milking the goats or bringing in the eggs. She'd hoped for some quiet time together over a cup of coffee and baked several kinds of goodies hoping to tempt him inside, but he always made his exit before she could invite him.

***

Amber fully recovered from her ordeal and was glad that Lauren was helping to care for the animals. They finished up the last harvest from the outside garden and picked all of the lingonberries they could stand to pick. The area was full of raspberries and blueberries and the two women ate their fill of them.

Frost was on the ground every morning and Sergei had

activated the heating system for the long winter run.

Kuzih and Nasnan came back from the gathering with a small pile of goods and several stories to tell. Lauren was touched to see some chocolate bars on top of the pile. She squirreled them away in her pocket when she thought no one was looking. Then she caught a wink passed between the couple and she knew they'd seen her.

As they told the two women about their harvest festival, Lauren realized their shyness was gone. They felt like old friends. She found she really enjoyed their company.

The two of them were a couple in every way and relied on each other for their survival as well as their place in the native community. She wondered what it would be like to have someone like that in her life. She couldn't imagine being with someone 24/7 and liking it. It wasn't the normal way of life in her world.

Sure her parents spent their days together now that they were retired, but their volunteer work and other activities weren't shared.

The closest relationship that Lauren knew of was her grandparents and they each had their own areas of responsibility. Her grandmother was usually in the house or the garden while her grandfather spent his days in the barn or the fields. They didn't do everything together like the TwoRivers.

"Lauren, I was wondering," Nasnan's voice broke into her thoughts. "What does your name mean?"

"I don't really know. I just know my mother had a famous actress she liked and I was named after her. I never really considered my name had any meaning beyond that."

"Interesting," Nasnan said. "Athabascan names always have meanings. They're supposed to define our personality. For instance, my name, Nasnan, means 'surrounded by song'."

"That's beautiful," Lauren replied, nodding. "You know Sergei's horse, Afon? His name means 'immortal' in Russian."

So, what does 'Kuzih' mean?" Amber asked.

He proudly puffed up his chest before answering her with a grin.

"It means, 'great talker'!"

The four of them burst into laughter at the obvious truth in his name.

***

An interesting revelation had come forth from Amber's misfortune.

When Carson picked her up, he flew her to Fairbanks to see the dentist. The dentist was an old friend of Carson's and was willing to work a trade for his services.

Amber received all of the care that she needed at no cost in exchange for Carson flying the doctor and his team out to some of the more remote villages for their program, "A Day of Dentistry". Carson figured he owed Amber much more than he'd ever paid her for her services and was happy to be part of the deal.

When it came time to bring Amber back to the homestead, Carson said "I'll be making an extra stop on the way."

He didn't share any more details and she didn't ask. After all, he was in the business of making deliveries.

He landed the plane on a rough airstrip and Amber was surprised to see several native children running from the trees towards the plane. She was even more surprised when she heard them shouting, "Dad! Dad" as they ran to greet their father.

Carson jumped out of the plane as soon as it rolled to a stop and was caught up in a group hug that expanded by the minute as the younger children joined in as fast as their little legs could carry them.

Everyone was laughing and talking at the same time and as Amber tried to take all of this in, she noticed a very pregnant woman waddling in their direction. The look on her face spoke volumes and Amber realized that this was the reason Carson had never responded to her attempts to move beyond the 'friend' stage. He was obviously a *very* married man with a large brood to show for it.

As the woman reached her children and her mate, Carson remembered his sketchy manners and stood up to introduce his family to Amber. He didn't say anything about her apparent surprise, but she could see he was enjoying her discomfort.

As he reeled off the names and ages of each of his children, he'd reach into his pocket and pull something out for them. He was just giving them little things like sticks of gum or pieces of candy, but it was clear that he was giving each child their own special treat. He saved his wife for last and patted her swollen belly as he presented her to Amber.

His wife received the last little packet from his pocket as he turned with her to walk towards the trees.

The children gathered around Amber and asked her question after question. She was delighted with their exuberant energy and soon they were playing a game of tag scaled down for the littlest ones.

The game ended when Carson came back and sent the children off to follow their mother home. He promised them he'd stay much longer on his next trip and hugged each one of them as they headed off.

When they got back into the air, Amber had only one question, "Why didn't you ever tell me about your family?"

"They're my family and my business. It's the Alaskan way to take care of your own business. You know that. It's in your blood too," he retorted. "People have all kinds of negative ideas and stereotypes about the native peoples. It's better for my family to stay right here in their own culture and I'll do everything I can to help them do that for their own sakes."

Amber knew he was right. It really wasn't any of her business. She wondered if he knew how much personal agony his privacy had cost her though. She knew he'd never given her any encouragement to fall in love with him and it was her own fault she'd suffered. Knowing what she did now didn't erase any of the hurt she'd carried for the last couple of years, but at least she finally understood why he stayed silent.

Chapter 10

Grady and Riley came through in mid-September for Riley's final expedition before he headed back to the lower '48. He asked Amber to make one final trip to the Horner Hot Springs with him before he headed home. She agreed and they planned an overnight camping trip.

Grady took this opportunity to convince Lauren to let him cook dinner for her. "I'll take care of everything for the meal and you can take some time away from the kitchen until I'm done."

"It's not that I don't like your cooking," he laughed. "I just want to give you a chance to eat something cooked by someone else. It's not like I can take you out to a restaurant to say thanks."

He surprised her with a wonderful 'bou stew' that he'd cooked in the electric pressure cooker.

"Wow!" she said on her first bite. "If I'd known you could cook like this, I'd have let you cook for me a long time ago. Where did you find roast beef?"

"Oh no," he protested. "That's not roast beef. That's caribou meat with your garden vegetables and some of the local herbs."

She took another bite and savored the tender meat.

"I don't know how you did it. When I tried to cook some of that meat, it was tougher than shoe leather and had no taste," she admitted.

"Aha! See! That's where the pressure cooker is your friend. The cooking process is so good that it can make even shoe leather taste good. I'll show you how to use it before I go."

The two of them cleaned their plates and ate most of the stew before they finally pushed themselves away from the table with a groan.

"I'd offer you some ice cream," Lauren said, "but I think you'd have to wear it. I can't imagine you have any room left to eat anymore."

Grady nodded at her comment and grabbed their mugs of hot cocoa before heading for the sofa. She saw him setting out the Scrabble game as she cleared the table. She put the last of the stew into the refrigerator before joining him. The dishes could wait until later, much later. *Like tomorrow*, she thought with a grin. *I'd rather spend time with this man.*

***

One day, the sound of Carson's plane surprised them all. Usually, he radioed or texted ahead that he was coming. Everyone scrambled for the pickup to meet him at the airstrip.

It was time for Riley and Grady to head back to base. Winter was coming and there was snow on the ground.

Lauren was anxious to see how Carson would land on the icy airstrip. It was rough enough landing on dirt and grass. She'd struggled to learn how to make the short trip from the lodgehouse to the barn on her snowshoes and it wasn't even very deep.

To her surprise, Carson's plane was outfitted with skis. He landed easily and swooshed his way across the snow to meet the truck.

Everyone turned at the chorus of barks, yips and howls coming from the other side of the clearing just in time to see Sergei emerge from the bare trees on the back of his sled.

Lauren missed the sight of Afon, but the beautiful huskie-mixes running as a precision team were as impressive in their own way. The dogs pulled the sled down the airstrip with looks of joy on their faces. As they responded to Sergei's command to stop, every dog dropped to their belly and looked back at him. His training skills weren't limited to horses.

Carson unloaded the few packages from the front of the plane and then he dragged out four *very* large boxes. Stamped on the outside of each box was a single word, 'Tampons'.

"Ladies," he began. "I'm sure there's some *logical* explanation for this."

Amber turned to Lauren with a pointed look.

"What did you do?" she asked.

"Uh, you told me to order you some more tampons," Lauren faltered. "I must have checked the wrong box on the 'Bush Mail Shopper' order form..."

"Uh, *yeah*! Instead of checking 'box' you must have checked 'case'. There're more tampons here than we could use in the next five years," Amber groaned.

The four men were trying to hide their amusement at this faux pas unsuccessfully and once Carson started laughing, everyone joined in. Everyone but Lauren. She was mortified.

"If that isn't a 'cheechako' move..." Carson started to say, but couldn't finish before a new wave of laughter came over him.

"Well...well, at least I'm not a 'sourpuss'!" Lauren shouted at him in her frustration. This brought another wave of laughter even louder than the first, that left her even more frustrated.

Showing support for her cousin, Amber gently correct her. "It's 'sourdough', not 'sourpuss,' though I've seen him act that way more than a few times," Amber said.

Lauren ignored everyone and walked back to the truck. She felt totally humiliated and wanted to go home. She didn't know what four cases of tampons had cost her, but that sign outside a shopping mall was looming ahead of her. *Only in Alaska would something like this happen*, she thought.

In the flurry of packing up their equipment and other belongings, Lauren's embarrassment was swept aside.

She cooked a nice supper in the hopes of redeeming herself. Everyone gathered at the table as soon as it was ready. Carson made an effort to be particularly nice to her, and he nearly succeeded in convincing her she was wrong about him, nearly.

Grady tried a couple of times to take her aside for a few private words, but something or somebody managed to keep that from happening. Lauren noticed that Grady seemed a little anxious and watched for some sign that he had romantic feelings for her, but since the others were present they acted in their usual friendly way.

The biggest surprise of the evening came when Sergei accepted Amber's invitation to join them for dinner. This was the first time he'd ever sat at their table and Lauren pulled out jars and cans of everything she could think of to throw together a nice meal.

Her crowning achievement came when she made Grady's 'bou stew' all on her own, much to everyone's delight. She happily shared all of the credit with Grady as her mentor.

Fueled by good food and the pleasure of the company, their talk lingered on long past supper and it was well after dark when Sergei headed home with his team.

Amber and Lauren urged him to stay, but he was

adamant that he needed to get back to his own place for the night. The other animals at his place needed to be cared for and there wasn't anyone else to do it. Besides, soon it would be dark for most of the day, except for a couple of hours of daylight. They all needed to get used to moving around in the dark.

The rest of them headed off to bed when Carson insisted on getting an early start in the morning. He explained that a large weather system was heading their way and it was possibly bringing a *lot* of snow. He wanted to be back at base before it hit the Interior.

***

True to his word, Carson was up before the sun and hustling everyone along. Gulping coffee and chomping on sourdough pancakes with reindeer sausage was interspersed with jumping up to run out and grab this or that forgotten cable or battery pack. There was no more time for idle chit chat.

The sun was just coming up when everyone piled into the pickup and headed for the airstrip.

Grady took charge of loading their gear on the plane while Carson went through his pre-flight checklist. He may have run his business in a slipshod manner, but he took his flying very seriously. A plane crash out here usually ended badly for the bush pilot. The sun was just clear of the trees by the time they were ready for take-off.

Rushing through their good-byes, Grady came over to Lauren and took hold of her arms. He paused for a long moment to look deep into her eyes. He leaned forward to kiss her and she kissed him back, upset at how sad she was to see him leave. She managed to say softly "I'm really going to miss you." And when he let go of her and turned away, she thought she saw tears in his eyes.

During his time there Grady had become more than a friend. Lauren was starting to realize that making a vow of 'no men' for a year may not have been the smartest decision. Now she was forced to admit that trying to keep him at arms length had been a mistake. She realized that if she hadn't been running away from the hurt of her break up that things between her and Grady might have turned out differently.

Now the chance to find out was lost as the men got into the plane and Carson started up the engine.

Amber and Lauren retreated to the warmth of the truck to watch their take-off.

Carson deftly maneuvered the plane to the far end of the runway and gunned the engine. The two women watched the plane ski down the runway and lifted off.

A final circle around the airfield, a last tip of the wings and the plane was gone. For the next few months, it was just going to be Lauren and Amber for most of the time. Carson would only come once a month and Sergei, well, he would come and go whenever he pleased.

Chapter 11

The cold of winter in Alaska is almost a tangible presence. Even in the warmth of the house, the cold could be felt pressing itself against the outer walls and windows. It sought out every crack and crevice around the doors and the logs of the walls trying to find a way to come inside. The heating system was good and they felt safe inside the buildings.

Going outside was a very different matter as frostbite and hypothermia were ever present dangers. Temperatures of forty or fifty below are normal for the Interior and it was important to always be prepared for the possibility that things could suddenly get worse. Add to that wind chill factors and death by cold was a risk they all faced.

The animals were safe in the barn and the horses and dogs all wore heavy fur coats of their own making. Amber feared for the horses until she took off her gloves one day and thrust her fingers deep into the thick coat on Petunia's side. As her fingers sunk into Petunia's hair, she could feel the heat of the horse's body and realized they were in no danger of freezing. The goats and chickens were at far more risk, but there was no reason for them to leave the safety of the heated barn most days.

The two women shared the outdoor chores in an effort

to reduce the amount of time they needed to go outside. There was no longer any danger of bears as they were hibernating in their dens sleeping off the winter, but the heavy snow brought the wolves in closer to the homestead. They knew the dogs would fight if it came to that, but not even the Shepherds were a match for a hungry wolf pack. Maggie was little more than wolf bait and she spent her days inside more than out.

***

They'd finally made it to the shortest day of the year, the winter solstice, when their frayed nerves snapped from boredom and the cabin fever that gripped them both. Lauren wasn't sure how the argument started, but it escalated faster than an avalanche on a sunny day.

They started arguing over whose turn it was to go outside and milk the goats and who was supposed to have made the coffee that morning. Even the tampon fiasco got brought up and thrown in Lauren's face, much to her amazement.

That was the last straw for her and she grabbed her gear to head outside. Usually Amber was the first to escape outdoors, but she'd headed back to her own room and slammed the door. Lauren could still hear her grumbling as she closed the door to the arctic entryway. It was time to put as much distance between themselves as possible.

To Lauren's surprise the day seemed much warmer than usual. The snow wasn't very deep and the little sunlight they had was enough to see across the clearing. She saw Trace first as he came over searching for a treat. Pulling out a sugar cube, she absently held out her hand to him. After he'd crunched it up, he nuzzled her again as if asking for more, but her pockets were empty. She headed over to the barn where they kept a few boxes of sugar cubes hidden from the goats. Trace followed her as if he'd read her mind.

Digging out a few more cubes from their hiding place, she noticed the bridle hanging next to one of the stalls and decided to put it on Trace and take him for a short ride. Usually it was too cold and snowy for such things, but today seemed perfect if she made it a quickie. She'd reached for the saddle before she realized she was wearing her bunny boots. There was no way they were going to fit in the stirrups and she didn't want to go back to the house to change. She figured she'd be okay without a saddle for a little jaunt. Amber seemed to prefer riding bareback. It should be fine for her too.

Trace seemed happy with her plan and lowered his head for her to put the bridle on him. Stepping up on a hay bale, she got on his back and off they went. At first she rode around the house, but the path towards the airfield beckoned to her so she made the turn and headed for that clearing. Trace plodded through the snow as effortlessly as if he was walking through shallow water. Her heavy boots swung against the horse's haunches keeping her level on his back like a pair of pendulums.

She traversed the airfield and came to a path that was worn down with tracks. She leaned over to see if she could figure out who or what was using the trail. Her first thought was moose, but then she realized it must have been a herd of caribou. Hoping to catch sight of them, she urged Trace down the trail and eagerly searched the trees around them for any other signs.

Focused on following the tracks, Lauren forgot to pay attention to where she was going and didn't realize that she'd crossed several other well-worn pathways. They'd traveled several miles before she caught sight of the flash of a caribou tail just ahead. Urging Trace forward, she tried her best to catch up to the herd. Despite her efforts the animals stayed about the same distance ahead of them leading her on a wild 'bou chase.

Two thoughts suddenly burst to the front of her mind with the force of a knockout punch. First, it was already starting to get dark and she didn't have any kind of light with her and secondly, wolves were known to follow the caribou herds and she didn't have any kind of weapon either. Both thoughts made her stop her in her tracks. She had an even greater problem....she was lost.

Sheer terror threatened to overcome her, but she knew this was no time to lose her head. She hoped she could follow Trace's path back the way they had come. She was sure they hadn't come *that* far. Carefully searching the ground she tried to pick up the trail. They weaved about in the snow for several minutes before she realized they were simply going in circles. It was getting dark a lot faster than she was making any progress towards home.

Considering her fight with Amber and the way she'd gone off without a word, there was no hope that anyone would come looking for her anytime soon. She'd be a popsicle long before a search party found her, even if there was anyone to launch a search party.

With the adrenaline pumping into her system, she started to hear rustling in the trees all around her and it took every bit of restraint not to give in to panic and fear. She struggled to think of a solution to surviving her stupidity. This was one time she'd have to agree with Carson about a 'cheechako' moment. She'd just topped every stupid thing she'd ever done before, with this single act.

As she tried to remember everything she'd learned about survival in the wilderness, she thought about something Mr. Dorman had told her when they first started riding. He'd said that Trace was the only one of the three horses that could find his way home. The one caveat was that she had to drop the reins to the ground and completely trust him to do it by himself.

She also remembered her sarcastic thought about

trusting any male. Now that she'd her survival depended on it, she had to put complete trust in Trace.

She leaned forward to have a talk with Trace. "Take us home, Trace boy. You know the way." He laid his ears back and seemed to listen but as she urged him to get going, he just stood there waiting for her direction. Tossing up a quick prayer that she was doing the right thing, she steeled herself against every broken promise, every betrayal and every deception she could remember, and she dropped the reins.

Trace immediately started walking. It wasn't the direction she would have chosen, but she didn't try and reach for the reins lest she fall off. Even if Trace didn't run away, she'd never be able to get back on him out here. He walked steadily for an hour and when it was full on dark, he kept on walking.

Lauren took in small sips of air as the temperature dropped and hunched herself down as close to the horse to stay warm. She didn't understand how the horse knew where he was going, but he was heading somewhere. The cold and the dark mixed with the adrenaline crash made her feel so sleepy and she struggled to stay awake. Her heavy boots were keeping her feet warm and her body balanced.

It wasn't until they were standing in front of the barn that she realized they were home. The barking and howling brought back her fears of wolves, but then the door opened and Sergei and Amber came running out. He was there to catch her as she fainted from exhaustion and he carried her back into the house.

***

It was late afternoon the next day, when Lauren finally woke up in her own bed. She could hear quiet voices coming from the kitchen. She slowly remembered all that had happened the day before. In a groggy state she spent a few minutes flexing her fingers and toes, then worked her way through her arms and legs without finding any problems.

Emotionally, she wasn't so sure as the last thing she remembered before waking up was the feel of strong arms cradling her against a powerful chest. She wasn't given to fits of fainting or histrionics like her mother, but she remembered fainting last night. She reasoned it was probably because of her extreme stress and exhaustion. There wasn't any way to explain her abject stupidity.

She was starting to get out of bed when her door was pushed open and Amber looked in on her. She got a brief glimpse of Sergei's worried face behind her cousin before he slipped back to the kitchen. Both of them were looked relieved.

"Oh, you're finally awake," Amber said hesitantly. "How are you feeling?"

Renee Hart

"I'm fine," Lauren sighed.

Suddenly she remembered the hero who'd saved her life.

"Is Trace okay?" she asked with a tremor in her voice. "I didn't hurt him, did I?"

"He's fine," Amber assured her as she came to sit next to her cousin on the bed. "Sergei rubbed him down and gave him some extra oats last night. I'm sure he's right as rain today."

The two women were quiet as they considered the events of the past couple of days and their parting words.

"I'm sorry," they both said at once. "This was all my fault..." and they laughed.

Sergei appeared in the open doorway again with a cup of tea in his hand and a bemused look on his face. Lauren was overwhelmed with his presence in her bedroom. Amber took the cup from him and pressed it into Lauren's hand.

"Here, drink this," she said. "It will make you feel better."

Lauren took a sip of the warm tea and realized that she hadn't eaten anything since yesterday morning. Her stomach gave out a loud grumble which caused both women to start laughing again. Sergei had already fled back to the kitchen.

"I need more than a cup of tea," she said. "I'm starving!"

"Well, come on. Let's get you something to eat! You might want to throw on a robe or something first," Amber called back as she went to the kitchen.

Lauren looked down at the baggy t-shirt and sweats she was wearing and groaned. She almost crawled back into bed and pulled the pillow over her head, but her stomach rumbled again.

As she staggered into the kitchen, she found Sergei and Amber standing close together in front of the wood stove. Their eyes were fixed on each other and neither of them heard her come in with her booties.

She cleared her throat to alert them to her presence. They both turned to her with a start and then hurried to get busy with other things. She sat down at the table where someone had been eating some goat cheese and bread and helped herself.

She'd eaten everything on the plate when she realized that Amber's mug was in her usual spot and her usual place was empty. With a start, she figured out she was eating off of Sergei's plate. She looked up to find him watching her with a grin on his face.

"Good stuff, eh?" he said.

Amber turned from the counter with a sandwich and a cup of soup when she realized what Lauren had done. She started laughing and that set them all off. Lauren offered him his chair and his empty plate, but he waved her off and grabbed another plate from the cupboard and some more bread and cheese. He obviously knew his way around their kitchen.

The three of them sat down and started piecing together the events of the past twenty-four hours. Each of them only knew a part of the story and it took all three of them to put it together.

Sergei had shown up some time after Lauren set off on her ride and he explained what happened then.

"After checking on the animals and finding the eggs hadn't been collected or the goats milked, " he said, "I came to the house to check on you two. I didn't notice that Trace was missing. I went inside and found Amber sleeping, and looked around for you. When I didn't find you, I woke Amber to try and figure out what was going on."

"I had no idea that you'd left with Trace," Amber said. I told Sergei that you were probably just hiding out somewhere trying to calm down after our argument. Sergei and I did the chores and it wasn't until we were putting out food for the horses that we realized Trace was gone. We didn't have any idea of where to look for you two. It was getting dark and we were really worried!"

Now it was Lauren's turn to fill in the blanks and she really didn't want to tell them what she had done. "There isn't any way to sugarcoat it. I didn't use my head when I got on Trace to go for a ride. I never should have left without telling you what I was doing."

Swallowing hard, she began to tell them what

happened. She didn't try to explain away her bad judgment or lack of forethought. She just told them what happened step by step.

Both of them were silent as she talked. Although Amber's eyes expressed fear, she kept it all in check. Sergei was also careful to conceal his concern throughout her story. When she was done, neither Sergei or Amber chastised her for being so thoughtless.

Finally, Sergei reached across the table and put his hands over the hand of each of the women and looked both of them intently.

"The moral of the story is this, you're safe and you've learned many things, nothing more to say."

Amber started to protest, but he gently squeezed her hand and put his finger to her lips.

"Shhh…" was all he said and Amber was quiet.

Lauren chuckled a bit inside as she noticed how the mysterious Russian had somehow worked his magic on her cousin. They obviously had strong feelings for each other.

Renee Hart

Chapter 12

The next few weeks passed in a blur and one day they woke up to the sound of water dripping from the edges of the roof. The snow was finally starting to melt. The sun was shining nearly all day now and the horses spent more time outside than in the barn. Everyone was eager for spring to come. Sergei came regularly and shared at least one meal a day with the women.

Lauren recognized the budding relationship between Amber and Sergei had slowly been coming together from the first time she saw him ride up on his horse.

He'd taken the Amber and Lauren back to his homestead a couple of times to show them the home and the workshop his parents had built. Sharing photos of them, he told them the tragic story of their lives and their deaths. They both knew that Sergei rarely talked about himself, so sharing parts of his life story with them meant they were special to him.

Carson came with the news that the Dorman's would return in a month since their research had finished earlier than expected.

With that news Amber and Lauren embarked on a flurry of spring cleaning. They wanted to return the homestead to the same condition it was in when they came. It was more a labor of love than a chore. Everyone's spirits soared with the warming days and sunshine.

One evening Lauren sat in front of her dusty laptop and reflected on what she'd learned from her year of living in the bush. She'd seen first hand that people, even relative strangers, take care of each other in times of need. She's been able to step into a world totally different from what she was used to and not only survive, but come out of it a stronger person, having lived in a place that few people experience.

She also learned that she doesn't need a man to make her happy. Yes, it would be nice to find *the one*, and she may have let a good man slip away. When she resumed dating she would go slowly and listen to her gut when things didn't feel right. She realized that making a vow of 'no men' was the wrong approach to exorcising Dylan from her life.

She was ready to go back to Boston, and was eager to see her parents and grandmother.

She'd had her adventure and completely healed the wounds of her ex's betrayal, but now it was time to move on with her life.

Alaska was wonderful, but it wasn't where her heart was. She'd always been a city girl and she wouldn't be happy out here trying to survive the hazards of the harsh and sometimes, unforgiving land year after year.

Her *great American novel* would just have to be written in some other part of the world.

Renee Hart

Chapter 13

Sitting at her desk, Lauren turned to look out the window. The view towards the harbor was fantastic and she couldn't look at it often enough. She sometimes missed the mountains and the endless forest, but she was happy to be back in the lively city.

"Excuse me, Lauren," her secretary said. "You have a visitor in the lobby downstairs. Shall I have him escorted up?"

"Please do," Lauren said without turning around. She was expecting a junior reporter for an interview.

A slight cough from the doorway startled her and she looked up into familiar brown eyes.

"Grady!" she exclaimed as she jumped up and ran around her desk to give him a hug.

He seemed slightly taken aback by her exuberance, but he hugged her back with equal enthusiasm.

"What are you doing here? How did you find me?" she asked, her questions running together.

He laughed and raised up both hands.

"I confess," he said. "I'm here looking for you and I got your contact information from Amber. She and Sergei were in Anchorage shopping for a wedding dress or something. I just moved to Boston. And since you're the only person I know here, I knew I needed a friend."

"Well, you've successfully found me and you've got a

friend. We don't have an Alaskan word like *cheechako* for people that are new to Boston, but there's plenty of pitfalls for the unwary in the big city. It's always good to have friends."

"Since you put it that way," Grady said, "how about I take you to lunch and you can fill me in on some of those pitfalls."

"Actually, I can't do lunch. I have an interview in a few minutes, but I'd love to take you to dinner. Where're you staying?"

With a quick exchange of info, Grady headed out as Lauren's secretary brought in her interviewee. As Grady passed her, the secretary mouthed to Lauren, *he's cute.*

Lauren grinned as Grady turned at the door to wave a quick good-bye. She hoped that her face wasn't too red as she tried to put on her professional demeanor.

***

Lauren selected a nice restaurant with an eclectic menu. There wasn't any 'bou stew', but she figured they'd find something interesting to eat. She chose a dark blue, fitted dress with a sparkly necklace and high heels that made her feel feminine and mysterious, but not too formal. She wanted Grady to see more than the woman he'd come to know in some of her worst moments.

The restaurant was within walking distance of his hotel

so they arranged to meet there. Grady came in right at the appointed time in a carefully pressed suit and tie. He was clearly attempting to upgrade her impression of him also.

He greeted her as an old friend with a simple kiss on the cheek and a half hug. She'd already ordered the wine and the waiter filled their glasses as they sat down.

At first, they acted stiff and formal as befitting their surroundings, but as they filled each other in on all that had happened to them since they'd last seen each other, the unfamiliar fell away and their friendship was renewed. By the time they reached dessert, they were back to their familiar rapport and laughed together easily.

"You know Grady," Lauren began. "I really didn't think I was ever going to see you again."

"I couldn't let that happen," Grady said. "It's really hard to find a good Scrabble partner that makes great hot cocoa."

At that moment, their waiter showed up with the check. Lauren reached for it, but Grady beat her to the grab.

"Oh, no you don't," he said. "This was my treat remember. You've cooked plenty of meals for me already."

"But none of them ever came up to the standard of 'bou stew'", she said with a grin.

"I don't know about that. You were a pretty quick study on that dish," he shot back.

As the waiter returned with the receipt and Grady's credit card, he said, "Thank you Mr. Grady. Please come back and visit us again soon," before he walked away.

"*Mister* Grady," Lauren repeated, "What's that about?"

"Sorry. I guess I never told you. Grady's my last name, but everyone's always called me that, so it's more like a nickname or something."

Putting on her best TV cop voice, Lauren said, "I want to see some I.D. Mister."

Laughing, Grady flipped open his wallet and revealed his Alaska driver's license.

Lauren grabbed it out of his hand to examine it more closely.

"Dylan P. Grady," she read out loud. "Your first name is Dylan?"

Lauren sat back in her chair in total surprise.

"So, what's the P. for?" she ventured to ask.

Leaning forward to take her hand, Grady grinned and said, "I think that's a subject for our next date. And then we can talk about what it will take to convince you to become Mrs. Grady."

THE END

A Summer Nanny In Fairbanks

Description: Third grade teacher, Mandy Hastings, is more than ready for the school year to end. She's almost certain that Brian, her boyfriend of 2 years, is about ready to pop the question. When he drops a bomb instead, Mandy wants to get as far away from her disappointment as possible. On a whim she applies for a summer job as a nanny in Fairbanks, Alaska.

Darren is raising his 12 year old daughter alone except for the help of his housekeeper, Mrs. Wilson, who has to take the summer off to settle her mother's estate. Since Darren's job on the North Slope keeps him away for days at a time there's no other solution except to send Katie to stay with Ms. Lipton in Massachusetts.

Katie desperately wants to stay in Fairbanks with her father so she takes matters into her own hands. She can only hope that the new nanny she secretly hired will meet with her father's approval.

A sequel to this story called *The River Home* follows *A Summer Nanny In Fairbanks*.

Chapter 1

"Ms. Hastings! Ms. Hastings, Billy is eating my crayons!"

The anxious voice broke into Mandy's thoughts as she was drawn back to her surroundings. Giving Billy a stern look, she soothed the anxious girl and helped her to gather up the remaining crayons from the table. She'd thought by the third grade these children would have moved beyond eating crayons, but there were always the ones that were a bit more challenged than the others.

She sighed and gathered the class to move to the next lesson. It was at times like these that the end of the school year couldn't come fast enough for her. They were all just counting down the final days until summer break signaled freedom.

As the children settled into their recitation of the multiplication tables, she sat down at her desk to check the messages on her cell phone. It wasn't her usual habit to engage in such activity during lessons, but Mandy was feeling the strain of the daily grind as much as her students. She paused as she noted a new message from Brian had just popped up. She quickly checked the text.

'Meet me for dinner tonight at Tandoori's?'

Mandy quickly texted him back, *'What time?'*

'Eight o'clock. I really need to talk to you.'

Mandy affirmed the time and added her own tag, '*I love you.*'

'*Ditto*', was the terse response she got in return...after a long pause.

***

Juggling the pile of schoolwork with the dress she'd retrieved from the dry cleaners on her way home, Mandy jabbed her door key at the lock trying to get it open before everything in her hands cascaded to the front porch. The door jerked open in that moment, unbalancing her load as her housemate attempted to come to her rescue. The two women groaned in harmony as papers went flying in every direction.

"I'm sorry," Tina said, as she knelt to the porch and hurried to gather the scatter homework. "I guess I was about ten seconds too late to avoid disaster."

Mandy rescued her dress from the dampness of the porch and went inside. Tina followed with the messy pile and Mandy's bag in hand.

"You're late," she said. "I thought you had gotten lost or something."

"No, the principal caught me on the way out and invited me to his office. He's got plans to make some changes next year and he wanted to run them by me. I think he's talking promotion!" Mandy said. "I'm really looking forward to seeing his new ideas implemented!"

"I hope so," Tina moaned. "These split schedules are killing me. It's hard to keep the students on track when no one's ever sure what track we're supposed to be on."

"I hear you," Mandy replied as she hurriedly checked her dress for any damage from their little mishap.

"What's with the dress," Tina asked.

"Brian texted me today. He wants to meet for dinner at Tandoori's. Says we need to have the *talk*."

Mandy's eyes grew wide at her sudden thought. '*The talk.....*'

"Do you think he means *the talk*," she turned to Tina with a wondering look on her face.

Both women stared at each other for a moment as they considered his meaning. As if their thoughts were synchronized, both of them reached for the other and they began to jump around and squeal with joy.

"This must mean that he's finally ready to make a commitment," Tina said gleefully.

Mandy was quick to agree with this idea. It wasn't as if he hadn't dropped enough hints as to his intentions. She ran from the living room to the kitchen and back again as her mind tried to process the moment.

It had been two years since their first date at Tandoori's and her relationship with Brian seemed perfect in everyone's eyes. He was a junior executive at a major corporation and had his feet firmly planted on the corporate ladder. His boss was so enamored with Brian's

Renee Hart

work that he'd taken a personal interest in the young man's career path. Brian was even invited to several social events that took place at the CEO's summer house in North Carolina. Very few of the employees at the corporate offices here in Atlanta could make that claim for themselves.

Mandy grabbed her dress and started towards her bedroom. She needed a shower and a long soak in the tub with that new bath milk she'd bought the other day. She wanted to look her very best for this occasion.

"Before you go," Tina asked. "Could you take a quick look at something for me? I've been trying to decide between these two summer job options and I'd like your opinion."

Tina pulled up the two ads and placed them side by side on her computer screen.

"This one's from a large hotel chain in the Cayman Islands for someone to work with the staff to improve their English skills. They're not paying a lot, but I'd have full use of the facilities and all of the amenities while I was there.

"That sounds like a lot of fun," Mandy agreed. "What's the other one?"

"Well, this one's a little more complicated, but I think it pays a lot more."

"So, where do you have to go and what do you have to do for this *more*," Mandy asked with a grin.

"Fairbanks, Alaska, and it's a nanny position for a

twelve year old girl."

"Wow, let me see. You can go to the Cayman's for three months and enjoy the sun, surf and sand while doing the easy job of improving the English of some hotel staff or you could go to Alaska and freeze your tail off while dealing with a prepubescent girl...."

"I don't think it's actually freezing in Alaska during the summer," Tina interrupted, "but you're right. If money's not the objective, the Cayman's sounds like way more fun. Thanks! I knew you'd be able to clear up my decision. I'm going to apply right now!"

Mandy laughed at her friend's quick decision and admired her willingness to toss caution to the wind and go off on an adventure. She sometimes wished that she could be that easygoing, but it just wasn't her style. Besides, if what they'd suspected was right, she'd be busy all summer with her wedding plans. With that thought, she hurried to her room to begin her beauty preparations.

***

Mandy arrived at the restaurant fifteen minutes early and carefully checked her appearance in the plate glass window of the store next door. She wasn't known for being late and rarely showed up early for anything. She was more along the lines of a 'just in time' sort of person. Her mother always credited her with being punctual if nothing

Renee Hart

else. *Mother was always more about being 'fashionably late' for everything, including her own wedding*, Mandy reminded herself. Pushing away unhappy thoughts, Mandy slipped inside the restaurant.

She was surprised to find Brian already seated at a table towards the back of the dining room. He wasn't known for his punctuality unless it was directly related to work. She'd gotten used to going into restaurants and waiting at the table for his arrival, so used to it in fact that she carried a book in her purse to pass the time while she waited. She hurried over to join him. It was clear from his glass and the look on his face that he'd started the evening without her.

He half stood as she approached and then quickly sat back down to empty his glass without pulling out her chair. She attributed this to his nervousness about the importance of this dinner. They'd never stood on formalities anyway.

"I hope you don't mind," he said, "I've already ordered for the both of us."

"No, of course not," she said with a smile. "That's very thoughtful of you."

She started to say more when the waiter showed up with two steaming plates of Tandoori Chicken Curry and a large bowl of rice. Forcing a smile, she thanked the waiter and watched in surprise as Brian dived into his plate with his fork and knife. He waved to the waiter to refill his glass and to bring her whatever she wanted to drink. She ordered an iced tea, sweet, and asked for some extra napkins. There was no way she wanted curry on her light blue silk dress. No dry cleaner in the world would be able to salvage a mess like that.

Brian had made a serious dent in his meal before he took his napkin and wiped his mouth. Taking a large swallow of his drink, he sat back and looked at her picking at the food on her plate cautiously. He watched her for several minutes before she realized he'd stopped eating.

"Is there something wrong with your food," he asked.

"Oh, no. I'm just not very hungry," she said.

"I thought you liked the curry here."

"Hmm," was all she said in response.

"I suppose you're wondering why I asked you to meet me here tonight," Brian began with a slight tremor in his voice.

Mandy noticed his hand reaching for his pocket, but she was disappointed to see that he'd only withdrawn a handkerchief to wipe the sweat from his brow.

"Early spring and it's already steamy in Atlanta," he joked as he shoved the cloth back into his pocket with a half-grin.

She stayed quiet and waited.

"I've been promoted," he announced, "to head of the Dallas sales office. I wanted you to be the first to know. You've been a good friend and very supportive during the past two years."

Mandy's thoughts reeled at the word, 'friend' as it clearly presented a lesser view of their relationship than her perspective. Even the simple addition of 'girl' to the front of that word would have sounded a lot better. Her women's intuition went into high alert.

"I also wanted you to be the first to know, well, the second," he scoffed, "that I'm marrying Vanessa Remington."

"Vanessa, *the CEO's daughter*, Remington," Mandy asked in shock. "You're marrying the boss's daughter?"

She couldn't stop her voice from rising at the end of her question. Her mind reeled with shock and anger at this unexpected public announcement of betrayal. A few diners sitting nearby tuned in to catch the drama playing out at their table.

How I could have been so taken with this man's charm to have missed this little twist, she thought to herself.

Brian was still talking, still trying to explain the full measure of his reasoning, but her ears were no longer listening. She managed to clear her thoughts just in time to hear his final sentence.

"I know that you love and care for me and would want the best for my life," he said without pausing, "and I think this is the best thing that could ever happen to me."

That was the apex of ignorance and deception.

All of Mandy's prim and proper upbringing snapped in

that single moment and she gave in to the basest instinct she'd ever seen on TV or in a movie. Rising to her feet, she raised her plate of chicken curry from the table and dumped it over Brian's head. In her most sarcastic voice, she asked him if he'd like a little rice with that curry before dumping the entire bowl of rice over him also.

He sat there in utter shock and horror as red curry dripped over his white shirt and light blue tie and bits of rice stuck to him everywhere. He looked like the worst version of a B-movie zombie in his new attire.

A few of the nearby diners had the audacity to applaud her briefly and none of the nearby waiters seemed inclined to hurry over to the scene to lend any assistance. Brian was too stunned to even move.

Gathering her wits and her purse, Mandy turned to deliver a final shot before making a quick exit.

"I never liked chicken curry, you fool!"

Storming out of the restaurant and leaving him in such a mess was the only real satisfaction to my whole evening, she thought back later.

Chapter 2

By the time Mandy got back to the house, tears were streaming freely down her face. She made no effort to contain them as her heart protested this sudden change in direction. She'd gone from being a blushing bride to a rejected old maid in the space of one dinner. Thankfully, it was dark and there was no one to see her undoing. She noted that Tina's car wasn't in the driveway as she pulled up.

Good thing, she thought. *I'm not ready to give any explanations yet.*

She went inside and hurried to her room to change. This was her favorite dress and she'd carefully saved it for this special occasion. Now she only wanted to get out of it and hide it in the back of her closet. She wondered if she'd ever have a reason or the desire to wear it again.

Her first thought was to crawl into bed and pull the covers over her head, but then she realized she'd had nothing to eat since lunch time and not even a broken heart was going to cover the emptiness in her stomach. One thing for sure, she'd never eat chicken curry again as long as she lived.

She walked to the kitchen hoping there was some ice cream lurking in the back of the freezer. She found a half-empty container of fudge ripple long past its prime, but the liberal application of some chocolate syrup and a few sprinkles perked it up to par. Eating it right out of the container while ignoring her mother's voice in her head, *Really Darling! That's not a proper way to eat ice cream,* she wandered over to look at the screen of Tina's computer.

The screen was still open to the job site where Tina had applied for the position in the Cayman's. Using the BACK arrow, Mandy clicked to the screen with the two jobs side by side. Considering the depth of her humiliation, all she wanted to do at this moment was to get as far away from Atlanta as her situation would allow her to go. Fairbanks, Alaska, in comparison, was a reasonable destination in her mind at that moment. She sat down to read the job description carefully.

"WANTED: Temporary Nanny for summer position in Fairbanks, Alaska. Job responsibilities include the care and feeding of a 12-year old with some light housekeeping and entertainment duties. All travel expenses will be covered round-trip first class and a monthly salary based on your qualifications. Please e-mail for further information."

In a fit of retaliation, Mandy entered the information required to apply for the job. Before her good sense could take hold of her, she hit the ENTER key and watched the screen change. It was done and whatever happened next would determine her direction for the summer. *Maybe* **North to Alaska** *wasn't such a bad idea,* she thought.

Darren Covington was fearless in the face of raging winter storms on the North Slope, hungry polar bears and the occasional defiant workman, but he trembled at the thought of dealing with his twelve year old daughter, Katie, when she was in a rage. The old adage, comparing the fury of hell with the scorned woman came to mind when he thought of such moments. He could only imagine what she would be like when she came of age with the head start she already had on this kind of behavior.

"I don't want to go back to Massachusetts and stay with Ms. Lipton for the summer," she shouted loudly enough for the neighbors to hear. "I want to stay here, in my home, with you! I spend the entire school year down in the lower '48. Alaska is my home. You've got no right to make me go back!!"

"But Katie," he said, trying for a reasonable tone, "I've already explained to you. Mrs. Wilson's mother died and she needs to go down and take care of the funeral and settle the estate. She's going to be gone all summer. There's no one here to take care of you when I'm out on the Slope. I can't leave you here alone."

Katie wanted to argue that point, but she knew it was true. Her father's job often took him away for several days at a time. There was no way she could stay alone in their big house on the Chena River. Too many things might go wrong and even in her anger, she knew she wasn't up to taking care of them. She cast around trying to think of another option, but their neighbors didn't present any viable alternatives.

"What if we hire a temporary summer nanny," she asked hopefully.

"Where are we going to find someone at this juncture? I'm not comfortable leaving you with some stranger."

"What if I got another teacher from my school to come up here instead of me going down to stay with Ms. Lipton? Would that work for you?" she asked.

"Do you have someone in mind that might be willing to come," Darren asked quietly. He didn't have much confidence in this avenue, but he thought it might give him a way to disarm her anger if he at least tried to listen to her ideas.

"I don't know, but will you give me a couple of days to at least try to find someone before you buy me a plane ticket," she asked with just the slightest hint of sarcasm in her voice.

Knowing it was useless to continue the argument, Darren relented to give her a few days. It wouldn't make any difference in the end. He'd already made the necessary arrangements with Ms. Lipton, and Katie had somewhere to go. If she could find an alternative, he'd be willing to change the plans. It would definitely make him happier to

Renee Hart

have her here in Fairbanks for the summer. He missed having her around during the long dark winter even if he did have to spend most of his days out on the North Slope.

***

Katie checked her e-mail for the sixth time that day looking for a response to her job posting. She was running out of time as Mrs. Wilson was nearly packed and ready to head south. If she didn't get a response today, her plan was about to crash and burn and she'd be packing her own bags and heading south, not a happy thought. She was excited to see that she had a message in her inbox.

Opening the message she was equally surprised to see this wasn't another dreary inquiry about pay, information, etc. This was an acceptance of the job with a full commitment. This person didn't bother to ask a single thing. Normally, this might have raised some serious questions, but Katie was too desperate to care about the details.

Using the information on the application and her father's credit card, Katie booked a round trip ticket, first class, from Atlanta to Fairbanks for a week from tomorrow. She left the return date to the discretion of the passenger hoping they could work out that little detail later. Putting all of their contact information and the flight info in an e-mail, she fired it off to her *new* nanny. Her last thought as she hit ENTER was, *I hope she's nice.*

***

Darren was surprised to find Katie up and waiting for him when he got home late that night. It had been a long time since he'd had the pleasure of coming home to anyone. There was even a plate of supper ready for him that Mrs. Wilson had set aside. Katie warmed it in the microwave by the time he got inside. She made small talk while he put his briefcase away and hung up his jacket. Grabbing the stack of mail off the hall table, he sorted through it as he walked to the kitchen. Katie followed along behind him talking about the usual stuff.

It wasn't until he was seated at the table chewing on green beans that the real reason came out for her waiting up. He listened carefully as she explained that a teacher, Mandy Hastings, had agreed to come to Fairbanks and stay with her as a temporary nanny for the summer. He realized later that he probably should have asked a lot more questions about this arrangement, but he was so happy with the news that he let the details slide. He should have known something was up. Katie was a little too full of vague details and short on specifics. His fatherly instincts must have been on tilt or something, he figured later.

***

Renee Hart

Mandy was idly checking her e-mail as she cleared out the rest of her things from her desk. Today was the last day of school for the teachers and all she had left to do was pack up a few personal belongings and head home. She'd been so engrossed in her personal misery and the drudgery of paperwork to close out the year that she'd almost forgotten about her moment of madness. She didn't even remember to tell Tina what she had done.

She was surprised to see an e-mail forwarded from the job service in her SPAM file. She wondered how long it had been there. She was even more surprised to learn that she'd been hired and all of her travel arrangements had been made and paid for already. As she scanned the message for more details, she nearly fell out of her chair in shock. She was scheduled to leave for Fairbanks in two days!

She struggled to take all of this in as her mind cast around for a million reasons as to why she simply couldn't go to Alaska. *My break-up with Brian was devastating, but common sense had to kick in sometime*, she thought. It's not like a person could just run off to the ends of the earth every time disappointment came their way.

As she stared at the e-mail, there was one little voice inside her head that rose up and pushed aside all the other voices. This voice didn't come to her very often, but she treasured whatever words that came in this one. This was her grandmother's voice and Mandy's eyes grew misty as her grandmother's face came into focus in her mind's eye. *Darling, you can do anything you set your mind to and I believe in you*, her grandmother's voice said quietly, *go to Alaska and have yourself an adventure.*

***

Mandy burst into the house with her arms full of shopping bags to find Tina trying on bikinis in front of the hall mirror. She collapsed on the couch under the pile of bags and gave out a loud groan. Tina hurried over to unbury her from the mound of sweaters and heavy leggings that spilled out of the bags. She held up a couple of pairs of wool socks and some mittens in amazement.

"What are you doing," she asked. "Getting a head start on a winter clothing drive for Siberia?"

"I'm heading north to Alaska," Mandy groaned.

"What? When?"

Tina looked at her housemate in astonishment. She knew Mandy wasn't one for making rash decisions or instant plans. Well, at least she thought she knew her friend...

"I'm leaving day after tomorrow."

At these words Mandy grabbed a stocking cap that had fallen from one of the bags and pulled it down over her face. She knew it wasn't the most mature response to her friend's questions, but she was feeling embarrassed and humiliated. She didn't want to admit to anyone how she'd let Brian's behavior drive her to make a complete fool of herself and take a job she didn't want, in a place she didn't want to go to, namely, Alaska.

For once, Tina was speechless. She just stared at Mandy half-buried in a pile of heavy winter clothing. Her mind raced as she struggled to understand the chain of events leading up to this. Suddenly, the lights came on as she remembered the job site she'd left up on her computer on the night of the *Tandoori crash*. Her eyes grew wide at the thought and she started to laugh out loud.

Mandy dragged the cap off her head and glared as Tina began to dance around the room in her cute little bikini. The stifling weight of the heavy clothes laying on top of her was causing her to break out in a sweat and an itchy rash too, she noted with alarm. *Don't tell me I'm allergic to wool*, she thought. *What else could go wrong today?*

Chapter 3

The landing in Fairbanks was as smooth as butter. Mandy looked out the window of the airplane thinking she'd see lots of snow on the ground. Unfortunately, it was two o'clock in the morning and she couldn't see much of anything beyond the lights of the airport. Looking at the ground around the airplane, she couldn't see any snow, but she was sure it was freezing out there. It just looked cold… and unwelcoming.

She gathered her carry-on bag and heavy winter coat from the closet. *No ugly overhead bins to wrestle with in first class*, she thought with a grin. This was her first time ever to fly anywhere in such luxury. She almost felt gracious and forgiving to have been brought to a summer job in this manner. Tina had to buy her own economy ticket to the Cayman's for her adventure. She stumbled towards the exit, as her legs were stiff from the long flights she'd had to endure. She nodded stiffly as the Captain and staff welcomed her to Alaska. One thing for sure, Atlanta was very far away.

It wasn't until she reached the luggage conveyor that she realized there'd been no mention of anyone coming to the airport to pick her up. She was overcome with a strong desire to run back to the plane and demand they take her right back home to Atlanta. Other people that flew first class were known to throw tantrums in public. Maybe it would be okay if she gave in to acting childish and silly.

Get a grip on yourself, she scolded herself in her best schoolteacher voice. *You're better than this.* For once, she had to agree with herself and there and then, she resolved to make the best of this situation. *Who knows, maybe something good would come out of all of this in the end.* With that thought she gathered her heavy bags and headed for the exit. If nothing else, she could call a taxi and show up on their front doorstep at three a.m.

***

Katie was in a real dilemma. Her father was away and Ms. Hasting's plane was landing at two a.m. She hadn't told him exactly when the new nanny was scheduled to arrive, mainly because she was trying very hard not to tell him anything about the whole situation that might tip him off to her little plot.

Mrs. Wilson was sound asleep in her bed long before ten and didn't like to be disturbed in the night. Katie had spent the last two hours trying to figure out how to get the new nanny back to the house and she finally came up with a plan.

Putting on her best grown-up voice, she called the Frosty Taxi Service and made arrangements for a driver to meet Ms. Hastings in the baggage pick-up area. She was assured that the driver would hold up a sign for Ms. Hastings. From there, the driver would bring the woman and her bags to the address she gave them. To conclude the matter, Katie gave them her credit card number to pay the fare with a generous tip for the driver. Now all she could do was wait to see if her plan worked.

She was rewarded with the sight of headlights in the driveway and hurried to open the front door. She'd nearly fallen asleep on the sofa a couple of times while she was waiting. Her hair was a mess and she couldn't stop yawning, but Ms. Hastings was in her driveway.

At that sight of the woman bundled up in a parka worthy of any Aleut hunter, Katie was speechless. She noted Ms. Hastings' heavy wool mittens hanging off those little clippie things, and the scarf wrapped tightly around her neck, with some amusement. Katie and the cab driver were wearing t-shirts and cut-offs in the early hours of the morning. *It's not exactly warm, but the poor woman must be roasting in that coat*, Katie thought. Katie helped the driver drag the heavy bags into the front entryway as Mandy struggled to undo the toggle buttons and zipper of her first parka ever.

Mandy figured she'd be leaving this in Alaska when she left as it would be of no use to her in Atlanta. *That is, if she can get herself out of it*, she thought as she struggled with the unfamiliar fastenings. Thank goodness she didn't have to deal with such things when it was time for recess with her students. She didn't know how the teachers would manage to get 20 or 30 students into their winter gear in the short span of a break and then back into the classroom. It was hard enough to deal with sweaters and boots when it rained.

Finally free of the confines of her coat, Mandy turned to greet the young lady who she presumed was to be her charge for the summer. She found Katie staring at her with a look of astonishment.

"You're very pretty," Katie said with surprise in her voice.

"Well, thank you," Mandy ventured. "You're very pretty too."

Katie blushed and turned her face away at the compliment. She wasn't used to such talk.

"I wasn't sure whether you'd want to stay here in the house or out back in our little guest cabin," Katie said. "You can have your choice if you'd like to take a look. Lots of people like staying in the cabin with it next to the river. It's really quiet."

With that question hanging in the air, Katie gave Ms. Hastings a quick tour of the house with a stop in the guest bedroom at the top of the stairs and then started to take her outside to show her the cabin. Mandy hesitated at the back door and looked outside fearfully.

"Are you sure it's safe to go out there in the dark," she asked the little girl.

Katie looked at the woman in confusion as the sky was already light enough for her to see all the way to the river.

"We don't have to go outside if you don't want to," Katie said. "You can just stay in the guestroom if you prefer."

Mandy nodded at that and turned back inside. Grabbing her overnight bag and one of the smaller cases, she headed upstairs. She figured she'd get the rest of her luggage in the morning. Later, she would attribute this oversight to jet lag, but it never occurred to her to wonder why her *greeting party* consisted of a lone little girl.

***

It wasn't long after Mandy and Katie had gone to bed that Darren came home. His plan to be home the previous evening got changed at the last minute. He figured he had just enough time to get a quick shower and some breakfast before he had to drive Mrs. Wilson to the airport. To his surprise, her suitcases were already in the front entryway. He was even more surprised when he realized how heavy they were when he picked them up. *She must have found a way to pack a moose in these bags*, he thought.

Since they were ready to go, he hauled them out to the garage and loaded them into the back of the SUV. Noticing the baggage tags, he wondered where she'd gotten tags from Atlanta. Her family all lived in Phoenix. Thinking to do her a favor, he cut off the old tags and tossed them in the bin on his way back inside. Heading upstairs for a shower, he noted the smell of coffee coming from the kitchen. He knew that meant Mrs. Wilson was already up and she would have some breakfast for him when he was done.

As he got dressed, he listened for sounds of life from Katie's room. He thought she'd want to go with them to the airport, but her room was quiet. Passing by on his way downstairs, he took a peek inside to see her still sleeping soundly. *She must have waited up for me last night*, he mused.

Darren was happy to find some hot biscuits with birch tree syrup and reindeer sausage on the table with a fresh pot of coffee. He was going to miss Mrs. Wilson's cooking. He didn't get to enjoy a lot of it, being away so much of the time, but he always enjoyed what she made for him. She filled him in on the details of the past few days and gave him a copy of her itinerary.

"I'm not exactly sure when I'll be back," she said. "It just depends on how long it takes to get the estate settled. I have to close up the house and all that, you see. You might want to worry I don't get a better offer down in Phoenix. These Alaskan winters can be long and hard for an old woman," she teased.

Darren laughed at her words, but deep inside, he had to wonder. With him gone so much and Katie away at school, Mrs. Wilson spent a lot of time here alone. It had to be hard on the woman. She had plenty of reasons not to come back to Fairbanks. It wasn't like she needed the money.

With her usual insight, she gave him a quick hug and announced it was time for them to head to the airport. She liked to be early with the hassle of security. She still wasn't used to taking off her shoes and having her purse searched for nail clippers and such.

"Katie said her good-byes last night and isn't planning to go with us to the airport this morning," Mrs. Wilson said. "I'm really going to miss my girl this summer after her being away all winter. I hope this new nanny you're getting takes real good care of her."

With those words, Mrs. Wilson picked up her suitcase from next to her bedroom door and headed towards the garage. Putting his plate and cup in the sink, Darren hurried to help her with the bag.

Tossing it in the back with the others, he closed the back of the SUV and opened the garage door. He didn't stop to wonder why his housekeeper needed four suitcases for her trip. A bright spring day greeted them as he backed out into the driveway. He figured he'd be back before Katie was up and maybe the two of them could spend the day together doing something fun.

∗∗

When they arrived at the airport, Darren parked next to

the curbside baggage check-in and went around to the back of the truck. Mrs. Wilson took her time getting out and he'd already lined up all of her bags in front of the clerk.

"How many are traveling, ma'am," the clerk asked as Mrs. Wilson handed him her ticket.

"There's just me," she said as she eyed the four suitcases in front of her.

"I'm sorry, ma'am," the clerk said, "but all of your suitcases need to be properly tagged. Here are the tags for these three. Please fill them out."

"But these aren't my bags," Mrs. Wilson protested as she turned to look at Darren in surprise. "Where did you get these bags?"

Darren looked confused and knelt to examine the bags. He had pulled off all of the labels back at the house, including the ones identifying the owner.

"I'm sorry. I thought they were yours," he explained. "I found them in the front entryway."

"No. I only have my one bag," Mrs. Wilson said. "You know I always like to travel light."

The two of them stood there staring at each other in confusion.

Suddenly Darren realized the new nanny must have arrived last night. He pulled out his cell phone and poked the icon for Katie's phone. After a few rings, the call went to voice mail.

"She must still be sleeping. There's no answer. I guess

I'll take these back to the house since you don't want to take them with you," he joked as he loaded them back into the truck.

Leaving Mrs. Wilson standing at the curb still scratching her head, he headed for home in a big hurry, wondering what he was going to find when he got there.

Renee Hart

Chapter 4

Mandy woke up feeling tired, confused and hungry all at the same time. The lingering aroma of coffee drew her out of bed. Her stomach rumbled as she pulled on a pair of jeans and a heavy sweater. A quick splash of water on her face from the sink and a few swipes at her hair was all she felt up to doing. She didn't know when she was going to meet her new employer, but she'd deal with that when the time came. *Besides, how much make-up would a nanny need to wear in Alaska*, she wondered.

Quietly, she opened the bedroom door, listening for movement elsewhere in the house. There was nothing that she could hear from where she stood. Moving to the top of the stairs, she stopped to listen again. Her nervousness was making her feel like a cat burglar. Still, no sound of anyone else in the house. She headed downstairs when she realized that her suitcases were no longer sitting in the front entryway. She picked up the pace as her eyes scanned the surrounding area for her luggage.

This is odd, she thought. *I'm sure Katie wouldn't have put them somewhere else. We both went to bed at the same time last night.*

She stood in the hallway scratching her head. The sudden sound of the garage door opening made her jump in surprise. She almost started to run back upstairs when she realized that would be silly. She had no reason to hide or to be afraid. She was the new nanny after all. Deciding to hold her ground, she turned to face the front door to greet whomever had arrived. She didn't hear the back door open.

"Hello?"

The sound of a deep male voice behind her startled Mandy, and she gave a little shriek. Spinning around to face this intruder, she lost her balance and started to fall. Two strong arms caught her mid-way to the floor and she found herself looking into an anxious pair of dark brown eyes. She had time to notice how they matched Katie's eyes before he lifted up and set her back on her feet. If he let go of her a bit too quickly, she didn't notice as she still felt the strength of his arms around her. Breathless, she put a hand to her chest and tried to still her heart.

"You frightened me," she said. "I thought you would be coming in the front door. I didn't think about there being a door in the back from the garage. Katie didn't have time to show me everything last night. I got in so late, you see...."

Her voice trailed off as she realized she was babbling. The man still hadn't said a word. He just stood there staring at her with a mixture of questions running across his face.

"Good morning."

The sound of Katie's sleepy voice from the top of the stairs drew their attention to her. She cautiously regarded the two of them as she made her way down the stairs.

"I see you two have met," she said.

A slight smile played across her face as she saw them together for the first time.

"Well, not exactly," her father said in a droll voice, "we haven't gotten that far yet."

Extending his hand, Darren attempted to interject some social protocol into the scene.

Mandy thought it best to play along and they acted out a very proper, formal introduction for Katie's benefit. If she caught the hint of comedy in their words, she didn't let on. She simply walked past them both and headed for the kitchen.

"Wow, I'm starving," she exclaimed as she tried to redirect their attention to safer ground. She was hoping to not have to make too many explanations today.

"Uh, Katie," Mandy called, "do you have any idea what happened to the bags I left here last night."

Katie stopped and turned around in surprise. She looked around the entryway.

Her father cleared his throat.

"I think I can explain that," he began. "Your bags are out in my SUV."

"What? Why?" Katie nearly shouted.

"Does this mean I'm leaving already," Mandy asked with a confused look on her face.

"No. No!"

Darren held up his hands in self-defense as he addressed the two of them.

"I made a mistake. I thought the bags belonged to Mrs. Wilson, ("Our housekeeper," he said in an aside to Mandy.) and I loaded them up this morning when I took her to the airport. When she didn't recognize them, I realized that someone else was in the house."

This last part was said with a pointed look at Katie, letting her know that sooner or later a more detailed explanation of all of this was going to be required of her.

"Wow, Dad," Katie groaned. "You never listen to me. I told you Mandy was coming."

"Yes, you did," he agreed, "but you still managed to leave out one little detail...as in, when!"

Mandy looked from father to daughter and back again. As a teacher, she was used to parent/child conflicts and miscommunications, but at school, she had some professional distance. Here, she was feeling a bit too involved, almost like she was being drawn in to their battle. It wasn't a comfortable feeling for her. She decided it was time to follow Katie's lead and change the subject.

"So, what's for breakfast," she quipped with a grin.

Picking up the lifeline Mandy was throwing her inadvertently, Katie turned back towards the kitchen.

"Dad's going to make us pancakes with reindeer sausage," she tossed over her shoulder.

"Sounds wonderful," Mandy said as she followed her

charge. "I've never had reindeer sausage before."

As she walked into the kitchen, she was able to see the entire expanse of the backyard which ended at the bank of the Chena River. The grass was lush and green and there wasn't any snow in view from where she stood. She gasped at the sight, as it was breathtaking in the bright sunlight.

"This is incredible," she said as she walked to the windows.

The entire back of the house was plate glass windows all the way up to the second story. Two French doors opened to a large patio made of fieldstone and the guest cabin was off to one side of the lawn. Spruce trees grew along the edges of the lawn, separating it from the neighbor's. Her closer view point revealed massive mountains in the distance clearly capped with snow. Mandy's entire perspective of Alaska was changed in that one instant. She hadn't expected anything like this.

Behind her Katie and Darren busied themselves with the task of getting breakfast ready. The two of them wrestled with their own thoughts as their new nanny took in the sights. If the air, seemed a bit frosty in the kitchen, well, this *was* Alaska.

***

Katie attempted to fill the air with small talk as she tried to keep Mandy from revealing too many details about how she came to Alaska. Every time her father asked a question, she'd interrupt either him or Mandy until they were both very suspicious of her. Finally, the two of them stopped talking and turned to look at her.

"Is there something you need to tell us," Darren asked, "because this isn't working for me."

Katie's face fell and she knew there was no point in trying to keep her secrets. She decided in that moment to come clean about the entire plan and hope for the best. She had no reason to expect anything after what she had done in deceiving them. Slowly she explained everything in exact detail, down to the amount she'd spent on a first class ticket from Atlanta to Fairbanks and the promise of a fair salary. (She did notice the two of them wince when she told them how much she'd paid for the air fare.)

Mandy listened to Katie's tearful confession in shocked silence. Realizing she was the unwitting party to an outright deception was disconcerting. She wasn't encouraged by the look on Darren's handsome face. He was carefully holding his tongue to give Katie enough time to tell the whole story, but the effort was showing. Mandy was sure she could hear the sound of him grinding his teeth.

When Katie was finished, Darren turned to look at Mandy. Her soft green eyes and strawberry blond hair reminded him of his late wife. He could only wonder at the affect this woman was having on Katie. She had the few

Renee Hart

pictures of her mother that were left in the house upstairs in her room. Just thinking of Karen made Darren sad as he tried to determine his next step.

"I'm sorry," Mandy said. "I think this is partly my fault. I took this job because I wanted to get away from Atlanta for the summer and Alaska seemed *pretty* far away. I was dealing with a major disappointment in my own life and didn't ask the right questions about the job."

She looked down at her hands, not knowing how to proceed and unwilling to look at Katie's tears. Although it had only been a few hours, she liked the little girl and didn't want to see her hurt.

Darren looked down at the table himself. Nothing in management training had ever prepared him for a situation like this. His daughter was openly crying now, and the young woman next to her looked ready to cry too. He was starting to feel like a buffoon in his own house. That wasn't helping anything.

Finally, the solution seemed obvious to him. Clearly, Katie had made some errors in judgment in bringing a stranger into their house and that had to be dealt with, but Mandy seemed like a decent person. Maybe this was as simple as putting their ducks back in the right order.

"Normally, when I hire someone, I do a background check on them and get some references first," Darren began. "Would you be willing to give me your information and a reference so I can take care of that?"

"Of course," Mandy said. "That's not a problem...if you really want me to stay after all this."

"If everything checks out and you're not a career criminal that goes around posing as a nanny for nefarious purposes, I think that would make Katie very happy and besides, my instincts tell me you're not a danger to us and they're usually pretty accurate. Anyone willing to eat five of my pancakes is a hero in my book."

Katie stopped sniffling and looked at her father hopefully.

"As for you, young lady, your punishment is to be determined," he said sternly. "Right now, I'm too full of pancakes to think of anything harsh enough to make atonement for what you've done to Mandy and my credit card balance."

Katie quickly looked back down at the table, but not fast enough for her father to miss the grin on her face. She wasn't too worried about any punishment her father could contrive for her. He wasn't that creative. She missed the wink Darren directed at Mandy over her head.

***

Being the CEO of operations in a large corporation comes with several advantages and one of them included a very efficient personnel department. Darren faxed all of Mandy's information to his hiring manager and received a full background report including a personal testimony from the principal at the school in Atlanta within two hours.

The woman was a highly regarded third grade teacher with a very impressive resume. As blind luck would have it, Katie had somehow managed to find an excellent nanny for herself. Darren didn't want to consider all of the things that could have gone wrong with this venture. He could only thank God that nothing did and Mandy had answered Katie's job ad.

Unfortunately with the report came another that required Darren's attention immediately in the field office. He dreaded seeing Katie's face when he told her he needed to head back up to the Slope. At least, he had the satisfaction of knowing she was in good hands. He went to see what the two of them were up to while he'd been working in his office and deliver the bad news.

***

He found them in the back yard where Katie was giving Mandy a look at the guest cabin. It was set up with sleeping quarters in the loft and a sitting area with a half bathroom downstairs. The river was very close and tall spruce trees surrounded it on three sides. It was pretty quiet most of the time. The float planes and boat traffic did occasionally disrupt the peace, but they were used to it.

Mandy was enchanted with the cabin, but she felt, with Darren gone so much of the time, it would be better for her to stay in the house with Katie. Secretly, she wasn't too sure about being out here alone, nor about how she'd feel going back and forth to the cabin in the dark. The wilderness aspect of Alaska wasn't very far away and Katie had already told her how moose and bear showed up at their place regularly. Alaskans considered the wildlife just part of the neighborhood.

Darren was relieved at her decision and didn't realize fear was a part of it. He didn't want Katie staying in the house alone either. He also didn't realize that Mandy knew very little about Alaska, including the fact it wouldn't ever get dark during most of her stay. She'd be lucky to see stars again before she headed back to Atlanta. The three of them had a lot to learn about each other in three short months. A small part of him was looking forward to it.

***

"What do you like on your pizza," Darren asked with a grin.

He knew Katie wanted pineapple and reindeer sausage. He didn't even need to ask. He smiled at Mandy as he tried to brush off Katie's hold on his arm. She was jumping up and down with excitement and shouting out her requests.

Mandy grinned back at him and wrinkled up her nose.

Giving him a wink, she said, "I think I'd like mushrooms and onions myself. With bleu cheese dressing!"

Katie turned to look at her with a look of total disgust on her face.

Mandy broke out laughing.

"I'm just kidding! Reindeer sausage and pineapple is fine with me as long as you add in extra cheese."

Nodding her head wildly, Katie jumped up and down again.

Darren laughed as he went into his office to place the order. He knew he wouldn't be able to hear a thing with Katie acting up like that.

***

The three of them ate pizza out on the patio while they watched the sun dance along the northwestern horizon. The gorgeous blaze as it slipped over the edge lit up the sky in brilliant colors of red and orange. Mandy realized as they were sitting there that even with the sun gone it wasn't really dark.

"What time will it get dark," she asked.

"Well, it really doesn't and since this is only the first of June, the days are going to continue getting longer until we reach the summer solstice," Katie explained. "Don't you know? This is the Land of the Midnight Sun?"

Mandy replied, "We hear things like that, but it's hard to imagine what it's like from Atlanta. To me, it's just some kind of romantic phrase. I've never seen a 24 hour day."

"I'm not sure 'romantic' is the right word for it," Darren said. "It can be hard to get used to for some people who find it hard to sleep when it's still light outside, and the downside is that in the winter we have days that are 20+ hours of darkness. Those can be even harder to get used to," he added soberly.

The three of them sat there quietly as each of them considered these extremes from their own perspective. Mandy didn't understand the sadness that came over her new employers, but she felt it.

Darren was the first to break the silence as he stood and began to gather the remains of their meal.

"I have to head up to the Slope first thing in the morning," he said. "Something's come up."

Looking at Mandy, he added, "This is our life and the way my business works. I hope you're okay with all of this."

Forcing a smile, Mandy looked back at him.

"Of course. I understand. I mean that's why you need a nanny, right?"

Darren nodded grimly as he carefully avoided looking at the disappointment on Katie's face. He knew she was anything but happy about this. He could only hope that she and Mandy would find a way to have fun on their own.

Chapter 5

The next morning, the sound of a helicopter landing in the backyard jarred Mandy out of her bed. She scrambled to the window, but her room looked out over the neighbor's house. She hurried down to the kitchen just in time to see Darren climbing in beside the pilot. She watched in amazement as the chopper lifted off and flew away over the river. If she caught his last worried look back towards the house as they left, it didn't really register with her.

She realized Katie was sitting at the counter watching her father fly away also. Listlessly stirring a bowl of oatmeal, the sadness on her face was evident. She brightened a bit as she turned to look at Mandy.

"Would you like some oatmeal," Katie asked. "I don't think there's anything else. No one's done any real grocery shopping in a while. Dad left us some money so we can go today if you want."

She pointed at two envelopes lying on the counter.

"One of those are for you," she said.

Mandy took the fatter envelope with her name on the front and peeked inside. The stack of hundred dollar bills inside made her gasp in surprise. A set of car keys tumbled out and clattered to the floor. She picked them and examined them.

"Those are for Dad's SUV. He figured you wouldn't want to drive the Hummer."

"No, of course not," Mandy agreed as she wondered if she would even be able to drive a 'Hummer'. Just the thought of doing such a thing nearly made her break out in hives.

"I think I'll just have some coffee this morning," she said absently.

Katie finished her oatmeal and the two of them made ready to go to the grocery store. Mandy opened the closet and looked at her parka.

"I guess I really didn't need to buy this, did I?"

She laughed at the look on Katie's face.

"I know. I know. I'm a teacher. I should know how to do basic research. I have to confess, I was in such a panic when I read your e-mail. I wasn't thinking clearly."

"Well, I hope you brought some lighter shirts and shorts, cause it can get pretty hot here in Fairbanks," Katie said.

"What do you mean *hot*?"

"We'll have days when it's in the eighties and sometimes, even the nineties," Katie added.

As she said that, Katie pushed the button to open the garage door. Mandy looked at the Hummer and laughed.

"I take it that isn't one of the million dollar Hummers!"

"No way! That hunk of junk is something my dad picked up at one of those surplus sales the army uses to clear out their closets. The seats are barely padded and there's no radio or CD player. I hate riding in it!"

Mandy turned her attention to the Range Rover parked next to it. Pushing the door lock button, she and Katie got in and put on their seatbelts.

"Uh," Mandy said as she looked around at the controls. "What?"

"I don't know how to drive a stick shift," Mandy confessed weakly. "I never learned. I never needed to learn."

She turned to find Katie staring at her in disbelief. The two of them took off their seatbelts and got out of the SUV. Mandy noticed a small tarp covering something with two wheels against the wall.

"What's this," she asked as she pulled the tarp away. "A Vespa! You have a Vespa!"

"Um, yeah, but its Dad's and he never lets me drive it."

"I'm sure if he was okay with me driving his SUV, he'll be okay with me driving his Vespa. We'll go to the grocery store on this!"

"Okay, but we're not going to be able to get a lot of groceries. I've only got two hands and unless you're a great driver, I'd like to have at least one to hang on to you with," Katie said.

"No worries! I've got this under control. Trust me," Mandy said as she wheeled the Vespa out of the garage. "Don't forget to grab the shopping bags and the garage remote."

Spying a pair of helmets on a shelf, she grabbed them

and put one of them on. Handing the other to Katie, she ignored the doubts playing across the girl's face. She might not know how to drive a stick shift, but she was a pro at scootering. The two of them got on and made it to the end of the driveway without mishap. Mandy stopped and turned around to look at Katie.

"Which way is the grocery store?"

Katie laughed and pointed to the left. Her spirits lifted as a sense of adventure overtook her doubts. They might not get a lot of groceries, but this was going to be fun.

The grocery store wasn't more than a few miles away and by the time they arrived, Katie was confident Mandy knew her way around on a scooter. A moose standing on the side of the road only caused her to wobble a little bit. Katie was glad it wasn't a bear. Finding a parking space near the front door, she parked the Vespa. As they walked into the store, Mandy was amazed at the shiny new expanse of the superstore and even more so when she saw the produce department with every kind of fruit and vegetable imaginable.

"This is as nice as anything we have in Atlanta," Mandy said. "I didn't expect this."

Grabbing a large cart, she started picking out strawberries and oranges and grapes by the bagful. Katie watched in surprise as she threw in milk and butter and bread. Her eyes grew even wider when Mandy picked out large cartons of juice and yogurt. The cart was soon piled with all kinds of food.

"How are we going to get all of this home on the Vespa," Katie asked as they were standing in the checkout line. "You do remember we came here on a scooter, don't you." This last bit was said with more than a hint of sarcasm.

"I told you. I have this under control. You just have to trust me."

"Okay," said Katie as she threw a couple of chocolate bars and some gum in the pile. She watched Mandy pay for the groceries in silence and then followed her outside.

Mandy stopped at the front door and pulled out her cell phone. She dialed a number and handed the phone to Katie.

"Get us a cab," she said.

Katie asked for a cab to come to the store as she realized Mandy's plan to get the groceries home. She had to admit, her new nanny caught on pretty fast. She started to laugh as Mandy gave her a wink.

***

Over the next couple of days, Darren checked in with Katie frequently, but he wasn't able to come home. He made several suggestions of things for them to do while he was away. Katie had her own ideas.

On this particular day, it was rainy and too cold for the Vespa so the two of them decided to stay at home. Katie was in her room putting some of her clothes away when Mandy came in to see what she wanted for lunch.

"What are all these for," Mandy asked, pointing at a large pile of brightly colored t-shirts.

Katie looked at the pile sadly. With a shrug she pulled it off the shelf and brought it over to her bed. Spreading the shirts out across the bed, she started explaining the importance of each one.

"This is from my soccer team in the first grade and this is from a relay race at the park. This one is from the swim team in third grade...they're all just old shirts from every sports thing I was ever a part of..." Her voice trailed off as she toyed with the pile of shirts absently.

Mandy picked up one of the shirts and looked at it carefully.

"So, there's a 2nd place ribbon sewed onto this one. What's that about?"

"That's from my mom. She was really into all this stuff and she wanted to remember what all the shirts and all the ribbons were about so when I won a ribbon, she would embroider it to the t-shirt that matched."

"What a great idea," Mandy said. "Did you have a plan for these since you've kept them all?"

"A plan? There was no plan. We just kept them and then she died and I..."

Katie looked so sad that Mandy wanted to cry. Her heart ached for the little girl's loss.

"Did you ever consider making them into a quilt or a wall hanging," Mandy asked. They would make a beautiful quilt and I can help you make it. My grandmother taught me how to quilt when I was about your age. It's really fun and easy to learn."

Katie's eyes brightened at the thought and she looked at the t-shirts with surprise. The idea of a quilt seemed like a great way to use them. She was sure her mother would approve as she loved making repurposed things herself. Maybe this was even what she had in mind when she started saving all of these t-shirts while Katie was still little.

"What do we need to make a quilt," Katie asked. "We have a sewing machine and some sewing stuff in the storeroom. We can use that. It was my mom's."

The two of them gathered all the shirts and some loose ribbons and hurried downstairs to the dining room. The large table would make a great workspace. Mandy carefully spread a blanket over the top of it as Katie ran to get the sewing machine and other stuff from the storeroom. Soon, the two of them were happily engaged in their project and forgot all about lunch.

While they worked, Mandy told Katie stories about her grandmother. She had many happy memories and stories to share about growing up. Her grandmother had been very important in Mandy's life and influenced her to become a teacher.

When she asked about Katie's grandparents, the child

confessed she didn't have the chance to know any of hers. Her father's parents died when he was a teenager. He stayed with an uncle on his ranch in Texas learning to be a wildcatter. That was where he met Katie's mother. The two of them eloped and ran away to Alaska against her parents' will.

"They never recod...record....uh, got back together," Katie finished sadly.

Mandy quickly changed the subject back to the tasks at hand.

Stopping to eat a quick supper, the two kept talking about their design plans and ideas. Katie had learned how to cut blocks from each shirt as Mandy worked on embroidering the stray ribbons in the right places. By the time they were ready for bed, they had an entire quilt top laid out on the living room floor waiting to be sewn together. The side of the t-shirt without writing was reserved for the backside of the quilt. With all the bright colors, their project looked like a work of art to Katie. She took dozens of pictures in her excitement.

"I don't think I'm going to be able to sleep," Katie yawned. "This is so fun. I don't want to go to bed."

Mandy laughed at her and started turning off lights. Together, the two of them headed upstairs.

As Mandy tucked Katie into bed, the young girl reached out and took her hand.

"Thanks for coming to Alaska," was all she managed to

say before her eyes slipped shut.

Mandy nodded as she turned off the light and went to her own room. Something inside her tried to warn her not to get too attached. *This is a summer job and soon, you'll go back to Atlanta*, she reminded herself.

Chapter 6

The next morning, both of them were up early and hurried downstairs to admire their work from the day before. To their surprise, Darren was already in the kitchen making pancakes. He'd cleared his schedule and made plans for them to spend the day playing *tourist* for Mandy's sake. Katie was overjoyed with this idea, but first she dragged him into the dining room to see what they'd been doing.

Katie bubbled over with enthusiasm as she showed him each quilt block and explained the importance of every one. He listened carefully and Mandy caught the look of pure gratitude he gave her when Katie wasn't looking. She even noticed him wiping an occasional tear from the corner of his eye when he thought no one was watching. She pretended not to notice, but inside she was happy for him.

Katie was on her second plate of pancakes before she realized her father's plans meant they wouldn't be able to work on her quilt. She looked upset.

"Don't worry," Mandy laughed. "We'll get it done. We need some things from the fabric store to finish it anyway. We have to buy some batting and a few other items. Quilts don't get done in a day."

"Sure, it's no problem," Darren added. "We can stop and get what you need while we're out. Now where do you think we should take Mandy today?"

"I know! I know! Let's take her to the Chena Hot Springs! We can visit the ice house and swim in the springs. It'll be fun!"

"Swim? I didn't bring a swimsuit," Mandy said.

"I was thinking about the riverboat tour," Darren said, "but it's up to you two. We could also call Max and see if he's available to fly us around in his float plane."

Mandy quickly shook her head no at that suggestion.

"I think I've had enough flying for a while," she said with a frown.

"So, it's the riverboat tour," Darren said.

"That sounds interesting," Mandy looked over at Katie.

Katie nodded her agreement and the three of them finished their pancakes and then made quick work of cleaning up in the kitchen together.

***

The riverboat tour didn't leave until 2:00 so they hopped in the Rover to make a trip to the fabric store. Katie took on the role of tour guide and pointed out some of the places they could visit in the coming days. Mandy was happy to have a chance to get a better look. It was hard to see everything while she was driving the scooter.

"How do you like driving the Rover," Darren asked. "I was thinking you might like to try the Hummer."

He said this last part with a grin as he snuck a look at Mandy's face. He was surprised to see her face had turned bright red and she was carefully avoiding looking at him. Katie started laughing in the back seat.

"We haven't been driving the Rover," Mandy said.

"What? How have you two been getting around," he asked.

"We've been scootering!" Katie shouted and burst out laughing.

"You been riding my Vespa?"

He looked at the two of them in astonishment.

"I don't know how to drive a stick shift," Mandy confessed.

"So how did you buy all those groceries on my Vespa," Darren asked confused.

"Oh, Dad! That's easy. We just called a cab to take the stuff home for us when we were done shopping."

Darren thought about this as he negotiated an intersection and shrugged.

"Good thinking," was all he said.

Pulling into the parking lot of the fabric store, he told the ladies he'd wait for them outside. He needed to make a couple of calls to make arrangements for the riverboat. They hurried inside to do their shopping.

***

Renee Hart

As they came into view of the riverboat, Mandy gasped in surprise. She'd never have guessed she'd find such a boat in Alaska. These kinds of boats she normally associated with the Mississippi River and stories about Tom Sawyer and Huck Finn. It was clearly a popular attraction as the large parking area was filled with tour buses already disengaging their passengers.

Darren took care of their tickets while Katie showed Mandy around the large gift shop. They stopped to take pictures with the large moose on display and the dog sled and were busy trying on hats when Darren caught up to them. He joined in the fun with some moose antlers and bear feet slippers to make them laugh.

Lunch was part of the tour package and they sat together at long tables and ate beef stew with the other passengers. Theirs was a lively table and soon everyone was sharing where they were from and what they liked best about Alaska so far.

One of the women made a comment about what a lovely family they were and Katie quickly looked down at the table. Mandy didn't catch what was said, but she noted Katie's discomfort and took her hand under the table. Katie smiled at her gratefully. No one thought to explain that Mandy was only the nanny.

***

When it was time to board the riverboat, Katie skipped ahead and hurried to the top deck. Darren took charge of Mandy as he kept a careful eye on his daughter. The three of them found seats together near the front of the boat. Katie resumed her role of tour guide and carefully explained their itinerary.

"How many times have you been on this trip," Mandy asked. "You appear to be an expert!"

"Only a couple of times," Katie admitted. "I know the route because this boat goes right past our house every day, and the places we're going and the people we'll see along the river are our neighbors. You just haven't seen it because we haven't been out in the backyard when it went by. It's an unwritten rule that we all have to wave when the boat goes by, so most of us try to stay inside until it's past otherwise, we find our pictures scattered across Facebook."

Mandy laughed.

"I hope you two aren't going to be bored with this," she said.

"Oh, no," the two of them chimed together. "We're going to enjoy this as much as you do. Especially the salmon spread on the way back!"

The two of them looked at each other licking their lips and began to laugh.

***

Darren spent the next few days in Fairbanks and the three of them enjoyed spending their evenings making dinner and eating on the patio. Sometimes they'd watch a movie or play video games together. The house was filled with the sound of their happy chatter as the three of them got to know each other. Katie always stayed up as late as she could trying to make the day last as long as possible, but inevitably she'd start nodding off and Darren would shoo her to bed. He told her she was much too big to be carried upstairs.

With Katie asleep, Darren and Mandy would sit on the patio and talk until it was very late and they were both yawning. The two of them soon found it easy just to sit and watch the river traffic go by in silence. When the occasional moose walked through the yard, Mandy would retreat to the back door while Darren laughed at her. She reminded him he wouldn't be laughing if it was a bear.

One evening, they were sitting there quietly when Mandy asked about Karen. Katie didn't talk about her mother very much and Mandy wanted to fill in the missing pieces.

Darren explained how they'd struggled when they first came to Alaska. He quickly got a job on the North Slope, but there was no place for his wife. She stayed here in Fairbanks alone most of the time until Katie was born. His job forced him to be away for weeks at a time.

At first they were happy and they adored Katie. They

lived in a 'Twinkie' house in North Pole and Karen stayed busy being a wife and mom.

"What's a 'Twinkie" house," Mandy interjected.

"Cheap Alaskan housing," Darren laughed. "Actually, it was a house trailer, but with the extreme cold up here, they coat the outside of the trailer with a thick layer of insulating foam. It dries brown and makes the trailer look like a 'Twinkie'."

Mandy laughed at his description.

Darren was silent as he considered how to finish his story.

"One of the hardest parts of living up here are the long, dark winters. Depression and suicide are a big problem. Each winter, Karen would get really sad and nothing seemed to help her. When Katie was nine, that year was especially hard. I was promoted to management, more money, but again, longer times away from home."

Darren paused.

"We went to see this doctor and he wrote out a prescription. We thought the drugs were safe. Karen started taking them and for a little while she seemed better, but then her mind started slipping. She complained that it was like being trapped in a fog. She couldn't think straight or remember large blocks of time. We were trying to settle a deal to purchase this house, but she wasn't able to focus or enjoy the idea of moving here."

Darren's voice choked and Mandy reached out to touch

his hand.

"You don't have to tell me the rest if you don't want to," she said.

"No, I think it's better that you know for Katie's sake. She doesn't fully understand what happened and if she wants to talk about it, I would feel better that you know the truth."

He took a deep breath and went on.

"One day, I was at work and I got a call from the hospital. A neighbor found Karen lying in the snow in front of our house. She wasn't breathing. When they checked for drugs or alcohol, they found she'd overdosed on this drug. I think she just forgot she'd already taken it and took it again three or four times that day. I don't think she was trying to kill herself. The bottle of pills was more than half full when the police came to check the house. They were going to take Katie away from me, but I fought them in court. There weren't any grounds to do that. Soon after, I finished the deal on this house and the two of us moved here. I hired Mrs. Wilson as the housekeeper and she's kept us going ever since."

The two of them sat there in silence for a long time.

Chapter 7

The summer solstice was nearly upon them and Fairbanks was packed with tourists. Scattered across the city were all kinds of celebrations focused on the longest day of the year. Katie had the newspaper spread across the kitchen counter, marking her favorites with a highlighter.

"Pioneer Park will have an open air bluegrass concert," she said as she colored it in. "Do you like bluegrass?"

"Sure," Mandy said absently.

"There's a fair with rides at the fairgrounds."

"Hmmm..." was the only reply to that.

Mandy was lost in her own thoughts as Katie chattered on.

They both jumped when Katie's phone rang.

Katie's friends were planning a trip to the movies and a sleepover. They wanted to know if she could come too. Katie looked at Mandy with puppy dog eyes and mouthed a silent, 'please'.

Mandy didn't see any reason why she couldn't go and nodded her okay.

With a shriek, Katie told her friends yes and hurried off to get ready. She yelled back at Mandy that Amanda's mother would be picking her up in half an hour. Her words were punctuated by the pounding of her feet up the stairs.

Mandy sighed as she folded the newspaper and put away the rest of the breakfast dishes. With Katie gone and Darren at work, she wasn't sure what to do with herself. With a start, she realized that she'd been in Alaska nearly a month already and she hadn't had a single day off in all that time, nor had there been any discussion of payment for her services. She frowned as she thought about how her role as nanny had quickly morphed into something else. The bigger problem was that 'something else' had no real boundaries or definition.

She and Katie spent their days together and when it was the three of them, they spent their time together acting like a ....a family, she realized. There was no way for her to deny she was enjoying her summer *job*. She liked being with Katie and if she was completely honest, she really liked being together, the three of them.

Taking the thought one step further, she admitted to herself, she especially liked the evenings she spent with Darren after Katie went to bed. The two of them seemed to be drawn to the patio every evening when the weather permitted and to the kitchen table when it rained. She was pretty sure Darren felt the same way as he often arranged his schedule to make time for them and always suggested things for the three of them to do together.

Amanda's mother showed up on time and Katie was out the door with her backpack and her new quilt for the sleepover. They'd just finished the binding a couple of days ago and Katie couldn't wait to show it off to her friends. She was sure they'd want to learn how to make their own quilt as soon as they saw hers.

With the house quiet, Mandy decided to do some laundry and then read a book. She was sorting clothes when she heard the garage door open. Surprised, she went to the kitchen just in time to see Darren coming through the door. His eyes lit up when he saw her.

"Surprise! I came home early to take my girls out for supper," he said looking around for Katie.

My girls, Mandy thought as she rubbed the back of her hand across her forehead, *Oh, this was getting more and more complicated.*

"Katie's not here," she explained crossly. "She's gone to a movie and a sleepover at Amanda's."

"Okay," he said hesitantly, "I have a better idea. How about the two of us going for a drive and I'll teach you how to drive a stick shift."

Mandy thought about saying no and telling him she needed a day off, but the words didn't come. Instead she said yes and went to her room to freshen up. Her original plan was to put on a fresh blouse over her jeans, but somehow that changed into a blouse with a skirt....and some make-up and a pair of earrings. When she looked into the mirror, she paused at her reflection. She wasn't looking at a nanny. She was looking at a young woman going on a long-anticipated...date.

Renee Hart

Her courage almost left her as he called from downstairs, "Are you ready yet?"

Willing herself to move, she walked down the stairs carefully noting his eyes as he caught her approach. She knew he wasn't seeing 'the nanny' either.

***

The two of them got into the SUV and headed into town. Darren pulled up next to an old beater in an empty parking lot. The owner of the vehicle was leaning against the hood grinning at them. He tossed a set of keys to Darren.

"Here you go, Boss," the young man said, "one *training* vehicle per your order."

Mandy looked at Darren, but he just shrugged.

"You didn't think I was going to teach you how to drive a stick in my Rover, didja?"

The other guy laughed and went over to the curb to sit down in the shade. He pulled out a cell phone and pretended to be invisible.

Darren and Mandy got into the beater. She was relieved to see the inside was in much better condition than the outside.

"Have you ever had any lessons in driving a stick," Darren asked.

Mandy shook her head.

"Well, here's the thing. Driving a stick shift is like dancing with a car. You've got to know the right steps and you have to listen to the music."

"What music," Mandy asked with confusion in her voice.

"The *music* is the sound the engine makes when you're in the right gear. When you're in the wrong gear, it's not musical at all. It sounds horrible and if your feet aren't doing the right steps, you're going to stumble along."

Mandy looked at Darren like he was crazy. She tried to think about his words as she'd watched him driving the Rover. Suddenly, it came to her how his words applied to what she'd seen him doing.

He spent a few minutes showing her how the gear shift worked and then explained the foot pedals. She listened to his instructions carefully.

"Okay, let's get the car started and I'll teach you the sound of music," he said with a grin.

Mandy was nervous, but Darren was so relaxed she couldn't help feeling easier. She started the car and pushed in the clutch.

As he helped her to tune in to the car's engine, she managed to get the car moving forward. Listening carefully to the gears, she shifted into second and popped the clutch in her excitement. The engine died and they lurched to a stop.

"That's why we're learning in this instead of that," he

said pointing back at the SUV. "It happens when you're learning, so no worries, we'll just start again."

After a half an hour of starting, stopping and making several rounds of the parking lot, Mandy was confident she was now able to 'dance with a car, truck or even the Rover'. She and Darren drove back to their starting point and returned the young man's car. Mandy pretended not to notice when she saw Darren slip the guy some money. The guy's face lit up and he hopped in his beater and drove off with a wave.

"Congratulations, Teacher! You've proved you can be taught," Darren said. "I think we need to fit in a little more practice out on the real road. Think you're up for that?"

Mandy grinned and nodded happily. She was flushed with her success and his nearness. She might not have had a day off in a month, but a day like this was worth a dozen day's off. He tossed her the keys and climbed in the passenger side. Pretending to sit back and relax, Darren watched her climb into the driver's seat.

"Where to, sir," she asked with a confidant air.

"Just turn right out of the parking lot and head north. The rest of your instructions will come in good time."

She nodded and got them on their way. He didn't explain where they were going and she didn't ask. It was good just to drive along quietly and enjoy the moment. Most drives, Katie filled the air with her happy chatter. The silence felt good for a change.

When he told her to turn onto a rough gravel road, she noticed the thick trees pressing up to the edges of the road. It was clear this road wasn't used very much. There wasn't even room for two cars to pass each other without brushing up against the heavy undergrowth. Noticing the scurry of rabbits and spruce hens back and forth across the road ahead of them, she was forced to slow down. Wrestling the Rover from side to side to avoid the potholes and washouts, the two of them were soon laughing.

"Where are we going," Mandy finally broke down and asked. "There's barely enough road to drive on. This can't be a good place for a beginner to drive a stick shift. If I mess up, we'll crash into a tree."

Darren laughed at her concern. "Trust me," was all he said.

***

Another half an hour of bumping along brought them to a very large clearing. Mandy could see ominous signs warning trespassers of dire consequences, and piles of dirt and gravel flanked by rusty digging equipment. An old log cabin stood on one edge of the open area and Darren pulled up next to it. He stepped out of the truck and honked the horn several times and called out, "Hello" in a loud voice.

An answering call came from somewhere off to the left

and Mandy was surprised to see a scraggly looking man with a long beard come walking out of the trees. He was wearing worn overalls over a tattered lumberjack shirt. Her eyes widened as she took in the large gun strapped to his side. She sat there frozen in her seat as he drew near to them.

Darren hurried over to greet the man and it was clear they were old friends. Waving to Mandy to get out, the two of them looked at her. Suddenly self-conscious about her 'date' attire and wishing she'd stayed in her jeans, Mandy got out.

"Clancy, this is Mandy, a friend of mine. Mandy, this is Clancy, an old friend and a real sourdough. This is his mine, The Dancing Dog. Clancy's way out here digging for gold."

Mandy's eyes widened at the thought of digging for gold. It was something she'd read about in books, but had never actually ever met anyone doing that for a living. She looked around at the piles of dirt and wondered how someone found gold. The two men laughed at the look on her face.

Clancy was busy working on his loader and didn't have time to show them around, but he told Darren to go ahead with his tour. Darren grabbed a couple of large dinner plates and headed down to the edge of a river. His friend had already disappeared back to wherever he'd come from in the trees.

Mandy was relieved she wasn't wearing high heels as she followed him down to the water's edge. He was scooping up some dirt with one of the plastic plates when she caught up to him. He added some water and started swirling the mud around in a circle. She watched his actions carefully.

When most of the water and dirt was gone from the plate, he came over next to her and tilted it from one side to the other in the sunlight.

"There...and here....here, too," Darren pointed at the sparkles of sunlight in the dish. "That's gold flake."

"Really? You mean, you walked down here and found gold just like that, with a dinner plate?"

Darren laughed at her words and the look of excitement on her face. He could feel her warmth against his arm as she strained to see what he was pointing at in the dish.

"Yep," he said. "That's how easy it is to find gold in Alaska and this isn't a dinner plate. This is a mining pan and the truth is, you'd probably starve to death before you found enough gold this way, but it's fun."

"Can I try," she asked with a glint in her eye.

"Of course, but maybe you don't want to get your skirt dirty," he smirked.

She stuck her tongue out at him.

"I do all the laundry anyway. My skirt will wash."

Mandy was jesting, but she noticed a shadow flicker across Darren's eyes at her words. He turned away quickly to get the other pan.

***

Darren resumed the role of driver on their way home. They'd spent a couple of hours fishing for gold in the river before hunger drove them to give up their pursuit. The trip home was nearly as quiet as their ride to the river. Mandy stared out the side window watching the scenery pass by as her thoughts battled. Her feelings for Darren and Katie were overwhelming. She would be going home soon.

"I'm starving," Darren groaned as they got back to civilization. "I really need to get something to eat."

Mandy's stomach agreed with him, much to her embarrassment. She was sure she could match him bite for bite in whatever he wanted to eat.

"I know this great place for bar-B-Q," Darren said. "Outside of Texas, you won't find better brisket anywhere. What do you say?"

Mandy looked down at her dusty blouse and skirt and tried to brush some of the dirt away.

"Never mind that. It's pretty dark in there. No one will notice a little dust."

Mandy gave him a nod and a grin.

***

The smell of roasting meat came to her nose before they'd even reached the restaurant. The parking lot was packed and the smokers were fired up. Her mouth was watering before the Rover was in a space. The two of them jumped out of the SUV and headed for the entrance. If she objected when Darren grabbed her hand as they crossed the road, she gave no sign of it. He let go when they reached the door so he could hold it open for her.

The waitress seated them and started to hand out menus.

"Nope. We don't need those," Darren said. "Just bring us two cowboy sundaes with brisket and a couple of root beers."

Mandy looked surprised at his words, but the whole day was an exercise in trust, so she figured she might as well trust him on this too.

The waitress headed off with a grin and they took a look around the place. The band was just starting to play and the dance floor was filling up.

"Do you ever dance with women or are you reserved for your Rover," she asked with a smile.

"I don't really know how to dance," Darren confessed weakly.

Grabbing his hand, Mandy pulled him out of his chair.

"Now it's my turn to be the teacher," she said. "It's easy. Just listen to the music and follow my lead"

Jumping on the end of a line, she pushed, pulled and

managed to get him through a line dance without hurting anyone. The two of them were laughing as they ran back to their table just in time to see their food coming.

"Saved by my sundae," Darren crowed as he got ready to dig in.

He grabbed his fork, but Mandy beat him to the first bite of hers. He laughed when her eyes grew wide with wonder and delight.

"This is amazing! Yum! I've never...."

She shoved another bite in her mouth and rolled her eyes. Once again, he followed her lead.

***

Nearly all the way home, Mandy talked about her first cowboy sundae. Darren was happy to listen to her exercise nearly every adjective she knew. He was quiet as he realized how much it meant to him to see her happiness. He hadn't thought of her as *the summer nanny* all day. *My thoughts seemed to have gone in an entirely different direction without my permission*, he thought.

They both grew quiet as they neared the house. Something had changed between them and neither one of them could explain it to themselves. They didn't want to think about it too hard. It was clear the road ahead of them was lined with potholes and perils.

Darren pulled the Rover into the garage and without

thinking, he shut the garage door. They both sat there for several minutes in silence. The two of them took their time getting out of the car. They were halfway to the kitchen door when the garage light suddenly went out leaving them in the dark.

Darren was walking behind Mandy. Surprised at the sudden darkness, she stopped. He bumped into her hard. On instinct, he reached out and grabbed both her arms from behind to keep her from toppling over.

Without thinking, he cradled her against him and pressed his face against the delicate curve of her neck. Inhaling the scent of her hair, he breathed in her very essence. Her warmth and softness fit against him and stirred a primal longing deep inside them both. He felt how much he needed her and sensed how much she wanted him. She settled into his embrace without resistance and the two of them stood there in the darkness.

The sudden buzz of his cell phone in his shirt pocket caused them both to jump. At the same time, the kitchen door was flung open to reveal Katie standing there. They couldn't see the look on her face with the light behind her, but her stance was clearly upset. They moved apart guiltily.

"WHERE WERE YOU?" Katie shouted. "I came home to an empty house! No one was here!"

Confused, Darren asked, "I thought you were at a sleepover. What are you doing home?"

"I wanted to come home," Katie stormed as she turned away from the doorway. "I felt sick! I made Amanda's mom drive me home and when I came in, you two were gone!"

The three of them made it into the kitchen as Katie punctuated her sentences by kicking the cabinets and slapping her hands down on the counter. Mandy watched her carefully. She wasn't sure if Katie was putting on a show or if she was really this upset about coming home to an empty house. She'd never seen the child act this way. She also had to wonder what Katie had seen when she opened the door to the garage and found them together in the dark. That might be the real reason behind her tantrum.

"Why didn't you call me to come and get you," Darren asked. "How long have you been home?"

"I called you right as I came in the front door cause the house was dark," Katie said.

"Katie, when my phone rang, we were in the garage. The house wasn't empty. We just got home ourselves. You must have drove up just after I closed the garage door..."

Darren stopped trying to explain when Katie started to cry. He looked from her to Mandy helplessly. Mandy frowned, but she wasn't sure how to handle this. *After all, I'm just the nanny and a temporary one at that*, she reminded herself.

Katie solved their problem by running out of the room.

Listening to her pounding up the stairs, the two of them stood there in silence. Finally, Mandy decided she would have to be the one to see to Katie. Darren looked like he didn't have a clue. She followed Katie upstairs and knocked on her door. There was no answer and the door was locked. Mandy thought it best to give her time to work things out. She'd talk to her in the morning. *It has turned into a very long day*, she thought as she headed to her own room.

Chapter 8

The next morning, Mandy woke up with a groan and a shudder. She'd had terrible dreams all night and didn't feel ready to face anyone. Running over the events of the previous day in her mind brought a rush of mixed emotions. Clearly she was in error in not sitting down and setting out the parameters of this job from the beginning. There was no way to reset this mistake and do things the right way. It was also clear that she couldn't just quit and run away from this mess. The damage to all of them would have far more impact than the effort of getting through the rest of the summer.

She knew Darren would pay her whatever she asked within reason, of course. Not having an actual work schedule or clearly defined job responsibilities hadn't mattered until now and the only reason that it mattered now was because she was falling in love with her boss and his daughter. There, she'd admitted it. Now the only question she had to answer was simple. What was she going to do about it?

Right now the only thing she could do was get up and get the day started. She couldn't stay in bed all day. Katie clearly needed her nanny.

***

Hearing the light clatter of dishes, Mandy followed the sound into the kitchen. She found Katie sitting at the breakfast counter with a bowl of cereal and her newspaper. Seeing Mandy, she said good morning somewhat sheepishly and busied herself with the paper.

There was no sign of Darren, not even a dirty coffee cup in the sink or leftover coffee in the pot. She realized he wasn't in the house as he was always the first one up. It almost looked like he'd left last night as he usually at least had coffee in the morning. She felt too shy about it to ask Katie.

She made some coffee and dug a container of yogurt out of the 'frig. Joining Katie at the counter, she sat down quietly and began to stir her yogurt absentmindedly. She realized the child was sneaking glances at her from the corner of her eye.

"So, what would you like to say," Mandy began.

Katie sighed deeply.

"I think I'm supposed to say I'm sorry," she began hesitantly. "And I am, sorry, I mean."

She paused to consider her next words carefully. Mandy waited patiently.

"When I came home last night and no one was here, I got really scared."

"I don't understand why, Katie. You know your father would never leave you. He loves you. He even went to court to fight for you when your mother died. What were you scared of last night?"

Katie stared at her cereal bowl and Mandy saw a tear slip down the side of her face.

"I was scared that something bad happened and you left," Kate mumbled.

Mandy was shocked into silence by her confession. She struggled between wanting to comfort the child or to try and explain how she would have to leave at the end of the summer. She knew there would be no comfort in that explanation.

"Katie, you know that I have a job, another life in Atlanta, don't you?"

She nodded sadly.

"This is a summer job and at the end of the summer, this job is over. I have to go home."

Katie nodded again as a few more tears slipped down her cheeks.

Mandy stopped talking and began to clear away the counter. She was overwhelmed with sadness at this situation. No matter how hard she tried to fix this, it wouldn't be fixed. *What would my grandmother do*, she wondered.

Without thinking any further, she went over and put her arms around Katie. As the little girl clung to her, sobs racked her body. Soon the two of them were crying as Mandy's heart broke for the child. She'd already lost so much in her life, but Mandy couldn't change any of that. She had her own responsibilities back in Atlanta.

***

For the next couple of weeks, Darren made himself scarce. He'd call and talk to Katie every day, but he never asked to speak to Mandy. He'd leave notes about things on the counter for both of them, but Mandy's notes were always carefully worded instructions about his schedule problems or needing something when she went to get groceries. There were no more excursions for the three of them or evenings together or quiet times on the patio.

Katie asked him time and again when they could do this or that together, but he was always tied up with something. He'd come in long after the two of them were in bed and leave before they got up. Mandy considered waiting him out on the couch, but realized she wouldn't know what to say if she did. She had to consider that maybe he really didn't want to see her and their day together was a mistake. She was sad, but she was also relieved as it took any burden away from her to end a relationship.

Then she recognized the real problem this situation was creating. In avoiding her, Darren was missing out on time with Katie and that wasn't fair to her. Mandy knew she had to confront him and find some sort of resolution. The question was how to do that and maintain a professional air between them.

She decided to use a creative approach. After Katie went to bed, she texted him a note.

"Dear Mr. Covington,

When I took this summer job, I expected to be treated in a fair and equitable manner. Since I began working for you at the end of May, I haven't been paid anything AND I haven't been given a single day off. It's now July and I'm deeply concerned about this matter. Please contact me to discuss this as soon as possible. Mandy."

Within the hour, he was standing in the kitchen with a very red face.

"I'm sorry," he said. "I'm really sorry. I've been horribly unfair to you."

"Actually," Mandy said, "I'm more concerned about how you're treating Katie. I'm not worried that you're not going to pay me. I know you will and I'm not worried about having a day off since this isn't like a real job. It's more like living someone else's life, if you want to know the truth. But, avoiding me is keeping you away from your daughter and that's what worries me. She doesn't deserve to be punished because we messed up."

"You're right. You're absolutely right. I've been a complete fool."

Mandy didn't try to rub salt in his wounds by agreeing with him, but on the inside, she agreed completely. She was relieved to know he could be taught also.

"How do we fix this," he asked. "What will make you comfortable?"

"Well, we can't go back to how we started out. That would make it harder on Katie when I leave at the end of the summer. I think you need to put some 'Katie time' into your schedule and explain to her how I need to have a couple of days off every week. I think she can understand and accept that."

Darren considered her ideas and agreed. They decided her time off would coincide with the days he was free from work and he would set-up things to do with his daughter during those days. Mandy would be free to do whatever she wanted without them. She saw the upside and the downside at the same time. She wondered what she would do to fill those empty days alone in a strange city where she had no friends.

***

At first Katie balked at this new arrangement. She understood that everyone was entitled to have a day off from their job, but she didn't like leaving Mandy alone. She'd beg Mandy to come along to wherever they were going or ask to stay home if Mandy couldn't go with them. The three of them struggled to come to terms with this each in their own way.

In the end, the adults basically forced it and no one was

really happy about it, but there didn't seem to be any other way. They made it through the month of July and slipped into August. The end of summer was in sight, but no one was counting the days, not even Mandy. She and Darren danced carefully around their feelings when they were around each other. When they were apart, they thought about nothing else.

***

One of Katie and Mandy's favorite haunts over the summer was Pioneer Park in the center of town. The two of them spent many happy days watching the crowds of tourists studying the rusting tractors and the old riverboat at the center of the park. They often brought a picnic lunch so they could listen to the music as the park hosted local talent weekly. By the end of the summer, they'd listened to many kinds of music from blue grass to jazz and everything in between.

Mandy was thinking this would be their last outdoor concert as the time for her to leave was drawing near. They secured their favorite picnic spot and started tossing the Frisbee around. The park was crowded with tourists as usual and Mandy kept a careful eye on Katie as they played.

Suddenly Mandy froze as she spotted a familiar face on a nearby bench. The man was staring at her intently. Katie didn't realize Mandy wasn't paying attention and she threw the Frisbee accurately for a change. Both of them were startled when it hit Mandy right in the eye. Mandy dropped to her knees in surprise and pain as Katie and the man rushed over to her.

"Brian," she exclaimed in pain and surprise. "What are you doing here in Alaska? How did you find me?"

Brian knelt down next to her as Katie took in the appearance of this strange man. His clothes appeared crumpled and dirty as if he'd been sleeping in them for days and he was unwashed and unshaven. He even smelled bad. She couldn't believe Mandy knew this man.

"Mandy, are you okay," Brian asked ignoring her questions.

She stared at him with her one good eye.

"Mandy, I've been a fool. I made a terrible mistake letting you go. I've come to find you and make this all right between us. I want to marry you!"

Katie was speechless at this stranger's words and stared at the two of them in dismay. She knelt down next to Mandy and put her arm around the woman protectively.

"You go away, mister," she said fiercely. "We don't want you here."

She looked at Mandy for confirmation that her words were true, but Mandy just moaned.

Brian leaned back on his heel and stared at her. He searched her eyes for any sign she still had feelings for him, but aside from the rapid swelling around her injury, he saw nothing to encourage him.

"Let me get you some ice for that," he said as he rose to his feet.

Hurrying over to the drink stand, he got some ice in a plastic cup. When he turned around, he saw Katie and Mandy quickly gathering up their things as they hurried to get away. He rushed after them as they headed for the parking lot. It was clear to anyone watching the two women were trying to get away from him.

They'd just reached the curb near the front entrance when a dark colored van raced up and squealed to a stop in front of the three of them. The door flew open and a large man in a suit stepped out with his hand in his pocket. He grabbed Brian's arm and told the three of them to get into the van in a very menacing tone.

Mandy and Katie dropped their things and slid into the back seat together. Brian and the large man climbed into the middle seat. Brian was blubbering as the man slammed the door closed and the driver took off in a big hurry.

"Mr. Remington would like to have a word with you," the large man said with a sneer.

Brian continued to blubber.

Mandy and Katie sat in the backseat quietly as they tried to figure out what was going on and how they'd suddenly gotten involved. Mandy had her arm around Katie and the girl was leaning over in her lap as if she was frightened or crying. The man wasn't paying any attention to them at all.

Suddenly Mandy realized what Katie was doing and put her arm about the girl's shoulders. She nodded quickly as Katie gave her a look and slipped the cell phone back into the pocket of her jeans. They both relaxed as they figured help would soon be on the way. Mandy's eye continued to swell and the ice was melting back on the curb at Pioneer Park. Brian was still blubbering.

They hadn't been driving very long when the van pulled up behind a hangar at a private airstrip. A Lear jet was parked next to the building and the hangar door stood open. The large man joined by his companion, the driver, ordered the three of them to get out. They all walked together into the hangar with Mandy and Katie at the front of the group.

"Who are you," a well-dressed man asked as he saw them come into the hangar.

Katie was the first to speak.

"I'm Katie Covington and this is my nanny, Mandy Hastings, and YOU are in a lot of trouble!"

The man's face froze as he took in the child's words and the woman's obviously battered appearance.

"What have you two idiots done," he growled.

His outrage was apparent.

The two men looked at each other in confusion as they held onto Brian's arms.

"We followed this guy like you said, waiting for the chance to pick him up quietly, but when he met these two, the three of them were running away. We had to grab them or take the chance on losing him."

Mandy and Katie turned in amazement to look at the man speaking.

"We weren't running away with him. We were running away *from* him," Mandy corrected the man.

At that moment, chaos erupted outside as the sounds of squealing tires and running feet came to them, overlaid with the noise of a helicopter and the clatter of guns. The men found themselves covered with several laser sightings as the shout came from outside to give themselves up. The two large men were face down on the floor in a hot second while Brian commenced blubbering again on his knees.

Several Alaskan State Troopers rushed into the building with Darren right on their heels. As the men were contained, Darren put his arms around Mandy and Katie and hustled them outside. He hugged both of them close to him as they hurried over to the nearest police car.

When they got to the car, he dropped to his knees and looked Katie over carefully to see that she was okay. Then he turned to check on Mandy and seeing her bruised face and battered eye, he got really upset and yelled for an ambulance. The paramedics rushed over with a stretcher, but she waved them off.

"I'm okay! I'm okay! It's not a big deal. I got hit with a

Frisbee," she said.

"Who hit you," Darren said fiercely looking around.

"I did," Katie laughed.

Darren looked at her in surprise and confusion. He didn't see anything funny about any of this.

"I've got to tell you Dad, that kidnapping app on my phone works great!"

***

The next few hours passed in a blur of explanations as the story behind their kidnapping was revealed in part by each participant. They learned the two goons were private detectives hired by Mr. Remington to catch Brian. They'd followed him to Fairbanks and alerted Mr. Remington they were about to nab him. He flew up in his private jet to meet Brian face to face.

There was sufficient evidence to convict Brian of embezzling funds from the company, but the evidence was mainly based on the testimony of Mr. Remington's daughter, Vanessa. She'd been left standing at the altar when the matter of the missing funds came to light and Brian had fled. Her father had some doubts about the whole business and wanted to talk to Brian before having him arrested and ruining his career.

Darren and Mr. Remington had a private meeting CEO to CEO to discuss everything while Brian and the two goons were held in custody. They didn't share any of the details of their conversation. Using his considerable connections, Darren thought it best to make this entire incident go away. Media attention would possibly put Katie at further risk if someone got the idea there was something to be gained by kidnapping her.

Mandy agreed with his assessment of the mishap and didn't want to pursue the matter either. She was glad to be rid of Brian and to see that he'd gotten what he deserved. There was a great deal of satisfaction in seeing how his plans had gone in the end.

The State Troopers got their own satisfaction in seeing the licenses of the two private detectives revoked. The four men involved were encouraged to leave the state immediately. Brian, in particular, was given a stern warning about not being welcome to revisit the state ever again. He simply nodded and left with Mr. Remington in his jet. The two goons had to buy their own tickets to go home.

***

The next morning, Darren was waiting in the kitchen when Mandy and Katie finally made their way downstairs. He'd made two stacks of pancakes with birch syrup and reindeer sausage. They giggled when they saw his handiwork. Each pancake was shaped like a heart. As they dug in and began to eat, Mandy noticed a message had been cooked into each one of her pancakes. Spreading them out on the plate, she began to read the words.

"Will....you....marry....me?" she read off of each one.

Katie looked at the two of them hopefully.

Mandy stared at the pancakes as her thoughts raced and a dozen voices chimed in her head in a noisy chorus of conflicting opinions. She knew in an instant all the reasons why this was a bad idea. It was easy to see why she should just say no, but there was one little voice that stood out from all the rest. This voice rarely agreed with the others and it always gave her the best advice.

In all her life, her grandmother had never steered her wrong, not one time.

Renee Hart

Epilogue

Mandy spun around once more in front of the mirror to check the back of her dress. The simple white dress flared out from her waist into a long, fluttery skirt. She felt like a princess. Her heart was dancing with excitement as she carefully checked her hair and make-up one last time.

Katie was watching the large crowd of people below as they hurried to find their seats on the deck. Tiny, sparkling lights danced from every part of the beautiful paddle wheel boat. The band was playing a lively tune that brought an air of excitement to the crowd. This wasn't going to be an ordinary wedding. She'd made great effort to see to it this event would be a wonderful memory for all of them. Her father and Mandy had given her free rein with the arrangements.

"Are you ready," Katie asked. "I think it's time for us to go. Are you ready to go yet?"

Mandy turned to look at her with a glint in her eye.

"I'm ready. Let's go!"

The two of them linked arms and left the captain's room together. Tina was waiting for them at the top of the stairs and she gasped at the sight of Mandy.

"You look wonderful," she gushed. "Are you ready for this?"

Mandy laughed.

"Will you two stop asking me if I'm ready! I'm ready! Let's do this!"

As they sorted themselves out, Tina signaled to her fiancé to let them know the bride was on the way. He waved at the musicians and they quickly ended the song they were playing and began the 'Bridal March'. Katie started down the stairs first, with Tina following close behind.

When they reached the bottom of the stairs, Katie was able to see her father's face as he stood at the makeshift altar next to the Captain. He looked so proud and happy as his eyes took in the sight of his beautiful daughter. Realizing that everyone had turned to look at them, Katie felt a moment of panic at finding herself the center of attention. Suddenly everyone stood up and Katie realized Mandy was coming into sight behind her. *They're here to see the bride, not you! Focus*, Katie reminded herself sternly.

As Mandy reached the bottom of the stairs first, Katie and then Tina carefully kissed her on each cheek. Then, with the bride walking a couple of steps ahead of them, the two bridesmaids fell in behind her and followed her to the altar.

Katie noted how her father's eyes were fixed on Mandy from the moment she appeared and he glowed with happiness at the sight of her. She fixed her own eyes on him as it helped to still the butterflies dancing in her stomach. If she felt slighted by her father's focus on his bride, it didn't register in her thoughts.

At the altar, the two bridesmaids stepped up next to the bride and presented her to the bridegroom. He gently took Mandy's hand and the two of them turned to face the Captain. The simple ceremony passed in a blur and it didn't take long for the Captain to announce, "I now present to you Mr. and Mrs. Covington!"

A cheer went up from the crowd and a flurry of rice flew from every direction as the new couple walked towards the back of the riverboat. Everyone was clapping and cheering and shouts of 'Congratulations!' came from every corner of the boat. The sudden blast from the riverboat whistle caused everyone to jump in surprise and then burst into laughter.

The reception area on the upper deck was nearly filled with tables with one end reserved for the dance floor. As the guests made their way upstairs, darkness began to fall over the river. Katie stood next to her father and his new bride in the reception line and greeted everyone. It was a long process as the guests made their way to the tables.

The riverboat made its way upriver and then down as the dining and dancing went on into the night. Just before they returned to the dock for everyone to disembark, a shout went up from one end of the boat and everyone looked around.

To their surprise and delight, the Aurora Borealis came

out to put a final stamp of approval on this happy union. Darren and Katie enjoyed the look on Mandy's face as she watched the ribbons of light stream across the northern sky.

"Katie! This is so amazing," Mandy whispered. "Your wedding arrangements are perfection!"

"Nah," Katie blushed, "I think I had a little help from Upstairs on this one."

"I get the feeling someone put in a good word for you," Darren said as he put one arm around his daughter and the other around his new bride.

The three of them stood together as one while the sky danced before them.

THE END

Ready for more of the Covington family? Keep reading for the sequel to *The Summer Nanny In Fairbanks* called **The River Home**.

The River Home

Sequel to *A Summer Nanny In Fairbanks*

Description: Mandy Covington has settled into her new role as wife and stepmom. She has resumed her role as school teacher, but with more variety than before.

Living through the winter in Fairbanks is proving to be quite a challenge, especially with some unexpected news to deal with.

Chapter 1

Mandy nearly dropped the vase of flowers as Katie ran into the kitchen screaming and waving around a large manila envelope. She barely managed to squeeze out a "sorry" as she continued dancing around the room. Mandy noticed the rest of the mail hadn't made it to the table in the hallway, but was scattered in a long trail leading back to the front door. Putting the vase in the middle of the table, she turned to find out what all the excitement was about, but the child was already outside in the backyard still waving the envelope around.

Stepping to the patio door, Mandy stood there with her hands on her hips watching her stepdaughter's celebration with a smile on her face. She couldn't imagine what could hold so much importance. Whatever had come in the mail was a source of great delight to the child.

Catching that thought, Mandy realized Katie was not really a child anymore as they'd just celebrated her thirteenth birthday which put her in the ranks of 'teenager'. This in-between age was already blurring the lines between childhood and the first major steps to becoming a young woman. A wave of sadness came over her as she knew how much she'd miss the little girl that had reached out and changed her life not so long ago. Her curiosity drew her outside.

"Okay! Okay! You've got my attention," she called. "Now just what is it that's got you all excited?

"We won! We won!" Katie crowed with joy as she continued to dance around the yard.

"Since Alaska doesn't have a lottery and I don't remember you mentioning any contests, what exactly did we win?" Mandy asked from the doorway.

"Do you remember Dad telling you about Family Day up on the Slope?" Katie gasped as she came and collapsed at Mandy's feet.

Mandy looked at her daughter with a furrowed brow and tried to remember anything relating to a 'Family Day'.

Impatiently, Katie shook the envelope at her and willed her to think back.

Shrugging helplessly, Mandy looked back at her hoping for a small hint.

"Family Day! That's when the workers up on the Slope get to invite their families to come and visit them. We get to have a big party and everything!"

"Oh, so why are you saying, 'we won'?"

"Because the only way we can go is if our names are drawn. There's a kind of a lottery because only so many people can go and in the past couple of years, Dad didn't even put our names in since I was away at school and there wasn't...."

Her voice trailed off into silence for a moment. Mandy

was used to these little moments and waited for the sadness to pass. She'd encouraged Katie to talk about her mother whenever she wanted, but the girl still tried to hide her loss at times like these.

Looking down at the envelope in her hands, Katie bounced up from the patio and walked into the kitchen. Laying it on the counter, she sat down on a stool and sighed.

"It's just that I've waited so long for this," she said sadly. Then, in an instant her mood changed again, "and now it's finally here!"

Jumping up from the stool, she headed off down the hall.

"Now where are you going?" Mandy called after her.

"I've got to figure out what I'm going to wear!" came echoing back down the hall followed by the stomping of feet up the stairs.

Mandy picked up the envelope and examined it closely. There was little on the outside of the envelope to give any indication of what was inside. It was simply addressed to 'The Covington Family' and bore the company logo as the return address. She laid it aside for Darren to open when he got home. If his daughter's excitement was an example of how important this was, she couldn't wait to see his response.

**

Renee Hart

Supper was ready when Mandy heard the sound of the garage door opening. She hurried to put the finishing touches on the table before checking her hair in the hall mirror. She caught the smile playing around the corners of Katie's mouth as she slipped the manila envelope under the edge of her father's placemat. Mandy wasn't sure why he would be surprised by this 'win' since he was an executive at the company. *Surely, the bosses knew who the winners are even before the envelopes are mailed out to the families*, she thought to herself.

Katie slipped into her chair and turned to face the door expectantly. She knew her father would have to kiss Mandy first and then come over to rumple her hair. His briefcase would be put in his office and he would go and wash his hands. Her foot tapped the floor impatiently as this familiar scene played out. Mandy grinned at her across the table knowing the wait was grinding on her nerves. Katie still hadn't worked out this matter of patience.

Darren sat down and looked around the table with a pleased smile. He couldn't believe his luck in finding a bride with a penchant for southern cooking. He'd already put on a couple of 'marriage pounds' or so he called them from a steady stream of home cooked meals. Mandy had even found ways to incorporate moose meat into her menus without compromising their style. She'd told him it was similar to venison and she just treated it accordingly.

Catching a look of sheer desperation on his daughter's face, he glanced over at his wife for a hint as to what was going on, but she carefully avoided his silent plea for help. There was no way she was going to fall into this drama. It was far better to stay on the sidelines and watch things play out between father and daughter. Uncharted waters had never been her forte.

Hoping to buy some time, he suggested that Katie say 'grace'. She dutifully folded her hands and bowed her head before blurting out a rushed prayer of thanksgiving. Darren barely had time to fold his own hands before she was staring at him again. He cast a swift glance around the table before noticing the envelope peeking out from under his placemat.

"Aha! What's this? Don't tell me it's time for grades to come out already," he mockingly asked before turning the envelope over. Seeing the return address, his eyes darkened for a moment before his face lit up.

Mandy caught the subtle pause in his reaction and wondered at it. There was clearly more to what was going on here than she'd been told earlier.

Darren looked at Katie and suddenly the two of them were up and out of their chairs. They began dancing a crazed version of the polka around the table while shouting a semblance of a celebration song. Mandy laughed as they danced first one direction and then turned to dance their way back to their chairs. Her ears were still ringing with their shouts of joy as they sat down.

The two of them turned to look at her expectantly and for a moment she was at a loss. Clearly this had a great deal of meaning for them, but she still didn't understand the significance. Shrugging her shoulders, she gave them a wan smile and waved her hand over the table.

"Why don't we continue this celebration by eating up all this good food," she laughed. To her relief, they agreed and the three of them got busy eating. She figured she'd learn more about this later after Katie went to bed. For now, she'd just try to play along.

***

Later that evening, Mandy slipped into Darren's office where he was doing some paperwork. She'd tucked Katie in and found her fast asleep half an hour later. It was time to find out the story behind today's events. He looked up with a smile as she came in and pushed his chair back so she could slip into his arms. Taking in the warm scent of her hair, he softly kissed her neck and worked his way around to nibble at her ears. She snuggled against him with her eyes closed.

Moments like these were treasured by both of them as their busy lives and crazy schedules made them rarer than they would have liked. Meeting the needs of a teenager also took up a lot of their time and attention. There'd never been a time just for the two of them with their ready-made family. Darren worried sometimes that Mandy had been a bit shortchanged in this deal, but she never complained and it was clear she loved Katie as her own.

Suddenly, Mandy sat up in his arms and looked at him expectantly.

"So, just what's the story behind this 'Family Day' business?" she asked brightly.

Darren groaned as his thoughts had gone in a completely different direction and he'd already forgotten the matter. He playfully tried to redirect her attention with some more kisses, but she was having none of it. Sitting back in his chair, he regarded her with a grin.

"Family Day. Where do I begin?" he mused. "How about we go make some cocoa and get comfortable before I tell you this story?"

Mandy nodded and got up to head for the kitchen. She couldn't help but notice the unopened envelope sitting on the corner of his desk. It seemed funny that no one had even bothered to check what was inside. *What if it's really about something else entirely*, she wondered.

Taking their usual spot out on the patio, Darren took a couple of sips as he gathered his thoughts. There were a lot of memories mixed up in this story and he wanted to keep the focus positive for everyone's sake. Dragging the past into their present carried a lot of sadness into their lives that Katie in particular didn't need. He cleared his throat a

Renee Hart

couple of times as Mandy waited patiently. The two of them stared out over the river as he began to talk.

"Family Day is an old company tradition. The original owners started it when the workers got upset over being away from their families all the time. The North Slope is dangerous and there isn't enough housing or facilities for people not involved in the work. The wives and children left behind here in Fairbanks are disconnected from the stuff going on up there. It seemed like a good way to bring the families up and let them see where everyone worked and the way they lived.

"When I first went to work on the Slope, I was nobody, just a kid that knew something about wildcatting...drilling for oil. They'd started 'Family Day" a couple of years before I came on board. Karen and Katie would get all excited every year when it was time for the drawing, especially Karen. Katie was too little to really know what it was all about at first.

"Every year when we didn't 'win', Karen would try to find out who got to go and eventually she and a few other of the wives figured out that it was mostly the bosses' families that were getting to go up to the Slope. The rumor got started that the whole thing was fixed and a lot of people got mad.

"As I built my own reputation and started moving up the ladder, the issue came to a head and for transparency's sake, the company hired an independent agent to do a 'lottery' based on some kind of anonymous system. That reawakened Karen's hope and once again she and Katie became passionate about 'winning the lottery'. It never happened and when she died, I actually stopped putting our name into the pool for several reasons of my own."

Darren paused here and drained the last of his cocoa. He sat quietly waiting for Mandy to process his story and come up with her own questions.

"So, what led you to put our names in the drawing for this year?" she finally asked.

Turning to face her in the dim light, he grinned at her shyly for a moment.

"I really wanted you to see where I'm at and what I'm doing when I'm not here."

Returning his grin, she stood up and headed for the back door.

"Where are you going?" he asked jumping up to follow her inside.

"I think I'm ready for the rest of those kisses," she called as she ran for the stairs. She could hear him laughing as he hurried to follow her lead. It was time for another kind of celebration.

***

With 'Family Day' two weeks away, Mandy blocked out the time on her schedule as a substitute teacher. Her reputation in the school district was growing steadily and her days filled up quickly. Skilled at teaching the younger students, she welcomed the chance to stretch herself with the higher levels. Working as a sub gave her the opportunity to try her hand at a variety of teaching, as well as control of her own schedule.

On a few rare occasions, she'd found herself at the Middle School working with Katie's teachers. They were happy to share their compliments on Katie's progress and readjustment to being back in Fairbanks. Much to her delight, Katie was always happy to see her in the hallways. She still called Mandy by her name, but always introduced her as 'my mom'. Everyone seemed to take that in stride without question.

She was throwing together a salad for dinner after a particularly stressful day at the kindergarten when she heard the sound of the garage door opening. She checked the clock as Katie was at the table finishing up her homework and it seemed too early for Darren. The door opened and Mandy was surprised to see Darren's face. His cheeks were flushed bright red and the rest of him looked pale. He almost looked like he was ready to fall down. She hurried over to his side, but he held up a hand to wave her off.

"You might want to give me some space," he mumbled. "I think I've got the flu or something. I'm just going to go upstairs and lie down for a little while."

Ignoring his noble attempt to spare her, Mandy hurried

over to put her cool hands to his forehead.

"Oh, dear. You've definitely got a fever. Is your throat sore? Stick out your tongue!"

As Mandy fussed over him, Katie caught sight of her father.

"Dad! You can't be sick. You've got to get better right now! Family Day is less than two weeks away!"

"Katie, your father will be fine long before it's time for Family Day. Don't worry," Mandy said as she led him to the stairs. "I'm just going to tuck him into bed and see to his needs. Why don't you finish the salad for me?"

Katie made a face as she watched the two of them go. She couldn't remember a single time when her father was ever sick. *It's just my bad luck for him to get the flu now*, she thought to herself in frustration. If he made them miss Family Day, she was never going to forgive him. Never!

***

The next few days tried everyone's patience as Darren was a terrible patient and Katie was beside herself with worry that he wouldn't get better in time. Mandy was stretched between the two of them as she juggled the roles of nursemaid, mother and kindergarten teacher. She almost wished she'd taken Darren's suggestion to find another housekeeper into deeper consideration. It was no wonder she was feeling a little under the weather herself by the time he was back on his feet.

Renee Hart

With less than a week to go until Family Day, Katie took one look at Mandy's face at breakfast and she wilted in her chair.

"Oh no! I knew it! You're sick, aren't you?"

Mandy tried to summon the energy to look anything but sick until a wave of nausea sent her running for the bathroom. She could hear Katie groaning behind her.

"I can't believe this! Four more days until Family Day and now this!"

Katie stormed around the kitchen hoping Mandy would reappear looking fine, but she knew there wasn't any chance of that happening. Her father was sick for four days. Even if Mandy was only sick for four days, this still ruined their chance of going up to the North Slope. They couldn't take the opportunity away from someone else if they weren't going to be able to make the trip.

The child struggled against the pull inside of her to do the right thing. Part of her wanted to throw a tantrum and rage against the unfairness of the world, but a more grown up side was emerging. Quietly, she began to make some peppermint tea as she listened for Mandy's movements in the house. Hearing her stepmother in the hallway, she put the tea on a small tray and headed upstairs.

Mandy was lying down with her face to the wall when Katie came to the door.

"Mandy?"

A small groan came from the bedroom.

"I brought you some peppermint tea," Katie whispered.

Mandy moved to sit up, but a wave of nausea forced her to lay still.

"Do you want me to call Dad?" Katie ventured.

"No. No, honey. I'll be fine. Just give me a few minutes, okay?"

"Do you want some tea? I put a little honey in it just like you did for Dad."

"That sounds nice. I'll try to drink some in a minute," Mandy said hoping this was true. She hated being the source of Katie's disappointment, but life didn't always work out the way people thought it should. Mandy knew it was better she learned it sooner rather than later.

***

Mandy felt a little better by lunchtime and she got up to see about Katie. She was happy to find the kitchen in order and some soup already on the stove for lunch. Finding Katie in her room, Mandy went in and sat down next to her on the bed.

"Are you feeling better?" Katie asked hopefully.

"I am."

Does this mean that you don't have the flu like Dad?"

"I don't have the flu. I'm sure of that," Mandy answered hesitantly.

"Does this mean we can go to 'Family Day' on the Slope?"

"I'm not exactly sure. I think I need to go see a doctor first," Mandy said. "But I have a good idea that we'll be able to go. I just don't want you to set your heart on it."

"Why?" Katie asked. "Is there something wrong?"

"Not exactly. In fact, I think there's something very right going on," Mandy said. "Here. Let me show you. Come with me."

Heading downstairs with Katie in tow, Mandy went to the hall closet and pulled out a bag from the quilt store in town. She turned and handed it to Katie.

"What's this?"

"It's our next quilting project," Mandy said with a grin. "Take a look inside."

Katie peeked into the bag and let out a whoop that rattled the windows.

Mandy put her hands over her ears and burst out laughing.

"How did you know?" Katie asked staring at Mandy in awe.

"Don't worry. Women just know these things."

"Wow! Won't Dad be surprised," Katie said excitedly.

"You bet! So let's make this quilt and have it ready for when he gets home. What do you think?"

"I think that right now I don't care about 'Family Day'," Katie said. "Becoming a 'big sister' is far better than that! Let's make a quilt!"

Chapter 2

Katie began folding up her latest quilting project to clear some room on their work table. Between the two of them, there was always something going on in their sewing room. When they weren't making quilts for the senior home, there were quilts for charity and quilts for friends in process all the time. They'd even finished one complicated pattern for a quilting contest at the State Fair, but it barely got an honorable mention. Neither of them cared as they'd enjoyed the challenge more than the end result anyway.

Mandy was sitting on the floor sorting through some bins. She'd packed up all of her grandmother's UFO's (in quilting terms: unfinished objects), when she'd made her final move to Fairbanks. The bins moved from her house in Atlanta to the workroom here where they became a place to stack other things. Katie edged closer to see what treasures had been hidden inside all this time.

"Where is it," Mandy fretted as she pulled out piles of fabric.

"What are you looking for," Katie ventured, moving even closer.

She was fascinated with the piles of hand-embroidered quilt squares and faded bits and pieces of fabric. These things represented the history of quilting for Mandy and, now, for her too. Katie learned to quilt alongside the stories of a grandmother she'd never know, but who lived on through the skills she'd passed to her granddaughter.

"My grandmother had a stash of baby stuff she'd been saving for me. Some of these prints are more than thirty or forty years old if I can find them," Mandy replied still sorting through the bins. "I'd almost forgotten about them until I was at the fabric store looking at baby prints."

Reaching the bottom of the last bin, Mandy let out a cry of delight as she held up a pile of pastels. Her eyes grew bright with tears as treasured memories came flooding back. Feeling a story coming on, Katie moved to sit down beside her stepmother. Her patience was rewarded.

"My grandmother loved "Mother Goose" nursery rhymes. I think she memorized them all long before I was born. She and I played games reciting them over and over testing each other. We were shopping for fabric one day and she saw this print. She didn't care for the pre-quilted stuff usually, but she wanted to buy this one specifically for her first great-grandchild she told me. She knew the old children's rhymes were falling out of favor and she wanted to hang onto them."

"Do you still remember them?" Katie asked gently, not wanting to break the mood.

"Sure," Mandy said, flipping the quilt over. "Here are the opening lines for all my favorites."

One by one she pointed at each picture and recited the words from memory, much to Katie's amusement. When she was finished, Katie looked a bit sad.

"I've never heard any of those rhymes," she said. "I wonder if my mom even knew them."

Mandy reached out and gave Katie a quick hug.

"She might have and she might not. Every family has their own traditions and memories. These are the ones my grandmother made for me. My parents didn't have time for such frivolities. I think this is the quilt we should make right now. It's easy and quick and we can have it ready by the time your father comes home. What do you think?"

"Yeah! That will be great! We can hang it on the back of the fourth chair at the dinner table and wait for him to notice it," Katie said with a big grin. "Won't he be surprised? Wait! He will be surprised, won't he?"

"He will," Mandy said with a smile that quickly faded to a slightly worried look.

Katie was quick to catch the frown and matched it with one of her own.

"You're not thinking he won't be happy about this, are you?" she asked Mandy.

After a pause to gather her thoughts, Mandy got up off the floor and looked around at the mess she'd made. She wasn't comfortable talking with Katie about such things. Sometimes, with Darren away at work so much, Katie moved into the role of friend more often than Mandy liked to admit. Both she and Darren worried that this pulled Katie too far into the grown-up world.

"Let's just say this might be quite a shock for him and leave it at that," Mandy said with a wink. "How about you get started on cleaning up the edge of this with the serger machine while I pick up this mess. Then we can work on the binding together."

Katie nodded happily and set right to work. She guided the fabric carefully through the machine with her tongue tightly clenched between her teeth. It always made Mandy smile when she saw the expression on Katie's face. She took everything very seriously for someone so young, Mandy thought to herself.

She laid aside a few more treasures from her grandmother's stash before closing up the bins. This baby was going to have plenty of quilts to grow up on. Her grandmother had seen to that. By the time she had the bins back in their spots, Katie was holding up the first phase of the quilt.

"How does this look," she asked, holding it out to Mandy.

Giving it a quick look, Mandy gave her a thumbs up and held out a couple of packets of binding for Katie to choose a color.

"We have this pink or dark blue," she said. "Which one do you like?"

Katie scrunched up her nose at the pink and asked the obvious question.

"Do you know you're going to have a girl?"

Mandy laughed.

"Not yet. It will be a while before we know that."

"Then we better not use the pink," Katie said. "If you have a boy, he wouldn't want pink."

"I don't think any baby is worried about pink or blue, but you're right. Let's play it safe and go with the dark blue. It'll look nice with the light green anyway."

Checking her watch, Mandy noticed it was getting late. She needed to get dinner going and asked Katie if she felt comfortable sewing on the binding by herself.

"I think I can do it. I just need to take my time to get it right. You go ahead and make dinner and I'll call you if I need help, okay?"

"Great! I'll check in on you after I get the meat in the oven," Mandy answered, heading off to the kitchen.

***

By the time Mandy finished setting the table, Katie came into the kitchen with the finished quilt. Stopping to admire her stepdaughter's work, Mandy was surprised to hear the sound of the garage door opening. The two of them looked at each other with wide eyes filled with mirth. Trying to contain themselves, Mandy ran to the mirror to check her reflection while Katie ran to the usually empty chair at their table to arrange the new quilt.

She'd scarcely finished and ran back to her own chair

when the back door opened and her father appeared in the doorway. Taking a deep breath, a big smile came over his face at the warm aroma filling the kitchen.

"I smell pot roast," he growled with a big grin on his face.

His eyes searched the table with a look of delight. Katie squirmed in her chair as Mandy attempted an air of nonchalance. The atmosphere in the room was charged with excitement. As he leaned forward to kiss Mandy, he gave her a careful look.

"Are you feeling better?" he asked quietly.

"I am," she said, and turned away so he wouldn't catch the big smile that came after those words.

Not being quite quick enough, Darren went over to the table to rumple Katie's hair. She dipped her head to hide the look on her face too. Catching the lack of her usual protest, Darren stopped and took a suspicious look around the room. Something was up. Clearly there was something he wasn't being told and no one was volunteering anything.

He headed for his office to drop off his briefcase and quickly checked the calendar in case he'd forgotten something important. Katie had circled the date for Family Day up on the North Slope so many times it was nearly a hole on the page. Maybe it had to do with Mandy feeling better so they wouldn't have to cancel the trip, he thought to himself. He knew how much it meant to Katie for all of them to go.

After washing his hands, he headed back to the kitchen hoping for a big slice of pot roast. Mandy truly knew the way to a man's heart. Her cooking was a source of constant pleasure in his life. He'd be hard-pressed to pick out his favorite meal from her extensive repertoire. As he came into sight, he noticed Katie was busying herself with re-folding the napkins while Mandy ladled food onto their plates. His heart swelled at the sight of his two favorite women. Taking his seat, he quickly gave the blessing before turning his attention to his plate.

Katie was trying to figure out a way to draw his attention to the fourth chair. She kicked the leg of it under the table, but the chair was too far from her. It barely moved.

"So, what have you two been up to all day?" he asked between bites.

"Quilting," they both exclaimed together.

As they attempted to stifle their giggles, he looked around suspiciously.

"And what's the latest project?" he hesitated to ask. He'd survived more quilt projects in the last year than he could count. Several of their projects found their way of incorporating themselves into the rest of the house, including his office at times. They claimed the light was better in there.

"Unable to contain her excitement any longer, Katie pointed out the new quilt with a flourish of her hand. As her father's eyes followed her gesture, she jumped up and ran around the table to hold up their surprise.

"Wow! That's pretty," Darren said nonchalantly. "Who'd you make that one for?"

Turning his attention back to his plate, he missed the look of frustration that passed between the women. Neither of them wanted to be the first to break the news. They'd hoped he'd catch on somehow.

"It's for you, **Dad**!"

Darren looked up at Katie in surprise and a look of confusion passed over his face. Carefully, he studied the picture on the quilt as Katie held it up for him. Turning to look at Mandy, he froze as his brain tried to bring the message of the quilt into focus. When his eyebrows shot up nearly to his hairline, the two women knew he'd finally gotten the picture.

"That's a baby quilt!"

Staring at Mandy, Darren put down his fork and picked up his napkin. Wiping his face carefully, he dabbed at a couple of imaginary droplets of sweat on his temple before speaking again.

"Are you sure?" he asked quietly.

"Yes, darling. I'm sure. I made doubly sure by taking a test, but I already knew."

Katie could scarcely contain herself with his subdued reaction and stomped her foot in frustration.

"Aren't you happy, Dad?"

Realizing his daughter was expecting far more excitement, Darren jumped up out of his chair and ran around the table. Sweeping her up in his arms, he spun her around and exclaimed, "Are you kidding me? I'm over the moon about this! Just the thought of having another baby in the house tickles me pink!"

Pulling away, Katie looked at him with confusion.

"I thought guys always wanted boys. You've already got a daughter. Don't you want a son?"

Darren laughed and moved to kneel down next to Mandy's chair. Gently taking her hands, he laid his head on her stomach.

"Hello, Little One."

"Oh, Dad. Really. It's not like he has ears yet," Katie said in disgust flopping back into her chair.

"That's true, but there's life inside of Mandy that needs to feel loved and wanted. I'm making sure of that starting right now."

Mandy smiled down at her husband and stroked his hair. She loved this man in that moment more than ever before. Far from worrying about the changes a baby would bring to their life, he was willing to step up and welcome this child without question. She was truly blessed in him.

As Darren returned to his chair, he had to take a moment to rumple Katie's hair. Making her usual protest, he grinned at the look on her face.

"You seem pretty sure that you're going to have a little

brother," he said. "What gives you that idea?"

"Well, I'd like either one, but since we don't know, I'm betting on a boy. What about you, Mandy? Boy or girl?"

"Hmmm...I don't know," Mandy replied. "I think I'd like one of each," she added with a wicked grin. "You know twins run in our family."

Darren laughed and added his own jab.

"They run on our side too."

Katie looked at the two of them in shock. Slapping her hand to her forehead, she fell back into her chair.

"Twins! We'd better get busy and make a lot more quilts and diapers and jammies and all that other stuff."

Darren and Mandy laughed at the look of distress on her face. This was going to be a very long nine months for all of them.

***

Later that evening, Darren snuggled into bed next to Mandy and carefully cradled her in his arms.

"Are you really happy?" she asked studying his face carefully.

"Of course. I'm just surprised. We haven't really talked about having more children. I don't know why, but I guess with Katie so grown up, I just put that idea aside. Now I realize that wasn't fair to you and I'm sorry about it. Are you happy?"

"I am. I didn't really think about it either. I think I messed up on my birth control pills and then when I realized I was pregnant, I could only hope you'd be as happy about it as I am."

"Well, I guess these things have a way of working themselves out."

"There is one problem," Mandy said hesitantly. "I'm not sure about the flight up to the North Slope. I'm really struggling with the nausea. I think I need to see a doctor and get a check-up first. I just don't want to disappoint Katie."

"That sounds like a good idea," Darren said snuggling a little closer.

"And...I want to have the baby here. At home," Mandy stated firmly.

"What?"

Darren sat up in surprise.

"You want to have the baby at home?"

"Yes. With me and you and Katie...and a midwife, certainly. And I want a water birth," Mandy continued firmly. "You're going to be my doula."

Darren found himself speechless as he sat there in the darkness trying to take all of this in.

"Well, it's clear you've put a lot of thought into this," he said. "I hope there's some room for discussion."

"Of course," Mandy retorted, "but these are the things I want for the birth of our child.

Trying to avoid a conflict, Darren asked the first question that came to his mind.

"Are you sure Katie's old enough to be part of the birth?"

"As her mother, well, stepmother if you want to get technical, I want her to be involved. A home birth can be a wonderful experience for the whole family. It's a natural way to welcome a child. I want Katie to be a part of that. I'm sure she's going to have some challenges when she's faced with us having another child. She's going to need to feel like she's a part of all this."

Darren lay back down and thought about this for a while.

"Weren't you a part of Katie's birthing?" Mandy asked in the darkness.

"No," came the answer. "I was up on the Slope and didn't make it back in time. I missed the whole thing."

The two of them lay there silently for a long while before sleep finally claimed them.

Chapter 3

The next morning, Mandy made an appointment at the nearby clinic. After a brief consultation, she was confident the trip to the North Slope for Family Day was a go. Dashing off a quick text to Katie and Darren, Mandy slipped in a quick trip to the bookstore. There was one special book she was hoping to find and she wasn't disappointed. Hiding away her treasure for a later date, Mandy took care of a few chores. She knew Katie would be too excited about their trip to think about anything else for the next couple of days.

***

"You two should be ashamed of yourself," Mandy exclaimed throwing her overnight bag onto the floor. "We'd agreed not to tell anyone about the baby and both of you broke that agreement! I can't believe you used me and the baby to get extra cherry pie!"

Darren and Katie stood frozen in the doorway at this unexpected outburst. Mandy wasn't given over to shouting anyway and she usually took their antics in stride. Both of them managed to look chagrined, at least until she'd stomped her way upstairs to the bedroom, and then they broke out giggling at the sound of the slamming door.

"This is all your fault," Katie said, punctuating each

Renee Hart

word with a poke at his stomach. "You're the one that came up with the idea of telling the hostess Mandy was pregnant and had an extra craving for cherry pie!"

"Not guilty! I was only saying it might work. You're the one that actually went and got the pie," he shot back at his daughter.

The two of them burst into laughter again and then hurried into the kitchen, hoping not to upset Mandy further.

"Do you think this is one of those hormonal things she warned us about?" Katie asked.

"I'm sure it is. I'll give her a little time and then go up and smooth things over. It might help if you make her an ice cream sundae."

"With extra cherries," they exclaimed together, and then clapped their hands over their mouths hoping she hadn't heard.

"So," Darren asked. "Did you enjoy Family Day? Was it everything you expected it to be after waiting all these years?"

"Actually, Dad. I thought it was kind of boring. I think it's probably better for the little kids and maybe the wives. I was ready to go home after about an hour into the tour. I really wanted to see a polar bear and some of those red foxes you're always telling us about. I guess they don't come around with all those people making so much noise."

"Sorry sweetheart. It's pretty hard to get the local

wildlife to conform to any kind of tour schedule. I'm glad you finally got to go anyway. Your mother would be really happy for you. She wanted to go more than anything."

The two of them sat there quietly remembering before Katie jumped up and headed to the refrigerator.

"I've got to make that sundae, and you've got some explaining to do," she said with one final poke at her father's arm.

Shaking off the past, the two of them got to work.

***

"Darren," Mandy called to him from the kitchen. "Did you add those appointments to your calendar I gave you for the birthing classes?"

Scrambling through the bits and pieces of paper littering his desk, he threw back a hasty "yes, dear" all the while hoping frantically his words were true. Not finding her list, he headed for the kitchen to copy down the dates again from the calendar on the refrigerator.

"I just want to cross check the dates again and make sure I've got them right," he said sheepishly as she gave him 'the look'.

Not even Katie was fooled as she snickered from the kitchen table where she was cutting out a baby's bib. Little scraps of fabric littered the floor and the table around her. Darren had lost count of the number of 'emergency' trips he'd had to make to the fabric stores this last couple of months. Something always seemed to be needed to finish a project.

"There! I've got them entered into the calendar on my phone," he said triumphantly. "Now you know you can count on me to be on time."

Mandy and Katie exchanged a look before turning back to their tasks.

"What was that all about," he asked in mock protest. "I said I would be there and you know I always do my best to keep my word. It's not my fault sometimes things just come up."

When nobody bothered to reply, Darren turned on his heel and headed back to his office muttering something about how he wasn't getting any respect. The silence he left behind had a lot more to say about the matter.

All told, he'd already missed the first ultrasound, two doctor appointments and the first meeting with the birthing center to choose the birthing team. Katie was pleased to step up and offer her support to Mandy, but they both knew the young girl was a poor substitute. It wasn't that Mandy didn't love Katie deeply, but this was a time when the presence of her husband was more important to her. It was beginning to feel like he had almost no part in this at all, well, beyond a small donation, Mandy thought with a feeling of helplessness.

**

"Mrs. Covington, is it possible your husband will be able

to fit the birth of your child into his overly full schedule?" Marilyn asked. "This is our third attempt to make the final selections on the birthing team and we've not yet had a chance to meet him."

Katie reached out to slip an arm around Mandy. Torn between wanting to support her stepmother or defend her father, she chewed her lower lip as she waited for Mandy's response.

Sighing deeply, Mandy sat up a bit straighter and squared her shoulders.

"Don't worry about him, Marilyn," she began. "He'll be okay with whatever we decide. Katie and I have made our own list of who we want on our team. We're going to go with these people."

With a little snort of disdain, the woman took Mandy's list and perused the list of names.

"This looks like an excellent team. All of these people mesh well together. I'm sure you'll be very happy with these choices. Therefore, we can conclude this meeting and consider the matter settled."

Marilyn left the two of them sitting in the small conference room. Katie felt her stepmother settle back in her chair in an atmosphere of defeat. She knew her father wasn't making a real effort to keep his word about being there for Mandy and didn't know how to defend him.

"I don't think your father really wants this baby," Mandy sniffled. "He hasn't said it right out, but his actions...well."

"I want to say you're wrong, but..." Katie sniffled a bit too.

The two of them sat there a while longer in silence before Mandy decided it was time to head home. As she stood up, she gave a little gasp of surprise and sat back down.

"What is it? What's wrong?" Katie nearly shouted in fear.

"Nothing, honey. I just felt the baby move. Here. Put your hand right here. He's kicking!"

Reaching out her hand, Katie pressed against the small mound gently. The look of hope on her face slipped to disappointment and she pulled her hand away.

"I don't feel anything," she pouted as she turned away to put on her coat.

"Sorry," Mandy offered. "The baby's still so small. It's hard to catch these little movements when they come. Just give him a few more days to grow bigger."

"Him? Are you thinking it's a boy?" Katie asked with new hope.

"I'm still not sure," Mandy laughed. "We're just going to have to wait a little longer."

***

If Darren had hopes of sneaking in late that night and

finding everyone in bed, he was sorely surprised to find Mandy wrapped up in a quilt on the couch waiting for him. Holding out a small bag as a peace offering, he attempted to look contrite.

"It's chocolate," he ventured wiggling the bag a little in front of her.

Patting the couch next to her, Mandy ignored his efforts.

"We need to talk."

His heart sank at her words. He knew she was going to be mad, but those specific words always seemed to go much deeper.

"I know what you're going to say and I'm sorry. Something came up and I couldn't get..."

Mandy held up her hand to stop his usual excuse from turning into an argument.

"I'm getting this overwhelming sense you aren't really on board with having this baby," she began, "and what's worse is that your daughter is of the same mind. We're both losing faith in you."

Darren winced at her words. The problem as he saw it was there was an ounce too much of truth in what she said. He'd known this from the beginning, but he'd hoped his feelings would change as the time ran out.

"It's not what you think," he said putting his hand on her swollen belly. "I love you and I love this baby. I just don't see myself as being a very good father. I wasn't there for Karen and Katie when they needed me and I'm afraid I'm going to let you and the baby down too."

Mandy swallowed hard at this unexpected burst of honesty. Darren was not inclined to speaking about such things so plainly. It was clear he'd given this situation some thought. Taking Mandy's hands in his, he moved to look directly into her eyes.

"I'm really sorry about missing all of those appointments. I've thought long and hard about what I need to change to be a better husband, a better father, and I realized my job isn't going to give me the room to do that unless I make some changes. I've moved one of my guys up in the ranks and I'm personally training him to take over my role as the hero. He's going to be the one to fly up to the North Slope all hours of the day or night to put out the 'fires' and save the day. I'm giving up my cape."

Mandy was speechless. This went far beyond anything she'd ever dared to ask for, let alone to hope. It went against everything she knew about her husband up until now. He loved his work, but he especially loved being the guy everyone counted on to save the day.

"Really," she finally dared to ask as she struggled to make herself believe in him again. "You would give up your superman cape for us?"

"How can I not do this?" he asked her gently. "It's breaking my heart to think that I might be breaking yours."

Mandy leaned forward and rested her forehead on his

shoulder.

"Oh!"

She jumped and moved back.

"What? What's wrong," Darren asked with alarm written all over his face.

"It's nothing," she laughed. "The baby just made his own declaration with a swift kick. Here! Put your hand right here."

Grabbing Darren's hand, she moved it to the spot where he could feel the tiny little foot moving against him. She laughed as his face lit up and he bent over to address the child they'd created between them. After a few well-placed kisses in the area of that foot, he moved up to work in a few along the side of her face. Claiming her lips, he relished the soft feel of her mouth against his.

"Does this mean I'm forgiven?" he whispered against her lips.

Pushing him away, Mandy gave him a stern look.

"I don't know," she said slowly. "It depends on what's in that little bag of yours."

"Well, it's not ice cream and pickles if that's what you're wondering, but I thought it might at least keep me from having to sleep on the sofa."

Handing her the bag, he laughed as her face lit up. *Food may be the way to a man's heart, but chocolate seemed to work better with women,* he thought, *well, at least with my women.*

Chapter 4

Darren checked his watch again and sighed. It wasn't like Mandy to be late for anything and he wasn't exactly early, more like "just in time" but there was no sign of her in the parking lot. He thought about giving her a call, but he didn't want to bother her if she was hurrying to get here. The roads weren't too bad by Alaskan standards, if she was taking her time...he didn't want to think of any alternatives.

Last winter, she'd struggled with driving in the snow and he'd spent far more time worrying about her than he would have liked. It was a huge relief when the roads finally cleared in May and things went back to normal for a while. She was proud to claim that she'd avoided any accidents the whole winter in comparison to him. He'd slipped off into the ditch a couple of times, but those were unavoidable he always tried to explain before everyone started laughing.

After their wedding, Mandy had looked into getting a teaching job, but the schools were already staffed for the year. She'd settled on working as a substitute after Katie's teacher complained how there were never enough good subs available. Much to her surprise, she found she enjoyed the challenge of working in the high school one day and teaching kindergarten the next. It also gave her the opportunity to find out which school and grade level she liked the best.

Darren had tried to explain that it wasn't necessary for her to take a job at all with his income, but she told him she needed to have something more in her life. His real concern was the challenge of getting up in the early morning hours when it was -50 degrees or worse to head off to work. Coming from Georgia, she wasn't used to dealing with the rigors of extreme cold, he knew. She brushed aside his concerns and learned the ins and outs of plugging in the block heater and using the remote starter.

Checking his watch again, Darren pulled out his cell phone only to find that the battery was dead. He decided to go inside the birthing center and ask about Mandy's appointment. With his history of not showing up, he'd probably look pretty silly if he'd somehow made an error, but with no phone and no Mandy....

The receptionist looked up with a smile as he came in the front door. Recognizing him, she looked down at her schedule with a frown.

"Didn't you get the message," she asked him as he leaned on the counter.

"No. Sorry. My phone picked this point in time to take a rest. I thought we had a two o'clock today. Did something change?"

"Yes. The Patterson's baby made an unscheduled arrival. Your birthing team is on-site with them and won't make it back in time for your appointment. I spoke with

Mrs. Covington this morning to let her know."

"Has she rescheduled yet?" Darren asked reaching for a pen.

"Not yet. She said she wanted to check with you first."

"Thanks," Darren said turning to head back to his car.

He was still wondering when his phone had stopped working as he got back in and headed towards home. It wasn't like Mandy not to call him when something came up. He didn't like to admit it to anyone, but the bungled kidnapping last summer had affected him far more than Mandy and Katie.

Whenever there was a glitch in their plans and either one of his women showed up late, he found it hard to take it in stride and relax. They had taken the whole business more like a bad prank they blamed on Mandy's former boyfriend and his stupidity. Darren, on the other hand, had really been fearful for their lives from the moment he'd received the emergency call from Katie's phone. It had taken him quite a while to be comfortable with them coming and going freely without him to look after them.

Realizing that he was driving a bit too fast for conditions, he forced himself to slow down and stop the fears, trying to push them into the back of his mind. He was sure everything would be fine when he got home. Repeating that thought at every stoplight, the short drive seemed to take forever.

Mandy was surprised at the sound of the garage door

opening this early in the day. Wiping her hands on a dish towel, she went to the hall mirror to check herself. Katie was busy in the sewing room working on her latest project, with the music blaring. Meeting Darren coming in the back door, Mandy reached out for a kiss and a hug. She was surprised when he gave her a quick peck and pushed past her to sit down at the kitchen counter.

"What's wrong?" she asked. "Why are you home so early?"

"I thought we had a two o'clock at the birthing center today."

"We did, but it was canceled this morning. I sent you a text. Didn't you get it?" Mandy asked.

Leaning his forehead on his hand, Darren muttered something about his phone being dead. He hated this feeling of being helpless to keep anything bad from happening to his family. He'd failed to keep Katie's mother safe and that would forever haunt him. It would drive him mad if something happened to Katie, Mandy and the baby.

Mandy realized he wasn't mad at her, but was wrestling with his past in that moment and came over to put her arms around him. As he buried his face in the crook of her neck, she felt the baby move and she jumped.

"Did I hurt you?" Darren asked worriedly.

"Oh, no. The baby just wanted to make a statement," she laughed.

Darren leaned over to kiss her softly rounded belly.

Katie walked into the kitchen and groaned at the sight of the two of them.

"Really?" she asked a bit sarcastically. "Are you two ever going to stop acting like newlyweds?"

"No!"

They both retorted at the same time and burst out laughing at the look of disgust on Katie's face. Making an effort to ignore her parents, Katie grabbed a yogurt out of the fridge and made a hasty retreat back to the sewing room. The two of them laughed as the music jumped up a notch, and shook their heads.

"I hope the baby likes loud music," Darren joked as he resumed kissing Mandy's shoulder.

"I figure he'll be used to it by the time he gets here."

"He? Are you saying "he", as in, we're having a son?"

"Well, the 'baby pool' at school is running three to one against him, but I'm still leaning towards a boy," Mandy laughed. "Of course, nothing's settled and I've told the doctor not to tell me anything, so we just have to wait."

"Wouldn't it be easier to know so we can buy all the right stuff and pick out the name," Darren asked with a grin.

"Maybe, but I'm a little superstitious about trying to get ahead of the game," Mandy countered. "I just want to wait until it happens and enjoy the surprise."

"Okay. We'll wait, but I confess I'm leaning towards a girl. I have some experience in that area and women are definitely easier to get along with," Darren said, heading for the fridge.

He burst out laughing at the look that came over Mandy's face. She wasn't buying anything he'd just said for a moment. He thought this might be a good time to change the subject.

"So, what's for supper or do I need to call for a pizza?"

Darren turned around just in time to avoid the wet dish towel she'd thrown at him.

"You might want to go spend a little time with your daughter and get out of my kitchen or you'll be eating peanut butter and jelly tonight!"

Taking her tone to heart, Darren grabbed a soda and headed for the music. Mandy laughed as she watched him dance into the sewing room. It was a relief when the sounds coming out of the room dropped several decibels.

***

"What's this?" Darren asked as he surveyed the large box blocking his entrance into the garage.

"That's the birthing pool," Mandy answered. "It was delivered today and I didn't want to have it in the house until I figured out exactly where I wanted to put it. I'm thinking the living room would be best, but I don't know. What do you think?"

"Sure. Whatever you want. I always thought it'd be great to have a swimming pool in the living room," Darren teased. "Much better than in the kitchen, of course."

"So, you're okay with all this?" Mandy ventured to ask.

"All this, as in having a baby at home in a swimming pool, you mean," Darren said rubbing his chin thoughtfully. "I have to admit I wasn't at first, but I read some stuff about it on-line and it's growing on me. The guys at work are asking me if I'm going to wear my speedo and stuff like that. They think it's pretty funny. I think they're just scared their wives might catch on to the idea and want to try it themselves some day."

"I think Katie's pretty excited about the idea. We watched a video of a live birth on-line the other day and she was quiet for a while afterwards. Then she had some good questions so we talked a lot about what her role would be during the birth."

"Do you really think it's a good idea for a 13-year-old to be a part of delivering a baby?" Darren asked wrinkling his nose.

"Sure. Lots of home births involve the whole family including small children and grandparents. Having a baby is a natural event and making her a part of it will give her a sense of family beyond anything else we can do for her."

"I'm going to trust your judgment on this," Darren said as he wrestled the box off to one side. "I'm having enough trouble trying to see myself doing my part without fainting and drowning in the process."

Mandy doubled over with laughter as Katie stepped out into the garage.

"Are you okay?" she exclaimed running over to check on her stepmother.

"Yes. Yes. I'm fine," Mandy choked out between gasps of laughter. "Your father is trying to hurry this baby up, I think."

"My friend, Kirsten is on the phone," Katie said. "Can we have a sleepover this weekend?"

"Sounds great," Darren replied. "I have to fly up to the Slope to check on a few things. You girls can have the run of the house and do all those girlie things you like to do."

Missing the shadow that crossed Mandy's face, he laughed as Katie ran back inside with a shout of joy.

***

As the headlights of his SUV passed across his house, Darren caught sight of several odd-looking snowmen spread over the front lawn. He stopped partway up the drive for a closer look and burst out laughing. It appeared the creator of these snow creatures was trying to convey a message, as each snowman was built with the largest snowball in the center giving them a very 'pregnant' appearance. He figured Katie and her friends must have had a very good time at their sleepover. He didn't dare try to think how Mandy had taken this display. Pregnancy had a funny way of crumbling the edges of her good natured response to some things in life.

Pulling into the garage, the thought came to him that he

hadn't made pancakes in a while and this might be a good way to get himself back into his wife's good graces. She'd barely kissed him good-bye as he made ready to head up north. He knew his absences were starting to wear on her as she struggled to deal with the cold and snow alone, on top of everything else. It pleased him to think about how his plans to change all this were well underway. His new 'hotshot' was really stepping up to the plate in his new level of responsibilities and Darren felt confident his days of flying up to the Slope every time something went wrong were coming to an end. Soon, everything would be different on the home front.

It didn't take long for the smell of pancakes and reindeer sausage to fill the house, and Katie was the first to appear in the kitchen. Keeping his ear turned to the upstairs, Darren filled his daughter's plate and gave over the other ear to her energetic account of the weekend's activities. She was on her second stack of pancakes before Mandy waddled her way down the stairs. Smiling at the sight of his very pregnant wife, Darren pulled her warm plate from the oven and invited her to the table. Pausing for a quick welcome home hug and a kiss, they carefully ignored Katie's groan from behind them. She chose that moment to bring up the artwork outside as Mandy glared at her. Darren resolved to stay out of the middle of this one. It clearly hadn't been well received on Mandy's side.

"We've got four more weeks of this if the baby stays on

schedule," Mandy said over a mouthful of pancakes dripping with syrup. "That's only two more classes and a quick check-up with the midwives."

"What else do we need to finish up before all that can happen?" Darren asked as he buttered his pancakes.

"The crib still has to be put together and the birthing pool has to be inflated and set up."

"Okay. I'll put that on Katie's list of things to do," Darren joked, watching his daughter's face.

Much to his disappointment, she just shrugged. Apparently, she wasn't in the mood for an argument.

"Have we decided on the living room for the 'big event' then?"

The two women looked at each other and nodded. It was clear the matter was settled between them at least. He was relieved to be left out of that discussion. The whole thing was still a mystery to him as to how it was all going to work without some serious water damage. He could think of a dozen things that could go wrong from a leak to a tip over of the pool flooding the entire downstairs with bath water. No. Correct that, *birth* water! The very thought of it gave him the shivers.

Pushing away his plate, he leaned back with a big grin and looked at his two favorite women in the world. As his eyes came to rest on the newest member of their family yet to appear, his thoughts softened and he sighed. *I truly have a lot to be thankful for*, he thought to himself.

Chapter 5

The next two weeks were busy as Darren juggled his work schedule and Katie's school activities. He was trying to keep Mandy at home as much as possible as the roads were pretty icy at this time of the year. The last thing he wanted was for her to end up in a ditch somewhere having a baby alone. He was secretly amused to find that Mandy had carefully scheduled the last two birthing classes to keep Katie in the loop. He wanted her to believe in his commitment to his being there for the birth, but it was clear she was hedging her bets on his behalf.

Katie had typed out long checklists of things to do when the time came with phone numbers and job assignments. The best part was in how she'd managed to assign several key tasks to herself. She was definitely planning to be ringside throughout the event. Duplicates of her list were posted on the refrigerator and spread around the house in every room. It wasn't unusual to come upon her going over the list at every opportunity and asking Mandy questions about this or that.

Despite his best intentions, the crib was in its box and the birthing pool was still in the garage. Mandy was distracted with her own concerns and didn't think to remind him about them. They both figured it would get done in his usual manner of, just in time.

He was finally ready to get to the tasks assigned to him after dinner one evening when the phone rang surprising them all. As Darren took the call, his face grew worried as he cast several glances at his wife. She could tell by the tone of his voice something was wrong and knew this meant he probably had to head up north to the Slope post haste. Her frown deepened as the conversation continued for several minutes longer.

When he finally hung up, Darren turned to find both women studying him carefully.

"There's been an accident up on the Slope. Several people are injured and there's some serious damage that my new guy's not ready to handle. I've got to go up...."

Darren's voice trailed off at the silence that met his words. He felt a flash of anger at being caught in the middle of something he couldn't control. This was his job and a man shouldn't be put between doing his job and taking care of his family. This wasn't his fault.

Nobody spoke as Darren turned to go upstairs to change his clothes and grab his overnight bag. Mandy took several deep breaths before she got up from the couch to follow him. Katie felt a couple of tears slip down her cheek before she gathered herself up and retreated to the sewing room. The shout of the sudden music followed Mandy upstairs.

The slump of Darren's shoulders as he stood in the shower told her everything she needed to know about his feelings in that moment. She waited there with his towel in

Renee Hart

hand as he stepped out.

"It's just a couple of days at most," he said quietly as he dried himself off. "You won't even know I was gone."

"It's fine. We'll be fine," Mandy said forcing a smile for his benefit.

She turned away in case there was a shadow of doubt in her eyes. This wasn't a time to send him off thinking she didn't believe in him. He could be facing a very dangerous situation up there.

"Jack's flying me up in the plane. The helicopter's already on site. He's going to stay until my return and fly me back. You know Jack. He's not one to take risks and he's flown the route hundreds of times in every kind of weather. I trust him with my life."

Mandy nodded as she gathered up some clothes for his bag and focused on rolling them into logs for packing. He stood there watching her for a moment before getting dressed in his long underwear. She laughed when she turned and caught sight of him in the red flannel he always wore.

"A few more pieces of my sweet potato pie and we're going to have to give you a new *nick*name," she giggled.

Looking down, he sucked in his stomach and flexed a few muscles for her benefit.

"I wouldn't be making any *fat* jokes, young lady," was his response, which only caused her to laugh harder.

"Besides that, unless this baby is planning to show up

early or pop out like a jack-in-the-box, you know I'm little more than a couple of hours away depending on the flight conditions. Even if you call me at the last minute, I can get here on time."

"You seem pretty sure of yourself," Mandy retorted. "I just hope you're right."

She didn't bother to remind him the baby had already started to turn over in the womb and was getting ready to shake things up a bit. He had enough to think about already. She watched him finish with his preparations before disappearing for a moment while his back was turned.

When he turned back around, she was zipping his bag closed. Taking her hands, he pulled her up from the bed and carefully put his arms around her.

Burying his face in her hair, he whispered in her ear, "I'll be back in time. I promise. You know I'd die before I'd break a promise to you."

Mandy pushed him away.

"Don't say things like that!"

Darren winced as Mandy turned and left the room. He could tell by the set of her shoulders, his words had only made things worse. Smacking himself in the forehead, he grabbed his bag and headed after her. *Sometimes, the word, 'stupid" seemed like an appropriate middle name*, he thought to himself.

The next couple of days were tense as Mandy and Katie tiptoed around the house waiting for the phone to ring or the sound of the garage door opening. Darren called in every few hours or so to update them on his progress. He was confident of being home in the next day or so. The women prayed that he was right.

It was late on the third day when the phone rang in the kitchen. Darren always called on Mandy or Katie's cell phones. The landline was only used for household business most of the time. The two of them looked at each other for a moment before Katie hurried to answer it.

"Mandy! It's for you," Katie called in a strained voice.

She waited impatiently for Mandy to haul herself into the kitchen and take the phone. Hovering nearby, Katie struggled to follow the conversation with fear in her eyes. She knew Darren's boss wouldn't be calling this late without a very good reason…or a very bad one, she warned herself. The sound of the doorbell ringing interrupted her thoughts.

Racing to the front door, Katie found her father's friend and co-worker pacing the front porch. She invited him in as Mandy came from the kitchen to join them.

Taking one look at her face, Tom took her by the arm and led her over to the couch.

"Let's not get ahead of ourselves here," he said gently. "We have no reason to think anything beyond the fact that we've lost contact with Jack's plane."

"What!?!"

Katie was nearly shouting as she hurried over to Mandy's side. She winced as she saw Mandy jump.

"What happened?" she continued in a much quieter tone, looking from Mandy to Tom and back again.

Mandy took her hand and gave it a squeeze.

Putting on a brave face, Mandy hurried to reassure Katie that it was just as Tom had said. Darren and Jack were heading home when they made an emergency call to the airport in Livengood that ice was forming on the wings of the plane. After that the radio went silent and all calls to them since then have gone unanswered.

"We've already got the chopper in the air heading north and Paul's assembling a rescue team to work out the search area," Tom said firmly. "We know when they left Deadhorse and what time the call came in. That will give us a very narrow path to work out where they went down. I don't want anyone jumping to any conclusions or getting over-excited."

This last part was said with a stern look at Katie and a sideways glance towards Mandy.

"What can we do?" Mandy asked quietly.

"Just do what you do best, Honey...pray."

Mandy didn't even bother to look up at her husband's friend. Prayer seemed like giving up somehow and leaving everything to chance. She struggled against seeing this situation in that light. This was just another time of waiting for Darren to come home like they always waited for him, she assured herself.

"Do you want some coffee?" she asked, trying to pull herself up off the couch.

"No. No, thanks. I'm going back to the office to keep an eye on the rescue team. If we can't pick up their location from the beacon, we're going to need another chopper. I'm frontline on this one."

Walking Tom to the front door, Mandy put her hand on his arm for a moment. He turned and looked at her carefully.

"How long do we have?" he asked casting a glance downwards.

"I don't know. A couple of days, a week...not much more than that," Mandy answered with a shake of her head. "This is my first time, you know, but I do know the baby's turned."

"Well, Hon, you know Darren. He's always been one of those just-in-time kind of guys," he laughed as he put on his coat. "I've learned never to count him out and he's never let me down."

After Mandy closed the door behind Tom, she went to the hall closet and pulled out her parka, boots, scarves, hats, and mittens, making a huge pile on the floor. Katie stood there watching her silently as she continued to search the closet.

"What are you doing?" Katie finally ventured to ask.

"I'm going after him," Mandy mumbled without looking up from her task. "He needs me and I'm going after him."

"But you don't know where he's at," Katie protested. "That's the whole problem. No one knows where he's at!"

"I'll find him."

"Mandy! You can't go out there. It can be 40 below or worse, and there's wind and snow and big trucks....and it's dark," Katie finished lamely.

She could see nothing she said was getting through to her stepmother. Katie tried to think of what to do when her best idea was simply to go along until Mandy came to her senses. Then, they would just turn around and come back home and everything would be okay. Grabbing her own coat and a hat, Katie threw them on while, out of the corner of her eye, watching Mandy struggle with her boots. It was almost funny, but Katie wasn't in the mood to laugh. Everything seemed to be spinning out of control right in front of her.

When Mandy was fully dressed, she turned and saw Katie standing there in her coat.

"You can't come with me. It's too dangerous," she mumbled through her scarf.

"I can too. You can't stop me and I'm not staying here alone. I'm too scared and you have to take care of me. You promised!"

"Promised. He promised. I, you..." Mandy broke off

and headed for the back door.

Katie followed behind closely on her heels. She was ready to get in the SUV when Mandy headed for the Hummer.

"We can't go in that," Katie protested. "That thing's not safe!"

Mandy didn't even turn around so Katie hurried to climb in the other side as the cold wind blew in the open garage door carrying a gust of snow. She prayed the Hummer wouldn't start, but it was as if the prayer was tossed away by the building storm outside. The beast roared to life and Mandy jammed it into reverse.

As soon as they hit the snowy driveway, the vehicle fishtailed wildly from one side to the other and Katie wondered if they were going to make it to the street. Mandy fought the wheel as she gunned the engine and they bumped over a large snowbank before coming to a sudden stop in the middle of the road. Shoving the gearshift forward, the grinding sound of the transmission was nearly drowned out by the wind.

Gripping the steering wheel tightly, Mandy focused her eyes straight ahead and got them moving forward. She made it to the main road and settled her feet into the patterns of dancing with the Hummer that Darren had taught her so long ago. Katie sat silently on her side and watched her stepmother's movements warily. A couple of tears slipped down her cheeks unnoticed in the darkness.

Chapter 6

Jack groaned as he tried to sit up a bit straighter in his seat. His left knee was jammed against the console and from the angle he had, his leg was broken. Trying to shake off the cold, he looked over at Darren in the darkness.

"Darren! Darren!! Are you still with me?"

A muffled reply came as Darren struggled to get free of a large pine branch poking in his broken window. As he moved a bit too violently, the plane gave out a warning sound and shifted a bit.

"Are we on the ground?" he asked in a shaky voice.

"Not exactly," Jack surmised. "Close though. It feels like we're caught up in some tree branches or something. There's a couple of flashlights under your seat if you can reach them."

Some scrabbling sounds in the darkness came as Darren felt around on the floor. The sudden flare of light as he found one caught them both by surprise. He handed the flashlight to Jack and searched for the second one. He'd just laid a hand on it when the plane shifted again and dropped little lower. It slipped towards the back of the plane.

"That one got away," he said as he sat back up in his seat and looked around. "So, what's it look like, Ace?"

"From here, it's hard to tell, but I'm sure from the cold

breeze on the back of my neck, we sheared the tail off and I'm also sure my leg's broken. Otherwise, your guess is as good as mine about the rest."

"Well, it's a safe bet we won't be flying out of here in this baby," Darren said grimly. "I don't have any broken bones, but there's some blood coming from my forehead."

"Here. Let me take a look," Jack said, shining his light in his friend's eyes.

Darren jerked away from the brightness and the two of them froze as the plane shifted violently beneath them again.

"Maybe we better find out just how high we are first," Darren said, cautiously turning to look towards the tail.

They were both relieved to see the pile of snow at the back of the plane. Apparently, they'd come to rest with the front of the plane stuck in a tree, but the back of it was clearly on the ground.

"That doesn't look too bad," Jack said trying to be funny. "A little duct tape and some superglue and she'll be back in the air in no time. There's a first aid kit strapped to the back of my seat. Can you reach it?"

Darren leaned over and pulled the kit free. The cold was starting to numb him and blood was running down the right side of his face. He could feel it dripping off his chin. Rummaging through the kit, he found a large bandage and some gauze and held it to the wound. Much to his relief, the damage was mainly superficial and quickly stopped bleeding.

Jack was fiddling with the radio, but there was only silence.

"Okay," Darren said, "let's figure out our options. Broken leg, no camping gear, no radio and it's too cold for a polar bear. Any suggestions?"

Jack rubbed his hands together for a moment before answering.

"My first thought was we shoulda stayed home. On second thought, I wish I'd picked a better landing spot. Other than that, it's gonna be a while before the cavalry comes riding in, so we need to get out of here and build a fire."

Darren agreed that this was a pretty good assessment of their situation and tried to work himself free of his seat. The smell of fuel dripping down outside his window caught his attention.

"Well, at least it'll be easy to get a fire started," he tried to joke.

Jack just gave him a dirty look.

***

Katie hunched down in her seat and stared out the windshield at the building storm throwing a whirlwind of snow in their faces. Winter in Alaska is harsh and often unforgiving to anyone daring to challenge its icy grip on the land. Most cheechakoes eventually learned respect and became sourdoughs, but some didn't learn fast enough and the penalty was usually bad, sometimes even fatal. Katie knew Mandy wasn't in her right mind as the lights of the city faded behind them. What she didn't know was how to reach through the fear gripping her stepmother and get them back home safely.

The icy road revealed little more than two tracks and the Hummer rolled along into the darkness as if there was no reason for concern. If they were headed for the grocery store or the fabric shop, Katie knew they were in little danger. Unfortunately, the last sign they'd passed put them north of Fox and she knew the road wasn't going to get better.

Mandy stared ahead into the driving snow without a glance to the left or the right. Her hands gripped the steering wheel as if it was her only way of holding everything together. The slap of the windshield wipers trying to keep up with the sticky snow on the flat windshield was the only sound. A passing snowplow threw up a thick cloud of snow and Mandy swerved to the right in her confusion. The Hummer slid sideways a bit heading off the road and she fought for control as Katie tensed with fear.

Suddenly the back wheel caught on a dry patch of pavement and turned the SUV around in a circle, coming to rest against a snow bank on the opposite side of the road.

As the cloud of snow from the impact settled around them, the two of them stared at the road ahead leading home and then turned to look at each other. Tears ran down Mandy's face as she realized the danger she'd put them in with this flight into the storm.

"I'm sorry, Katie," she cried reaching out for the young girl and drawing her into a hug. "I don't know what's wrong with me!"

"I do," Katie managed in a muffled voice, "You're pregnant! That's enough to drive anyone crazy and then my Dad manages to get himself lost in the wilderness!"

Katie's voice choked on her last words as Mandy let go of her and tried to open the door. Katie grabbed her arm.

"Please! Let's go home," she cried out.

Mandy looked at her sadly and nodded.

Checking for lights or any sign of traffic, Mandy took a deep breath and slowly let out the clutch. Much to their relief, the Hummer rolled forward without any problems and they found themselves in the path of the snowplow heading home. Katie was relieved to see her stepmother looking around and acting more like herself. She stayed silent as she waited for any lights to come into view through the darkness of the storm. With the wind at their back, the snow didn't seem so fierce and the snowplow wasn't far enough ahead of them for the path to fade away yet.

Neither of them spoke another word until they were

turning into the driveway. Mandy stopped as they stared at the snow packed garage. Suddenly she started to laugh.

"What's so funny about that," Katie demanded. "You know Dad's going to be mad!"

Suddenly, the shock and the adrenaline of the last couple of hours drained away and Katie started laughing too. The two of them sat there choking on their laughter until the last giggles died away and the Hummer was silent.

"At least you remembered to close the kitchen door," Mandy mumbled half to herself.

The thought of the kitchen filled with snow set them both off to giggling again and they laughed until Mandy started to hiccup.

"Oh, no," Mandy groaned, holding her swollen belly with both arms.

"What! What's going on?" Katie nearly shouted with panic in her voice.

"I've got to go to the bathroom," Mandy said with a grin. "Now!"

The two of them eyed the path through the garage to get to the kitchen door and then surveyed the equally hazardous trek to the front door.

"Let me go first," Katie said, "I can break a path for you. I'm thinking the front door's going to be easier. Do you have your keys?"

Mandy scrunched up her face and shook her head no.

Setting her shoulders, Katie pushed the Hummer's door

open and stepped out into the snow. The drift filling the front of the garage easily stood above her shoulders. She had no idea how deep or far into the garage it went or of how she was going to fight her way through it. Making her way to the edge of the opening, she felt her way along the wall climbing up over the mound.

Mandy watched as she disappeared over the top and the light came on inside the garage. Struggling to get out of the driver's seat, she found the snow was already knee deep in the driveway. As she followed Katie's path to the garage, the baby gave a sudden lurch and her already strained bladder gave up the fight. She stood there feeling her boots fill as Katie's head reappeared at the middle of the drift.

"There's less snow right here," she called out. "If you can get over this high part, it's not too bad to make it to the kitchen."

Mandy nodded grimly and waddled over to the waiting girl. As Katie pushed aside snow, Mandy pulled herself over the drift and slid down on the other side. Pulling themselves along the path inside that Katie had created, they nearly fell through the door into the kitchen where they both collapsed on the floor and lay there trying to catch their breath.

"I thought you had to go to the bathroom," Katie muttered as she sat up and started pulling off her boots and coat. She glanced over at Mandy still lying on the floor looking like she was in no hurry to get up.

"Uh, yeah, I did," Mandy mumbled without moving. The look on her face said the rest and Katie froze.

"Are you kidding me?" Katie demanded.

"Sorry, darling. Just part of the process, or so I'm told."

Katie jumped up from the floor with a look of horror as she surveyed the scene.

"Don't worry," Mandy said. "I think most of it's in my boots and the rest has soaked my snow pants. You're safe."

Recovering her composure, Katie ran to get some towels from the laundry room and came back to help Mandy sort out the mess they'd made of the floor. She tried not to watch as Mandy wrestled out of the pile of wet winter gear. By the time Mandy was down to her underwear, Katie was back with some clean towels and her robe.

"Can you check and see if anyone's called while I take a shower," Mandy asked as she headed for the stairs.

"Got it," Katie mumbled to the empty room as her stepmother disappeared.

***

Darren tossed a few more sticks on the fire before pulling back the tarp to check on Jack's condition. His friend was sleeping restlessly as the warmth of the fire eased the stress of their predicament for a little while. Darren shivered a bit in his jacket as the sound of a wolf howling in the distance drifted towards him in the darkness. With his thoughts turning towards home, he wondered at how Mandy and Katie were doing. He wasn't sure how much wilderness stood between him and his family, but without a plane, a radio or any mode of transportation to get out of here, the distance seemed impossible to overcome.

Forcing his thoughts back to the fire, he checked his pile of sticks and moved to gather a few more around the edges of the circle of firelight. Jack's landing wasn't the best, but the location now had plenty of firewood thanks to the plane crash. He'd set up camp a short distance from the plane to avoid any chance of setting everything in the area on fire due to the leaking fuel. The resulting blaze would create a huge signal fire if there was anyone around to see it. Unfortunately, it wouldn't last long enough to keep them from freezing to death before someone came to investigate the source, if anyone came at all.

He added his sticks to the pile and in the darkness pawed through the small pile of stuff he'd gathered from the plane. *Would it have been too much to stash a box of granola bars or a bag of beef jerky on the plane*, he grumbled to himself. Finding nothing to eat, he turned his attention back to the fire. There was still a couple of hours left before daylight that would allow him to survey their surroundings in search of better shelter. He leaned back against a large rock warmed by the fire and closed his eyes for a moment. *Things always looked better in the light of morning* was his last thought as he drifted off to sleep.

"Darren....Darren! Wake up!"

Trying to stay in his dream, Darren pushed the hand away from his shoulder and turned back to look into Karen's eyes. She smiled at him sadly and began to turn away. He felt something cold and wet touching his face as he reached for her. He knew it was up to him to keep her safe and he wasn't going to fail her again. The word *again* rang out in his mind as he struggled to remember how he'd failed her already. Suddenly everything came flooding back as he opened his eyes and felt the cold that was seeping into his legs. The fire was nearly out and Jack was staring at him with fear in his eyes.

"Thank God," Jack exclaimed as he closed his eyes and relaxed. "You've got me wrapped up in this tarp like a burrito and I thought you'd gone to sleep forever."

Darren wiped the snow from his face and neck that had fallen onto him from the tree and started to work the stiffness from his arms and legs. Finally, he figured he could move without falling over into the snow, so he grabbed a handful of sticks to build up the fire. Turning his attention to Jack, he loosened the tarp and helped him sit up against a rock.

"How's the leg?" Darren asked pulling back the tarp to take a look at his handiwork.

"Well, it sure ain't going to win any scouting awards, but it'll do for now," Jack smirked as he tried to shift his weight a bit.

The look on his face said more than any words about how he wasn't going to be hoofing it out of here on his own. Darren stood up and stretched as he surveyed the area around them. The light was dim, but considering the time of year, they weren't going to get much more that day.

"I'm going to walk around the camp in a spiral pattern to see if I can get a clearer idea of what's around us," he said as he knelt down next to Jack and handed him a small metal container of melted snow.

"Coffee, sir," he quipped with a grin.

Jack drank a couple of swallows and handed it back.

"I think we've gotten too casual about making this flight. There's no food and very little in the way of survival gear in this plane," Darren said. "I can't find the tail so I don't know if the homing beacon is working or not and the radio is useless. Basically, we're going to have to work this out on our own."

Jack nodded grimly as he stared down at his broken leg. Darren's use of the word *we* was cutting the situation a little thin in his opinion. He was feeling about as helpful as a duck's webbed feet on a frozen lake. He reached forward to grab a couple of sticks to add to the fire and groaned as pain shot up his leg into his hip. Darren carefully turned his face to hide his concern.

***

Renee Hart

Mandy moaned as a wave of pain forced her awake. The dim light in the bedroom gave her no indication of the time or of how long she'd been asleep. The events of last night came flooding back as she struggled to sit up on the edge of the bed. She ran her hands over her swollen belly and felt the baby stretching. She nearly grunted as a well-placed kick caught her at the bottom of her rib cage. If this wasn't a boy with a dream of playing soccer or football, this young lady had her own aspirations for sports with a kick like that. *Or maybe the baby's getting anxious about getting out of his or her cramped quarters*, Mandy thought to herself. *I know I'm well past ready myself.*

Tears came to her eyes as she wondered again where Darren was and if he was going to make it back on time. Another kind of wondering lingered in the shadows but she pushed it way fiercely. This was not the time to let such thoughts run amok. She waddled to the bathroom as she listened for any sound that Katie was up and about. Usually there was music on wherever she was, but this morning the house was silent.

As she was making her way downstairs, the smell of coffee drifted to her, and she began to hurry towards the kitchen as hope sprang up in her face. Turning the corner at the bottom of the stairs her eyes swept the kitchen only to find Tom sitting at the counter with a cup of coffee and Katie busy at the stove making breakfast. The two of them turned and froze as she came in and seeing her face darken with disappointment at the sight of them, they both knew what she'd been thinking.

"I'm sorry Mandy," Tom said quietly as he came over and put his arm around her. "I stopped by to check on you two and found the garage door standing wide open. I came in to see if you were okay as the kitchen door wasn't locked and found Katie making breakfast."

Leading her to a chair, he stepped back as Katie slid a plate in front of her with some toast and a cup of juice. Mandy's face burned red as she considered his words. She knew Darren wouldn't be too happy to find out how she'd taken care of things.

"We...I...uh...went to...." Mandy paused to think of a plausible excuse as Katie moved nearer with her own ideas on how to explain things. "The grocery store!"

"The quilt shop," Katie said at the same time.

"Uh...to get," Mandy started to add as she cast a desperate look at Katie, "fabric!"

"Ice cream," Katie exclaimed at the same time.

"And the garage door must have got stuck," Mandy finished lamely, her words trailing off as the look of confusion on Tom's face overwhelmed her ability to lie any further.

Remembering the real reason Tom was in her kitchen, Mandy attempted to change the subject.

"Is there any word on the plane yet?" she asked

hopefully.

"Nothing yet, but they started at the top of the search grid at first light," Tom said brightly. "We're hoping to find them within a day or so..."

His words trailed off as lying didn't come any easier to him and there was a lot of wilderness to be searched in the limited hours of daylight. The three of them carefully avoided looking at each other as the sound of the back door opening drew their attention to the snow-covered man standing there.

"We've got the driveway," the man said, then after clearing his throat, "and the garage cleared of snow. Is there anything else you want us to do before we head in to work?"

Everyone froze as Mandy gave out a groan. All eyes were fixed on her as she rubbed her hands over her aching mound. She looked up just in time to catch their worried glances.

"No. No! It's nothing! I'm fine," she protested. "The baby is just moving around a lot today."

After a brief moment of silence, Mandy turned to the man in the doorway.

"Would you like some coffee or cocoa, or something?"

The man mumbled, "No, thanks, ma'am," a bit nervously and looked at his boss.

"Could you put the Hummer back in the garage for me?" Mandy said, and paused. "Oh! There's one more thing I need some help with," she added. "There's a big box in the garage that I need moved into the living room. Can you bring that in for us?"

The man nodded and hurried to absent himself from the kitchen to do her bidding. The three of them listened to the sound of the Hummer as it roared to life and growled its way back into the garage. A couple of minutes later the door opened again as two men wrested the large box inside. No one spoke as the men tried to work out their snow covered boots and the clean kitchen floor.

"Never mind," Katie interrupted them. "We can get it to the living room by ourselves."

The two men cast her a grateful look and slipped back out the door.

Mandy sat at the table breaking her toast up into small pieces as Tom and Katie pushed and pulled the large box into the living room.

"What is this?" Tom asked as they rounded the corner into the living room.

At Katie's reply, Tom fell silent and didn't dare ask another question.

***

Darren retraced his tracks back to the camp with an armful of firewood. His efforts to find better shelter hadn't revealed anything as of yet, but he did manage to find the broken tail flaps from the plane. As he had feared, the beacon was badly damaged when the tail caught on some rocks during the crash.

He took some time to stamp out an SOS in the closest clearing and line it with pine branches, but in the dim light of winter, he knew a plane or helicopter would have to fly directly over it and be looking in the right direction. It was basically little more than a shot in the dark.

When he came into sight of the camp, he saw Jack looking around anxiously.

"Ho, my friend! It's just me," he called out.

"Whoa! Am I glad to see your ugly mug," Jack growled. "I've been hearing noises for the last hour or so and been expecting a moose, wolf, or bear to come crashing out of those woods with me lying here like a felled tree. The best I could do would be to pelt 'em with snowballs."

Darren grinned at the pile of ammo Jack had worked up next to his pallet. Seeing his smirk, Jack picked up one of the snowballs and nailed him right in the forehead with it.

"There! You see! I'm not just laying here doing nothing," Jack exclaimed as he laughed at the look of surprise on his friend's face.

"I take back any thoughts I may have had about that," Darren said wiping snow from his hair and face. "You're clearly armed and dangerous! Too bad your ammo isn't good enough to get us any food out here in the wilderness."

His answer came in the form of another snowball

hitting him squarely in the back. He wisely decided to ignore it.

"So, did you find anything out there worth talking about?" Jack asked after Darren sat down.

"No shelter in sight, but there is a pretty rough trail off to the east. Could be a trap line," Darren said quietly. "I also found the broken tail pieces. The homing beacon is missing. I don't know if it's working or not since I couldn't find it."

The two men sat there quietly considering their options.

"On one side, logic says stay with the plane," Jack began, "but on the other side, we don't have adequate shelter and we're not sure how long they'll take to find us. This is a tough call, but it's up to you if we stay or go. I'd sure hate to sit here and freeze to death waiting for rescue if I could walk out of here, but I'm not going to be walking anywhere soon."

Jack's voice trailed off as Darren stared into the fire without answering. His thoughts were back in Fairbanks. He'd promised Mandy to be there when the baby came and he meant that promise with every fiber of his being. He didn't want to think about how the news of the crash was affecting her right now or Katie either as she faced the prospect of losing her dad after enduring and recovering from the death of her mother. His dream of Karen last night made him aware of just how close death was in this place. Sleep too long, let the fire go out, the wrong animal and it was all over just like that. He realized Jack had stopped talking and looked up.

The look of uncertainty on Jack's face spoke volumes of the fear he was fighting himself.

"Don't worry, buddy," Darren said. "If anyone leaves here, we're leaving together. I'm not ready to lose my favorite pilot...well, maybe my second favorite now."

He quickly dodged another snowball before returning a couple of his own.

"Enough! Enough!"

Jack quickly surrendered and lay back against the rock. The flush on his face told Darren that he didn't have the leisure of waiting much longer on making a decision. His friend was clearly hurting.

Chapter Seven

After Tom headed back to the office, Mandy sat at the table and stared at the crumbled toast. Katie puttered about the kitchen setting things back into order and slipped sideways glances at her stepmother as she waited for some indication of what was to come next. Mandy finally got up and went into the living room. Katie took a moment to clear the table before following her to find Mandy staring at the large box in the middle of the room.

"Let's have a hot tub party," Mandy suddenly announced, startling Katie. "We'll fill this tub and put on our swimsuits and eat pizza and wait for your father to come in and surprise us."

Katie didn't know what to say. She stood there rubbing her ear and tried to think of what was a person supposed to do when somebody was missing, maybe even…. The thought stopped there abruptly as she slammed the door on it and considered the alternatives. She supposed they could sit around and worry or cry, but what good would that do for anyone.

"We'll put on a video! You know. One of those girlie romance movies your dad hates," Mandy continued, as if she could put enough distractions together to make all this bearable.

"And we'll eat chocolate," the two of them exclaimed

together as they danced in a small circle.

"Ugh," Mandy groaned as she suddenly stopped and wrapped her arms around her middle.

Katie quickly guided her over to the couch.

"What is it? What's wrong?"

"Nothing's wrong," Mandy answered her gently. "This is just nature's way of telling us we're running out of time. You remember our training. We expected this to happen."

Katie nodded solemnly but her eyes were wide as she stared at the baby bulge and sucked in her cheeks. She'd secretly hoped her dad was going to keep his promise and take charge, but it was looking like things might not work out the way she wanted them. *Having a baby is going to be a lot more complicated than watching a video*, she thought to herself.

Much to their amazement, setting up the birthing pool didn't take them very long and Katie headed out to the garage to find the garden hose. She paused at the sight of the carefully swept garage dispersing any telltale evidence of last night's little misadventure. Unless one of them told, her dad would never have to know about what happened. She quietly wondered to herself if there was a reason for him to know as she dragged the hose back into the kitchen. *Maybe parents don't always have to hear about those things they weren't around to stop from happening anyway*, she mused. *How many drives have Mandy and I gone on over the last year that were never talked about?*

Focusing on hooking the hose up to the kitchen faucet, she put the matter aside. There were more important things to think about right now as she dragged the other end of the hose into the living room.

***

Darren spent most of the night staring into the fire as sleep evaded his grasp and his thoughts ran around in circles. His decisions in the next few hours could very well determine whether he and Jack would live or die. He didn't mind making hard decisions, but the outcome here had far more implications than just his death. Leaving Mandy alone with two children to raise seemed terribly wrong to him and Jack wasn't going to make it on his own. He also had a family that would miss him if Darren couldn't get him home safe. The bottom line out here in the wilderness was that neither of them could survive the frigid cold much longer with just a couple of tarps and a small fire. They needed to find better shelter and they had to do it soon.

With the matter settled, Darren threw a few more sticks on the fire and settled back against the warm rock hoping to catch a few minutes of shuteye. The sound of Jack coughing jerked him awake and he realized the fire was nearly out. It was clear he'd fallen asleep at least for a little while. Turning his attention to Jack, he made his friend drink some water and checked his leg for swelling. They were both quiet as the first light of the day came and their hungry bellies growled with neglect.

"I've made a decision," Darren began, "we need to try and find better shelter. I'm going to pull one or both of the landing skis off the plane to make a sled for you. We'll head out as soon as it's light enough for me to set a direction."

Jack gave him a weak grin and merely nodded his agreement. He trusted Darren's judgment and was willing to go along with whatever plan seemed the best. The two of them would see this through to the end.

Darren set to work gathering the stuff he needed and by the time it was light enough to see they were ready to move out. He helped Jack settle himself on the makeshift sled and the two of them set off in search of shelter. As Jack watched their campsite fade away, he prayed the two of them would find someplace better, and soon.

***

Mandy woke up and looked around the bedroom hoping to see Darren coming from the bathroom. She'd been dreaming and it was as if everything was normal and he was at home with them. Her dream seemed so real and she hated waking up and finding that it wasn't true.

Their little hot tub party last night didn't really keep

them from worrying about their fears, but the warmth of the water had taken away at least part of the physical stress. Katie had tried so hard to make it look like she was having fun. They'd both laughed when she'd suggested they keep the hot tub in the living room for the rest of the winter. It was a bit unconventional, but nothing topped a hot bath when it was cold outside.

Mandy winced as her abdomen contracted and the baby gave a kick in protest. The birthing team leader was coming by today for a routine check on her condition. She wasn't due yet, but the early labor was a constant reminder of the ticking clock. The baby wasn't going to be deterred by Darren's absence one way or another. It was up to her to keep her focus on the birth as much as possible. There was nothing she could do for her missing husband right now.

She heard a light tap at the bedroom door and turned to find Katie peering around the edge of it.

"Are you awake?" the young girl whispered into the darkened room.

Mandy struggled to sit up as Katie hurried over to the bed.

"What is it? What's the matter?" Mandy asked breathlessly.

"Nothing. There's nothing wrong. I just wanted to tell you Tom called and said they haven't found the plane yet. They'll be back in the air as soon as it's light again. Did you get any sleep?"

Rubbing Katie's back as the young girl sat down next to her, Mandy nodded and asked, "You?"

"I did. I barely got into bed before I was dreaming about swimming babies and dog sleds racing over the snow."

Mandy puckered her lips as she tried to figure out the connection. She lost her train of thought as another contraction took all of her attention for a moment.

"How will we know when it's real and not just some kind of early labor thing?" Katie asked with a frown.

"That's why we have a team of experts," Mandy laughed, "to help us figure that out. Susan's coming over this afternoon to check things. She'll be happy to see we've got the birthing pool ready. I think she was starting to worry that your Dad's 'just in time' way of doing things wasn't going to be on time at all."

The two of them laughed for a moment before they each sank into their own thoughts concerning Darren's "just in time" ways.

"Do you think he's going to make it back in time for the delivery?" Katie ventured as her lower lip trembled.

Mandy gave her a quick hug and said, "You know your Dad better than I do, and he's made a promise. We both know he'll do everything in his power to keep that promise. Now let's go have some breakfast. I'm starving!"

***

Darren quickly found the trail he'd noticed yesterday and set his mind to moving as fast as possible with the sled bumping against his heels. Jack was quiet and the only sound was the shush of the ski over the snow. There weren't any signs indicating anyone had come that way in a while but the trail was clearly being maintained by somebody. The underbrush was cut back on each side just enough for the sled with Jack to pass through without him being slapped by stray branches.

They'd gone along for about an hour when an old cabin came into sight. It wasn't much more than a large shed, but there was firewood stacked along the front and smoke coming from the stovepipe. Darren quickened his pace and hailed the house. He was surprised by the sight of a burly man at the door who appeared equally astonished to see someone outside his cabin.

"Where'd you come from?" the man asked, staring at Darren's frosty face before realizing that another man was with him.

"Our plane went down somewhere near the other end of your trap line," Darren explained. "We followed it in search of some shelter. Do you have a radio?"

"We?"

Darren moved aside so the man could see Jack and made a stab at introductions.

"Let's get you two warm. My friend's call me Dewey. Come on inside. Don't mind the dogs. They're friendly.

The two men helped Jack into the cabin where several dogs filled most of the floor space around the tiny woodstove. Dewey crowded them to one side to make room for Jack in front of the stove as Darren stood next to the door shivering with a mixture of cold and relief.

"I don't have a radio. This here's just a place I keep for overnight when I'm running my line," Dewey said as he filled a couple of battered cups with some hot coffee and a healthy dose of sugar. "My main cabin is quite a ways from here and I was just getting ready to head home."

He pulled out a box of pilot bread and offered it to them. The two men eagerly grabbed a couple of the stale crackers and gobbled them down. Dewey threw a couple more logs into the stove and watched as Darren pulled back the makeshift bandages covering Jack's leg.

"Broken?"

"Yeah," Darren nodded and grabbed another cracker. "How fast can we get to a radio?"

"It's a few hours to my cabin, but there's no way for all of us to go on my sled," Dewey said rubbing his chin. "In fact, it's a pretty rough trail and your friend won't be too happy for it. It might be best if you two stay here and I'll head home and call in a rescue chopper for you."

"Here's the deal," Darren said. "My wife's about to have a baby at any minute and I really need to get home. How fast could your team get me to the main road heading down to Fairbanks?"

"You don't want to go to the main road," Jack said from the floor. "If you can get to the Chena, it'll take you straight home faster than the road will from this direction with a dogsled and a good team."

"I've got a great team," Dewey boasted, "and they know that route downriver better than any team in this area. They'll get you home faster than the north wind."

"Well, how about you two stay here and I'll take the team and head for home," Darren ventured, "and when I get to the first radio I find, I'll call in and have a chopper sent to pick you both up."

"That would be at Milo's place," Dewey said. "He's downriver from here and usually at his cabin. He's pretty easy to find if you stick to the river close. You just follow the dogs."

Darren quietly reviewed the little he knew about running a team. He'd played around with his neighbor's dogs a few times but had limited experience of running them outside of groomed trails. He didn't want to admit to Dewey his lack of real training as the desire to get home was stronger than any other thought in his head at that moment.

Sitting in the little cabin and waiting for Dewey to get home and call for their rescue would take several hours and in that same amount of time he could be at Mandy's side.

The calculated gamble to keep his promise seemed like a fair trade to him. Jack was safe and help would be on the way to him within hours if Darren could simply drive a team of dogs to the finish of this little misadventure. Feeling the strength coming back into his body with the food and the warmth of the fire, he squared his shoulders and pushed away his fears.

***

Mandy hissed as another contraction caused her to grab onto Susan's arm. The midwife finished her examination and shook her head.

"It's time to call in the birthing team," Susan said gently. "This baby's looking to make an appearance sooner than we expected, but everything's fine."

Mandy shook her head in frustration. Everything wasn't fine as far as she was concerned. There was no word from the search team and her husband was still missing. This wasn't going by the plan at all. A couple of tears slipped from the corner of her eyes before she could stop them. Susan rubbed her hands and arms gently and shushed away her fears.

"We're a team and we'll get through this as a team," Susan said. "The beauty of being a team is that the job gets done even if one member isn't able to be here."

Mandy nodded sadly and turned her face towards the

window. She listened as Susan gave Katie the news and set the first steps of the birthing plan in motion. The young girl listened quietly and squared her shoulders before heading off to the kitchen with her marching orders. She cast a worried glance towards her stepmother as she left the room, but Mandy was lost in her own thoughts.

***

Darren listened carefully as Dewey harnessed each dog to the lines in order. The dogs were eager to head out on the trail and danced in their places with barely controlled energy. Darren knew they would leap forward with a strength far beyond their small size and it wouldn't matter to them who was standing on the back of that sled. It was in their hearts to run like the wind for as long as they were allowed.

Jack was quiet inside the warm cabin as the stress and fear of the last few days drained away from his tortured body. He fully believed Darren would accomplish this mission and come out looking like a hero like he had always done in the past. He only hoped the man would get home in time to welcome his new child into the world. The timing for that was the one thing beyond anyone's control on this earth. He threw up a quick prayer for Godspeed and a safe journey for his friend before drifting off to sleep.

Dewey ran through some last minute instructions

before handing the reins over to Darren and pointing him in the right direction.

"This trail leads right to the river and the dogs know it well," he said. "All you have to do is hang on and keep the sled level. The dogs will do everything else."

Darren nodded and swallowed hard. He was about to give the order to head out when Dewey reached out and put a hand on his arm.

"These dogs," Dewey said pointedly, "they're my family. Take care of them."

Darren put his hand on the other man's shoulder and gave Dewey his word to do everything in his power to keep them all safe and get them back home. With that said, he turned to face forward and gave the order to head out. The dogs leapt forward almost as one and the sled jerked from its spot nearly leaving Darren sitting in the snow but he somehow managed to hang on as the sled quickly smoothed out. They were on their way home!

Chapter 8

As the last member of the birthing team arrived, Katie finished putting together the last veggie platter with some hummus and dip. She'd carefully planned a variety of snack foods for the team with everyone's tastes in mind. The table was heavily laden with finger foods and simple bite-sized appetizers. She took a step back and surveyed her work proudly. One thing for sure, no one would be hungry in their house today.

With that thought in mind, she moved to the living room to work on the next step of her plan. Her ear was turned to the sewing room where Mandy was spending some quiet time working on one of her unfinished quilts between random contractions. She'd made it clear to everyone she needed some *alone time* to prepare for the challenge ahead of her.

The other members of the team busied themselves with their own distractions as everyone waited patiently for the baby who was now calling all the shots. Katie was amazed at how each person somehow found a way to blend into the background as she worked on the next step on her list.

Two of the team members were resting in the guest bedroom. The midwife, Susan had taken over a corner of Darren's office where she'd set up her computer to keep notes on the progression of Mandy's labor. Another member was in the rec room downstairs in the basement watching something on her laptop. Katie bustled from the kitchen to the living room and back as she gathered her supplies. She felt like she was the only one making noise. The sudden sound of the phone caused her to freeze mid-step for a moment. She'd been so busy with her preparations, she'd nearly forgotten about her missing father.

As she jumped for the phone, she caught sight of Mandy in the doorway of the sewing room watching her. Tom didn't take long to convey the message that there was no message before hanging up. Katie looked at Mandy and shook her head slowly. She didn't get any response as Mandy turned away with a detached look on her face. Katie knew there wasn't anything more to say that would change anything so she went back to her list. It was better to be busy.

***

Darren was relieved when he broke free of the thickly wooded path onto the openness of the river bank. The dogs had settled into an easy lope early on, but the wide space seemed to bring them into a new level of calm as their random barks grew fewer and their stride seemed to smooth up even more. The sled slipped along easily behind the team, with the occasional bump from stray rocks and chunks of ice.

Darren didn't realize how tightly he'd been holding onto the sled until he tried to lift one hand to wipe away some snow from his face. His hand was frozen to the grip inside the iced glove and he couldn't pull it loose. Concerned, he tried to pull the other hand loose. It was equally stuck and Darren suddenly realized he had no way to stop the dogs without the use of his hands unless they responded to his voice command and that usually didn't happen without the use of an anchor. The dogs enjoyed running too much.

As he pondered this new predicament, he suddenly realized the light of the day was fading. Dewey had given him a headlamp to use in the darkness, but with his hands frozen to the sled grips, he had no way to get it out of his pocket and put it on. He prayed there was going to be enough light from the moon and stars to keep him on the river's path until he realized the dogs were the ones keeping them going in the right direction. He wasn't much more use to them than the sled.

The dogs continued along the river in the gathering darkness. Darren spied a glimmer of light in the distance and hoped the dogs would have an interest in stopping. He'd ceased struggling against the frozen gloves to avoid pulling his hand out into the frigid air and find himself unable to get it back inside, but the hope of contacting someone with a radio caused him to renew his efforts.

Dividing his attention between his hands and the swiftly

approaching light, Darren didn't notice a patch of broken ice ahead of them. The dogs ran through it without pausing. The sled wasn't as accommodating as it bounced over the bumpy ice and Darren lost control tipping the sled onto its side. The sudden braking effect of the tipped sled dragged the dogs to a stop, leaving him lying in the snow as they quickly laid down to take advantage of the break.

On the upside, the fall had broken his gloves loose from the grips. He was finally free of the sled, but his body didn't seem capable of getting up from the ground. Feeling the cold seeping deeper into his bones, he closed his eyes and thought to rest for a moment. His thoughts slipped home and he wondered how Mandy and Katie were faring without him. He sensed time was slipping away as he thought about the baby.

He felt someone nearby and turned his head to see who had come but the image was blurred. Straining his eyes in the darkness, he was surprised to see Karen staring down at him. His feelings of regret were overwhelming as he stared into his dead wife's eyes.

"Darren! You must wake up! This isn't the time to sleep," Karen's voice came to him though he never saw her mouth move.

Darren froze as she moved closer as if to kiss him. He closed his eyes, waiting for the touch of her lips. The cold wetness surprised him and his eyes flew open to find one of Dewey's dogs had pulled free from the team and came back to lick his face. He knew the dog was only looking for the promise of a treat, but the timing had saved his life. Struggling to his knees, he crawled over to the sled and pulled out the rations Dewey had stashed for the dogs.

Sharing the meaty snacks out among the dogs, he tried to work the stiffness out of his limbs. He'd lost sight of the light he'd seen before the sled tipped over and the dogs were anxious to get back on the trail. Righting the sled, he checked the dogs' lines and worked to get the stray back into position. His cold hands fought his efforts to force them back into his gloves, but after several attempts he finally got them back on.

Within a few minutes, Darren had the sled back on course for home. He wasn't sure how far he'd come or how far there was left to go, but he was convinced that Someone was looking out for him on this trip. He was losing track of the number of times he'd cheated death in the past few days. He knew this story would go far in the lore of family legends some day if he lived to tell it.

***

It was dark when Susan gathered everyone with an update on Mandy's progress. Katie listened intently as the midwife reviewed their roles during active labor. Her eyes were wide as she pushed away the fears trying to undermine her confidence. *Mandy believed in me enough for the both of us*, she reminded herself. *We've trained for this and now it's time.* She stood at the patio door for a moment, staring out over the river. Her thoughts searched the darkness for some sign her dad was on his way home to them.

"Come on, Dad! We need you," came the cry inside of Katie's heart. On the outside, she set her shoulders and moved to light the candles she'd carefully placed around the living room. The gentle light danced on the still water of the birthing pool. Katie turned to see Mandy's face as she heard her come into the room. Mandy's eyes sparkled as she surveyed Katie's efforts to make the room calm and welcoming. Giving the girl a quick hug, Mandy walked around the room to admire the different candle displays Katie had spent months collecting.

"I think we need to get some pictures of this for your father," Mandy said quietly. "Have you got all our cameras ready?"

Katie moved to show her the video camera across from the birthing pool and the digital cameras on each end table.

"How about music," Mandy asked. "Are we set up for something quiet and soothing?"

"Just like you wanted," Katie laughed, "something old, very old."

She turned on the music for Mandy's approval just as another contraction came sending Mandy into a controlled breathing exercise. Katie moved over next to her and stroked the back of her neck.

"Does it hurt a lot?" Katie asked worriedly as Mandy visibly relaxed.

"Only for a moment," Mandy said, trying to appear lighthearted.

"What were you making in the workroom?" Katie asked, trying to change the subject.

"A quilt for Darren....I felt he was cold," Mandy said this last bit in a distant voice with a touch of sadness.

Katie shivered at the sound of her words.

"I'm sure Dad's going to love it," was the best she could come up with.

The sound of the phone ringing drew both of them to the kitchen. They stared at the phone as the ringing continued. Neither of them wanted to be the first to reach out and pick it up. The decision was made as another contraction sent Mandy into a breathing exercise. Katie grabbed up the phone to answer with anxious eyes on her mother-in-law.

"Hello....yes....no....okay, I'll let her know," came Katie's side of the conversation before she hung up the phone.

Mandy looked at her expectantly.

"It was Tom. They've called off the search because it's dark, and they will continue in the morning," Katie reported in a flat voice.

The two of them stared out into the darkness as they took in the thought of another long night of waiting. Only this time, there was little chance that Darren's absence would be their focus. Another Covington was going to be taking center stage tonight if everything went by the book.

**

Darren strained to see the path ahead using the dim light of the headlamp. The low batteries barely reached beyond the ears of the lead dog. Fortunately, the dogs weren't hampered by the darkness and it appeared they'd found the tracks of another sled or snow machine to ease their way. The brief pause and quick snack a few hours back seemed to boost their energy level up to what they'd had at the start of this trip and the wind whistled past his ears.

His eyes searched the darkness for any sign of light. He was sure they'd come far enough to start seeing actual signs of human habitation. The path the dogs were following was fresh, probably made that very day. Darren just hoped it would continue heading in the right direction. He didn't want to find himself pulling up to some remote cabin in the middle of the night.

Suddenly, another light came into view as a musher came up running parallel to him on the other side of the river. Darren kept his eyes on the other sled as their paths drew closer together. The dogs from both teams drew off of each other's energy and began to compete. Darren held on tightly as the sled lurched and bobbed over the uneven ice. He wanted to slow down, maybe even stop so he could talk to the other musher and find out where he was, but he dared not loosen his grip on the sled. A fall at this speed wouldn't be in his best interests.

Darren noted the other guy seemed to be urging his team onward as if he was also enjoying their race. Hanging on to the grips, he resolved to enjoy this moment until the other musher called it to come to an end. The unexpected competition went on for half an hour before the other team started to fall behind. Not wanting to lose an opportunity to talk, Darren called to his team hoping to get them to slow. They seemed to welcome a chance to rest and fell into a gentle run.

As his fellow musher drew up alongside, Darren watched his actions carefully. He was able to match the man's moves and the two teams came to a rest alongside each other. Both men were careful to keep some distance between them to prevent any altercations, but the dogs were quick to sink into the snow for a brief respite. Darren's team had covered a lot of miles already that day. He pulled out some more rations for them and tossed them each a snack before heading over to meet the competition.

As they got close, each of them pulled back the hood of their parkas and stared at one other in surprise.

"Darren? Is that you?"

Darren stared at his neighbor in surprise. He was

overwhelmed with emotion as he realized just how close to home he'd come in the last few hours.

"I didn't know you were running a team," Jessie continued as she drew closer. "When did you take up mushing?"

"Actually, I haven't," Darren choked out the words. "I'm just trying to get home and keep a promise."

Jessie looked at him in confusion as Darren realized she probably didn't even know he was technically missing and possibly dead. The company would have avoided any publicity until the conclusions were inevitable.

"Well, you're nearly there," the woman continued. "It's only a few more miles to the edge of the city. Look you can see the light pollution of the town from here."

Darren turned to look in the direction she was pointing and saw that what she said was true. The sky was glowing directly ahead of them and it wasn't the Northern Lights.

"That's a great team you've got there," Jessie added. "Really gave my boys a run for their money. Whose dogs are those?"

"They belong to a trapper named Dewey. He loaned them to me so I could get home before Mandy has our baby."

"How much time do you have?"

"Don't know. I've been out of the loop," Darren chattered as the adrenaline in his system was overwhelmed by the biting cold.

Jessie went back to her sled and grabbed a thermos.

"Here. You look like you desperately need something warm to drink. How long have you been out on the river today?"

"By my watch, about ten hours or so," he said after taking another long swallow of the tea. "I don't know how much run the dogs have got left at this point."

"They look pretty good to me. Let me get them some water and food. When they're done, I'll lead you the rest of the way home."

Darren nodded his head gratefully and moved aside to let Jessie see to the dogs. He felt a bit guilty about not helping, but his strength was nearly gone. It was all he could do to lift the thermos to his lips and take a drink. Turning to look north, he caught a glimpse of the Northern Lights dancing on the horizon.

Jack!

The original plan to call for a rescue chopper got bogged down in the frozen gloves part of the ride and no one was on their way to rescue the pilot yet. Darren struggled over to Jessie and asked her if she had a cell phone with her.

"Sure. You might even get a signal out here since they just put in a tower for that new development on the west edge of town," she said handing him the phone.

Darren's first thought was to call home, but he was close to getting home and it seemed better to see to Jack's needs first, so he decided to call Tom. That's when he realized he didn't know a single useful phone number as everything was programmed into his phone and his battery was dead. He handed the phone back to Jessie when she'd finished tending the dogs with a quiet word of thanks.

"How long will it take to get to my house," he asked the woman.

"Less than an hour at an easy pace," she ventured. "Faster if we let the dogs have their own lead though yours are pretty tired right now."

"Well, I have a pretty strong feeling I'm being missed right about now. How about we give them a chance to enjoy one last run for the night?"

Jessie laughed at the look on his face and agreed. The two of them called to their dogs and grabbed up their anchors. Within minutes, the race was on as the dogs tried to outperform each other on the last leg of this race to the finish.

***

Katie hovered nervously in the background as Mandy received word that she was nearly through transition and the baby was moving into the birth canal. She'd been in and out of the pool a couple of times in the last few hours and her contractions were steady and strong. The baby's heart was beating with its own rhythm and the midwife sat nearby keeping careful watch over everything going on in the room.

A random phone call at the start of the transition phase upset Mandy so Katie quietly turned off the ringer, figuring what was going on here was more important than anything else right now. The midwife had given her a nod of encouragement when she saw what Katie was doing. It made the girl feel good to know she'd thought to do this on her own.

The plan for the birth was for Darren to get in the pool with Mandy and support her. The backup plan would put Katie in that role, but she was hesitating. Nothing felt right to her and she didn't want to upset Mandy again by debating the matter. She'd pulled one of the others aside in the kitchen and asked if it mattered for her to be in the pool or not. The woman assured her Mandy was fine and she had enough support without Katie in the pool.

Mandy was focused on giving birth and wasn't caught up in plans or thoughts of anyone else in the room. Even the noise of the garage door opening and barking dogs didn't seem to get through to her as she counted the rise and fall of each contraction.

Katie went to the kitchen door just as it opened and the familiar figure standing there coated in ice and snow forced a cry from her lips that she quickly moved to stifle with both hands. Tears came to her eyes as her father threw back the hood of his parka and held out his arms to his daughter. She closed the gap between them in two quick steps and buried her face in his chest as gibberish came to her lips.

Suddenly, she remembered what was happening in the other room and pushed him away.

"The baby's coming," she choked out grabbing at his outer clothes in an effort to free him from them. "You've got to get ready or you're going to miss everything!"

The surprised face of the midwife appeared around the corner. She took one look at the frost covering his face and hair and his obviously battered appearance before coming over to help Katie pull off his boots. The idea of him getting into the pool with Mandy was out of the question. First, he was much too cold and the shock of the hot water might kill him, and secondly, with his injuries and near-hypothermia, he would interfere with the birthing process and cause Mandy more discomfort.

"Katie. It would be better for you to get in the pool behind Mandy and support her and your father can help from in front. He's too cold to get in that water right now."

Katie swallowed hard and nodded. They'd trained for this moment and with her Dad here, Katie knew she could do whatever it took to get this baby into the world. She grabbed her camera and followed Darren into the living room to catch the look on Mandy's face when she saw her husband. She wasn't disappointed as Mandy's eyes lit up with sheer joy as she took in Darren's face.

"I knew you would get here," she started to say, "just in

time!"

They finished her sentence in unison as Darren knelt down in front of her and gently stroked her face and arms. She pulled away from his cold hands so he plunged them into the pool hoping to warm them quickly. The pain was overwhelming and brought tears to his eyes as his skin screamed at the touch of the hot water but he fought the urge to pull them out.

"It's better to take this in small steps," the midwife said to him quietly. "You're here and that's the most important thing."

Katie moved to climb into the pool behind Mandy and slipped in behind her stepmother. She was rewarded with a soft sigh as the girl's arms formed a gentle circle reaching around Mandy to grasp her father's shoulders. The three of them breathed together as Mandy started another contraction. The large mirrored area at the bottom of the pool showed the baby's head was crowning nicely.

Mandy stared down in the water and watched the head pressing through. The pain was lost in the vision she was focusing on and the touch of Darren's forehead against hers. It was as if the whole world had somehow come into perfect alignment and everything was right again.

When the contraction ended, she leaned back into Katie's arms and inhaled the gentle scent of the girl while staring into her husband's eyes. In that moment she knew how much her daughter meant to her and gave thanks.

The next contraction delivered the head and the three of them watched in fascination as the baby's head turned. A few breaths later and the final contraction came with the baby slipping out fully and floating towards the bottom of the pool. Mandy reached down with both arms and scooped up the infant, gently bringing him to her chest.

The three of them stared at the miracle sandwiched between them, and tears slipped down their faces unnoticed.

"Mr. Covington," Mandy said softly, "may I present your son."

Darren trembled as the baby opened his eyes and stared at these strange new creatures. Katie would later swear the baby smiled at that point, but no one could confirm that as the moment was lost in wonder.

It wasn't until the baby was carefully wrapped and Mandy had finished the birthing that Darren remembered to put in a call to Tom and give him Jack's location. He excused his lapse by saying there was no way the helicopter could get to his friend until morning anyway, but no one was upset with him. Jack was picked up and transported to the hospital before noon the next day.

It was in the wee hours of the morning after the birthing team had gone to bed and Darren had taken a long hot shower that he came downstairs and found Katie putting away the leftover food in the kitchen. Mandy was upstairs snuggled under the covers and sleeping soundly, with their son in his cradle at the side of the bed.

"Your Mom tells me you did all this food and the candles and music arrangements by yourself," Darren said proudly. "She also said the two of you set up the pool together."

"Yeah, Dad, but don't be thinking that means we didn't miss you around here."

Pulling Katie into his arms and rubbing his face into her hair, he didn't respond.

"You almost blew it, you know!"

"The key word there is *almost*," Darren laughed, "and you know me. I'm the just-in-time guy!"

"That's it!"

Katie began to laugh and dance around the kitchen, much to Darren's amusement.

"That's the perfect name for my little brother," Katie crowed. "That way he'll always have a great story to tell about how he got his name!"

The two of them stared at each other with wide eyes filled with glee.

"Just in time!" The two of them exclaimed the name at the same time and burst out laughing.

Remembering the pair asleep upstairs, they clapped their hands over their mouths. They were going to have to learn some things it seemed with a new baby in the house.

Taking a look around the table, Darren was overwhelmed with hunger and grabbed a couple of trays

Katie hadn't finished clearing yet.

"Join me for a late, late night snack," he invited her, "and I'll tell you what I learned about mushing."

The two of them sat there at the table and ate their fill as the early light of dawn appeared.

A faint cry from upstairs reminded them of other hungry mouths waiting to be fed so they put together a tray for Mandy and headed up to be together. Slipping into the bedroom, Darren knelt down next to his wife and son. The baby suckled noisily, much to their amusement, as Katie stood hesitantly in the doorway with the tray.

When Mandy looked up, she held out her hand to Katie inviting her to come and be with them. The four of them snuggled together in the quiet bedroom and stared at the newest addition to the Covington family for some time before anyone spoke.

"In all the madness, we never found time to pick out a name for this little guy," Mandy whispered into the quiet.

"We've got the perfect name," Darren and Katie burst out together startling the baby.

Mandy gave them the *look*.

Continuing in whispers, the two of them made their case for the perfect name as Mandy watched their son fall back to sleep with milk still clinging to his rosebud lips. When they finished talking, the room was quiet as they waited for her reaction. She gently stroked the baby's cheek and watched carefully as his little chest rose and fell softly with each breath. *Justin Tyme Covington*, she thought to herself, *what a wonderful name, but I think we'll call you Ty for now.*

After what seemed like a very long time, Mandy turned to look at them and smiled. All three of her charges were sound asleep, curled up next to her. She lay back in the midst of her family and listened to their quiet breathing. Surely, life couldn't get any better than this.

THE END

Renee Hart

Homer: End Of The Road

Description: With Lou's boat in dry dock in Anchorage for repairs, and fishing season already underway, finding employment on another boat is the only way to make enough to get the troller, Lindy Lee, back in action.

A fishing boat captain in Homer in desperate need of crew members, provides a lucky break.

Chapter 1

Lou checked messages on the cell phone again hoping to hear from anybody looking for crew. The salmon season was already in full swing and most of the boats were already out there fishing. No one was looking for an extra hand at this point, at least not in Anchorage.

Sitting out the season wasn't going to earn Lou any money for the repairs needed on the Lindy Lee and the damages were too extensive to be overcome with duct tape and super glue. That last storm had nearly put the troller at the bottom of the ocean and the crew along with her. Fortunately, the coast guard arrived in time to get a line on the boat and tow them back to shore. Otherwise, Lou wouldn't be needing a job on somebody else's boat.

The Lindy Lee was sitting in dry dock looking war torn and weary. She'd been stripped of her trolls and the wheelhouse looked like a bomb had gone off in it. There wasn't a single unbroken window anywhere and the door was barely hanging on by one hinge. The rust on her hull just added to her sad and broken appearance, and Lou could barely stand to look at her without wanting to cry. *Lou's dad probably would have, as he loved that boat as if it were his only child*, Lou thought a bit sarcastically.

***

Renee Hart

Ray scratched his head and wondered how he was going to make any money this fishing season if he spent his days stuck at the dock. If it wasn't one thing wrong, it was another, and nearly all of his crew had walked off and joined other boats. They came down to Homer looking to make money during the salmon season, not to sit around watching him working on the engine. Now, only he and Jonesy were left to sort out the problems keeping them in port.

Jonesy was an old salt that came with the boat. Ray's father and Jonesy took to the high seas together back in the day when a man could make a year's salary during the summer season. The two of them stuck it out during the lean years and lived rich during the golden ones when the salmon ran so thick you didn't have to move the boat to catch 'em. The old man kept threatening to retire, but Ray figured he'd rather go down with the boat than sit in a rocking chair.

Banging his knuckles on the manifold for the fifth time that day, he growled in frustration. This old boat wasn't going to give him an inch without a pound of flesh to pay for it. His father had the *touch* and kept this motor purring long after another man would have sent it to the scrapyard. Sadly, Ray hadn't gotten that as part of his inheritance, just this rusty old boat and a crusty old deckhand firmly set in his ways.

Finally, he spotted the problem with a wire making a faulty connection. He was sure that he'd checked all the wiring first thing and couldn't figure out how this one had gotten past him. The wiring sheath was pulled over the end of the wire as if to hide the break. He stared at it for a while trying to make sense of how that could have happened. Shrugging his shoulders, he gave up thinking and fixed it. The engine rewarded him with a roar as it came back to life.

Hoping this would be the last hurdle keeping him tied to the dock, he pulled out his cell to check for messages. He'd put out the word all up and down the coast, he was looking for crew. So far, there'd been no response and without a couple of first rate hands, he and Jonesy would be working double shifts. It wasn't a pleasant prospect for either of them.

The old guy was feeling his years and needed more time to rest. Ray kept him on more out of respect for the old-timer's relationship with his father than for his speed on the nets. He really needed two, maybe three more hands to bring in a catch that would cover his expenses and keep the boat running.

Finding a message, he opened it up and quickly scanned through it. He was relieved to see a guy named Lou Alberts was looking for a job up in Anchorage. He'd posted his resume link with a couple of references for back-up. Ray decided to jump right on this guy and sent him a text. He figured if the guy was all his resume said he was and he really needed a job, he'd be in Homer by tomorrow. If he wasn't Ray would figure it out when the guy was leaning over the rail puking his guts out.

***

Lou nearly fell off the chair when the cell phone began vibrating. Pulling it out, the message was short and sweet.

"Heading out tomorrow from Homer. Find the Seabiscuit by nine if you want a job."

That was the word, Lou wanted to hear. Picking up the rucksack from the dock, it was out the door and down the road as time was short and Homer was three hours away with a good ride. Longer if no one was headed to 'the end of the road' at that time of the day. Maybe Lady Luck would come along for the journey south.

***

Ray was on the boat by seven going over the nets and checking his supplies. He planned to stay out as long as he could to make up for the missed days. The reports trickling back said the fish were running well. He was never sure how much you could trust some of the stories as fishermen were well known for telling fish tales. *That just came with the territory*, he figured.

He jumped at the sound of a voice calling from the dock.

"Ahoy, on the boat!"

Standing up to see the caller, he was surprised to see a young woman with a rucksack thrown over one shoulder. She looked to be about five foot eight with blond hair pulled back into a ponytail and eyes like the gray of the sea on a stormy day.

"Permission to come aboard."

It was clear she wasn't really asking. It was more like observing the formalities as she stepped on board without waiting for him to respond. He was just standing there like an idiot staring at her with his trap hanging open.

"Lou Alberts reporting for duty, sir," she said extending her free hand to him.

"You're a woman!"

Looking down at herself, she did a quick once-over and looked him straight in the eye.

"Last time I checked, you're right. I'm a woman. Is that a problem for you?"

Realizing there was no right answer for that question, he wisely shut up and pondered his next move. He'd never had a woman on the boat and neither had his father. Jonesy wasn't going to be happy about this at all as he was old school and always said women on a boat were bad luck.

"You've got a pretty impressive resume," he said lamely.

"You mean, for a woman," Lou asked.

She couldn't help the trace of sarcasm that crept into her voice. Running her own boat kept her from having to deal with this whole sexist thing and she wasn't used to it. She had a strong reputation built up with the other captains around Anchorage, but apparently, he hadn't bothered to call any of her references to check up on her. Otherwise, someone would have clued him in one way or another.

Attempting to cover up his awkward beginning, he decided to back pedal and start again. Maybe he could keep himself from having to deal with a lawsuit over discrimination.

"Excuse my surprise. Your name threw me off. I was expecting a man with a name like Lou. Sorry. My name's Ray. Welcome to the Seabiscuit."

Shaking his outstretched hand, Lou gave him a grin and said, "No harm, no foul. Let me stow my gear and I'll give you a hand with those nets."

The two of them were busy with the final checklist when Jonesy came along. When he caught sight of Lou with a gaff in her hand, he stopped short and stared. She noticed the glare on his face and decided to ignore him. Latching down the gaff, she picked up the rest of the gear she was packing away and continued working.

Ray saw Jonesy staring at Lou and hunched his shoulders as he knew that look meant he was about to get his ear chewed off. Calling out a good morning to the old salt did nothing to soften the look on his face. He turned his glare to Ray and mouthed a few choice words. Ray shrugged and waved the old man to come aboard.

"Let's go, Jonesy. I want to get out there before the fish are all in somebody else's boat. We're already late for heading out."

Without a word, Jonesy turned around on his heel and marched off. Ray watched him go in stunned silence. He knew there was no chance the stubborn old coot would get on this boat with a woman on board.

"Looks like you need another crewman for this boat," Lou said dryly.

Ray just shook his head in frustration. Another fishing day down the drain and the clock was ticking. If it wasn't for bad luck, he wouldn't have a claim on any kind of luck at all.

"I think I can fix this pretty quick, if you're okay with that," Lou said pulling out her cellphone.

Ray just nodded and turned away. He was out of ideas on his part.

Fifteen minutes later a cab came screaming up to the dock and Ray was surprised to see a younger, taller version of Lou jump out and come running down to the boat.

"Permission to come aboard, Captain," she panted as she wrestled her hastily packed rucksack off her shoulder.

Ray couldn't help but notice some lacy bit of women's underwear hanging out of a side pocket. He looked at Lou helplessly.

"Captain Ray, I'd like you to meet my little sister, Adrian. She's got plenty of experience crewing and as I learned last night, is fresh out of a job. The two of us have been working on our father's boat since we could hold a line by ourselves."

Ray scratched his head. *This was a fine kettle of fish*, he thought to himself. Heaving a sigh, he gave the order to cast off and the two women hurried to make it so. It was clear to him, they'd both done this kind of thing before, and it wasn't long before they were heading northwest out of the harbor.

As the two women settled themselves in for the ride, Ray was left alone with his thoughts.

Chapter 2

"Daddy! Daddy! Swing me around again," Ray cried.

His father was happy to oblige him and the little tyke squealed as his legs flew straight out behind him. Strong hands covered his in a tight grip and the boy trusted in his father's strength. The man was a lumberjack and could fell a tree in a few mighty strokes of an axe. To Ray, his father was as solid as a rock and nothing could bring him down.

The two of them were left alone when Ray's mother decided the life of a lumberjack's wife wasn't for her. She took off before the boy's fifth birthday looking for something better. Ray's father just shrugged when he found out and took the boy with him when he had to go to the woods. He never talked about the woman again that Ray ever heard.

A couple of years went by before Ray's dad realized his son was supposed to be going to school. Living so far away from the nearest town, there wasn't a school within a day's ride for the boy to attend. That settled it for the man and he packed the two of them up and headed north to Alaska with a solid grubstake in his pocket and a dream of a new life for the two of them. He'd always wanted to try life as a fisherman. With Lady Luck smiling down on him, he'd get them a boat and they'd learn a new way of life.

Ray cut the engine and took a look around the area. There wasn't another boat in sight as far as he could see and this was his spot. He could feel the fish beneath him just itching to get in his boat. His father used to laugh at his special feel for the fish, that is, until he realized Ray had a gift. The boy was always right and their catch was all the proof he needed to believe.

The two women stepped into action as soon as the motor was cut and started hauling out the gear to lay the nets. They were hanging gillnets for Sockeye and it was clear they knew exactly what to do. Ray didn't even need to give them any orders. He watched the two of them carefully as they worked the lines and played out the nets at a nice even speed. They worked out any tangles long before they happened and the whole operation went as smooth as butter. All he had to do was keep the boat moving in the right direction, and soon they were hauling in salmon. They worked hard for several hours until the light was gone. It was time to have some supper and call it a day.

"Either of you know anything about cooking," Ray asked with a grin. "Not that there's going to be much of that out here, but all I'm really good at is opening a can."

"Well, one thing for sure, you don't want to trust any cooking to Lou. She can mess up a bowl of water in a microwave," Adrian laughed as she poked her sister in the ribs.

Lou grimaced at her sister and turned away to stow a couple of stray buckets. She didn't sign on this gig to be the cook. *Let Miss Smarty-mouth step up*, she thought.

Adrian caught her thinking without a word and headed down below to see what was for supper. Not expecting to find much, she wasn't disappointed. It was clear Captain Ray wasn't much for food shopping.

Finding some mismatched cans of beans and a few more without labels, she called up to her sister for a couple of 'smalls' to incorporate into a decent meal. She was rewarded by the sound of a splat as a fish came flying into the galley and landed on the counter. The unexpected arrival of a couple more caught her in the chest, and she briefly considered throwing them back. Thinking better of it, she quickly filleted them and arranged a nice plate of sushi. Mixing up a pan of beans, she tossed them on the stove and looked for some kind of bread. No luck there.

She had the table laid for three by time the others had washed their hands and came down to see what she'd thrown together. Without a word, the food disappeared quickly and their dirty dishes were the only sign there'd been a meal at all. The three of them sat back simultaneously and groaned in unison. At the sound, they all burst out laughing. Ray was finally feeling his luck was changing for the better.

"I cooked, so that means you got the dishes," Adrian shot off at Lou.

"Naw, for a meal like that I'm happy to do the dishes. You two go get some shuteye and I'll take the first watch," Ray said with a grin.

Lou looked at him with a raised eyebrow, but didn't protest his decision. *He was the captain of this boat, after all*, she thought. The two women were gone before he could say, "Halibut."

***

Ray had the galley cleaned and coffee made before the two women got to dreaming about whatever came to them in the night. He was pleased with the outcome of the day and felt good about his prospects for the morrow. The two women knew their way around the boat and performed their duties without a lot of silly chatter. That was more than he could say for his last crew. It seemed somebody was always moaning about the weather or the fish or how someone else wasn't earning their pay. He hadn't heard a single word of complaint all day.

About the time he realized that he hadn't discussed the watch times, Lou came into the wheelhouse looking bright-eyed, with a cup of coffee in hand. Relieved at the sight of her, he stood up and stretched before passing her his seat.

"I guess I should have known you'd know the watch

schedule already," Ray said. "I was just trying to figure out how I was going to wake one of you to take over for me."

"No worries, Captain. This ain't our first rodeo as I'm sure you can see for yourself. Go find your bunk and leave this to me."

With that, Lou turned to take a look out at the sea sparkling in the half light. This was her favorite time to be on watch. She listened as Ray quietly took his leave behind her. *If he was feeling dismissed, well, it wasn't personal,* she thought.

***

Adrian showed up for her watch right on time. She brought Lou a fresh cup of coffee knowing her sister wouldn't go back to sleep. The two of them would have some quiet time before the Captain was up, she figured. It had been a while since they'd had a chance to catch up on each other's news.

"Thanks, Sis for dialing me in on this gig. I really need to earn some money if I'm ever going to have my own plane," Adrian said.

"Well, if you hadn't come along, I don't think the Captain would have sailed with just me, and the other crewman walked at the sight of me. The Lindy Lee is so busted up, there's no chance of getting her back in the water this season. I'm in the same boat as you. I need the money."

"Have you considered that maybe the Lindy Lee isn't meant to go back out again," Adrian asked quietly. "I know you love her and feel an obligation to Dad's dream, but maybe it's time for a dream of your own..."

Adrian's voice trailed off at the look on her sister's face. Lou wasn't given to crying, but she sure looked on the verge of it this time.

Taking a long slow sip of her coffee, Lou avoided looking at her sister's face. She'd thought a lot about the question her sister had just asked, but the real problem she found wasn't the boat. In trying to figure out her next step, she was surprised to realize she didn't actually have a dream of her own.

She'd been so busy living her father's dream that she'd never taken the time to find one for herself. Now, here she was past thirty, with a busted up boat and nothing else to show for her life. Heck, she didn't even have a bank account or a place of her own. She spent her time on land drifting from her friend's places to her sister's house in Homer like a ship without an anchor.

"Good morning," Ray said from the door of the wheelhouse. "Ready to grab something to eat and get back to work. I made some oatmeal...well, actually I boiled some water. The oatmeal's that instant kind."

He missed the grimace Adrian cast at Lou as he turned to go out. *First order of business when they got back to port was to get some real food on this boat*, the two women agreed without a word spoken.

***

Their second day matched the success of the first and Ray was pleased with how smoothly the two women kept things running between them. They seemed so in tune with each other that words weren't necessary for them. More than once, he saw one of them hand the right tool to the other for the task at hand without a sound. He marveled at their ability to do that.

They took a quick break for lunch and ate cold beans straight from the cans. Washing them down with cool water, they did a quick assessment of the day's catch so far, and decided the hold would be filled in one more day if their luck held and they'd need to head into port to off load it.

"Are you two twins," Ray blurted out. "I mean, I've never seen two people communicate without words the way you two do."

"No, we're not real twins. Actually, though," Adrian laughed, "we *are* Irish twins."

"Oh, so you're Irish," Ray said looking confused.

"No, we're *Irish twins*."

"I don't understand."

"We're only ten months apart in age. That's what some

people call Irish twins. We just grew up doing everything together. That's why we can almost work together as a single person. Until I got married, I'm not sure we'd ever been away from each other more than a couple of days our whole lives."

"You're married," Ray asked, looking at Adrian in surprise.

"I am, five years already and I've got twins of my own... real twins, a boy and a girl. They're three and a half."

"Are they with their father," Ray couldn't help but ask.

"No. My husband's with the Coast Guard. He's on a two month training mission out on the Aleutians. The twins are with their grandmother back in Homer."

Ray felt like he'd stepped off land onto a loose dinghy and looked for a way back to solid ground. He pitched his empty can into the trash bin and tossed the spoon into the sink.

"Well, that was fun. Let's go see what we can drag up this afternoon," he said before turning to head topside.

The two women looked at each other and grinned before following his lead. Soon they were hard back at it and the fish were practically jumping into the boat on their own accord. It appeared Lady Luck had come along on this ride.

***

Their third day was a repeat of the first two and the hold was filled to the brim by late afternoon. Ray decided to make a run for the cannery in Homer so they could off load first thing in the morning and be back out by early afternoon. He related his plan to the crew and they made ready to get underway. Leaving them to secure the last of the gear, he went to the wheelhouse to radio in his schedule and make a couple of calls.

There was a long way to go before he made up his late start, but they'd put a dent in the problem. Now he just needed to keep this going for a while. He sat down at the wheel and checked his heading and the weather. It all looked good for a late evening arrival. Adrian had asked permission to spend the night at home with her kids. Lou said she would stay and help him to unload. He was grateful for that. There was no reason the two of them couldn't handle the job. The woman worked as hard as any man he'd ever worked with, both of them did.

Adrian jumped off onto the dock as soon as they touched down and tied the boat up in a slip. She waved good-bye and disappeared from sight. Lou stepped off the boat and took a look around at the other boats tied up nearby. She got a few terse nods from the other men working on their boats, but most of them ignored her.

A couple of old-timers came over to talk to Ray. Jonesy had said some pretty rough things down at the Salty Dog about the situation. They wanted to hear Ray's side of the matter. He didn't feel like it was any of their business how he ran his boat or picked his crew. He cut them off pretty quick. They went off in the same snit as Jonesy did. He figured they'd tell their own version of things no matter what he said anyway.

Seeing Lou walking back his way, he suddenly realized he was hungry. They hadn't bothered to do anything about supper and their lunch of beans had long since run out.

"You like bar-be-que?" he called to her. "There's a pretty good place at the other end of the Spit. They make a mean brisket sandwich with a side of baked beans."

He laughed at the look on her face.

"I think I'll just have my sandwich with a side of coleslaw if you don't mind," Lou grinned.

"Same here," Ray said as he stepped onto the dock.

Giving the boat a quick once-over to see that everything was locked down properly the two of them headed off. They figured nothing could go wrong if they were only away for an hour or so.

***

Ray and Lou were making their way back to the Seabiscuit when they both saw her bobbing in the ocean about fifty yards away from the dock.

"What the..." Ray gasped as he ran down the dock. "I thought you two knew how to tie up a boat!"

He knew if the Harbormaster caught sight of his boat out there dancing on the waves there'd be hell to pay. Looking around for a handy skiff or even a kayak, he noted a few faces watching, but when they saw him looking, they'd turn away. He couldn't believe no one was going to help him. A sudden splash behind him made him turn around.

Lou had stripped off her shoes and emptied her pockets before diving into the icy cold water. She was swimming like a champion towards the drifting boat and as Ray watched, she closed the gap in record time. He noted that more than a few men had stood to watch the drama unfolding before them. There were few among them that would be willing to jump into the water for their own boat let alone somebody else's.

Ray was relieved when she hoisted herself on board and disappeared from sight. He figured she might want to get out of her wet clothes before doing anything else so he sat down in the slip where the boat had been tied up. As he sat there feeling like a horses' butt, his eyes caught sight of a piece of rope. Any fool could see the rope had been cut loose as the cleat hitch was still firmly in place where Adrian had tied it. His thoughts grew dark as he wondered at the kind of man that would cut another man's boat loose and set it adrift. This was the act of a criminal.

***

Renee Hart

Ray sat on that dock for more than an hour, much to the amusement of the other sailors. He could hear snippets of their conversation as the Seabiscuit slipped a little further from shore with the tide. It was clear they were talking about him. His ears burned as he strained to shut them out and listen for signs that Lou was okay.

It was fully dark when the engine started and Lou nosed the boat back into the slip. He tied up the boat again noting the cut end on the side of the boat that matched the one in his hand. As he jumped on board, Lou came out of the wheelhouse dressed in sweats and a hoodie. Her hair was still wet and she appeared to still be shivering a bit. He hurried to make some coffee for them.

Grimly, he showed her the bit of rope he'd retrieved from the dock. She didn't look surprised. Mostly, she just looked sad.

"Any idea on who might have done this," she asked quietly.

"Not really. There's been a lot of things like this happening lately. Just little things like missing gear and stuff left in places where it could hurt somebody, but nothing I could really pin down. I just thought it was Jonesy being careless, or plain old bad luck. I'm sorry about what I said."

"No worries. It's a natural thing to blame the 'new guy'. I would have blamed you if you'd been the one that tied up the boat."

The two of them laughed at the thought, but their faces quickly grew grim as they considered there just might be a saboteur out there lurking in the shadows.

"Do you think this might be worth reporting to the authorities?" Lou asked.

"I don't have much more than a cut piece of rope and a lot of little mysteries," Ray said. "I don't think that's going to get me much traction with them. They like hard evidence. Besides, I don't want to have to explain why my crew member jumped into the sea and saved *my* boat. It should have been me swimming out, not you!"

Ray was trying to make that last bit sound funny, but his concern was evident. Kachemak Bay wasn't known for being a popular swimming hole, even if it was July. Most people wouldn't even attempt it without a wet suit at least. The water was barely above freezing when the sun was shining on it and the tide was coming in over the black sand. Here at the docks where it was deeper, there was no warmth in it at all.

"It's not a real big deal. I'm a strong swimmer and it wasn't very far. My dad taught us to focus on the goal and ignore the pain. Funny way to raise up girls, I know, but it works. That wasn't my first dip in the ocean. I'm just really glad you've got a hot shower on this boat!"

"Does your dad raising you to be tough have anything to do with naming you Lou?"

"Oh, no. That's my mother's fault. She loves to read and her favorite author when I was born was Louisa May Alcott. She named me after her, but I hated the name cause no one could ever say it right. When Adrian was little, she used to call me 'Weesa". I didn't want to be stuck with that so I made everyone call me 'Lou', and when I was eighteen I had it legally changed, much to my mother's dismay. I'm not sure she's over it yet."

Ray laughed as he sat back and considered the young woman sitting before him. She was easy on the eyes and soothing in her own quiet way. He'd only known her a couple of days, but he found himself wanting to know more. The two of them sitting there in the wheelhouse made him realize how lonely his own life had become since his father died.

Sure, he'd dated a few women over the years, but most of them weren't interested in boats or fishing. He never watched TV or cared about sports or any of the other things they wanted to talk about. Reading was his only diversion and he was happy with a dime store western. He wasn't what most people would consider cultured in any way.

"Well, I figure we're safe for tonight, but we'd better still keep watch. I don't want anything to come between this load and the cannery tomorrow morning. I'll take first watch and we'll switch when you wake up. I figure I owe you that much."

"A little extra sleep is what I get for saving your boat,"

Lou scoffed. "I hope you're not thinking of skimping on my paycheck too."

Ray laughed as she turned and headed off to her bunk. The sound of the closing door echoed in the wheelhouse. He winced at the sudden emptiness she'd left behind.

***

The two of them were up early and had the boat at the cannery before it opened. They were the first to unload and had their payout in hand when Adrian pulled up in a taxi. They watched in surprise as she unloaded several bags of groceries from the back of the car. Lou hustled over to give her a hand as Ray watched in amusement.

"I take it we won't be eating beans for the next few days," he laughed.

"Not if I can help it," Adrian teased him right back. "If I'm gonna work, I'm gonna eat something I like!"

Pulling out a bag of M&M's she tossed it to him.

"Like chocolate," she crowed.

Ray laughed and tore the bag open.

"I get all the blue and green ones," he said as he pawed through the candy.

"Why's that," Lou asked grabbing the bag out of his hands.

Trying to snatch it back, Ray nearly lost his balance and fell overboard.

Seeing him safe, the two women laughed and disappeared below to stash the food. They were eager to head back out and get to work. Ray noticed a couple of guys staring at him from the dock as he turned away to untie the boat. He wasn't sure who'd been poisoning the waters here around Homer, but he was feeling a little bit like an outsider. He could only wonder what was going on as he headed back out to sea.

When the two women came topside a little while later, they'd already cleared the harbor. Ray was wondering what was going to be for lunch as they appeared with a stack of sandwiches.

"If I'd known what I was missing out on by not having women crew members, I'd have jumped overboard and drowned myself. Who would have thought there was more to life than cold beans from a can?"

Adrian laughed as she handed him a sandwich dripping with sprouts. Taking a big bite, he started chewing carefully. He couldn't say what he was eating exactly, but it was a darn sight better than beans. He grunted and took another big bite. *I could get used to this*, he thought.

Chapter 3

Lady Luck stayed with them on this trip and within three days, they'd repeated their opening success and were heading back with a full hold again. With this kind of action, they'd be making their quota for the season despite the late start. They were in high spirits as the land came into sight.

Adrian once again requested shore leave to check in on the twins and Lou committed to helping him offload the catch. Ray didn't have anywhere else to be so the arrangement suited him just fine. He figured it would be best to call for a pizza delivery this time though. They agreed it was better than leaving the boat unattended and having a repeat of the last trip's little adventure. The water hadn't gotten any warmer in the last few days.

As they sat on the deck eating pizza and watching the twinkling lights of the shore bob up and down, the two of them chatted like old friends.

"So," Lou asked, "why'd you name your boat after hard tack?"

"*Hard tack*? This boat's named after a horse!"

"A horse? You mean, *the horse*, Seabiscuit, the horse! How'd that happen?"

"It's a long story."

"Well, we've got all night and I like good stories. So tell me."

"Okay. Well, my dad was a lumberjack in Oregon. He'd go out on the job for three months at a time and when he was done, he'd get his pay in one lump sum from the company. He'd pay off the company store and whatever bills we had and then he'd take the rest and go find this bookie he knew."

"Wherever Seabiscuit was running, no matter the odds, my dad would bet everything on him to win. He'd win some and sure, he lost a few times, but my dad never bet against him. He'd say to me, "Son, this horse is always being counted out, but I tell you, he's got the heart of a champion. He's gonna get me my boat.""

"My dad would take all of his winnings and sock them away and one day, he felt he had enough, so we moved to Alaska where he got his boat. There was no other name for it in my dad's mind. So here we sit on the original Seabiscuit."

"That's a pretty good yarn....for a fisherman," Lou said as she yawned and stretched. "Do you think we need to keep watch tonight?

"I'm thinking it's pretty quiet out here and we should just try and get some sleep. I don't think anyone will try anything knowing there's someone on board."

Lou nodded and paused before heading below.

"Good night, Captain. Thanks for the pizza."

"My pleasure," Ray said with a smile.

He started to reach out for her when he realized that she was an employee, not a date and jerked back his hand. Quickly, he turned away and started to gather up their trash. He didn't hear her leave.

Stepping to the dock, he hurried over to a nearby trash can and crammed the pizza box inside. The can was nearly full to the top with paper and boxes he noticed. He walked back to the boat and ran a practiced eye over the deck. Seeing that everything was in order, he went below hoping to catch some sleep before he had to deal with the cannery in the morning. He feared his mind was too full of the wrong kind of thinking to let him sleep, but soon he was sawing logs in his father's best tradition.

***

He wasn't sure how long he'd been asleep when the smell of smoke began to choke him. He could see the blaze of orange right next to the boat and he leaped out of his cot.

Running topside, he saw the trash can he'd walked to earlier right up next to the boat and tipped on one side. The paper and boxes inside smelled of gasoline and were blazing fiercely. He could see the dock was already starting to catch where the gas had soaked into the wood.

He turned to grab the fire extinguisher from the bracket on the wall, when he realized Lou was standing right next to him. She pulled the pin and started spraying the fire. Fearing it wouldn't be enough to keep the fire from spreading, Ray grabbed a gaff hook and tried to move the can away from the side of the boat. There was no room to push it off the other side of the dock without endangering someone else's boat.

The two of them worked together frantically trying to contain the fire. They were relieved when a couple of men from nearby boats came to assist them. Trying to fight the fire from the deck of a moving boat was difficult and having men on the dock soon got the fire out completely. The boat escaped any damage, but the dock was missing a large chunk that had to be chopped away. Ray knew there would be questions this time. No way to get around the fact this was an act of arson. He was pretty sure it was directed at him.

The fire wasn't out very long when a firetruck pulled up. The firemen checked to make sure the fire was completely out. Examining the trash can, they noted the evidence of gasoline used to start the fire. They took several samples of the dock where the fire had burned clear through the wood. There was no mistaking the fire had been set deliberately.

They were followed by another car and a man in casual clothes came over to look at the scene of the crime. He was followed by two Homer police officers in uniform who got busy taping off the area. They interviewed the two men that had helped Ray and Lou put out the fire. The first man came over to talk to Ray and Lou about the incident. They were still a bit shaken with their close call.

"Good evening, folks," the man said, "I'm Detective Ryan Sanders with the Alaskan State Troopers. Looks like you've had a pretty scary night. Can you tell me what happened here?"

Ray gave his account of the evening including the fact the trash can hadn't been that close to the boat when he went to bed earlier. Lou couldn't confirm that as she'd already gone below when Ray took out the trash. Detective Sanders took detailed notes as they talked. Looking pointedly at Ray, he asked if there was any reason someone would set a fire next to his boat.

Ray just looked at the detective and shrugged.

"If there is a reason, I don't know what it is," he said.

Turning to Lou, Detective Sanders asked her the same question.

"Ryan, you know I don't have any reason for someone to try and kill me. Not even you would be that mean!'

"Wait a minute," Ray said. "Do you two know each other?"

"We do," they both said simultaneously.

"We were engaged to be married, oh, about ten years ago or so, but Ryan wanted to be a cop and he didn't want a 'fishwife', if that's even a word," she finished lamely.

Ray stared at the two of them in surprise. He couldn't think of how this night could get any stranger. His head was reeling and it wasn't just smoke inhalation.

"I take it you two are working the salmon run so you'll be in and out of the harbor," Detective Sanders said. "I need you to check in with me when you're in port in case something comes up or I have any further questions. Is that clear?"

"Are we suspects or something," Ray asked.

"No, I don't see it that way. At this point, you're probably closer to being heroes. Who knows how far the fire would have spread if you hadn't woken up when you did. Some people around here have reasons to be thankful."

With that said, Ryan closed his notebook and stood up.

"Lou would you mind walking me back to my car," he said.

She nodded stiffly and followed him off the boat.

Ray watched the two of them walk away and then turned back to the mess on the deck of his boat. He had one busted gaff hook and a fire extinguisher that needed to be replaced. Thank God that was all. This problem had just moved to a whole new level with this single act. There would be no more sleeping without someone on watch.

***

The next morning, Ray and Lou were both up early and once again, they were first in line at the cannery. They were already back on the boat having coffee when Adrian arrived. She had clean clothes for the three of them.

"Mom took care of washing them last night. She's hoping you'll come by next time we're in port. She misses you," Adrian said to Lou.

Noticing the blackened paint on the side of the boat, she took a step back and asked what had happened. Lou hadn't told her about the first incident and didn't relish telling her about the second. She didn't want her sister worrying about anything else. The woman already had her fill of worries with her husband away and the kids at home.

"Aw, it's nothing. There was a fire on the dock last night. We were parked a bit too close," Lou said trying to pass it off.

Ray's eyebrow went up, but he didn't try to correct her. He figured she knew her sister far better than he did. If she didn't want to talk about it, he wasn't going to either. Thinking it was time to change the subject, he tossed the rest of his coffee over the side and gave the order to cast off. He was ready to put Homer behind them.

***

Ray picked a new fishing spot this time out thinking the other one might just be played out. His *fish sense* wasn't working for him and the sea felt empty. Pulling up an empty net only confirmed what he already knew deep inside. There was nothing here for them. After an entire day, they'd come up with barely enough fish to cover the bottom of the hold.

He thought it might be best to move on to another spot in the morning. The women said it was his boat, his call. They knew there were fish out here. They just needed to find the right spot to drop the net again.

The next morning, he headed off to another area before the women got up. He wanted to be ready to get to work as soon as they finished breakfast. He'd fished this area before and the currents usually worked in his favor. He was hoping things would go his way once again.

Just before he got to his spot, he heard the door open behind him. Turning, he caught sight of Lou coming in with two cups of coffee in hand. She came and stood next to him and together, they watched the sun slip up over the horizon. He wondered what it would be like to watch the next ten thousand sunrises with this woman standing at his side. His face turned red as he realized he would like to do that.

"So, what's the plan, Captain," she asked quietly.

"There's a spot here with a trough and a high ridge. The currents sometimes push the fish to run alongside the ridge for about a mile in this direction. I figure if we start here, we can bring in a pretty good load, maybe make up for yesterday."

"Sounds like a plan," Lou said as she gathered their

empty cups and headed down to the galley.

Ray wasn't feeling any fish moving below, but he sure was feeling her presence on his boat. He'd never been more aware of another person in his entire life. It was like she was slowly creeping in under his skin or something. The thought scared him more than a little bit.

***

After a hasty breakfast, the two women jumped to work on the nets. Their poor catch on the previous day weighed heavy on their minds as they worked. Everyone was feeling tense and jumpy as net after net came up empty or nearly so. It was clear Lady Luck hadn't come along on this ride.

Finally, in frustration Ray called for an early supper and went down to take a nap. He didn't know if sleep would help, but he needed to shut down for a little while and give his brain some time to cool off. He couldn't even think straight at this point.

The two women cleaned up the deck and stowed all the gear. No point in getting sloppy and risking somebody getting hurt. Their father was always quick to remind them fishing didn't come with any guarantees. It wasn't worth getting all worked up about things you didn't have control of in the first place.

Adrian pulled out some chocolate and a deck of cards. *A few hands of five card stud ought to draw the attention of Lady Luck back to the boat*, she figured. Lou caught her thoughts as usual and the two sat down to play.

When Ray came out from his nap, he was tempted by the M&M's to join in the game and soon had captured far more than his fair share of the bag according to the ladies. They wouldn't let him quit playing until they'd won some back. The game went on far too late and soon everybody was yawning.

Ray said he'd take the first watch and they'd split the watch times. It wasn't the best arrangement, but they were in good spirits after the fun, so everyone agreed. The two women headed for their bunks.

When Lou came up to take her turn, she looked pretty groggy so Ray made some extra strong coffee before he headed to the sack. Adrian dragged in when it was her turn to watch, making Lou laugh. The three of them were a mess and the day just might be another wash, but at least everyone was in a better frame of mind about it.

Ray decided to move the boat to the far end of the ridge and head north from there. He hadn't gone very far when his *fish sense* went into overdrive. He knew this was going to be a very good day for them. He powered down and took a quick scan of the area. He didn't see another fishing boat in sight.

The two women were already getting busy setting the gill nets and despite their broken sleep, their enthusiasm was evident. They could sense the fish for themselves. As they brought up net after net, the hold filled up quickly. Some nets were so full, they were straining under the weight of the fish. Ray was praying his equipment would hold out longer than the salmon run as he watched the fish pour into the boat.

He was so busy keeping an eye on the women, he forgot to keep an eye on the weather. Suddenly, he realized the sea was getting pretty choppy and the sky to the west was dark. Dialing up the weather scanner, he learned a storm was heading their way pretty fast.

He was debating whether or not they could outrun it and make for the harbor or could they batten down the hatches and ride it out when a rogue wave swept across the deck catching Adrian off guard. She went down with a crash and nearly took Lou with her. The two women scrambled to secure their gear as they took in the darkening skies over them. There wasn't going to be any running. The storm was already on them and they were in for a bumpy ride.

The women raced to secure the hold and the nets before the storm hit. Ray caught a few angry looks cast his way as Lou knew it was his responsibility to keep them apprised of the weather conditions. He'd put them all in danger by not paying attention. He was just as aware of that as she was, but there wasn't any way to fix it now. He was fighting to keep the boat in alignment with the racing wind and currents. He was relieved when the two women made their way to the wheelhouse.

Turning to see if they were okay, his eyes met Lou's. The storm he saw there was far more frightening than the one outside his windows and he quickly looked away. He was expecting a torrent of recriminations, but she was silent as she pulled out the first aid kit and began to bandage her sister's arm and right leg. The injuries were minor, but nothing was left to chance when at sea. Small cuts could turn into big problems if not treated properly.

Ray wrangled the boat like a wild bull as together, the two of them fought against the storm. The women braced themselves into a corner and watched without comment. As Lou had said once before, this wasn't their first rodeo. This storm would pass and others would follow. It was the life of a fisherman or woman.

***

After an hour of raging winds and gusts of rain and even some snow, the storm passed and the sea lay calm in the light of the setting sun. Ray's whole body ached as he staggered to a chair and collapsed into it. Adrian headed to her bunk to rest her aches and pains while Lou headed to the galley to make some fresh coffee and rustle up something to eat. She surveyed the mess below decks and figured it wouldn't take much to set things right.

Heading back to the wheelhouse, she pondered the

situation. She'd been angry at Ray for not keeping an eye on the weather. It was the captain's responsibility to keep the crew safe.

Unfortunately, for her, she'd made the same error a few months ago and her boat was a wreck. Ray put an enormous effort into keeping the storm from taking the boat under and deserved a lot of credit for it. Her crew was saved, but the credit for that really went to the Coast Guard. In all fairness, she didn't have the right to take him to task for making the same mistake she did. Sometimes, things out at sea just went south in a big hurry.

She carried the tray with food and coffee inside and found him slumped over in the chair. Putting her hand on his shoulder, she shook him gently. He roused slowly and looked at her cautiously.

"Here, try drinking some of this," she said, holding a cup of coffee to his lips.

He stared deep into her eyes looking for any sign of anger. There was nothing there but concern for him that he could read. He took several sips of the heavily sweetened coffee before taking the cup from her hand.

"I'm sorry," he said quietly. "I should have been watching the weather closer."

"It's not your fault. Things happen out here that are beyond our control. That's one of the first lessons we all have to learn as captains."

Handing him a peanut butter and jelly sandwich, she

shrugged her shoulders.

"You never asked how I came to be looking for a job on your boat," she said.

"I didn't think it was any of my business."

"Maybe not, but I want to tell you. I made a very similar mistake a few months ago. My boat nearly went under. The Coast Guard arrived just in time to tow us back to port. If it hadn't been for them, I wouldn't be here telling you this sorry tale. My boat's in dry dock wondering if she'll ever ride the seas again. I'm starting to wonder the same thing myself," she added dryly.

"I...I'm glad...you're here...telling me...this sorry tale," Ray said as he leaned towards her. Thinking he was about to kiss her, Lou closed her eyes in anticipation. She was very surprised when he passed out and fell into her arms. Gently she lowered him to the floor of the wheelhouse. It was clear the man was beyond exhaustion.

Summoning Adrian, the two women hauled him off to his cot and tucked him in. Lou sent her sister back to bed and took charge of the wheelhouse. The sea was dead calm and there wasn't much point in keeping watch, but she didn't want to leave anything to chance. Lady Luck was playing a pretty fickle hand this time out.

***

Lou knew the holds were only two-thirds full, but with

Ray and Adrian under the weather, so to speak, they could use a break. If they stayed and tried to keep fishing the same spot, the holds would be full long before the day was over. If they went in and offloaded what they had, Ray and Adrian could get some rest while she piloted the boat in and back out again.

With the holds empty and those two back on their feet, they could get a fresh start and only lose one day at most. It was a gamble every way she figured it, and the real problem was Ray's reaction to her making an executive decision. Under normal circumstances, she wouldn't dare to overstep her bounds as a crewman. As a captain, she wasn't sure how she'd respond to a crewman stepping up like this, but she'd never been one to just sit around.

Checking her GPS, she pointed the boat for Homer. With clear skies and a calm sea, they'd be at the cannery by morning. She settled in for a long night at the wheel. *There wouldn't be anyone coming up to relieve her anytime soon*, she figured with a sigh.

***

Waiting in line at the cannery, Lou checked out the boat for any damages from the storm. Tightening down some loose gear, and after clearing up the mess in the galley, the boat was sea-worthy. Adrian came up on deck as Lou was looking over the tally sheet. Aside from a few bruises and some stiff muscles, she looked good to go also. The two of them debated on what to do about Ray. Lou had peeked into his cabin earlier, but he was still sound asleep. She slipped away quietly to let him rest.

"So, you didn't tell me what happened with your job at Air & Sea Tours," Lou asked her sister quietly.

Adrian scoffed and shook her head.

"That jerk, Winchell, that runs the operation, he thought he was going to take me for a ride."

"What do you mean," Lou asked as she watched Adrian closely. She wasn't one to let someone take advantage of her little sister.

"I signed on in hopes of flying some of the tour groups. Well, that was supposed to be the job anyway, but he wanted me to go to the local pubs and restaurants and hustle up the customers too. He had this idea I'd find the clients, fly the tours and collect less than half what they were paying while he sat on his butt in the office. Thirty percent was the number he was throwing around. I told him it was a crap deal and walked. I wouldn't make enough money this summer to put a down payment on anything."

"Good for you!" Lou slapped her sister on the back and regretted it instantly as Adrian winced in pain. "Sorry."

"No worries. What's one more bruise between sisters?"

The two of them looked at each other and burst out laughing. Suddenly, they noticed Detective Sanders heading their way. It was clear he was a man on a mission as he zeroed in on the boat. Lou stepped out on the dock to head him off.

"Lou, can I have a word with you...privately," he said with a side glance at Adrian.

Lou tried not to laugh as her sister stuck her tongue out at Ryan's back. Giving her sister a warning look, she turned to follow him a short distance away from the boat.

Adrian couldn't hear their conversation, but she could read their body language well enough to see that Ryan was trying to stand a little too close and her sister wasn't having any of it. He did all of the talking and when he was done, Lou started to turn away. He reached out a hand to stop her.

"Lou, I know you're still mad at me for breaking off our engagement and I'm sorry. I was a fool and I know that now. I'm wondering if you'd be willing to give me another chance," Ryan said softly.

Lou paused and turned to look into his eyes carefully. At one point in her life, this man had shared her heart with a boat. Now, the boat was a wreck and her heart was patched together with bailing wire and pitch. She searched through the wreckage trying to find a spark of feeling for him. She turned back to the boat without another word, leaving him standing there.

Much to their relief the cannery guy waved them in to offload and they were able to make quick work of it.

Stashing the paperwork in the wheelhouse, Lou made the boat ready to head back out while her sister made a quick call to check on the twins. They still hadn't heard a peep from Ray's cabin so they let him rest.

***

They were halfway back to their choice fishing hole when Ray finally made an appearance above deck. Adrian was taking a turn at the wheel while Lou was catching some shuteye. He took in his surroundings with bleary eyes as he tried to get his head clear.

"How long have I been out," he asked.

"I'm not sure," Adrian considered. "I think somewhere between twelve and fourteen hours. Lou would know better than I. She's the one who's been taking care of everything. I lost some time myself last night."

"Where's she at," Ray asked.

"She's sleeping right now. Last night, she brought the boat back into Homer while we were both out. We offloaded the holds this morning at the cannery, paperwork's in the drawer there, and headed back out right after.

Ray pulled out the paperwork and gave it a quick scan. Shoving it back into the drawer, he headed to the galley for some fresh coffee and a bite to eat.

"You want some coffee," he threw back over his

shoulder as he left.

"Sure, thanks."

Stepping in the galley, he was surprised to find Lou had just finished making a fresh pot. She grabbed another cup off the hook for him without asking.

"I hear you've been keeping things going while I was out," Ray mumbled.

"Yeah," Lou said without looking at him. She didn't know what to say. Her feelings were all jumbled up like a school of dancing fish.

"Well, I guess the least I can do is say 'thanks'..."

Lou turned to take some coffee to her sister when Ray reached out a hand to stop her.

"I mean it, you know. I really appreciate you stepping up and helping me out."

Lou looked into his eyes as she considered his words. There was a warmth mixed with confusion as Ray's feelings warred with his thoughts. Her eyes slipped down to his mouth and she considered what it would be like to kiss him. She blushed as she realized how much she wanted to feel his mouth on hers. It had been a long time since she'd been kissed, too long maybe.

As if he'd read her thoughts, Ray leaned towards her and...BANG! The galley door knocked into both of them as Adrian pushed it from the other side.

"You two have got to come up and see this," she said excitedly waving them topside.

They both hurried up to see what her excitement was all about.

In the late afternoon sun, they found the boat surrounded by a pod of whales. It appeared they were headed in the same direction, and the humpback whales easily kept pace with the boat. The three of them were entertained for the better part of the next hour as the mammals played in the water alongside.

When the whales decided they'd had enough, the pod quickly disappeared from sight. The three of them realized it was way past time for supper and Adrian headed below to rustle them up some grub.

Chapter 4

They arrived at their fishing hole about the same time as they finished their meal. The two women were ready to get back to work and started laying out their gear. Knowing it wouldn't be getting dark anytime soon, well at least for the next few weeks, they voted to fish until they were tired. Then they'd take a break and get some rest and get back at it again. With any luck, the holds would be full in the next couple of days and they'd be heading back to Homer.

Hanging the gill nets took them less time than eating supper and the fish were once again pouring into the boat. Ray carefully divided his attention between the fish, the women and the weather as he maneuvered the boat to keep the nets in line with the current. The three of them worked together like a seasoned team and Ray was encouraged to believe Lady Luck had returned for the ride.

The holds were more than half full when Ray called for a break in the action. Adrian hurried below to make some coffee and sandwiches for the three of them while Lou checked over the gear and put the deck back into some semblance of order. She didn't care to leave a sloppy deck when the work was done. *Just made the next shift a little bit harder*, she thought to herself.

They ate together in the wheelhouse in companionable

Renee Hart

silence as they watched the sun take its late night dip below the horizon before it started to climb back into the sky. Summer was short in Alaska, but the long days drove everyone to make the most of it. The dark days of winter left plenty of time for sleeping.

"So, what was Ryan all worked up about this morning," Adrian asked casually.

Lou slipped a sideways glance at Ray before answering. She'd forgotten about her little chat with her ex-fiancé already. She noted Ray's sudden interest in the conversation.

"He wanted to let us know the fire on the dock wasn't a criminal act aimed at us specifically. It seems some fool dumped some oil cans full of dirty gas into the trash bin instead of disposing of them properly. Then another idiot came along and dumped something hot into the overstuffed bin and when it caught fire, he kicked it over thinking the whole thing would fall into the ocean. Instead, it rolled down the dock and ended up against the side of our boat. He ran off fearing he was in for a lot of trouble leaving us to deal with his mess. That was his story anyway. Seems there were enough witnesses to put the story together."

Ray listened to her relate the detective's version of the events without comment. Even if the fire wasn't an act against them, that still left the cut rope and a few other mysteries to be explained away. He couldn't shake the feeling someone was trying to cause him trouble.

Clearing away the remains of their supper (breakfast?), the two women headed back to the deck to put in another shift. They figured one more good haul would earn them some shuteye, and then they could decide on their next move.

Apparently, the fish had decided to hang around for a while longer and soon they were back in the rhythm of working the nets and stacking the fish in the holds. Ray wrangled the boat with a smile on his face in the choppy sea as the two women worked steadily. He was pleased to hear the holds were full when the two women brought in the final catch and filled the deck with fish for the last time. It had been a very good day and thanks to Lou's quick thinking, they had another load for the cannery already.

The three of them cleaned up the gear together as Ray pitched in to help everyone get settled in for the 'night'. It was time for some well-earned rest. He would take the first watch as the two women hit their bunks. He set course for Homer once again.

***

At the end of his watch, he was surprised when he saw Adrian slipping into the wheelhouse. He'd been expecting, hoping to see (if he was being honest), Lou come in for the second watch. Adrian came and stood next to him and surveyed the area around them. There weren't any other lights or boats in sight and the sea was nearly dead calm. Swallowing his disappointment, he nodded to her before surrendering his seat and headed for his own bunk.

As he lay in his cot, Ray thought about his feelings for Lou. He'd never expected to find romance in Homer, especially with a member of his own crew. He'd had some vague dreams about marriage and a family, but never considered how to make them a reality.

His world was a fishing boat and the stink of fish combined with a deep love of the sea. The sea was a demanding mistress and most men found that women weren't willing to compete with her. The hold she had on the men that loved her went far too deep for the average woman. He'd never met a woman caught up in that same grip, or so he thought of Lou.

She was clearly at home on a boat, but he wondered if she'd leave it if given the chance for a home on dry land. Ryan Sanders clearly had an interest in changing her mind, if he'd read the man right. *What did I have that could compete with a man earning a steady paycheck every month*, he wondered.

Pushing away his thoughts, he struggled to find the sleep that tried to elude him. His body was tired, but his mind wouldn't let him rest. Every time he closed his eyes, he would find himself looking into a pair of stormy gray eyes or focusing on a mouth waiting to be kissed. *That was the trouble with having women crewing on the boat*, he thought angrily, *they're a distraction!*

With that thought, he slipped into an uneasy sleep.

***

He felt like he'd only been asleep for a few minutes when someone began shaking him and calling his name.

"Ray! Ray! You need to wake up! There's trouble."

Ray forced his eyes open to find Lou standing over him as she tried to wake him.

"What's the matter," he groaned still groggy from the bad dream that had overtaken him.

"There's a boat in trouble off the portside. They've got a fire on board and there's smoke everywhere. It's *The Maiden*, out of Soldotna, I think from what I can see and make out on the radio. The captain put out a 'Mayday', but the Coast Guard's at least two hours out on another call. We're the closest boat."

Ray swung his legs out and tried to sit up. Lou stepped backwards out of the way and turned to head topside. It was his call on how to help the other boat. They'd be able to take on the crew, but the question remained to be decided on how far he could go to save the other boat without risking his own.

Struggling to pull on his pants, he realized the sea was picking up as the boat pitched back and forth. Getting the crew off the other boat and onto his own wasn't going to be as easy as walking across a plank. That was clear as he made his way topside and noted the wind rising from the west.

Lou had maneuvered the Seabiscuit within shouting distance of the distressed boat and they could see the white faces of the crew between the clouds of billowing smoke. Ray couldn't make out the source of the fire from their vantage point. There wasn't much to burn on these fishing boats beyond the fuel and some of the trappings. If the fuel did catch, however, the explosion would be deadly to anyone on board.

He tried to raise the captain of *The Maiden* on the radio, but there was no answer. He watched carefully for some signal on the situation. A life raft came over the side and three crew members lowered themselves down into it. They quickly paddled the raft towards the Seabiscuit and Lou tossed them a line from the deck.

Adrian lowered a rope ladder and the three men scrambled aboard. One of them hurried to the wheelhouse to apprise Ray of the condition of the other boat. Ray was surprised to find himself face to face with Jonesy.

"The fire's out on *The Maiden* but the motor's toast. We think it was the wiring that caught. The captain wants to stay on board, but thought we'd be safer with all the smoke over here. The Coast Guard's on the way. They can tow him in. He says you can wait or go on your way and he'll catch up with us in Homer."

Jonesy relayed all this without looking at Ray's face.

"It's good to see you Jonesy. I've been wondering how you've been," Ray said with a grin. "Looks like you found yerself a much better post."

Jonesy didn't say anything and Ray figured he'd said enough. Signaling to the other captain, Ray got them back on course. There was clearly no point in wasting time sitting out here. He had more important things to do.

***

The three men made themselves comfortable on the deck and Ray was amused to see Adrian bringing them some coffee and sandwiches. Those men probably wouldn't have been nearly so accommodating if the situation had been reversed and the women found themselves on *The Maiden*. Ray noted that even Jonesy took a couple of sandwiches when they were offered. Maybe the man wasn't as much an old fool as Ray thought, or perhaps he was just really hungry.

They made it into Homer as the line was forming up for the cannery. The three crewmen from *The Maiden* gave a hurried thanks as they disembarked and walked off. Adrian wasn't far behind them as she wanted to see to the twins. She had a rucksack stuffed with dirty clothes thrown over one shoulder. Once again, Ray and Lou found themselves alone together on the boat with nothing to do, but wait.

They hadn't been docked very long before Ray noticed Detective Ryan Sanders coming towards the boat. He had a determined look on his face. Lou didn't see him approach as she was busy coiling up some rope on the deck. He called to her from the dock. Hearing his voice, she turned towards him and Ray tried to catch the look in her eyes. He barely caught a flash of something before she'd looked away from him.

"Lou, do you have some time? Can you take a walk with me," Ryan asked.

If there was a hint of desperation to Ryan's voice, Ray couldn't help but feel the echo of it in his own thoughts. He really wanted to hear Lou tell the guy to buzz off, or worse. Instead she turned to look at him with a question in her eyes and he just nodded. She shrugged her shoulders and stepped up on the edge of the boat. Ryan offered her a hand down, but she ignored it and jumped to the dock. The two of them walked off as Ray watched them go. He couldn't remember ever feeling so helpless about anything in his life before.

Lou was back before their turn came to offload and Ryan was nowhere to be seen. Ray took that as a good sign, but Lou was pretty tense and avoided his eyes. He had the distinct impression the conversation between the two of them didn't go very well, but he dared not ask any questions. As the captain, he was supposed to at least try to maintain some professional distance from the crew. At least that was what he kept telling himself. Only a fool would listen to such nonsense.

After they weighed their fish in and received the payout, Ray considered the idea of taking an extra day off since they'd made such a good haul. They were well on their way to making quota for the season and everyone was pulling their weight. *It wouldn't hurt to give the women a day off and take one for himself at the same time*, he figured.

He shared his thoughts with Lou and she actually looked relieved at the idea. He planned to stay on the boat, but she was free to go to her sister's house for the night. Almost quicker than the words were out of his mouth, Lou was heading for the dock with her phone in hand. She was climbing into a cab by the time he'd gotten used to the idea of her going.

***

Sitting on the deck of the Seabiscuit, Ray soon found himself with company. The word was out on *The Maiden's* SOS call and Ray's good deed, so a few of the other captains stopped by with beer to chew the fat and swap fish tales. It appeared the salmon run was holding up well for everyone and they each took a turn at bragging up their hauls.

A couple of the guys tried to tease him about his new crew, but he didn't take the bait. He was quick to point out to them how he was on track to make quota same as them so he had no complaints. Besides, he was eating something other than cold beans from a can and that was a big step up for him.

As the group thinned out, the two guys left stopped talking and started to fidget. Ray could tell something was on their minds, so finally he just told them to say what they had to say and get over it.

"We thought you should know that State Trooper, Detective Sanders has been snooping around and asking a lot of questions about you specifically," one of the guys said quietly.

"Yeah," the other one pitched in, "and he hasn't been too subtle about it. It's like he's trying to find something to pin on you. What'd you do...steal his girlfriend?"

Ray leaned back in his chair, but didn't answer. It had been a lot of years since he'd run into trouble with the law and he didn't feel like repeating that experience. Guys like him never came out on top when cops got it in their head to make a case. It didn't even really matter if he'd done anything wrong. They could make it look anyway they wanted it to look.

As the conversation died, the last two guys packed up their empties and headed for their own boats. Ray sat there a while longer wondering what he'd gotten himself into with Lou. If Sanders was looking for a way to take Ray out of the picture so he could go after her, he was probably on the right track. Sometimes, a man's past had a way of catching up with him when he least expected it.

Chapter 5

The next morning, Lou and Adrian were back on board before Ray's feet hit the floor. They had clean clothes, groceries, and some sticky buns from the Sister's Bakery. Ray could tell at a single glance they hadn't brought enough sticky buns. There was gonna be a fight over them for sure. He was even considering if he could get away with pitching the women over board so he could have them all for himself.

As if reading his thoughts, Adrian grabbed one for herself and headed for the far end of the deck. Lou followed suit and hurriedly jammed it into her mouth licking at the caramel as it dripped down her chin. Ray had one in each hand and took a big bite out of both of them as a sign of ownership. The three of them made funny sounds as they devoured the gooey treats.

Soon they were all laughing at the sight of each other's sticky hands and faces. There was nothing like sticky buns to bring out the inner child in someone was the thought they all shared in that simple moment. Cleaning up the mess took longer than making it had taken them as they scrubbed caramel and cinnamon from their hands and faces and a few other places it had dripped.

When they were done, Ray headed for the wheelhouse and they were headed back to sea in search of more salmon. Their spirits were high as they looked forward to another good haul from their favorite spot. The weather was clear and the two women made themselves comfortable on the deck.

"So, what's going on with you and Ray," Adrian asked her sister quietly.

"Nothing really. I keep thinking something's going on, but every time we get close to testing that theory, somebody comes along and messes us up...like you and the whales the other day. I was sure he was just about to kiss me and I wanted him to, then BANG! You hit us with the galley door."

Adrian busted out laughing at the look on her sister's face.

"Well, you know my timing never was that great, and besides, whales rock! You didn't want to miss them, did you?"

Lou stuck her tongue out at her sister and finding a stray smear of caramel at the corner of her mouth, she tried licking it off. It had been a good long while since she'd had sticky buns, but they hadn't lost their appeal. *Good thing she didn't live in Homer full time*, she thought with a grin, *or she'd have a 'sticky bun' butt!*

***

Ray decided to check out another one of his favorite

fishing spots on this trip. Heading a little farther north, he focused his 'fish sense' on the water below, hoping to tap into another good haul. Passing a few other fishing boats along his route, he gave them a wide berth. He found it always worked in his favor to respect the other captains and their crews. The horizon was clear and the sea was choppy under a brisk breeze.

Reaching a spot he liked, his feet began to itch as they sensed the fish moving along below the boat. Ray signaled to the women to start hanging out the nets and they jumped to work as usual. Soon the three of them were in sync moving like a well-oiled machine and the fish starting coming in a steady stream. The numbers were slower than their past couple of runs, but the women were busy on the deck.

After several hours, the nets started coming up nearly empty and Ray called for them to take a supper break. He was pretty sure this fishing hole was played out and they'd have to move on to find another.

Adrian headed below to throw together a meal while Lou cleaned up the deck. Ray stepped out to inspect the nets and equipment, but mainly, he was looking for an excuse to be near Lou. She didn't pay much attention to him as she was focused on getting her work done.

"How are the nets holding up," Ray asked.

"No problems that I can see so far," Lou answered him absently.

"I'm thinking this spot is played out and we're going to need to find another one," Ray added as he tried to get a conversation going.

Lou just shrugged and turned away to stow some gear.

Ray stared at her back in frustration and then turned to go to the wheel house. It was pretty clear to him, she wasn't interested in talking.

Lou listened to him stomp off and fought back the urge to call after him. Knowing that sooner or later she was going to have to face this situation head on, didn't make her feel any better about ignoring him. She always felt better when she had a clear destination in mind. This was more like traveling in uncharted waters in the dark and she didn't like it at all.

Adrian called them to come down to the galley to eat. She made a couple of starts at a conversation, but gave up when she got no response and they ate in silence. She threw Lou a couple questioning looks, but her sister carefully avoided looking at her. Ray jumped up when he was done eating and put his dishes in the sink. Mumbling something that sounded like 'thanks' and 'I'll take care of these later', he headed topside without another word.

"Okay. Now what's going on," Adrian asked sarcastically. "Being stuck on this boat with you two is like being trapped in a high school soap opera. Why don't you just kiss him and get over it?"

"I don't think it's a really good idea to kiss the captain.

What if he takes it the wrong way or worse what if he's a terrible kisser and wants to kiss me again?"

Adrian burst out laughing at the look on her sister's face.

"Girl, I don't know what to tell you, but I'm certainly not going to kiss him for you so you can find out. This is one 'fish' you're going to have to reel in by yourself."

The sound of the motor trying to start and failing caused them both to pause and listen. Engine problems were never good, but a problem this far out could quickly become a serious matter. They held their breath as Ray gave it another try. Once again the starter ground down to silence as the motor didn't catch. The two women came up from the galley as Ray stomped towards the engine compartment with a grim look on his face. He avoided looking at them.

They watched him poke around for a bit and jiggle a few wires here and there. There was nothing jumping out at him right off the bat.

"Do you want me to take a look," Lou asked hesitantly. "Sometimes a second set of eyes on a problem helps.

Ray shrugged and took a step backwards. He watched carefully as she poked around in pretty much the same way he did and jiggled a few wires herself.

"You want to go and give it another try while I stay here and see if I notice anything out of order," she asked.

Ray obediently turned and went to the wheelhouse. He

didn't expect anything to be different, but one never knew with these things. Sometimes it turned out to be a loose wire and other times, it was just one of those mysteries that came along without warning and left the same way.

He pressed the START button and the motor roared to life as if laughing in his face. He looked out at Lou and gave her a big 'thumbs-up'. If it was just plain dumb luck, that was good enough for him. He headed the boat north as the women went below. Plagued by this strange feeling, he figured they were talking about him. On that count, he was wrong.

"Sis, how did you know Gage was the right man for you," Lou asked quietly.

"Hon, even if I could tell you that, it wouldn't necessarily apply to you," Adrian replied. "As much as we're alike, we're still two very different people. You like captaining your own fishing boat. My dream is flying in the Bush. I wanted a family. You're still trying to figure out what you want. Gage and I were moving in the same direction and it felt right for us to do it together. You're not going to find that with a guy whose life plan doesn't have room for the things you love.....like Ryan," she added.

Lou looked at her sister with storm tossed eyes as she considered her words.

"Ryan's telling me he made a mistake and he wants to try again. He's hinting that there's something about Ray that I should know about, but so far he hasn't told me what's bothering him."

"Maybe you ought to go and ask Ray about it yourself. If he tells you, then you've got one up on Ryan and he can't use his info to play you, if that's what he's trying to do, I mean."

Lou nodded thoughtfully and filled two cups with fresh coffee.

"You're right. I think it's time to step up to the wheelhouse and have a chat with the captain. Maybe he'll be glad to see me coming and maybe he won't, but I'll give it a shot."

Adrian watched her sister go and then took a look around the galley. *I guess this mess is up to me since I made it*, she thought.

***

Ray heard the door to the wheelhouse open behind him. Smelling the fresh coffee, he turned and looked hopefully into Lou's eyes. She gave him a wry smile and handed him a cup.

"Don't worry. I didn't make it," she said with a grin.

Ray laughed and took a swallow.

"So, where are we heading Captain?"

"I've got another spot I like a few miles north of here. I thought we'd check out the fishing there. Should be there within the hour."

The two paused and sipped their coffee for a bit.

"Can I ask you a personal question," Lou asked hesitantly.

"Sure. You can ask me whatever you want. Fire away."

"Ryan's throwing around hints like you've got some deep, dark secret in your past that I should know about. He thinks I'm falling for you and he's trying to warn me off."

"Are you?"

"Am I what?"

Ray considered her with a raised eyebrow and a half grin on his face.

Lou decided to sidestep the question.

"I'm not good with uncharted waters. I like to know what I'm getting into before I get into it, if you know what I mean..."

Ray turned to fiddle with some instruments and check his heading while he considered his answer. If he was getting into something here, he knew it was better to go in with a full disclosure. Ryan was in a position to undermine any chance he had with Lou and he had the opportunity right here to shut the guy off at the pass. It seemed like a good idea to take it.

"Ryan has probably tapped into my police record. It's not a big enough deal to scare anyone outright so he's just dangling it like bait. The bottom line is that I do have a police record for a crime I did commit."

"So, you admit you're a criminal," Lou said, "and are you willing to tell me about this crime you committed or do I have to guess."

Ray scratched his head and then he rubbed his arm. Reaching for his cup he took another sip of coffee as he avoided looking at Lou.

She got the distinct impression, he was about to start laughing.

"If I tell you, you have to promise not to tell anybody else," Ray warned while trying to look serious. "I don't want this to get out and ruin my reputation."

Lou crossed her arms in front of her chest and leaned back against the wall.

"You might want to sit down for this," Ray said. "It's another long story."

She didn't move so he went on.

"I finished up my high school years here in Homer. One of the traditions at graduation is to go down on the beach and have a big bonfire. That usually involves beer...."

"Of course," Lou agreed dryly.

"It also usually involves some of the guys getting their cars or pick-ups out on the sand at low tide and goofing around doing donuts and skids, you know, silly movie stunts without the camera tricks."

Lou nodded.

"Well, I had an old Ford pick-up and I was out there playing the fool like everyone else. The tide was starting to come in and we were splashing through the inlets. Water was spraying up in the air like crazy. Everyone was laughing and having a great time and I got a little too carried away with it all. I'd like to blame it on the beer, but I was just being stupid."

"What happened?"

"I was too far out and I hit a rock pretty hard with the right front wheel. It busted one of the tie rods and the wheel was turned out almost at a right angle. Some of my buddies were trying to get a tow line on me to pull the truck back in, but with the tire wedged up against the rock and sideways, we couldn't move her."

"Let me guess," Lou added. "The tide caught you out and the truck went under."

"Yeah, the local authorities get pretty nasty about stuff like that and I got hit with all kinds of charges about damaging the environment and messing up the ocean with the oil and gas from the truck. You know the drill. They threw the book at me to make an example. I ended up with some big fines I couldn't pay and a year's probation, and because I was already eighteen, a police record that won't go away. It never mattered that much to me. I worked for my dad and I've never had to explain my past to anyone."

"But, it's there for someone like Ryan to make light of it, if they're looking to make trouble for you," Lou finished for him.

"Yeah, exactly," Ray said watching her closely.

"So, I'm guessing your effort to try the criminal lifestyle didn't actually take and you decided to live the straight and narrow from that point on…"

Lou took a couple of steps toward him.

"You're right about that. A couple of hours sitting in a jail cell thinking my dad was going to kill me for drowning his truck was more than enough to convince me not to go down that path."

Ray stood up out of his chair.

"Good thing you were wrong about that…"

"About what," Ray asked confused as he took another step closer to Lou.

"That your dad was going to kill you," Lou said with a grin, "or we wouldn't be standing here having this conversation."

As she finished her sentence, the two of them closed the gap between them and Ray reached out to take her into his arms. He paused to look carefully into her eyes checking the weather before they closed and he leaned down to kiss her gently. Lingering to take in the scent of her and the feel of her warmth against him, he kissed her once more and then gently set her away from him.

She looked at him curiously, but he turned his attention back to the boat.

"We need to get back to work," he said a bit brusquely. "This is the spot I wanted to try next."

Lou stared at the back of his head for a moment unable

to hide her confusion. Not knowing what was going through his mind, she turned and left the wheelhouse.

Ray listened to the door close behind her before he punched the wall next to him. Focusing on the pain in his hand, he tried not to think about how much he'd wanted to just keep kissing her. In that moment, he saw an opportunity for a whole other kind of life ahead of him, and he wanted that life. The questions he was afraid to face were all jumbled together like a heap of stinking fish. He didn't know where to begin to clear that deck.

Chapter 6

Lou nearly ran down Adrian as she hurried to go below just as her sister was coming topside. One look at her sister's face and Adrian knew everything there was to know in that moment. It was also very clear that Lou wasn't ready to talk about it. She was beyond words as she wrestled with a flood of emotions and thoughts. Adrian was smart enough to leave it alone...for now.

***

The two women easily stepped back into the rhythm of hanging the gill nets and hauling in their catch without any words. They were in another good spot and the fish were coming in pretty steady.

Ray was glad to be back in safer territory as fishing was all he really knew. The sea life and keeping this boat running was enough of a challenge for him. The idea of letting go and making a new life for himself was terrifying. The hope that he and Lou could make a life together out here as a couple even more so. Kissing her had set loose the wild idea in him of the two of them getting married and having a couple of kids as a real possibility. He'd never considered that with any other woman.

Lady Luck was riding shotgun on this run and the holds were full once again. Ray was satisfied that his season was back on track and he'd make full quota for the salmon catch this year. Setting course for Homer, the three of them settled down for a nice meal and a quiet trip back to port. With clear sailing, they'd be at the cannery ready to off-load by morning.

Adrian was looking forward to seeing the twins and getting some news on her husband. His training mission was supposed to be over soon and he would be coming back to Homer with his new orders. She was also ready to get away from her sister and Ray for a couple of days. They were dancing around each other, being polite and trying to pretend there wasn't anything going on between them. The only people on board being fooled by that act was the two of them.

Ray announced they would spend a couple of days in Homer and the two women were free to head home. He would stay with the boat and take care of his business while they took care of theirs. When he got the pay slip for this haul, he told them they'd get their percentages and they'd start the next month anew. Everyone was happy with that particular piece of news. It's always good to get paid.

The next morning, Ray was good on his word and the sisters headed home with a smile on their faces and a month's pay in their pockets. He tried not to watch as they headed off, but a part of him wanted to go along with them too. He'd gotten pretty used to having the two women around.

With a sigh, he turned back to the business at hand. The paperwork in the life of fishing vessel was a job all by itself and Ray had let it get ahead of him. He had catch reports to file and bills to pay before he could take some time for himself. The good news was the boat and his equipment was holding up and he didn't have any repairs to make or equipment to replace. That wasn't always the case with some crews he'd had in the past.

A couple of advantages that came with this crew was how they'd taken on his dirty laundry with theirs and the way they always came back with plenty of groceries for the three of them. He couldn't remember how long it had been since his last can of cold beans. If he was being honest, he'd have to admit he wasn't missing them.

***

Ray spent the better part of the day getting all his paperwork brought up to date. It was pretty late when he realized the day was nearly gone and his stomach was growling big time. Breakfast was a distant memory and lunch had slipped by him without comment. Dinner needed to be something a bit more substantial than a can of beans. He headed for the galley to see what he could scrounge up.

A sudden call from the dock surprised him and he found a familiar face staring at him over a pizza box and a six pack. Jan was an old friend that had moved to Kodiak when her husband was transferred. He was happy to see her.

"Ray! How've you been? Bill and I have missed you! What a stroke of luck that you're in port at the same time we're here. Bill's uptown for a meeting, but he should be back soon. I just grabbed a pizza, care to share?"

Jan reeled all this off while stepping aboard with her load.

Ray laughed as he reached out to give her a hand. She hadn't changed a bit. The woman was a spitfire in high school and she still ran in high gear. He gave her an awkward hug as they juggled the pizza between them.

Soon they were catching up on each other's news as they crammed slices of pizza in their mouths. By the time Bill showed up, there were only a couple of gnawed crusts left in the box between them.

"Good thing I didn't come back hungry," he laughed looking at the remnants. The two of them talked a bit longer before Bill said he needed to get back to their boat and take care of a few things as they were heading out early. Jan lingered behind for a little while.

As she was getting ready to leave, Ray stepped out on

the dock with her. Throwing her arms around him, Jan gave him a big hug and a sound kiss on the cheek.

"It was so good to see you, Ray. I'm really hoping you'll have some time to come down to Kodiak and visit us before winter sets in. We'd like to show you what we've got going on down there, see if you might be interested in joining up with us."

Ray hugged her back and laughed.

"I'd like that, Jan. Let me see what I can do when this season is over. There's actually someone I'd like you to meet."

"Ooh...are you telling me there's a woman in your life?"

She jumped up and down in excitement at this juicy little tidbit and gave him another hug.

He blushed and looked down at his feet.

"I've got my hopes," he said quietly.

Neither of them noticed the cab that pulled up near the dock and the face watching the two of them from the window. They didn't notice when the cab left and no one got out. As Jan headed back to her boat, Ray took a long, slow look around at the quiet harbor. *It must be nice to be going home to somebody waiting for you*, he thought sadly as he headed for his bunk.

***

Adrian looked at her sister curiously as she dragged into

the kitchen the next morning. The twins greeted their aunt with high excitement. It was a special treat for them to have Lou in the house. Her visits were usually few and far between with her boat running out of Anchorage. This summer, the only person missing was their father and he was due home soon.

Their enthusiasm filled the air with happy chatter that masked the silence coming from Lou's corner of the table. Adrian had heard Lou leave the house last night and come back within the hour. She figured Lou was going to head back to the boat and spend the evening with Ray. When her sister came back early, Adrian could only wonder what had gone wrong. It was clear something wasn't right.

***

Ray was up earlier than usual and wondered what to do with himself for a whole day. He was idly checking over some rope on the deck when another captain stopped by to chat.

"I don't know if you heard, Ray, but Jonesy's up at the hospice on the hill. He's not doing too good they say. Thought you might like to run up and have a word with the old guy. I know he was like 'family' to you and all."

Ray didn't need to hear any more. He locked up the boat and headed for the hospice. Since his dad died, Jonesy was the only link Ray had to any kind of past.

Losing him would set Ray totally adrift and he didn't want it to be like this. The only reason Jonesy wasn't sailing with him was his own stubbornness, but Ray wasn't going to keep that from seeing the old salt and giving him a proper send-off when the time came for it. He owed it to Jonesy and to his dad.

Grabbing a cab on the Spit, Ray sat back and thought about how Jonesy was the one person that came along just in time. Ray's dad didn't really know anything about fishing. He'd been a lumberjack all his life. He just got it into his head to become a fisherman and Ray was along for the ride.

When they put the down payment on the Seabiscuit, Jonesy happened along the dock as they were looking at their fishing gear. Most of it came with the boat and neither of them had a clue about anything. The old salt took one look at them staggering around the deck and started laughing out loud.

"Let me guess," he roared with laughter, "you two have never been on a boat before in your life and now you're planning to be fishermen."

Ray expected his dad to get mad at this rude man, but instead he welcomed the sailor to come aboard and offered him a beer. Jonesy declined saying he never touched the stuff, but he did come on board and soon the two men were talking like old friends. Seems he was *between positions* as he put it and was willing to come alongside and teach them how to sail the high seas for a share in the profits.

Ray's dad thought that was a fine plan and took him up on his offer. Ray couldn't remember a single fishing trip without Jonesy on board, until he stomped off the day Lou came to crew. *That must a nearly broke the old man's heart*, Ray thought sadly. He felt guilty when he considered how easily he had let the old salt go. Maybe he should have run after him and tried to reason with him. It was too late to take it back now.

The cab pulled up in front of the hospice and Ray handed the driver a five dollar bill. One of the perks of Homer was that a ride anywhere in town cost five bucks. Didn't matter where you were going, as long as it was in town, you just handed over that bill and you were done.

He got out and stared at the familiar building in front of him. This was the same place his dad had left this world from, and Ray wasn't too keen to go inside. All things considered, if he didn't go down with the Seabiscuit this just might be the place he spent his last days. Shaking off that grim thought, he went inside to the front desk.

Walking down the hall to Jonesy's room, Ray wondered if he should have brought the guy some kind of gift. It wasn't like the guy would light up at some flowers or a plant, but there must be something he could have brought. The only thing that come to mind was a dead fish and he figured the hospice would have smelled that coming a mile away.

Renee Hart

The old man's face was turned to the wall when Ray walked into the room. He was laying so still that for a second, Ray thought he might be too late.

A nurse came in behind him and announced loudly, "Well, Jonesy, looks like you've got yourself a visitor here!"

Jonesy turned to look at Ray in surprise and just for a quick second, Ray caught a spark of happiness before the old man quickly covered it up with a hoarse cough.

"If you've come to spit on my grave, son, yer a might too early. I ain't dead yet."

"Aw, Jonesy, you know it ain't like that between us. Why do you have to be so mean?"

Addressing the nurse, Jonesy said, "You know, this here pup, he gave my job away to a she-male!"

The nurse just rolled her eyes and finished her notes on his chart before taking her leave. She was clearly resigned to the old salt's gruff mannerisms.

"Women taking away a man's job. What's this world coming to?" Jonesy grumbled on to himself.

"Now you know it wasn't like that," Ray said. "We needed another hand and then you up and quit on me and I needed to hire me a second woman to boot. If it wasn't for those two women, I wouldn't have had a chance of making the salmon run."

"Yeah, and that first one ya hired", Jonesy chortled, "she sure could swim, eh?"

"And what do you know about that?"

"Well, I know enough to say she saved your sorry tail."

Jonesy had the decency to look guilty at that point.

"Don't be thinking I'm gonna apologize for cutting the Seabiscuit loose. You deserved it far as I was concerned. Yer Pa must a been turnin' over in his watery grave at the way you treated me."

Ray just shook his head. *Another mystery solved and no satisfaction in the solution*, he thought to himself.

"Well, don't be thinking I'm going to apologize for hiring Lou either!" Ray shot back with a quick one across the bow.

At the look in Ray's eyes, Jonesy saw far more than the young man had intended to reveal.

"Lou, is it? I can see it didn't take long for her to find a way in under your skin. You're sweet on her, ain't ya?"

Jonesy started to laugh. "I always told you, Boy, women and boats don't mix well."

Considering the topic of conversation, Ray didn't feel like arguing. He decided to change the subject.

"What are you doing in here?"

"Dying, they tell me. I just wish this old body would get it over with. I'm sick of hanging around this place. Need to get me back to the sea where I can die in peace. You promise me when my time comes you'll take care of it just like we done yer pa. You promise me!"

"You got it, Jonesy. You got my word on it."

"That's good enough for me."

Renee Hart

Chapter 7

Adrian looked up in surprise as a cab pulled up in front of the house. She heard the screams of the twins long before she caught sight of her husband coming up the front walk with a duffle bag over one shoulder. He had a twin hanging off each arm when he reached the front porch, and the neighbors had to be looking out their windows at all the shouting.

She ran to the front door and threw herself into the melee of joyful homecoming. Her husband laughed as she and the children rained kisses and hugs on him from every direction. Everyone talked at once and Lou and her mother came from the kitchen to add their welcome.

Gage was surprised to see his sister-in-law as she was a rare visitor during the fishing season.

The children dominated the next couple of hours as they brought their dad up to speed on everything they'd done since he'd headed out. The adults didn't even try to get a word in edgewise. They figured eventually the torrent of words would run out and they'd have a chance to talk then. It wasn't until the kids were tucked into bed that their time finally came.

Gage started off with his news.

"I've got leave, thirty days, and we've been transferred to Kodiak. I thought we could relax for a while and hang out with the kids here in Homer and then head south to find a new place, get them enrolled in school, all the usual stuff."

"That sounds great, Darling, but we've got three weeks to go in the salmon season and we're crewing on a boat for a guy named Ray. We can't just up and quit on him. We need to finish out the run."

"About that," Lou piped up, "I was wondering how you'd feel about taking my spot on the boat Gage. I really need to head back up to Anchorage and see what I can do about the Lindy Lee. I've been away from her too long. You and Adrian could take it like a working honeymoon where you're getting paid to be together."

Gage looked like that idea appealed to him. He liked fishing and while it wasn't a job he wanted full time, it would be fun for three weeks to work alongside his wife. He turned to look at Adrian to see what she thought. The look on her face brought a frown to his.

"Something going on that I need to know about," he asked.

Adrian stood up and started clearing the table. There were a lot of things she could have said in that moment, but words weren't going to fix this. If Lou was going to run away from a good thing, she could just get going.

"So, you'll do it, take my place?" Lou asked, directing her question at Gage.

"Uh, sure, Lou. If that's what you really want and

Adrian's okay with this. I'll do it."

He figured Adrian would fill him in on the details later. It was clear she didn't approve, but the reasons why weren't being put on the table at this point.

***

The next morning Adrian and Gage headed down to the dock. Lou was gone before anyone else got out of bed. The twins were sad to see all the adults leaving again, but Grandma had plans for the day and soon they were caught up in them. Adrian was so grateful for her mother's relationship with the twins. She made all of this work for them with their crazy lifestyles.

Ray was surprised when Adrian and Gage came on board. He was even more surprised to learn that Lou had headed north and traded her spot on the Seabiscuit with Gage. He wanted to ask more questions, but the look on Adrian's face didn't encourage him. She seemed to be saying to him to just let it go. Shrugging his shoulders, he gave the order to cast off and headed to the wheelhouse. There were fish out in the sea waiting to be caught. *With any luck, he'd be the one catching them*, he thought sadly.

***

Adrian and Gage didn't quite have the same fluidity in

working together that Ray had enjoyed watching between the two women. They were forced to use a lot more words and sometimes got in each other's way, but they were good-natured about it and used it as an opportunity to sneak a kiss or grab a hug. Ray tried not to watch them as closely as he'd watched the two sisters as it made him feel self-conscious, like a third wheel on his own boat.

He'd found them a good spot and the fish were coming in steady. Ray tended to his duties as the captain, but his heart was in Anchorage. After his day with Jonesy, he'd worked out in his own mind what he really wanted in his life and it wasn't to die alone without a family to remember him and carry on his name. He'd been awake most of the night trying to figure out what to say to Lou to make her come around and see things his way.

While a boat didn't need two captains, she was confident enough to stand beside him and let him wear the hat. He knew she was ready, willing and able to step up whenever he needed her. There hadn't been any problems with this arrangement so far and if there were in the future, well, like other couples, they'd just work things out.

Suddenly, Ray knew what he had to do. He'd wasted enough time avoiding life already. It was time he stepped up and got this boat back on course. Signaling to Adrian to pull in the nets and secure the deck, he plotted his course north. With Lady Luck on his side, they'd be in Anchorage by morning. They could off-load whatever was in the holds already and he'd find a way to reel in *the one* that got away.

As if Adrian read his mind, the nets were stowed and the deck was clear within the hour. The two of them headed below as Ray got them underway. The fish would still be there when they got back.

***

The next morning, Adrian handed Ray a cup of coffee and a piece of paper with two addresses on it.

"She could be here or maybe, here. I can't really say. You've got her number if she'll pick up, but I wouldn't count on it. She can be pretty stubborn. Good luck."

Ray stuffed the piece of paper in his pocket and swallowed the coffee before heading out. He wasn't sure what kind of reception to expect or even why she'd jumped ship, but he was going to find out. He figured, he'd start with the Lindy Lee. As a captain with a broken heart, he knew that was where he would be hiding out.

Checking in at the office of the boatyard, he got directions to the Lindy and started heading in her direction. He saw that blond ponytail first as she stood in front of the wreck talking with another man. The two of them were just finishing up their conversation as he approached them. They shook hands and the man handed her an envelope. She saw Ray as she turned to head out and stopped short.

"What are you doing here," she asked in surprise.

"I came to find out what you're doing here," he replied.

"Just tying up some loose ends," she said avoiding his eyes.

"Were you planning on tying up all your loose ends or just the ones here in Anchorage?"

"What's that supposed to mean," Lou said a bit sarcastically. "Isn't one woman enough for you?"

Ray looked at her in surprise.

"What are you talking about?"

"I saw you...the other night. Hugging and kissing that woman on the dock!"

Ray looked confused as he tried to think what she was talking about.

"Oh, Jan! You saw me hugging Jan, *Bill's wife, Jan.* What were you doing? Spying on me?"

"Spying on you! Bill's wife, Jan! No, I came back to the boat that night to bring you some dessert. I wasn't spying on you!"

"So that's what this is all about? You saw me hugging some woman so you *assumed* I was with another woman. Is that the kind of guy you think I am?"

Ray looked hurt and a bit angry, and Lou knew she'd done him wrong by not giving him a chance to talk before running away. Letting her feelings make the course correction her head couldn't work out, she reached for him. Pulling him close, she kissed him gently. He kissed her back before taking her by the shoulders and moving her back a bit.

"Does this mean you're sorry," he asked with a grin.

"I am. I'm very sorry for making a stupid assumption and I'm sorry for making you come to Anchorage, but I'm not sorry for falling in love with you."

Ray stared deep into those stormy gray eyes. Seeing the truth of those words, he pulled her close and kissed her again.

The two of them sighed deeply as he pulled her close and held onto her tightly. His chin rested on the top of her head as they stood there, and he looked at the Lindy Lee.

"This is your boat, eh?"

"Not anymore," Lou said. "I've decided I don't want to be the captain anymore.

She leaned back and looked up into his eyes.

"I've found I prefer crewing."

Epilogue

Ray laughed as he watched his son wrestle with the salmon on the other end of the line. The little guy was committed to bringing in this fish all by himself, and Ray wasn't sure what was going to give first, his strength or his vow. Lou came up on deck just as the fish surfaced and she leaned over to see what her firstborn had on his line. Their daughter giggled as she saw the fish splashing about in the water. Ray handed her over to Lou as he got the net ready for his son. If he let this one get away, there would be tears for sure.

Ray Jr. crowed with pride as his Dad scooped the fish up out of the water. His little feet were stamping the deck as he congratulated himself. Lou could barely contain her amusement as his excitement spilled over to his twin sister. The two of them danced around in a circle together as Ray secured the fish and held it up for inspection.

"We have fresh salmon for dinner tonight," Ray exclaimed as Lou snapped a picture of the three of them with the fish.

"Again, Daddy! I want to catch another one," Ray Jr. demanded.

Ray obliged him by baiting his line and getting him in position.

"Do you want to try, Lindy," Lou asked her daughter.

The little girl shook her head. She wasn't as taken with fishing as her brother, but she loved to drive the boat while sitting on her Daddy's lap. Ray Jr. wasn't one to sit still for very long so she didn't have to contend with him for that position. She'd tell anyone that'd listen about how she was going to drive the Seabiscuit all by herself someday.

As Lou stepped over next to Ray, he slipped an arm around her waist and drew her close. This was the one he'd almost let get away and without her, well, he didn't want to think about the road not traveled...better to focus on their life here in Homer, at the end of the road.

THE END

Together in the Wild

Description: Former building contractor, Graham, has escaped to the Alaskan Bush after a messy divorce. He builds a single room cabin and takes up the Bush life near a native village. He's learning that surviving in the wild is a lot harder than it looks.

He's desperately working to get enough wood cut and split before winter comes when his friend, an Athabaskan elder named Ravensong, brings Graham some mail that will change his life forever.

The pressures in Graham's predicament keep mounting, until an intern named Ashley throws him a lifeline which he desperately needs. Ashley can only hope that Graham will see the situation for what it really is and do what needs to be done.

Renee Hart

Chapter 1

Graham stared at the broken chain for several minutes as he worked through his next move. There was a time, not so long ago, when he would have thrown down the busted tool in disgust and stormed away in anger. He liked to think he was past such childish behavior, but there was just enough doubt left in him to make him wonder when things went wrong. An old acquaintance used to say, "Sure, people can change, but not that much." and then he'd snicker as if it was the best joke ever told.

Busting his chainsaw wasn't on his list of things to do before winter came storming his way. At this point, he figured he had about half the firewood he needed to make it until spring. Without a chainsaw he wasn't going to be setting any records cutting down trees and hacking them up into pieces he could maul. His nearest neighbor, Ravensong, had warned him to buy spare parts for his tools. The problem was that spare parts didn't always fit into a budget with barely enough room for simple things like....food.

With one end of the chain wrapped tightly around the spindle and the other end pinched in the gap of the fallen tree, Graham was faced with the problem of how to rescue the saw without doing further damage to it. He knew his cutting techniques were pretty lame, as he tackled trees far beyond his skills with tools not built for the demands he placed on them.

His former life as a building contractor included a lavish budget for the best tools available in the marketplace. Breaking an expensive saw meant little more than losing a handful of nails back then. Here in the Alaskan bush, losing a handful of nails could mean the difference between a rock solid roof and one that flapped in the wind all winter long. It wasn't like you could run down to your local hardware store and pick up some spares any time you felt like having a jaunt.

Poking and prodding the mess he'd created wasn't revealing any way to work the chain free from the tree. Settling back on his heels, he closed his eyes and pushed away every ounce of worry, fear and distress that came at his mind. Ravensong told him the answer to every problem was here in God's creation. A person just needed to clear away all the confusion and noise in their head and learn how to listen.

As the sounds of the birds worked their way into his head, he reached a little deeper until he could hear the wind whispering in the trees and brush around him. The distant sound of a barking dog drew his attention home, but he let go of that thought. It wasn't time for him to go home yet. His cart wasn't full. Not finding anything in the darkness behind his eyelids, he opened his eyes and looked around the area again.

Focusing on the chainsaw, he realized that if he loosened the paddle from the chainsaw, the chain itself would be free. It might not give him a way to get the chain out of the tree, but it would save the chainsaw from any further damage. He loosened the two bolts holding it in place and almost laughed as the paddle slipped free of the chain and in the process released the chainsaw from its precarious position beneath the damaged tree.

With the chainsaw out of the way, Graham saw how to move the far end of the log he was cutting. This simple move released the chain, leaving him with a broken chain link to resolve and nothing more. Wiping the sweat away from his brow, he gave into the small sense of satisfaction that came when he fixed a problem without a tantrum. These were small steps, but every one counted as he looked for the evidence to prove he was clearly a new man.

Every day he overcame one of his old ways became a day to celebrate in his new life. Coming to Alaska was originally intended as an escape from everything that was wrong with his world. Unfortunately, his life out here in the bush had a way of bringing all those wrong things into a very different kind of focus. It hadn't taken too long to learn how the problems that brought him here were still very much a part of him. He didn't escape from a single thing on this journey. It was all just part of the baggage he carried along with him.

Gathering up the pieces of his chainsaw, he loaded his

cart with them and the few chunks of cut wood. It made a pitiful load for a day's work, but he whistled cheerfully as he headed off down the trail towards home. Tonight, he would find a way to fix the chain and tomorrow would be a fresh start. *There was no reason for him to be upset*, he reminded himself sternly. *All was well.*

The sounds of his sled dog team barking and yipping drew him through the tightly packed trees. He didn't like bringing them out into the woods when he was cutting firewood. The dogs loved running down rabbit trails and harassing squirrels as he worked, but they were blissfully unaware of the danger of falling trees. A near death experience finally convinced him they were better off staying home.

Saber, who was supposed to be his lead dog, was almost killed when a misdirected tree bounced off another and fell close enough to the dog to knock him head over heels. By the time Graham reached Saber, he was up and shaking himself from head to tail looking pretty confused about his tumble. Except for a few nasty scrapes, he was unharmed, but Graham's nerves were shot for the rest of that day.

Graham was interested in having every part of the Alaska wilderness experience, and dog sledding seemed like an important part of that vision. When he arrived in Alaska and found a place to call *home,* he'd dutifully bought an old dog sled and four dogs intending to train them to be a crack team. He was assured by the breeder that Saber was born and bred to be a champion lead dog. Somebody apparently forgot to clue the dog into this little factoid. He was much better at herding the other dogs than he was at leading them along a trail.

Without a leader to direct the team, the four dogs quickly found interesting ways to tangle themselves up as they headed in different directions. Graham spent more time shouting expletives than commands, and the dogs were always confused. He eventually realized he was as much a part of the problem as the dogs. Confessing to himself that he didn't know anything about sled dogs or how to train a team was the first step towards a better relationship with them.

When he became completely honest about his dogs, they were less inclined to pull a dog sled and more interested in their favorite spot on his bed. It didn't take him too long to realize his dogs were all in the category of 'rejects'. He figured those kennel owners saw him coming a mile away as they extolled the virtues of the dogs they sold him, knowing full well those dogs were useless for anything beyond being chowhounds.

Eventually, he parked the sled in the corner of the yard hoping to sell it someday. After a couple of winters sitting in its parking spot, one of the runners pulled itself loose and the squirrels chewed off all the lashings. Now, it was only good as a place for stacking up logs to be cut for special uses.

In the cold of the first winter, the dogs quickly abandoned their private little *shacks* in exchange for a spot next to the wood stove. From there, they eventually squeezed themselves onto the corners of his bed and the five of them slept cozily through the cold winter nights. Graham didn't want to think about what his relationship with his dogs would mean if he was ever again romantically involved. *What woman would be willing to share her bed with me and four rangy dogs that snored?* he wondered more than once.

As he drew closer to home, the frantic sounds of barking and whining increased. It was clear to anyone listening someone or something was coming. Out here, he was fairly confident that *someone* was just him. There wasn't another human being within miles of his homestead most of the time. The dogs served as his welcoming committee whenever he left them and came back. He dared not think of what would happen to them if he didn't.

As the trail opened up into the clearing he called *home*, Graham took a deep breath as he carefully scanned the area. While it was a pretty sure thing the dogs were just barking in anticipation of his arrival, it wasn't a good idea to depend on that. He'd seen enough bear and moose poking around the edges of the clearing when he was safe inside the cabin. It was always at the back of his mind to avoid walking into the clearing and finding it already occupied.

So far, he'd managed to keep up a good relationship with his *neighbors*. They minded their business and he kept out of their way. Taking care of his trash and burning anything that might draw the bears to investigate as a possible food source was a priority. The moose were fairly shy of him and weren't inclined to spend much time in his clearing. His garden was well-fenced and the dog enclosure next to it served fair warning to them. Any smaller animals were on their own as far as he was concerned, as the dogs loved giving chase to whatever happened along.

Seeing nothing unusual in the area, he pulled his cart over to the wood stacked along one wall of his cabin. The dogs were frantically barking to be let out as soon as they caught sight of him. He hurried over to set them free hoping they'd run off some energy and let him get some work done before the end of the day. Of course, each dog needed a scratch and a belly rub accompanied by an explanation of why he'd left them behind.

Saber waited for the other three to finish before adding his complaint and getting his back scratched. It was a silly routine, but it was one thing that made him feel like he actually mattered to four other living beings. He knew letting the dogs stand in the place of his two children was a cheap substitution, but he had no other recourse. Their mother used every legal resource at hand to make sure he would never be a part of their lives again. He'd finally convinced himself she was right and they were better off without him.

Admitting to himself that he missed them was one step closer to giving in to the thought of how much he'd failed at being a husband and a father. It was better out here not to think about the past and stay focused on what needed to be done to survive what lay ahead. Winter was always coming or upon him and this was life or death. Nothing else needed to be given any room to trip him up.

***

Supper wasn't fancy out here in the bush. He wasn't so far off the grid that he couldn't get to a store, but everything he bought had to be packed in on his back or his cart. Having a working sled dog team might have made things easier, but since what he had worked for his needs, he figured there was no demand for improvement.

His gardening skills were sub-par and he just barely managed to grow salad greens, cabbage and kale with a few carrots and tomatoes if he was diligent. The nearby river provided plenty of fish for the taking and a moose kill or caribou lasted a long time between him and the dogs. The dogs added some of their own variety by snacking on whatever squirrels or rabbits fell into their clutches. He was glad for that as it saved his greens from the little '*fur-bites*' as he liked to call them.

He figured with his small needs and limited cooking skills, he was doing okay. If he wanted to call a can of beans *supper*, that's what he did. This was just a part of his new lifestyle and he never really needed a burger and fries anyway. He did occasionally miss out on having a big plate of fried chicken with mashed potatoes and gravy, but that was a part of another life. *Food was simply the fuel needed to get through the day's work*, he would remind himself when those memories started to get to him.

After supper, he'd sit at the table and work on whatever little project had taken up residence on it. Tonight it would be the chain from his saw that held his attention until he was sure sleep would hold him captive until dawn. It didn't pay for him to go to bed too early. Lying there awake gave him too much time to think about things best left unthought-of, and he was careful to avoid doing that.

Chapter 2

Graham was poking what was passing for breakfast around on his plate when Pylon gave out a little whine. Figuring the little beggar was looking for a handout, he didn't bother to look up. Feeding these four off his plate would put him in a world of hurt as he barely managed to eat enough to keep up his own strength at times.

The sound of a throat clearing right in front of him had him on his feet and reaching for his gun in one swift move. As his eyes met those of his friend, Ravensong, he was embarrassed to realize the man had been standing there for several minutes already. He could never figure out why his stupid dogs never barked when this Athabascan Native was headed their way. They always barked when he was coming home. Everyone else coming down that trail received a loud welcoming chorus of barks and howling.

Ravensong walked into the clearing as if he owned the place and the dogs recognized his authority. It drove him literally crazy when he thought about it. It's not like the guy came once a week, or even once a month, but when he did, it was the same every time.

"Brother! I don't know how you do that, but I wish you'd either stop it or tell me," Graham growled at his friend. "It makes me feel stupid when my dogs have more respect for a stranger than for the guy they sleep with every night."

"You sleep with your dogs?" Ravensong asked, wrinkling his nose in disgust.

Graham shoveled in the last bite of his breakfast and ignored the question.

Ravensong tossed a very large packet on the ground in front of him. The bold blue and white colors of the USPS tape barely held the bundle in check. When one of the seams burst, mail slid out at an alarming pace and scattered across the dirt. Graham groaned at the mess.

"Grayling says there's no point in having a post office box if you're not going to come in and clear it out once in a while. She can't hold this stuff forever, you know."

"It's not like I get any real mail anyway," Graham grumbled. "I'm willing to bet everything in that pile is either marked 'Resident' or some other junk mail descriptor."

"You're lucky I'm not a betting man or I'd take you up on that and you'd owe me big time. I happen to know for a fact Grayling tossed all that extraneous junk away to make room for this fire starter, and you should be grateful to her cause she'd get in trouble if anyone knew she did that for you."

Graham reached out and grabbed the nearest pile of mail and began sorting through it. Sure enough, every credit card offer and discount mailer was addressed to him personally. He wondered how they'd managed to link his name and post office box here in Alaska to the man he used to be back in Illinois. Even way out here in the bush, the system managed to keep their clutches on his life.

Knowing this was a pointless exercise when everything here was just going straight into the burn bin unopened, he barely focused on the return addresses flashing by as he flipped through the envelopes.

Most of his attention was on Ravensong as he strolled around the clearing checking on Graham's progress. He would have been embarrassed to admit he was hoping for some nod of recognition or a word of praise on the work he had accomplished. His own father had been stingy with such words and quick to find fault with anything he was doing. He'd given up hope of pleasing the man by the time he was fifteen. By then he knew he was a disappointment.

He paused in his sorting as Ravensong picked up the chain saw and noted the mend on the chain. Picking up a file laying nearby, he scraped a couple of edges on the mend, smoothing them out and then laid it aside.

"Good repair," was all he said, but it was *gold* in Graham's ears.

Noting the unfamiliar feel of heavy paper, (the kind lawyer's like to use), Graham looked down at the envelope in his hands. Sure enough. It was from that fancy legal firm his ex-wife liked so much. He sat there feeling like that moment when the sky is heavily overcast and there's this tiny little gap that lets the sun peek through and then just as quickly it's gone again.

Ravensong caught the change in the air and turned to look at him.

"What is it?"

"I don't know."

"Well, are you going to open it or do you have some other method of divining what's inside?"

"Maybe I should just toss it in the burn bin with the rest and say I never got it..."

Graham turned the thick letter over and over in his hands as his friend watched him struggle with an avalanche of conflicting emotions. He thought all of this was over and behind him. It had been more than five years since their divorce and the custody hearings. She'd gotten everything including his business, their home and most importantly, their family. *What more could she be looking for from me at this point?* he wondered to himself.

His hands tightened on the letter as his inner battle grew. The emotions raging inside him looked for an outlet and he considered ripping it up into little pieces and casting it to the wind. The image tailing behind that thought broke the grip of the anger and he chuckled. As his friend watched him carefully, he could only chuckle harder, picturing his dogs running about the clearing chasing little scraps of legal paper as if they were errant butterflies let loose among them.

"I'd ask what was so funny, but it's pretty clear to me

you don't really know."

Graham looked up at his friend with a big grin on his face and tried to figure out a response. Coming up with nothing, he realized Ravensong was right. Until he opened this letter and read it, he had no idea what it contained. Heck, maybe she'd had her lawyers track him down to say it had all been a big misunderstanding. *Yeah, right. Good luck with that angle*, he couldn't help thinking. *I couldn't forgive myself. Why would anyone else?*

Pulling out his pocket knife, he slit the end of the envelope and pulled out a sheaf of paperwork. Carefully, unfolding the stack, he quickly scanned the top letter. Pausing at the bottom, he shuffled through the rest of the papers and then went back to read the letter again slowly.

Ravensong was silent as he repeated the same process two more times before he looked up with tears in his eyes.

"My ex-wife is dead. She died of cancer in March. This is her will giving me full custody of our two children and enough money to take care of them for the rest of our lives..."

Graham paused and swallowed hard as he considered the ramifications of all of this for him. He was a father again, just like that.

"She died in March?"

"Uh huh."

"You do realize it's June? Is there some kind of expiration date at work here?"

Graham froze at the question and looked back at the papers in his hand. Finding nothing to clear up the matter, he fell to the ground and began sorting through the rest of the mail. It didn't take long to find two more letters from the legal firm, two from his ex-wife and another from his former in-laws.

Clearly, a great deal of effort was put into resolving this while Graham remained blissfully unaware of the tragedy. He checked the mailing dates hoping to find the most recent information. The letter from his former in-laws won the prize and he slit it open. Scanning over the letter, he groaned in dismay and hurried to grab a pack from inside the door.

"You said it's June. What's the date? Do you know?" he asked as he grabbed a few things close at hand and stuffed them in the pack.

"Of course. It's the seventeenth. Why? Are you going somewhere?"

As Graham rounded up the dogs and rushed them into their pen, he ground out the words from a tightly clenched jaw, "My ex-sister-in-law is on her way here as we speak with my two children. She's supposed to be in the village today!"

If Ravensong had a startled expression, Graham figured this was as close to it as he was ever going to get. It was a two hour walk to the village. He knew it wouldn't be good for the woman to arrive without Graham there to meet them. She would probably get the wrong impression right off the bat and make more trouble for him.

"No worries," Ravensong said with a grin. "My UTV is just over the hill."

Graham looked at his friend and shook his head. The guy was full of surprises. In five years, he still didn't know all that much about him and everything he did know, didn't add up. The only thing he could be sure of was that when there was a need, Ravensong would be there with a solution. He'd proved that out so many times since they'd met, Graham had long since stopped counting.

Chapter 3

As they headed off to the UTV, Graham thought back to the first time he'd met the lanky Athabascan. His first winter in Alaska, he'd barely gotten the cabin built before winter was upon him. He hadn't cut enough firewood to keep the place warm for more than a couple of days. Trying to keep up with the demand kept him out in the woods for long hours, and the cold was brutal. It didn't take long before he fell sick and by the time his neighbor came along and found him, he was in dire straits.

Ravensong didn't say much in those days. He just showed up one day with an old woman and a load of firewood. The woman was a healer and his mother-in-law, though Graham didn't learn that until much later. She slept on a pallet on the floor and spooned some nasty concoction into his mouth every hour until the fever broke.

When he finally realized he was still alive and warm, he'd lost track of time. The woman stayed until he was able to care for himself, and Ravensong checked in on him at least once a week for the rest of the winter. Graham knew he owed his life to the two of them and it was a debt that could never be repaid. He'd tried to speak about it once, but Ravensong clucked his tongue and turned away from him. *Some things weren't meant for talking*, the man said as he walked away. Graham never brought it up again.

The UTV cut the trip to the village down to twenty minutes. From Graham's perspective hanging onto the back of the bucking four-wheeler, it was a rough ride. Under ordinary circumstances, he'd have happily made the hike on his own two feet. He wasn't sure if the need for speed was his current crisis or this was his friend's normal way to drive.

Ravensong was as wild a rider as any teenager in the village and drove without a care through grabby branches and thorny bushes. He actually laughed and shouted with joy in a few places. Every stream or puddle was attacked with enthusiasm and Graham was sure there were a few detours to catch at least a couple of them. The two of them were splattered with mud within the first couple of miles.

It was a relief to finally come in sight of civilization where the village elder regained a sense of decorum and started driving responsibly. Their relief was short-lived, however, as they came in sight of the building that housed the post office, community center and grocery store. The dusty, battered limousine parked next to the weathered building looked crudely out of time and place on the gravel street.

Graham wondered how his sister-in-law had managed to find someone willing to drive her all the way out here in

that when he spotted her. She was waving her arms around like a windmill and screaming at the hapless fellow charged with security in the village. The look on his face never wavered as he stared at her pathetic performance. He'd seen plenty of screaming, hysterical women acting in drunken rage in his day. A wise man did his best not to provoke a woman on a rant.

They both looked up as the UTV roared to a stop next to them. As her eyes took in Graham and his companion in their filthy state, they narrowed with contempt and hatred. Both men felt their guts tighten as they prepared themselves for a full-on assault from this *she-lion*.

Graham had the thought to save his friend and send him off before she launched her attack, but the words died in his throat. The two of them stood there frozen in their tracks by the look on her face. For a long moment, no one spoke and just when the suspense got to the point of unbearable, the door to the limo opened. The four of them turned their attention to the car. Graham's breath caught in his throat as his son and daughter climbed out. The two of them stood there hand in hand staring at their father.

The driver also chose that moment to step out of the car and came around to the rear and opened the trunk. He calmingly began unloading a small mountain of luggage as if nothing out of the ordinary was happening.

Ignoring the others, Ravensong went over and knelt down in front of the two children. Speaking to them quietly, he introduced himself and asked them their names. Focusing their attention on him, the children answered him politely while watching their aunt from the corners of their eyes. It wouldn't do to draw her ire by doing something inappropriate. Of course, in this strange place, it was a matter of confusion to them as to what was actually considered appropriate.

"Are you our father?" Lacey asked.

At that moment, Celia decided to take command of the situation and stamped towards the three of them.

"Get away from those children! You filthy..." she demanded.

Her words died as she came within arm's length and Ravensong stood to his feet.

Graham would have dismissed what happened next as a bit of dust in his eye or a slip of imagination except for the look of fear that passed over her face as she fell back two steps. His friend wasn't a tall or imposing man in any way, but when he stood up to face her, he literally towered over her with the shape and the bulk of an enraged grizzly. The illusion was complete with raised claws and a mouth gaping open in a roar showing glistening teeth.

To make it seem even more extraordinary, his children had shifted to put the 'grizzly' between themselves and their aunt. It was clear to them which was the least danger.

As fast as it happened, Graham barely had time to take a step forward when he saw only his friend and his children

Renee Hart

facing a silent woman.

She turned her attention to the pile of luggage the limo driving had unloaded.

"Not those! You stupid man! All of the pink luggage is mine! Put it back into the car! I'm not staying here!"

The driver hurried to comply as she advanced on him, preferring a weaker target. The paltry mound left on the ground would easily fit on Graham's cart and he wondered why she'd even bothered to bring anything at all for them.

Turning her attention to Graham from the safety of the limo, she seemed to consider her parting words carefully.

"The filthy man over there, that's your father."

The children looked at Graham as she got back into the car and slammed the door. The limo driver shut the trunk and made as if to tip his hat to them before he hurried to get in himself. The car started and began to move away before anyone could react.

It hadn't gone very far when the brakes were suddenly put on and her window opened. Holding Lacey's doll by one leg she threw it out of the car violently. The four of them watched as the baby doll spun head over heels and smacked into a tree. The resulting crash smashed the doll's delicate porcelain head into a dozen pieces. The car continued on its way as if nothing had happened.

Tears dripped down Lacey's face as she stood there holding her brother's hand. She made no move to collect her doll, so Ravensong walked over and gathered up the remains. He carefully wrapped the bundle in a handkerchief he'd pulled from his pocket to hide the broken face.

Graham continued to watch the limo pick its way down the rough gravel road. He was amused to note one of the shocks or a leaf spring was broken on the right rear. This ensured his sister-in-law was taking a beating for the rest of her trip. He was surprised at the calm that surrounded him.

In his past, her actions would have set off a rage in him that would have resulted in bodily harm for someone. Now he could only wonder at the wickedness oozing from his former sister-in-law from every pore. The woman had no boundaries of decency.

He'd been warned by his friends about the twin sisters with the "Jekyll and Hyde" personalities. His ex-wife was gentle and sweet and kind. Her sister was anything but and did everything she could to break them apart. He was sure it was her efforts that finally turned his wife against him. Given, he had piled up the charges against himself fully on his own merit and couldn't blame anyone else for that. However, the final resolution had all the hallmarks of the revenge of a spurned woman. *She'd gotten her due in the guise of helping out her poor little sister*, he reckoned.

Turning his attention back to more immediate matters, he listened as Ravensong explained to Lacey about the special doll hospital that existed right here in this tiny native village. The man assured the little girl her doll would be restored to better than new if she was patient. Somehow the six-year old entered into the faith of the man without question and she actually smiled at him.

His son, Devin wasn't so easily convinced. He stood there stony-faced as everything played out around him. The pathetic pile of bags and boxes laying in the middle of the road represented what was left of his life. He was three when his father left and two men standing before him, well, one was as complete a stranger as the other. Being rid of his aunt was a relief, but even in her rages, he knew her.

Graham walked over to his children and knelt down in front of them. Everything in him wanted to wrap his arms around them and gather them in, but he knew that wouldn't be welcome at this point.

"Hello Lacey, Devin," he said as brightly as he could muster. "Welcome to Alaska. I'm Graham, your father."

"You're my real daddy?" Lacey asked in a trembling voice.

Graham nodded as the lump in his throat threatened to choke him. He was surprised when she let go of her brother's hand and threw her arms around his neck. Hugging him tightly, she clung to him for several minutes before letting go and stepping back.

"You're awful dirty," she said, attempting to brush the mud from his shoulders.

"Well, if my trip here was any indication of my friend's

driving skills, you're going to be about the same before we get you two home."

Graham said the last as he cast an eye at Ravensong. He knew the elder had clearly caught his meaning when he turned away to hide his grin.

"We're going to need a little help with all this," Ravensong said as he turned to go into the community center. He managed to round up a couple of people with UTV's and trailers to help them haul everything out in one trip while Graham emptied the little store's shelves of every can of ravioli and anything else he figured kids might eat as part of the load.

"Are you two hungry?" Graham asked wondering when they'd eaten last.

"Devin's always hungry," Lacey piped up with a grin at her brother.

Graham looked at his son for confirmation, but the boy refused to meet his eyes.

***

Graham groaned as he dropped the last load of stuff to the ground in front of the cabin. Having spent an entire day dealing with an unexpected and inexplicable situation left him mentally and physically spent. His emotions were simply raw. He figured if he wasn't so exhausted, he'd be in a panic over this turn of events.

His two children mostly sat on logs near the front door and watched him come and go for over an hour. The dogs welcomed their new playmates and would occasionally interrupt their own play to run from one to the other trying to get them to throw sticks or give out a scratch. The children were happy to oblige.

Ravensong stayed in the clearing and watched from a corner of the yard as he whittled on a piece of wood. Occasionally, he'd pull something from his pack and examine it carefully before putting it back. He didn't try to engage the children, giving them time to work out their surroundings.

They hadn't been too impressed with the outhouse at first, but Graham pointed out how the spring-fed sink worked by gravity. A quick demonstration made them laugh as ice cold water splashed forth freely while they washed their hands and faces.

Somehow the return trip to the cabin managed to involve a lot less mud and Graham had his own suspicions on that account. The children only needed a quick wash to be clean. He was going to need a whole lot more in the way of a scrubbing, including his clothes.

Taking a moment to sit down on a log of his own, Graham pulled the packet of letters out of his bag. *I really need a word with their mother right now*, he thought to himself. He knew her options for the children's care had been limited. Her parents lived in a retirement home.

There was no place for the children with them even if they had the ability to care for them. His parents were dead and he had no other family.

Graham was relieved she had enough sense to not leave them in the care of her twin sister. He wouldn't leave one of his dogs in that woman's hands. That left only the state to care for his children and Illinois had less than a stellar reputation there. The system was understaffed, underfunded and over-capacity.

Slitting open the envelope, he found himself engulfed in the memory of her scent. The woman rarely wore perfume, but she never needed any in his opinion. She smelled like a cool breeze on a hot summer's day. He took a deep breath as he carefully unfolded the sheaf of papers. Taking in the first few paragraphs, his eyes filled with tears and he quickly refolded the sheets, stuffing them into his pocket. *This isn't the time to do this*, he thought gruffly.

With a quick look around the clearing he caught the children yawning as they drooped on their perches. He realized it was long past time for them to be in bed. The summer sun made it weird to keep an ordinary day/night schedule. Ravensong was still hard at work in his corner of the yard. The dogs were all stretched out doing their own version of a nap.

Graham took a hard look at the cabin as he considered sleeping arrangements. Clearly two more bodies, even if they were only children, weren't going to fit on his bed.

Renee Hart

Subtracting himself by moving to a pallet on the floor probably wasn't much of an improvement for them.

When he built the cabin, he'd originally planned to create a loft bedroom for himself. He'd built the loft and a ladder to get to it, but it never made any sense for him to be going up and down just to sleep. It's not like he needed the space where he slept downstairs for something else. The entire place contained just enough furniture to meet his needs, a table and two chairs, a platform bed and an empty bookshelf.

He'd put in a counter with a sink and a two burner propane stove that he didn't use. He'd never gotten around to buying a tank of propane for it, and cooking on the woodstove was too easy. A couple of shelves loosely nailed to the wall held his few dishes and various cans of food.

He had to blink his eyes a couple of times to clear away the mist, but suddenly he saw just how precariously his life was balanced on mere subsistence. He'd created nothing of value here. This was not a home. It was little more than a glorified camping spot and the children needed more from him. The weight of this undertaking nearly took him off his feet as it hit him hard.

As he mentally staggered, Ravensong came up and stood next to him.

"Life is given to us one day at a time, my friend," he said quietly. "This one's over."

Handing Graham the bundle in his hand, he turned and

started to walk away. Feeling panic at the thought of being alone with the children, he turned to call the elder back, but the man was no longer in the clearing. Looking to the left and the right, he almost laughed out loud at his friend's strange abilities. The Athabascan came and went almost as if he were a spirit already.

Graham quickly pushed away that thought as a shiver went down his spine. Turning over the bundle, he found himself looking into the delicately hand-carved face of Lacey's doll.

Taking his friend's advice, he put the children to bed and made a pallet for himself on the floor. They were asleep before he was done. Remembering the doll, he carefully placed it under Lacey's arm as she slept. He couldn't help but notice the doll's face was a perfect image of his late wife.

Renee Hart

Chapter 4

The next few weeks, Graham stumbled from one challenge to the next with the children. He learned their likes and dislikes, sometimes in unexpected ways. They tested his patience and resolve as the two of them struggled with the lack of structure in his world. Morning cartoons and afternoon video games bracketed their mealtimes in their old life and without these, the children were cast adrift in a sea of meaningless time. He couldn't even figure out a way to set a real bedtime for them.

Devin still wasn't talking to him unless he was forced to do so and Lacey talked all the time. Her constant chatter made up for her brother's silence, but most of what she talked about, Graham didn't understand. He noticed both children were more inclined to listen when Ravensong talked to them.

Graham partially divided the loft into two sleeping areas so Devin could have some privacy but leaving him within a whisper of his sister. At night, he would lay below them and listen to Devin tell her stories until she fell asleep. He couldn't make out the words, just the comforting drone soothing her to believe all was well with them.

The dogs couldn't climb the ladder, much to their dismay, and stayed below with him until he built a small staircase against the back wall. Pylon and Driver quickly learned how to negotiate the narrow stairs while Saber and Lance stayed below with him. This division worked out well for him especially and he slept the better for it. He found it was smarter to wake up clear-headed as this gave him a chance to get ahead of their morning scramble. Otherwise, he'd wake to find six pairs of hungry eyes regarding him balefully from around his bed.

He was still fighting against the approach of winter and had to get back to the task of cutting firewood. The children were too young to leave at the cabin alone and he feared having them out in the woods with him. The thought of them wandering off was his biggest fear at first, but he quickly learned the one thing his dogs were really good at doing. They knew how to find the children and loved playing hide and seek with them. The dogs took to the children like ducks to water and soon they were inseparable.

Graham finally determined his best option was to begin by widening the path to his clearing and keep the children and dogs at home. He knew there wasn't enough firewood in this for another season, but he'd deal with next year when it came. He'd barely maintained a walking path since he didn't have anything more than his cart. Making the path wide enough for a UTV would give him plenty of firewood and keep him close to home.

Sorting out his financial situation took some finagling,

Renee Hart

but the end result gave him enough money right off the bat to get his own UTV with a trailer, some furnishings and a few other things with a solid nest egg to fall back on if needed. He felt he'd been given back everything he'd lost and more. *It's the closest I'll ever get to being given a second chance in life*, he reminded himself often.

✱✱✱

One of the biggest changes in Graham's lifestyle was his new commitment to eating healthier meals. The children expected to eat three times a day and had clearly defined ideas on what foods constituted breakfast, lunch and dinner. He tried to get away with serving cereal for supper or sandwiches for breakfast a few times, but Lacey was profoundly upset.

He understood her need for 'normal' was hyper-sensitive at this point and decided to try harder to meet her expectations.

Devin was a lot more flexible about such things. He was happy to eat marshmallows and peanut butter sandwiches all day. He wasn't as keen on canned beans as his father unless they were warmed over a campfire. Graham was happy to oblige since it got him out of cooking, but had enough parenting left in him to feel guilty about all the shortcuts.

Two more mouths to feed and a wider variety of food

needs required a now-weekly trip to the village to lay in supplies. The three of them quickly advanced to a first name basis with the people who worked in the small grocery store. They also managed to meet everyone living in the village after about a dozen trips as Lacey was a shameless Miss Busybody.

She'd introduce herself to anyone she didn't know, much to Graham's amusement and Devin's embarrassment. Her best skill was in remembering everyone she met and greeting them by name on their next visit. Everyone was amazed and delighted with her outgoing mannerisms.

On one of their weekly visits, a young woman came into the store while they were checking out. Lacey promptly stepped in front of her and held out her hand.

"Hello, I'm Lacey. This is my brother, Devin. We live with our father in a bush," she said proudly.

The woman knelt down in front of her and took her hand.

"Hello, Lacey. My name's Ashley and I've been wanting to meet you. I've heard so much about you."

"You have? Why? Who's been talking about me?" Lacey demanded in a mocked-up show of outrage as she looked around the store.

Ashley leaned back on her heels and laughed at Lacey's antics.

"Well, you do know that two children *living in a bush*

with their father is big news in a little town like this, don't you?"

Ashley winked at Graham as she said this. He felt a tingle run up his spine.

"Besides, it's my business to know. I'm the coordinator for Bush School," Ashley said as she stood up. "It's my job to help people get the resources they need for home-schooling or on-line education, things like that."

Graham stood there feeling like a complete idiot. He was stuck in the worries of establishing simple routines like eating and washing clothes and bodies. The idea of school was still out there in the vague future like the end of summer vacation. Of course, his children needed an education and it wasn't like they could go to the village school on the sunny yellow school bus. That didn't exist out here.

Catching the look on his face and the shadow of fear in his eyes, Ashley reached in her bag and pulled out a card.

"Don't worry. There's plenty of time to get things set up before school starts. Just give me a call when you're ready."

"I, uh......I don't have a phone," he stammered and turned red.

"Oh. Okay. Well, do you have time to step over to my makeshift office and talk about your children's education?" she asked politely.

Graham felt trapped and uncertain about his response.

Something needed to be done, but he didn't have a clue on this matter. He felt like he'd just stepped off the bank onto an iceberg in a swiftly moving river. As the floor rocked beneath him, he realized Lacey was yanking on the leg of his pants.

"Daddy, Daddy, please can we have some ice cream?" she asked over and over as he stood lost in thought.

He nodded absently as he pulled some money from his pocket.

While the children ate their treat, Graham listened to Ashley's spiel about the resources he had available to help him with their education. She opened a file on each of the children on her laptop and made some recommendations based on their ages. As she talked, Graham relaxed finding her calm manner and casual attitude refreshing. It had been a long time since he'd felt comfortable around a woman.

By the end of their meeting, Graham had a large box of books and other school materials to begin their schooling in the bush. On top of the pile was a parent's handbook to guide him in getting started. He headed out to the UTV feeling vaguely confident in this new venture.

The real boost came at the end of the meeting when Ashley assured him, she would be with him every step of the way. Her words resonated in his mind all the way home.

As Graham was unloading their latest haul from the UTV's trailer, he noticed Devin wasn't lending a hand. Calling for his son to come outside and help, Graham looked around the clearing to see where the boy had gone. Lacey was happily playing with the dogs. She wasn't interested in her brother's whereabouts.

Checking the cabin, Graham finally heard the sound of sniffling coming from the loft. Poking his head upstairs, he found Devin sitting in the corner with his head down.

"Devin, why aren't you helping me unload the trailer?" he asked quietly.

"I don't want to," he mumbled.

"Why not? You always help me unload."

"I just want to go home," he mumbled.

Graham didn't know what to say to this. Knowing this moment was coming did nothing to prepare him for when it arrived. Devin hadn't said anything when their aunt dumped them in the village. He didn't complain about the cabin or the food. He talked to Lacey, mostly when Graham wasn't around and he talked to the dogs. He listened to Ravensong and sometimes, he'd ask him a question, but he rarely spoke to his father.

When he did, it was usually to ask for more cereal or another sandwich. The only important thing he'd ever asked was to be taught how to drive the UTV. Graham indulged him every now and then out on the trail by letting him sit in front and steer. He was too weak to fully control the vehicle at this point. The best he could manage was to move it slowly forward on his own.

Graham figured the boy had very few memories of the time before he'd left. He had no idea what he'd been told in the intervening years. His mother's letters didn't reveal much about what she'd told the children to explain his absence from their lives. He expected their aunt might have had a few choice words to say about him, but her effect on the children was limited. It appears she'd only stepped into the picture when her parents grew desperate to locate him on the children's behalf.

"Devin, you are home. This is your home now," he said quietly as he came in and sat down next to his son.

"No! This is not my home and you're not my father!"

"Son, why do you think I'm not your father?" Graham asked quietly.

"My father was a monster with a voice that roared when he spoke. I remember...," Devin said ending in a half-sob.

Graham sat quietly as he contemplated his son's words. His boy was right. He was a monster back in those days and he yelled far more than he ever talked to anyone. In his mind, he flashed back to a scene over dinner where some little thing was wrong and he was yelling at his wife. He remembered catching sight of his son's face at the table. His eyes were big with terror as he stared at his father's rage. Graham had turned away from the look on his son's face that day seeing the reflection of his own childhood as he endured his own father's rants. All that anger over nothing and no way to take it back.

He searched his mind for some happy memory, something to reconnect him to his son. There weren't any happy family photos to pull out and no stories he could recollect. A tear slipped down his cheek as he struggled to find some way to make this right. His son was just as broken as Lacey's doll had been that day in the village. He wondered if Ravensong knew of a hospital nearby to fix broken childhoods. He could sure use some help himself.

"Devin, you're right. Your father *was* a monster, but that monster is gone," Graham said gently. "I don't know how to make your bad memories go away, but I do know how to make good ones now. I am your father and I love you."

He reached out to touch his son, but Devin shied away from his hand. Graham thought it best to give him some time alone and headed back down to finish unloading the trailer. He was nervous about leaving Lacey outside on her own for too long. He came downstairs to find his worst fear realized as there was no sign of his daughter or the dogs in the clearing. It was as if they'd vanished.

He looked about the area frantically and called for the dogs. No answer. He shouted for Lacey and listened to the silence. He ran around the cabin and partway down the trail looking for any sign of them. *I wasn't upstairs for that long*, he thought to himself in frustration. Running back to the cabin he found Devin standing in the doorway with a pale face.

"Your sister's playing hide and seek," Graham said trying to sound jovial, "come and help me find her!"

The two of them ran around the cabin in opposite directions and met again at the front. Graham kept calling for the dogs as they were more likely to come running at the sound of his voice. Devin called for his sister over and over as he ducked in and out of the trees on the paths they'd worn playing. She loved playing this game, but the dogs were always the best at finding them. Without a single dog, the two of them were on their own as they searched an ever-widening circle around the cabin.

They'd looked for over fifteen minutes when Lance came wandering back into the yard. He flopped down in front of the cabin and started licking his paws. Graham hurried over to check out the dog and noticed his feet were stained with blueberries. Calling for Devin, the two of them raced down the path to the nearest berry patch.

With branches slapping him in the face as he raced through the darkening forest, Graham prayed no bears were out hunting berries today. His chest hurt as he ran as fast as possible in the dim light looking for any sign of his daughter. He didn't stop to think of his gun strapped to the UTV back in the clearing.

Devin struggled to keep his father in sight. His short little legs were no match for Graham's and he soon found himself falling behind. He was relieved when Lance came up and walked beside him. *At least I'm not alone*, he thought with a shudder.

As Graham crested the rise, the sight of his dogs lying in a circle around Lacey was the first thing he saw. She lay on the ground unmoving and his heart jumped in fear. As he drew closer, the dogs rose to greet him with their usual joy, but he was focused on Lacey. He was relieved when she yawned and stretched. She was simply asleep.

He watched her for a moment as he struggled to regain his breath and calm his fears. With the dogs completely at ease, his concerns about bears were put to rest. Watching the gentle rise of her chest, he noted the blueberry stains around her mouth and all over her hands. She'd apparently eaten her fill.

As Lance came along to join the others, Graham turned to see Devin hurrying towards them. He realized that his hasty dash through the forest had left his son behind. The boy only had eyes for his sister and he ran straight over to shake her awake.

"We found you and you're a BAD girl!" Devin shouted at his startled sister.

Her eyes flew open and she stared at her brother. As his fear spilled over into anger, his voice rose and he shouted several more things at her before Graham took hold of his shoulder and turned him away. Lacey started to cry as Devin fought against his father's grip.

"Devin. Devin, look at me," Graham said gently as he knelt down in front of his son. "Lacey's okay. We don't need to scare her or be angry."

The little boy jerked away from his father and turned towards his sister.

"You don't understand," he wailed in anguish. "It's my job! Mommy made me promise to take care of her. It's my job!"

Grabbing Lacey's hand, he pulled her up from the ground and turned to go back to the cabin. The dogs fell in behind the two of them while Graham knelt there in the mud. He took a deep, shaky breath before rising to his feet to bring up the rear. The boy never wavered from the path and no one spoke along the way.

Chapter 5

Over the next few days, the two children were strangely quiet. Graham wasn't sure how to approach Devin's fears or his obligation to care for his sister. He was hoping for some wisdom to come along in the form of Ravensong, but his friend was inexplicably absent. They all went on pretending everything was okay though Graham happened on Devin scolding Lacey a couple of times. They'd go silent when he came into sight.

Hearing a UTV coming along the trail one morning, he opened the door expecting to find his friend. He was surprised to find himself looking into the blue eyes and muddy face of Ashley. He saw his friend, Ravensong grinning in the background. Without a doubt he was responsible for the mud on her, Graham realized with a grin of his own.

"Good morning," Ashley said brightly.

Graham was speechless as he considered his next move. Lacey saved him in that moment as she stepped forward and greeted their guest. As she was welcoming the woman, Graham moved to one side so Ashley could enter. As he did, his eyes swept the interior of the cabin. Groaning inside, he realized it would have been far better for them to go outside and greet their visitors. The place was a mess.

Ravensong took up his usual seat in the corner of the

yard. He rarely came inside the cabin on any of his visits, preferring to sit outside. Devin hurried to sit near him. Leaving the door open, Graham stepped outside also. The cabin felt crowded with Ashley inside. He could hear Lacey chattering as she gave Ashley the 'nickel' tour. The two of them stepped back into the yard and the dogs gathered around for their share of the attention as Lacey introduced them. The three males watched from the safety of their corners.

Addressing Graham, Ashley pulled a thick stack of workbooks from her backpack.

"I found some additional workbooks that I thought you might like to have for the children," she said. "The lessons are based on popular storybook characters."

She held them out to Graham. He took them awkwardly and stood there not knowing what to say.

"Have you had a chance to look at any of the stuff I gave you last week?" she asked, apparently unfazed by his lack of speech so far.

"Uh, no," he stammered. "I've been cutting firewood."

"Can I see what you brought?" Lacey asked holding out her hand for the books.

Graham handed them to his daughter and the two of them watched as Lacey sat down on her stump and sorted through the pile. As she read the titles of each workbook, Graham was amazed at her ability.

"You can read?" he asked in surprise.

"Of course. Everyone at Miss Mary's school can read," she quipped.

"Cannot!"

Everyone turned to look at Devin's angry face. He flushed and turned away.

Ashley went over and knelt down in front of him.

"What are you saying Devin?" she asked gently.

"Nothing," he said and turned further away from her.

She looked to Graham, but he had no idea what his son was referring to either. The children hadn't come with any books and until they'd run into Ashley, there weren't any children's books in the cabin. Graham hadn't thought about it until just this moment. He'd heard Devin tell Lacey stories every night. He'd never thought about where he'd learned the stories.

Ashley moved back to Lacey's side and pulled a small reader from the stack.

"Would you like me to read you a story?" she said as she sat down on a nearby stump.

Lacey bobbed her head up and down wildly. Graham moved to his woodpile and picked up his maul. He didn't know what else to do. Ravensong kept his seat as he whittled on a piece of wood while Devin watched him carefully.

Ashley read the short story in a voice just loud enough to draw Devin's attention. At first, he struggled to listen from his perch, but his father's work added just enough noise to make him miss key words. From the corner of her eye, Ashley watched him find ways to slip closer. By the end of the story, he was standing at her shoulder watching as she turned each page.

"Would you like to take a turn?" she asked him quietly.

He backed away.

"I would," Lacey chirped brightly.

Ashley handed her the book and pointed out her stopping place.

The little girl continued on without a flaw as the two of them listened. When she got to the end of the story, she closed it with a happy sigh.

"That was a good story," she said.

"Would you like to read for me?" Ashley asked Devin again.

"Devin can't read," Lacey said. "He doesn't like reading. It makes him angry."

"That's not true," Devin shouted as he ran over and pushed Lacey off her stump.

She fell to the ground in surprise and started to cry. Ashley was too shocked to move as Devin ran behind the cabin. Graham dropped his maul and ran over to check his daughter. Finding her unhurt, he followed his son's path to get this sorted out. He'd never seen the boy do anything to harm his sister before. If anything, he was extra careful around the little girl and always watched over her.

Finding the boy crouched down next to a log pile, Devin

cowered at the sight of his father's approach. His eyes were filled with tears.

Graham walked over and sat down on the ground next to his son.

"Devin, I'm not going to hurt you," he said gently, "but you know I can't let you hurt your sister. That's not okay."

The boy was silent.

"I really need for you to tell me what's going on," Graham continued. "I can't help you if I don't know what's wrong."

Devin just shook his head.

Ashley came around the corner of the cabin holding Lacey's hand. The little girl was chattering brightly as if nothing had happened. Devin watched their approach from the corner of his eye.

"I'm sorry, Devin," Lacey said kneeling down in front of him. "I didn't mean it. Will you come and play a game with us?"

Devin took his sister's hand and got up. The two of them headed back towards the front of the cabin leaving Graham alone with Ashley.

"Do you have any idea of what the problem is?" she asked.

"No. I haven't been a part of their lives for the last five years. He may have dis...dix... uh."

"Dyslexia?"

"Yeah, that's it. Runs in our family. I have it. My

father had it. Devin may have it too."

"Where did he start school?"

"I'm afraid I don't know that either. His mother and I didn't have any contact until she reached out from the grave and made me a father again."

Ashley looked at him strangely, but he was beyond making any more explanations. He turned and followed after the children.

"Graham."

He stopped but didn't turn back to look at her.

"Graham. I can help him. This is what I'm trained to do," Ashley said gently. "He doesn't have to suffer like you did..."

Graham's back stiffened as he fought against the urge to push her away. He'd been pushing this problem away his whole life. *And look where that's gotten me,* he thought to himself, *maybe I need to help Devin not to become a monster like me. Maybe it's time to admit that I need help with this, with my children...*

Turning back to look at Ashley's face, he saw the compassion in her eyes. He nodded and quickly moved towards the front of the cabin. He could hear her following, but she didn't speak anymore.

Before Ashley headed back to the village with Ravensong, she made a plan to come out and work with the children two days a week. When they came to the village for their weekly shopping trip, she'd set aside some time to work with them on her computer. It was only a small beginning, but somewhere deep in Graham's heart he felt a glimmer of hope.

***

Ashley was true to her word and showed up early to spend time with the children. She ran several tests disguised as games to determine their learning skills. They'd play together until it was time for lunch and then Graham would come and join them. He'd join in with some of the simple word games, but Ashley always took the lead.

In the evenings, Lacey would play teacher, much to the guys' amusement, and read them all a story. This was all done under the guise of *helping* Lacey with her homework to give Devin some much needed confidence and it seemed to be working.

After several weeks, the children looked forward to Ashley's visits and she was spending far more than a few hours a week with them. Graham had to admit even he was always listening for the sound of her UTV as he went about his chores. The firewood cache was growing a lot slower than it needed to be with winter coming, but he ignored it.

***

One afternoon they were enjoying a picnic with Ravensong near the river. The children were playing together while Ravensong sat off to one side watching them. Graham and Ashley took a walk down the bank. It was the first time the two of them were really focused on talking to each other without the children hanging around.

"Graham," Ashley began, "you know I'll be heading back to the lower '48 soon."

"What do you mean? I thought you lived here in Alaska."

"I was only here for a year to complete my internship. My work is done at the end of the summer. I'll be leaving in September."

Graham looked stricken as the thought of her leaving struck his heart like a knife. He reached out for her like a drowning man seeking a lifeline. She grabbed hold of his hands. Pulling her towards him, he buried his face in her shoulder as he tried to breath. His mind wrestled with the fear of losing her.

"Ashley, I don't want you to go," he groaned. "I...the children, we need you."

She didn't say anything as he held her tightly, but he could feel her trembling. Taking her silence as rejection, he let go of her and moved away.

"Graham, I have a different plan for my life. I love Alaska, but I don't want to live out here in the bush. It's not the kind of life I dreamed of for myself. This is too harsh and demanding. I can't do it."

Ashley's voice trailed off as she saw Graham's jaw clench in frustration. She knew her words hurt him, but not telling the truth would be even worse. She'd trained to be an educator and wanted a life and a career. Hiding away from the world wasn't a part of her vision. He'd come here to escape from the world she wanted to embrace. What chance was there for the two of them to be together?

"I understand," he said sadly. "You have a right to your own dreams."

He turned to head back the way they came when he saw Devin and Lacey hiding in the bushes. They'd snuck along hoping to surprise the two grown-ups, but from the looks on their faces, they'd gotten enough of the conversation to be unhappily surprised on their own.

Ashley knelt down in front of them and reached out her arms. Lacey ran to her and started to cry, but Devin ran away. Graham hurried after him far enough to see him run to Ravensong. He stopped and stood on the trail looking back and forth at his daughter and his son wondering how he could help them when his own heart was tearing into pieces.

As they packed up the remains of the picnic and prepared to go home, Ravensong watched the four of them quietly. He knew they were running out of time, but he couldn't interfere. It was up to them to make the right choices. Graham didn't look up as they drove away.

***

For the next several days, Ashley didn't come out to the cabin and Graham couldn't make himself go into the village. The children had gone silent again, speaking only when necessary. Devin wouldn't meet his eyes and stopped doing any of his schoolwork. Lacey made a big show of doing hers whenever she had Graham's attention. Unfortunately, he was trapped in a place of indecision and lost in his own thoughts most of the time.

At night, Devin would talk to Lacey until she fell asleep. Graham was tempted to sit on the stairs so he could hear better what was being said, but feared causing further distrust in their relationship. He would lay awake long after the children were asleep wondering about their future.

When he'd made the choice to live out here in the bush, he was alone and thought he would always be alone. Having his children out here with him forced him to face up to the harsh realities of life in the wilderness. He was barely able to survive the winters on his own. How would the children survive the long winter days and the bitter cold? There were so many dangers that lurked just outside their clearing. Graham stopped himself from making a list of them.

Chapter 6

One morning, the children were arguing over their cereal and Graham couldn't handle their bickering anymore. Jumping up from the table, he grabbed his chainsaw and headed for the door. He told them to stay near the front of the cabin as he needed to clear some more trees near the back. They didn't say anything as he went outside.

He wanted to clear the trees farther back from the outhouse so he had a clear view of it from inside. These trees were larger than usual and he was running the chainsaw for long periods of time. He'd been at work for a couple of hours before he decided to take a break.

Walking around to the front of the cabin, he saw the dogs were still in their pen. This surprised him as the children usually let them out when they did their morning chores. He went into the cabin to see what they were doing. There was no one downstairs and no one answered his call.

Stepping back outside, he looked around the clearing. The UTV was usually parked on the far side of the cabin. It wasn't there. He ran over to take a closer look and saw the trailer had been unhitched, but the UTV was gone. He listened carefully to see if he could hear the sound of it, but there was only silence punctuated with the chatter of birds.

He sat down on a stump and considered his next step. His first thought was that the children went to find Ashley. It would take him two hours to hike to the village and catch up to them. He knew Devin wouldn't have been able to fill the gas tank and the UTV was nearly empty. There was a good chance they might be stalled somewhere between here and the village. In that case, he would catch up to them sooner.

Jumping up, he grabbed his pack and his rifle. Letting the dogs out of their pen, he headed off down the trail in search of his children. He didn't want to think about what else might be out there hunting for them if they ended up on foot.

Graham was certain Devin and Lacey were headed to the village. The dogs started heading down the river trail when they came to it, but he whistled them back. He didn't think they would go back to the river. He figured the dogs were following the scent from their last picnic.

He ran as long as he could and then he'd walk for a while to catch his breath. The dogs circled around him weaving back and forth across the trail ahead and behind him. Every once in a while, he'd stop and listen for the sound of the UTV, but there was only silence. Fear tried to take hold of his thoughts, but he stayed focused on the path.

Coming into sight of the village, his eyes searched along both sides of the widening path. There were really only two places for them to be, he figured as he ran along. The grocery store/community center was where they usually met Ashley, and Ravensong's place at the other end of the village were their usual destinations. Beyond that was the road leading back to civilization, but he saw no reason for them to go that way.

He reached the village center and looked around for his UTV. Ravensong was on the porch talking to another man as Graham came into sight. The elder stared at his friend's sudden appearance and realized something was terribly wrong. He was at Graham's side in an instant.

"Are...Devin...and...Lacey...here?" Graham gasped out slowly.

"No. I haven't seen or heard anyone come this way all morning," Ravensong replied.

"Where's Ashley?"

"She's in the center, doing paperwork, I think."

At that moment, Ashley came out on the porch and stood there staring at the two men.

"What's wrong? Where are the children?" she called out to them.

"They've run away. We need to go and look for them," Ravensong said as he hurried inside.

Graham walked over to the porch and sank down on the edge of it. His dogs came and flopped down on the ground around him. He pressed his hands over his face and tried to think how he could have missed them. He'd been so certain they'd gone to the village. They must have missed a turn or taken a different trail by mistake. It was so unlike Devin as the boy had an uncanny sense of directions and never needed to be told where to go.

He looked up as two UTV's roared up and came to a stop in front of him.

"Let's go!"

Ashley shouted at him from the back of Ravensong's UTV. The two of them raced off down the trail as Graham climbed on the back of the other vehicle. His dogs ran along beside the machines as they hurried back towards the cabin.

As they reached each cross trail, they'd stop and Graham would urge the dogs to find Devin and Lacey. The dogs would run about sniffing the air and then continue heading back towards home. This continued until they got to the turn-off for the river where the dogs took the lead and headed that way.

When they came to the river, the dogs started running along the bank, but Graham called them back. He wasn't sure the dogs were on the trail of the children as they'd never gone any further down river. They got off the machines and searched the sandy bank for signs the UTV had gone in that direction. It didn't take Ravensong long to find their tracks in the sand.

Racing along the bank, they didn't have to go far before they found the abandoned UTV. The children weren't anywhere in sight. Graham stared at their little footprints in the sand heading off along the riverbank. *Surely, they couldn't have gotten that far away*, he thought to himself.

The dogs circled the UTV and continued running ahead of the others. Every time they turned a corner and disappeared from sight, Graham strained to hear the welcoming barks he knew would come when they found Devin and Lacey. There was no sounds from the dogs and when they reached a wide stream feeding into the river, the dogs were milling in a circle of confusion. The children's tracks were lost in the mess of paw prints.

The stream looked too deep for the children to cross here. Settling the dogs, the four adults searched for footprints in a careful pattern. The area was very rocky and it took several passes before they found a print heading upstream into the woods. The trees came right down to the edges of the water so there was no room for the UTV's.

"I think two of us should head upstream and see if we can find them," Graham said. "The other two can wait here in case they come down on the other side and we miss them."

"I'm going with you," Ashley blurted out, much to Graham's surprise.

Ravensong simply nodded.

Sending the dogs ahead, Graham grabbed his rifle and started working his way through the thick brush. It was slow going and the narrow path showed no signs of the children.

Suddenly Ashley cried out and pointed to the middle of the stream. Following her lead, Graham saw something white bobbing along in the water. He recognized Lacey's doll. Thinking he could easily step into the water and retrieve it, he slipped down the bank and rushed into the shallows. Without warning, he quickly sank to his hips.

"Quicksand! Ashley stay back," he warned her.

Tossing his rifle on the bank, he looked around for a branch or anything to grab onto, but he was too far from the edge. Ashley grabbed branches and tested their strength but everything was old or rotten and broke off in her hands. She turned to see that Graham was still sinking as he fought the urge to struggle.

Thinking quickly, Ashley turned away and stripped off her jeans. Graham tried not to stare at her pink polka-dot undies as he wondered how this was going to help. Tossing him a leg, she held tightly to the other and braced her feet against a tree root.

"You're going to have to lay forward and pull yourself along a little bit at a time," she said as she gritted her teeth.

Graham wrapped the denim around his arm and put his trust in her strength as he did what she said. It was a slow, pain-staking process as he slowly freed himself from the morass, but it was clearly working. He reached the bank soaking wet and covered with muck. Ashley's pants were equally soaked and dirty. She turned away to put them back on as he tried not to think about what would have happened if she hadn't pulled him out.

The sound of the dogs barking their 'happy' barks caused the two of them to try to push through the brush to find the dogs. As they rounded the bend, they saw Lacey straddling a log. It was obvious they were trying to cross the stream, but she'd gotten scared. Her arms were locked in place around the tree. Devin was trying to coax her free, but the excitement of the dogs was creating havoc for him.

He froze as his father and Ashley came into sight.

"Daddy! Daddy," Lacey cried in relief at the sight of her father.

Graham hurried over to grab hold of her before she fell into the stream. Ashley reached out for her as he then turned to check Devin over. By shear luck they were both unharmed by their misadventure. Devin had a look of relief on his face as he avoided looking at his father.

The four of them kneeled down on the bank and tried to catch their breath.

"Why are you two all muddy?" Lacey asked.

"Your Dad found some quicksand," Ashley said with a smirk.

Ignoring her attempt to be funny, Graham attempted to face this head on with his son.

"Would you like to explain where you thought you were going with your little sister?" Graham asked looking hard at Devin.

"I was taking her home," he retorted in a defiant tone. "We want to go home!"

"Devin, do you have any idea how far you'd have to walk to get anywhere out here?"

"Ravensong told me the city was up this river!"

"Sure, Son, but it's hundreds of miles of wilderness until you get there and then you'd be in a city where you don't know anyone. Your home is here with me now."

Devin folded his arms across his chest and stared at the ground.

Graham sighed in frustration and got up.

"We need to get back to the others and head home. It'll be dark soon and the trail's pretty rough."

Ashley took Lacey by the hand and the two of them led the way. Devin fell in behind them while Graham whistled in the dogs and brought up the rear. It wasn't long before they saw the faces of Ravensong and his friend watching their approach. As they drew near, the Elder stood up with a small bundle in his hand. Lacey was delighted to be reunited with her doll once again.

"You found my baby doll," she crowed with delight as she snuggled the wet bundle.

"You're lucky the doll hospital gave her a wooden head. She was floating down instead of swimming along under water," Ravensong said with a wink at Graham.

Noticing how Graham and Ashley were soaked and covered in muck, he raised his eyebrows in a question, but they both ignored him. The six of them headed back to Graham's UTV without any further comment. The dogs were pretty tired and the men were forced to slow down so they could keep up with the UTV's. Stopping to put some gas in Graham's vehicle, they hurried to get on their way as everyone was cold, tired and hungry.

At the river turnout, Ravensong paused to let Ashley speak to Graham, but their conversation was brief. She headed back to the village with the two men. Graham didn't even think to ask her to come back to the cabin with them. He didn't feel like he had any right to ask her for anything more.

When they got home, he made some soup for the children and sent them off to bed. He sat at the table a long time after they'd gone upstairs and thought about the events of the day. His children were safe, but their situation was far from resolved.

Devin wasn't convinced that this was their home and Graham was starting to understand why. If he had to worry about the children running away every day, he was going to be more in the role of a prison guard than a father. They clearly didn't understand the dangers of wandering about in the wilderness and he didn't want to use fear to control them. Maybe they were just too little to understand. Their situation was clearly at an impasse and he couldn't see a way out from where he sat. On that thought, he gave up and went to bed.

Chapter 7

Graham let a couple of days go by before he proposed a trip to the village. Lacey was excited and hurried to get ready. Devin didn't say anything, but his dawdling showed his reluctance to face Ashley and Ravensong. He was the last to get his shoes on and walked outside dragging his feet all the way. Graham ignored the way he was acting thinking it would pass once they got to the village.

The skies were clear and they set off early enough in the day to be back before dark. They made good time and reached the village before anyone had to use the bathroom for a change. Devin didn't ask to drive this time.

Graham went to see Ravensong first as he hoped his friend would have some words of wisdom for Devin. The boy seemed to have far more respect for the Elder than for his own father. Ravensong was really Graham's last hope in reaching his son. If this meeting failed, Graham wasn't sure how he was going to make it as a father to his own children.

Ravensong was sitting on his porch when Graham drove up. The three of them got off the UTV and sat down beside him.

"Greetings, my friends," Ravensong said. "What brings you to the village today?"

"Daddy's UTV brought us," Lacey piped up.

The two men laughed at her comment.

"I was hoping you might like to take a walk with Devin," Graham hinted to his friend.

"That's a fine idea," Ravensong agreed. "There are some things I'd like to show him."

"Great! Lacey and I are going over to the Community Center. You can meet us over there when you're done."

Graham and Lacey hopped back on their ride and headed back the way they'd came. Devin hunched his shoulders as he waited for the scolding he knew he deserved. Ravensong was quiet as he cleared away the shavings from his latest work. He realized how much Graham was relying on him to find a way to reach the boy.

Finally, he stood and held out his hand.

"Come with me, Devin. I'd like to show you some things."

The boy rose without a word and followed the Elder down the path.

***

As Graham stopped near the Center, Ashley came out onto the porch with a large box in her hands. He noticed she was packing a small trailer that was already half full.

"Hi, Ashley!"

Lacey ran over to the woman and stood before her.

"Can I help you?" Lacey asked.

"No, darling. Just let me put this in the trailer and we can get some ice cream, okay?"

"Are you moving?"

Lacey's eyes grew wide as she put the idea together with the conversation they'd overheard by the river.

"What is all this?" Graham asked quietly.

"Oh, this is all the extra teaching materials that need to be returned to the main office. Clearly, there's not as many students out here in the village as the registration indicates. I think most of them moved to the cities with their families last year and didn't remove their names."

"Do you have time for a cup of coffee?"

"Sure. Just help me load the rest of my boxes and we can sit down and take a break. I've been at this all morning."

Graham settled Lacey on the porch with a book and helped Ashley finish up her packing. As they worked, they tried to talk about anything but what had happened a few days earlier. With the extra hands, their task was quickly finished and they sat down just out of Lacey's hearing.

"Ashley, I didn't get a chance to thank you for saving my life the other day."

"That's right! You didn't and I don't want you to think I'd go and take my pants off for just any ole guy!"

Graham smiled grimly at her attempt to deflect the situation with humor.

"I also want to thank you for everything you've done for

me and Lacey and Devin. You've come to mean a lot to all of us. I know I don't have anything to offer you, but I want you to stay."

"I can't do that. I've already told you that my dreams for my life don't work out here in the bush. I want more than a cabin in the middle of nowhere. As much as I care for you and the children, I know I wouldn't be happy just trying to survive every day. Besides, I think this is too much to ask of your children. I know you're punishing yourself by hiding away out here, but what have they done to deserve to live like this?"

Graham was shocked into silence at her words. She'd never expressed any disapproval of his lifestyle before this and he wasn't sure how to take it. He'd never considered his move to Alaska as a way of punishing himself, but from her perspective, he could see her point. Especially when he considered it in light of Devin's reluctance to embrace this world. The children were dragged from everything and everyone they knew and dumped in a strange world without clocks and televisions, schools or shopping malls. They had absolutely no choice in any of this.

Lacey got out of her chair and came over to stand in front of them.

"Are you two having a fight?" she asked.

"No, honey. We're not having a fight. We're just talking," Graham said sadly.

He looked up to see Devin coming with Ravensong. The

two of them were walking side by side and Graham could definitely see a change in his son. It was as if the boy was charged with a new sense of confidence and wisdom. His gaze was no longer fixed to the ground and he appeared fully engaged with the world around him. Graham knew that once again his old friend had pulled forth the right words from the Creator.

Reading the looks on the faces of Graham and Ashley, Ravensong's heart sank. He knew their conversation hadn't gone in the right direction. Taking charge of the children, he invited them to the store to get some ice cream. It wouldn't give those two much time to find their path, but it was the best he had to offer.

"Where are you going when you leave Alaska?"

"My family's from Idaho. My mother's there and I have some property near the town of Lewiston. Graham, please, let's get married and go live there together. We can come back here for vacations in the summer..."

Ashley stopped at the look on Graham's face. He appeared shocked as he tried to take in all that she'd just said. His mind was struggling with the idea she was leaving and he knew he wanted her to stay, but getting married and being a family was too many steps for his brain.

His thoughts reeled as her words overwhelmed him. He knew those were all logical steps for normal people, but he wasn't a normal person in his mind. He was a failure as a husband and a father. Why would a woman as smart and confident as Ashley want to marry someone like him? The question rolled around in his head like a loose wrecking ball and he just sat there stunned.

Ashley took his silence as rejection and got up to go inside the Center. She'd laid all her thoughts and feelings out on the table. As far as she was concerned, there was nothing more to say to this man. Obviously, he didn't feel the same way about her. She fought back tears as she hurried to be away before the children came back outside. There was no way she could face them without crying now.

Graham was sitting on the UTV when the children came back outside with Ravensong. The Elder knew with one look that things hadn't gone well for his friend. His heart was troubled as he took in the distant sound of thunder.

"A storm is coming, my friend," he said. "It might be best to stay here until it passes."

"No. We need to get home. We'll be fine, just the three of us," Graham said grimly.

Ravensong knew he wasn't talking about the storm and he watched them drive away helplessly.

***

They hadn't gone very far before the wind started to pick up and blow leaves and dirt around them. The trees were whipping back and forth in the heavy gusts. Dead branches littered the trail ahead and behind them and Graham was forced to slow down. The sky grew dark and heavy with clouds. The children were clutching their father with tight grips that hampered his movements.

Suddenly, a tree on the right side of the narrow path snapped off. Graham heard the crack and barely caught the sight of the tree falling towards them. With his left hand, he tried to shove Lacey out of the way as his right arm came up to deflect the blow. The violent crash threw her off into the bushes and Graham took the full weight of the massive tree on his right side. Devin was knocked backwards and escaped injury.

Fortunately, the tree bounced off Graham and landed across the trailer. He was seriously injured, but his main concern was to find Lacey. She wasn't making any sounds he could hear over the noise of the storm. When he tried to stand up, he fell back to the seat as he stifled a scream of pain.

"Devin, are you okay?"

The boy shook himself a bit and nodded at his father. His eyes were wide with fear as he looked at the blood on Graham's face. He knew his father had taken the blunt of the falling tree and was badly hurt.

"Devin, you need to find Lacey for me," Graham said as calmly as he could. "Don't move her. First, we need to find out if she's hurt. Can you do that for me?"

Devin nodded and crawled over to the side of the trail to

look for his sister. He found her curled up against another tree.

"Lacey. Lacey! Are you hurt?" he asked into her ear.

She turned her head and looked up at him with glazed eyes, but didn't speak.

"Daddy! She's right here, but she won't talk to me."

Graham forced his body to move and collapsed to the ground next to Devin. He knew his right arm was broken. It was possible some ribs and his collarbone were also broken, but he was more concerned about his daughter. He needed to assess her injuries before he figured out his next step.

Stretching out alongside Devin, Graham felt over Lacey checking for broken bones or blood, but there was nothing he could find. Calling her name, he noted her glazed response and considered that maybe she'd hit her head on the tree.

"Devin, can you get me the sleeping bag from the trailer?"

His son disappeared from view and came back a few moments later with the bag and the first aid kit. Graham spread the bag around Lacey and had Devin tuck it under her. Using the bag, the two of them pulled her out of the bushes and cuddled her next to her father. The effort and the pain overwhelmed him and he shut his eyes.

"Daddy! Daddy! Wake up!"

Graham opened his eyes at the sound of Devin's cries

and looked into the face of his son.

"I'm here, Devin. I need you to look at the UTV and the trailer and tell me what's wrong with them."

The boy hurried to comply and Graham could hear him moving around behind them.

"Dad!"

Graham forced his eyes open again.

"The trailer's smashed under a big tree. I can't move it, but I can pull the hitch pin like I did before back at the cabin. The UTV's okay, I think."

"Devin, do you think you can make it back to the village and get us some help?"

"Yes, Daddy. I can do that. I can find Ravensong and bring him here. He'll help us."

As Graham lay there in the middle of the trail next to his little girl, he realized that his stubbornness was the cause of all of this. Ravensong tried to get him to wait for the storm to pass, but he wouldn't hear of it. He listened to the sound of the UTV as his little boy fought to find a way through the brush around the fallen tree. The engine stuttered as Devin struggled to control the heavy machine.

As the sound faded with Devin's departure, Graham turned his attention to the noises around them. The wind was still blowing, but the storm was moving away from them. He could pick up some bird sounds nearby. Mostly there was silence. He tried to talk to Lacey. She didn't respond. The effort to talk nearly made him pass out so he decided it was safer for him to stay quiet.

He didn't know how long the two of them laid there before help arrived. He'd lost all track of time as he faded in and out of consciousness. Their rescuers seemingly appeared out of nowhere and went to work while he was completely out of it. He didn't fully become aware of anything until they were loading him and Lacey into the rescue plane. His awareness was brief as pain once again shut down his brain and all he managed to understand was that they were all safe.

Chapter 8

The next few days were touch and go for Graham. He had a major concussion, several broken bones and some serious internal bruising. Lacey only had a minor concussion and she was much quicker about getting back to normal. She'd made several friends in the hospital long before her father was fully aware of his surroundings.

Ashley divided her time between their two rooms. She berated herself for caring about this man when he didn't care about her, but she couldn't just walk away. She'd made the decision to leave Devin in the village with Ravensong. It was a difficult choice, but the plane only had room for one more person and it didn't make sense to send an eight year old.

With Lacey out of danger, Ashley turned her attention to Graham. He was asleep most of the time as his injuries took their time to heal. She'd sit and watch him sleep. Sometimes, she'd talk to him about their summer and the things they'd done together. He never gave any indication he was listening. The doctor told her this was caused more by the heavy pain medication than his injuries.

***

About a week after the accident, Graham woke up to

find the nurse running through her checklist. Seeing his eyes open, the woman began talking to him like they were well acquainted. Graham listened to her words carefully for some clue as to his condition. Her words weren't giving him any clarity.

"Good morning! It's good to see those eyes of yours open for a change. You just missed your wife. She went home to check on your little girl. She sure is a devoted woman trying to watch over you and your little one all this time. I don't think I ever saw her take more than a few minutes to go to the bathroom the first three days after you two were brought in. You must love her very much..."

"My wife?" was all Graham managed.

"Oh, don't worry. She said she'd be back within an hour."

This last statement was said as the nurse headed out the door to let the doctor know Graham was fully alert. She didn't notice the look of confusion she left in her wake. When she returned with the doctor, Graham was trying to move himself to a sitting position. The effort left him dizzy and disoriented and he groaned as he lay back down.

"You're going to need to take your time," the doctor said. "You've got some serious internal bruising to your right side. We don't want to cause anything to start bleeding by moving too fast. Can you tell me your name?"

Graham was certain about that and gave the correct answer.

"Do you know the date or maybe what day it is?"

The blank look on Graham's face was enough of a response.

"Do you know where you are?"

"Hospital?"

"Can you tell us what happened to you?"

Graham thought back to the last thing he remembered. The accident was clear in his mind. Everything that came after was a blur until this point in time. He was just about to answer when Ashley came into the room with Lacey.

"Daddy!"

Her little voice burst forth with excitement at seeing Graham awake. She hurried to his side and rubbed his good arm. He wrapped it around her ignoring the pain in his side and pulled her close.

"Hello Darling! How are you? You look like you've been eating something with ketchup."

"I did! We had some French fries for lunch."

Graham looked up at Ashley who'd come to stand behind Lacey. She was looking down at him with a worried look. Before he could react, she leaned over and plopped a kiss on his forehead.

"It's so good to see you awake, honey," she said in a fake kind of way.

"You see," the nurse said, "I told you your wife would be back within the hour."

The doctor scribbled a couple of notes and headed out

the door. The nurse was right behind him as Ashley pulled up a chair next to the bed.

"My wife?"

"Oh, Graham, I'm sorry. They wouldn't let me stay with you and Lacey unless I was a family member. They wouldn't even let me on the rescue plane, but Ravensong told them I was your wife. I was so worried about you and Lacey so I went along with it…"

Graham grinned at her embarrassment.

Lacey was watching the two of them anxiously. She wasn't sure what was going on between them. All she was sure of was how much she wanted Ashley to continue to be a part of their lives. The last few days reminded her of the void her mother's death had left in her life. It was nice having a mom.

Suddenly Graham's face darkened.

"Where's Devin? Is he okay?"

"Don't worry. He's safe. He stayed in the village with Ravensong. There wasn't any more room on the plane for him. He's back there basking in the praise of the elders for rescuing you and Lacey."

"Yeah! He's a real hero," Lacey piped up. "He saved us from the tree!"

"You bet he is, Sweetheart! I can't wait to tell him how proud I am to be his dad."

The three of them talked for a little while longer before Graham started to drift off. He wanted to thank Ashley for staying by his side, but the words wouldn't come. As she and Lacey got ready to head out, he hugged and kissed his daughter. Ashley stood back shyly, but the nurse came in at that moment. The two of them made a show of saying good-bye for her benefit. Lacey just looked at their performance in confusion.

Waiting until they were outside, Lacey asked, "Are you going to marry my daddy? That would be okay with me."

Ashley didn't know what to say so she just kneeled down and gave the little girl a hug.

"I'd like for you to be my mommy," Lacey whispered quietly.

Ashley pretended not to hear the little girl.

***

Graham spent another two weeks in the hospital before the doctor would even consider releasing him. Ashley took Lacey back to the village to check on Devin during that time. She needed to finish taking care of her business and make preparations to leave Alaska. With the two children in her care, it was hard to hide from them what she was doing. They didn't know how to grasp the idea of her leaving with the thought of wanting her to be with them as a family.

Ravensong and Devin brought the dogs into the village and found a temporary home for them with another man.

This fellow had an experienced team and quickly integrated Graham's dogs with his own. He was interested in making a deal to buy them. They'd matured into reliable sled dogs and needed very little training to take to the trail with his team.

When word came that Graham was going to be released from the hospital, Ashley flew up to Fairbanks to bring him home. She left the children with Ravensong's family. The short flight gave her very little time to think about her next step. She could only hope he'd be able to handle the challenges he faced with his injuries.

Staying at the cabin this winter wasn't going to be possible with his arm and shoulder in a cast for the next couple of months. Without his strength, she knew that even if she agreed to stay with them, she couldn't handle what it would take to get them through the winter. He was being forced to make some hard decisions by this situation.

She decided to head straight for the hospital when she arrived in Fairbanks. Finding his room empty, she headed to the nurses' station. The nurse directed her to the physical therapy room. As she stood looking in the doorway, she watched Graham working with the therapist on his balance. He was still a bit shaky on his feet. A cast covered his right arm from the wrist up over his shoulder with straps across his back and chest.

Sensing someone watching him, Graham turned and saw her standing in the doorway. His face lit up at the sight of her and the therapist looked around to see what was going on.

"You can come in," the therapist called to her.

Embarrassed at being caught watching, Ashley blushed, but came over to greet Graham. She put her arm around his good side and kissed his cheek. Surprised when he returned the hug, she stumbled a bit, but he caught her.

Turning to his therapist, Graham proudly introduced Ashley.

"This is my wife, Ashley," he said with a big grin.

"Well, why don't you show your wife the exercises I've taught you and then you can be done for the day."

"That sounds like a deal," Graham said. "I could sure use a break from this torture."

Going through his routine until the therapist was satisfied, Graham was finally given the green light to head out. Ashley walked alongside his wheelchair as he was driven back to his room. She filled him in on things back at the village while they walked. As she talked about the children, he reached up and took her hand for a moment. Giving it a squeeze, he let go when she smiled at him.

Once he was settled in his bed, it was time for supper. She was invited to join him and two meals were brought for them. As they sat there eating, Graham studied her face carefully. He wasn't good at making long speeches, but this was one time in his life, he knew he needed to say the right things. Taking a deep breath, he laid down his fork and

Renee Hart

looked her straight in the eye.

"Ashley, I'm not good with words," he began. "I came to Alaska and built a cabin way out in the woods thinking I'd never have to talk to anyone ever again. I never expected to be a father again and I really didn't expect to fall in love..."

Ashley's eyes widened as she listened.

"The bottom line is that I do love you and I want the four of us to be a family, and we can live wherever you want. I know what you said back in the village is true and my children deserve to have more than I can give them out in the bush, and you deserve more..."

Ashley's eyes filled with tears as she looked into Graham's.

"So, what do you say? Can we make this 'wife' thing official?"

"I'd like that," was all Ashley needed to say.

Epilogue

Ravensong looked up as an unfamiliar pick-up truck came to a stop in front of him. As the young man got out and came around the front of the truck, the old elder laid aside his knife. The carving in his hand dropped to the floor when he stood up.

"Devin! My boy, it's so good to see you, but you're not a boy anymore, are you?" Ravensong said with a grin as he stepped forward to grasp the young man's hand.

"No, my oldest friend. I'm not a boy anymore. Thanks to you, I'm a man," Devin replied as he pulled the elder into his embrace.

"It's been a long time since you or your father has come back to the village."

"True. It's been a very long time, but we're going to make that up to you this summer," Devin said. "My Dad and Mom are on their way here as we speak with the younger children. We came on ahead to get the cabin ready."

"We?"

At that moment, a young woman opened the passenger side door of the truck and slipped out to the ground. Her obvious belly made its own statement, much to Ravensong's delight.

"Ravensong, this is my wife Lisa and our baby, yet to be

unnamed," Devin said proudly as he put his arm around her.

"Lisa, this is the man who gave me back my childhood."

"Oh, and just how did he manage to do that?"

Devin grinned widely as he said, "Let's just say he took me out back of the woodshed and showed me the error of my ways."

He and Ravensong winked at each other and began to laugh as Lisa pondered the humor in his statement. At that point, she was more interested in finding the nearest bathroom, and the two men hurried to direct her accordingly.

"Have you been out to the cabin lately," Devin asked as they sat down on the porch.

"Actually, I was out there this morning. I wanted to check on the preparations. I sent two guys out there a few days ago to make sure everything was ready for your arrival."

"What do you mean? Who told you we were coming," Devin asked as he looked confused.

Ravensong bent over to pick up his carving from the porch. Turning it over in his hand, he noted the cuts he still needed to make to finish it.

Devin realized he wasn't going to get an answer. He looked around at the nearby houses and the paved road.

"There's been a lot of changes since we were here last," he said.

"Oh, sure. There's a road out to the cabin now and we have electricity and a bigger store. It's been more than ten years since your last visit. Will Lacey come?"

"She's planning to show up in a couple of weeks. Her fiancé is supposed to come up with her and she wants to get married here. She claims this is the place she learned about love."

"I think that's probably true for both of you, am I right?"

Devin looked at his friend as he considered the question. He'd learned a lot of things that summer when he was eight. Love wasn't the first item on his list, but it was clearly a part of everything that happened. He found his father and gained a new mother. The time he'd spent with Ravensong helped to put his feet on the right path and finally, he'd found himself. The Elder showed him how to be a little boy again and from there, he grew up in a good way.

"I'd have to say yes to that," Devin stated firmly.

"And just what are you agreeing to," Lisa teased as she waddled around the corner of the porch.

The two men rose as she came up onto the porch.

"I'm agreeing with my friend here that we've been away from this place too long and we should come back to visit more often," Devin said with a wink at Ravensong.

"I'd like that," Lisa agreed, "but first, we're going to have to make some improvements to the plumbing!"

The three of them burst out laughing. It was clearly going to be an interesting summer.

THE END

About The Author

Renee Hart is the author of the Alaska Adventure Romance Series. She writes clean Alaskan adventure romance and romantic comedy. Renee lives in the Alaskan Bush with her husband and their dog and cat. When shes not writing you can find her quilting, baking bread or sipping hot cocoa by the wood stove with a good book.

Made in the USA
Middletown, DE
13 February 2019

VICTORIAN ANTIQUES

Katharine Morrison McClinton

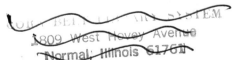

Wallace-Homestead
authoritative books on antiques & collectibles

Published By

Wallace-Homestead Book Company
1912 Grand Avenue
Des Moines, Iowa 50305

ACKNOWLEDGMENTS

A number of friends and colleagues in Museums, Libraries, and Historical Societies have helped in locating material and photographs needed in the preparation of this book. Special thanks are due to Nancy O. Merrill, Curator of Glass, Chrysler Museum; Richard Carter Barret, Director-Curator, The Bennington Museum; Marvin D. Schwartz, Curator of Decorative Arts, The Brooklyn Museum; R. C. Morrell, Curator, and Muriel G. Harris, Librarian, The American Clock and Watch Museum; Bradley Smith, Ass. to the Director, Shelburne Museum; E. P. Hogan, Historical Research Librarian, The International Silver Co; S. Kirk Millspaugh, Vice-President, Samuel Kirk & Son; Ann Hogan, Gorham Mfg. Co; Janet Byrne, Ass. Curator, Print Dept., The Metropolitan Museum of Art; Amelia E. Mac Swiggan; Carolyn Scoon, Curator of Decorative Arts, Arthur Carlson, Curator of Maps and Prints, Shirley Beresford and the library staff of The New-York Historical Society; Elizabeth Usher and the library staff of The Metropolitan Museum of Art; also to the staff of the Art Reference Room of The New York Public Library, and the Reference Staff of the Welwood Murray Memorial Library, Palm Springs, California. A special thanks for photographs to the Index of American Design; Hallmark Cards Inc; The Old Print Shop; The H. V. Smith Museum of The Home Insurance Co; and to The Henry Ford Museum. To Carlton Brown, George O. Bird, and particularly to Gerald G. Gibson, Curator of Decorative Arts, and Katharine Hagler, Assistant, of The Henry Ford Museum, who gave so generously of their time.

TO MY FRIENDS AT
The Henry Ford Museum,

AND PARTICULARLY TO
THE EXECUTIVE DIRECTOR
Donald Shelley,

TO THE
CURATOR OF DECORATIVE ARTS
Gerald G. Gibson,

AND TO
Katharine Hagler, Assistant,

WITHOUT WHOSE CO-OPERATION
THIS BOOK COULD
NOT HAVE BEEN ILLUSTRATED

CONTENTS

8 · CONTENTS

COLLECTING AMERICAN VICTORIAN ANTIQUES

I. FURNITURE
(1840–1900)

THE dates for the Victorian period in America are approximate, for the style evolved gradually and the beginnings of the designs are seen at the end of the eighteenth century. Although the Victorian included many different styles used simultaneously, in each case the style was an interpretation of earlier styles and designs. It was an age of borrow and copy, and the American furniture maker and manufacturer, although he got a late start, excelled at the game. Indeed, Victorianism had its most successful blossoming in America, according to Rita Wellman in *Victoria Royal*.

Victorian furniture and Victorian design in general involved the use of motifs from the whole history of art. These motifs were revised and elaborated. Along with this look toward the past and the revivalism of older styles, there was the influence of industry in the mechanical innovations such as patented tilting chairs, automatic spring sofas, and beds that pulled out of bookcases. Industry also promoted the use of materials other than wood for the construction of furniture. The

Parlor from the Robert Milligan house, Saratoga Springs. Rococo styled carved furniture made by E. Galusha, Troy, N.Y. Carved marble mantel, carved gilt mirror. Crimson damask draperies hang from gilt cornices. The floral pattern carpet is crimson and gold. (*Brooklyn Museum*)

11

present-day popular iron, wire, tubular metal, and rattan furniture had their beginnings in the nineteenth century. Also such products as gutta percha and papier mâché were used by Victorian furniture makers. Comfort and usefulness were important factors in the design of such pieces as the ottoman and the Turkish overstuffed chair. The history of Victorian furniture in America is the history of a gradual change from individual craftsmanship in a small shop to mass production in the factory. Duncan Phyfe (d. 1854) employed as many as a hundred workmen although he himself directed the design of the furniture made in his shop, and Lambert Hitchcock (d. 1852) had started the shift to quantity production early in the century.

Although there were many different styles of Victorian furniture, there were only two major influences—French and English—and all the styles can be grouped under these major divisions plus the native American influence brought about by the taste, manners, and customs of rural America which produced the individual and original country Victorian. The French influence in American Victorian furniture is seen in the styles of Victorian Empire, Louis XIV, Louis XV, and Louis XVI and later in Art Nouveau. The influence is at first classic in the Empire, then rococo and baroque. The two woods used in making French-inspired American Victorian furniture were mahogany and rosewood, and later metal and exotic woods were used in Art Nouveau. The second influence to dominate American Victorian furniture was the English influence. This is seen in the Gothic, Renaissance, Elizabethan, and Eastlake furniture, and in the later Mission and Golden Oak which Grand Rapids made out of the Ruskin-William Morris efforts of reform. Country furniture was a simpler, less expensive popular expression, but it followed the influences of the more sophisticated pieces.

The first indications of the Victorian style in America were seen in the early 1830's. In the beginning the design influence was largely French. As the period opens we see a modification of the classic Greek forms of the French Empire Period. There is a similarity in structure, but the Victorian Empire is heavy and degenerate. Awkward, ungainly scrolls replace the round columns and claw and ball feet on tables, bureaus, and wardrobes. However, the workmanship and materials were generally good. Designs for this Late Empire furniture are shown in John Hall's book, *The Cabinet Maker's Assistant,* published in Baltimore in 1840. The book shows furniture with "C" and "S" scrolls for supports, legs and backs of sofas and chairs. These designs were intended for the use of the band saw, which had recently been invented, and carving was reduced to a minimum. Actual furniture of similar design is illustrated in the broadside of Joseph Meeks & Sons printed in New York in 1833. This style continued in popularity until the 1850's.

Alongside the classic forms was the use of historic ornaments of other periods, namely the Gothic, Elizabethan, and Renaissance; French Louis XIV, Louis XV and Louis XVI. The Gothic, although a favorite with Downing and the architects, was never used extensively in homes. Architects designed Gothic chairs for churches and public buildings. In the house Gothic furniture was thought suitable for the hall and library, but a few bedroom sets were also made and used.

The Louis XV style was the most important American Victorian furniture style. The outstanding maker of this type of furniture was Belter, who made furniture in his shop in New York City between 1844 and 1863. Similar furniture was also made by Charles Baudouine, M. A. Roux and Leon Marcotte in New York; George J. Henkels in Philadelphia, and A. Eliaers in Boston; Elijah Galusha in Troy, New York; S. J. Johns in Cincinnati, Ohio; and later in factories in Grand Rapids, Michigan and other large cities. This French rococo was especially popular in New Orleans and there were several cabinetmakers of French extraction working there, including Francis Seignouret, A. Seibrecht and Prudent Mallard, and later A. Debruille and Pierre Abadie. The Frenchman Anthony G. Quervelle was making furniture in Philadelphia from 1820 to 1856. The known pieces of his work show a combination of classic and Gothic motifs of design. As the interest in nineteenth century furniture increases the names of many more furniture makers and manufacturers will become known and much more furniture will be recognized and attributed to known makers in various parts of America.

The Gothic style developed early through the enthusiasm of the architects who themselves designed furniture. By the middle of the century the Renaissance style appeared in the exhibitions in London and Paris, and at the Philadelphia Centennial in 1876 the Eastlake style and the Turkish influence were the most dominant in the furniture exhibits. The majority of these exhibits were in bad taste. The furniture was covered with elaborate ornament mostly made by machine, and decorative motifs were used in indiscriminate combinations of various historical styles.

But there were tastemakers in the nineteenth century. The bad design and poor taste of the majority of the articles exhibited at the various World's Fairs from the Crystal Palace Exhibition in 1851 down to the Philadelphia Centennial, was criticized, especially by writers in the *Journal of Design* and the *Art Journal,* and efforts were made to improve the design. One of the best known reformers was John Ruskin and his writings did much to start the movement toward improvement. In America, the architect Andrew Jackson Downing criticized the taste of Americans and in his books sought to raise the level of the furnishings, especially of country houses, by suggesting the suitable decoration and styles of furniture. William Morris and his group of pre-Raphaelite painters contributed important suggestions but their work was never made for mass production. However, one of William Morris' followers, Charles Locke Eastlake, wrote *Hints on Household Taste* which went through many editions in England and reached America in 1872. Whatever Eastlake's good intentions may have been, his ideas and their adoption and commercialization by American manufacturers produced some of the worst examples of furniture design ever inflicted upon the American public. The fact that the American public embraced this bad taste and misuse of materials was due, to some extent, to the cheapness with which it could be manufactured, and so vast was the output that Eastlake was accepted in every home in America. The arts and crafts movement of Elbert Hubbard, the magazine *The Craftsman,* and the art of Louis Tiffany reached only a small audience. However, their efforts at improvement are recognized and admired today.

Parlor of Clinton Inn, Greenfield Village, Dearborn. Victorian Empire furniture. Argand lamp on table. (*The Henry Ford Museum*)

Victorian Empire (1840–50)

MUCH of this late Empire furniture was made by cabinetmakers who worked with hand tools, but although they continued to use earlier Empire forms, the furniture was heavier in style and ornamentation and had lost the most of its elegance of form. Metal decorative mounts as seen on the early Empire furniture of Duncan Phyfe and Charles

15

Honoré Lannuier were not used, and although Downing shows a chair with sphinx-carved front legs, such carving or animal legs are seldom to be seen. Victorian details such as machine-made wavy molding and applied flower and leaf carving replaced the finer details. This furniture has been ignored for years because it was inferior compared to the earlier Empire furniture. However, much of this furniture is of good workmanship. It is made of heavy mahogany or mahogany veneer over pine. Some pieces were made of rosewood and country pieces were made of maple, butternut, or other hard woods stained red or brown. This is furniture which is available for the average collector today, and while one may not want to assemble rooms full of examples, a few pieces can be used with good effect in the furnishings of any room and the prices are within the reach of the small pocketbook. This is the furniture that antique dealers scorned a few years ago. So far, few articles have been reproduced. The one drawback to Victorian Empire is chipped veneer which is expensive to replace. The collector should have certain information about the forms, the motifs of design, and the woods used. Since the chair is the piece most available and most popular, we begin our guide to collecting with the chair.

ABOVE. Victorian Empire mahogany ottoman with bracket feet. Similar ones made with "C" and "S" scroll feet. (*The Metropolitan Museum of Art*)

LEFT. Victorian Empire mahogany gondola side chair. (*The Henry Ford Museum*)

Victorian Empire *chairs* were of klismos type with concave back and curved saber legs. The open back of the side chair is "U" shape with the top rail arched in a flat curve, finger-molded, or crested with a carved leaf or flower and sometimes pierced with a central finger hole. The splat in the center of the back may be plain with finger-molded edge or serpentined with a carved center design; or sometimes the center splat is vertical vase-shaped or pierced with a cut-out design. A similar chair was made with cabriole legs. This type of chair was also made with rockers and there was an upholstered armchair with covered back and seat, open arms, and concave curved rear and front legs.

Victorian Empire *footstools* have "C" or "S" scroll legs and upholstered seats. Sometimes the cushion seat is upheld by a rectangular base with plain or serpentine skirt edged with plain or wavy molding, and has four bracket feet with casters.

Sofas have straight or serpentine backs, roll-over arms, and scroll, bulbous, or bracket feet. The front rail may be plain or serpentine with wavy machine molding. There is usually no carving, but the structure is outlined in ponderous bands and scrolls of pine veneered with plain and figured mahogany. The sofas are from five feet to six feet six inches in length, and the seat and back are fully upholstered, originally in haircloth. These sofas date from 1830 to 1855. A small armless love seat with scrolled or bracket feet is 40 to 44 inches long.

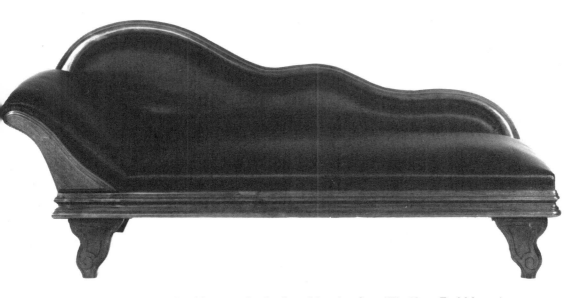

Victorian walnut couch with serpentine back and bracket feet. (*The Henry Ford Museum*)

Victorian Empire *tables* retain the lines of early Empire tables. The center tables and the folding-leaf card tables are supported by a bulbous pedestal or a lyre support that rests on a rectangular-shaped base with four scrolled feet. Sometimes these tables have flower and foliage carving, but more often there is no carving and the tops have a gentle serpentine curve. They are made of pine with mahogany veneer. Pedestal extension tables and circular or oval tilt-top tables of the Victorian Empire had a round pedestal with four cyma-curved feet. The pedestal of the extension table is hollow and contains a turned leg for support when the table is extended. These tables are made of rosewood, mahogany or black walnut. The tilt-top tables are often found in cherry or maple as well as mahogany and black walnut. There was also a rectangular drop-leaf table with four tapering turned legs which was made of black walnut or maple, or such fruit woods as cherry or butternut. This was made in the Middle West as well as on the East Coast from 1840 to 1865. A two-part dining table with each part supported by four legs and a center extension leg was made of black walnut, veneered mahogany, and maple, cherry or butternut. The legs are turned baluster-shaped or have bulbous fluted shafts.

BELOW. Victorian Empire mahogany pedestal table. (*The Henry Ford Museum*)

Empire cherry table. (*The Henry Ford Museum*)

The Victorian Empire *sideboard* often incorporates some of the finer details of earlier periods such as inlay panels, turned columns, and heavy claw feet together with wavy machine moldings. There is usually a rectangular backboard, plain or with a crest of carving, or it may be in the form of a broken arch ending in a carved rosette. Knobs are of stamped brass, wooden mushroom turned, or pressed glass. These sideboards were not factory made, but were usually made to order by a local cabinetmaker. Such sideboards are shown in the broadside of Joseph Meeks & Sons, New York cabinetmaker.

Victorian Empire mahogany card table with "S" scroll support. Mahogany chairs, rococo influence. (*The Henry Ford Museum*)

Square-top *sewing tables* with a baluster-turned or a plain tapering center shaft are supported by four scroll-cut legs.

The *desks* and *secretaries* of the Victorian Empire period are straight line with two or three drawers and a writing flap-shelf. The feet are bracket type or they may have short turned legs. They are made of mahogany veneer or native hard woods stained red.

The Victorian Empire *chest of drawers* began as a straight line piece but later incorporated the heavy cyma curve. Early in the period the chest had plain straight line construction with four tiers of drawers with mushroom-turned wooden knobs, bracket feet and a valanced skirt. The chest was made of mahogany, maple or black walnut, with drawer fronts veneered. Sometimes the top set of small drawers are recessed to the back of the bureau top. Often these chests have bulbous wooden legs and the corners are decorated in split-ball turnings. The drawers may be surrounded with wavy moldings or the top drawer may be ogee-molded. Some of these bureaus with two small side top drawers have round mirrors attached by a center base, or octagon mirrors attached by wooden knobs to a pair of "S" scrolls. Later these bureaus had heavy "S" scroll legs and feet extending down each side of the front.

The *bed* which matched these chests of drawers was the sleigh bed

Victorian Empire walnut bureau similar to one in John Hall's *Cabinet Maker's Assistant.* (*The Henry Ford Museum*)

made of veneer mahogany or rosewood, or pine or other soft woods painted. Head and foot boards were of equal height with curving top rails supported by flaring cyma-curved legs ending in heavy block feet. These beds are often smaller than average so that the standard modern box spring and mattress is too large and one must be made to order. When originally used the beds were usually set with the long side against the wall and a draped canopy was hung over both ends. Heavy beds with turned posts and head- and foot-boards of turned spindles were also made. A bed with massive turned posts ending in a heavy triangular finial and with a solid wood head- and foot-board was advertised in the *New York Directory* of 1840 as Gardiner's Premium Bedstead. The posts on later beds were shorter and had spool turnings. These were usually made of a combination of maple, birch, or pine, rather than mahogany, and date from 1840 to 1865. Empire *melodeons* and *pianos* were made in great quantities, according to the advertisements. The melodeons had lyre end supports and a scrollwork stretcher which upheld the lyre-shaped pedal support. The Victorian Empire spinet piano and early square piano has massive tapering octagon legs and heavy circular feet. The recessed pedal-frame is lyre-shaped. This piano is made of mahogany and rosewood veneer.

Victorian Empire sleigh bed, mahogany. (*Henry Francis du Pont Winterthur Museum*)

Victorian Baroque and Rococo (1840–1870's)

"MODERN French Furniture and especially that in the style of Louis Quatorze stands much higher in general estimation in this country than any other," says Downing in *The Architecture of Country Houses*. This furniture was really a combination of various French styles from Louis XIV to Louis XVI. All styles were made simultaneously, separately, and with mixed contours and details. It is impossible to separate them completely. At the beginning, the straight line baroque Louis XIV was favored. The chairs had straight baluster legs and a

Rosewood Victorian rococo parlor set. Carved mirrors and matching cornices. (*Campbell House Foundation, St. Louis, Missouri*)

high rectangular back with carved cresting. Elegant and expensive sets were made of rosewood, mahogany, and walnut. This furniture was made by cabinetmakers such as Meeks in New York and S. J. Johns of Cincinnati, who operated factories supplying furniture in great quantities. The ornate carving was often produced by separate carving factories. However, this furniture did not hold the popular eye for long. Instead, it was the rococo curves of the lighter Louis XV style that was demanded by the rising wealth of the middle class and this became the most popular French type. So much was manufactured that a great deal of this cabriole-leg Louis XV furniture with its elaborate scroll "C" and "S" curves and naturalistic carvings of fruit, flowers, foliage and birds exists for the collector today.

One of the remarkable developments in furniture production at this time was the creation of sets. There were sets of furniture for parlor, boudoir, bedroom and library as well as the dining room. French rococo was especially favored for the drawing room, and sets to be used there consisted of one or more sofas, a center table, an ottoman, an étagère, at least two arm chairs, and four side chairs. Downing names Alexander Roux and Platt of New York as the best known local makers, but there were many more including Leon Marcotte, who was listed in the New York directories from 1850, and who advertised furniture of "Black wood and gilt, Rosewood and satin, carved center tables, marble tops, marquetry." There were also makers in Boston, Newport, R.I., Rochester, Troy, Philadelphia, and as far west as Cincinnati, Ohio, and south to New Orleans.

Most of this furniture was made of rosewood, mahogany or walnut, but some was made of bird's-eye maple, chestnut, zebra and other woods. It was not only carved but often decorated with dull or matte-finished gilding. Cheaper sets were made of chestnut, oak or dyed maple.

While it is impossible to name all of the manufacturers of this rococo furniture, for they finally increased to the hundreds, there are a few who were working in the early 1850's whose ads give us definite information about the overlapping of styles and the furniture made in a specific year. In 1853 George Henkels of Philadelphia advertised

Victorian rococo walnut turned-spindle side chair.

Victorian rococo open-arm chair with floral carving. (*Carren Limited*)

Rococo walnut ladies' chair, 1850–1870. (*The Henry Ford Museum*)

Rococo carved rosewood chair. E. Galusha, Troy, N.Y. (*Munson-Williams-Proctor Institute*)

"Furniture in every style, Louis XIV, Louis XV, Elizabethan, and Antique with sculpture carving; ('called Renaissance in France but Antique in America,' says Samuel Sloan in *Sloan's Homestead Architecture,* Philadelphia, 1866) and Modern Style in Rosewood, Walnut, Mahogany, Satinwood and Maple." Henkel's shop burned in 1854, but he rebuilt and in the advertisement of 1857 he makes this interesting statement which probably was the reason for the shift of woods. "Walnut is now more used than all others. The supply of mahogany and rosewood is diminishing, maple has not met with much favor. Oak is in great favor for dining and library furniture." The ad which appears in Bigelow's *History of Mercantile and Manufacturing,* vol. XI, shows a cut of the shop with an extension table in the center. Henkel's rosewood furniture was elaborately carved "by the best European artists." It was usually upholstered in satin, and the tables, consoles and étagères had tops of "Siena marble." The furniture was not cheap.

Edwin Smallwood of Boston, in an ad of 1853, states that he

LEFT. Victorian rococo mahogany side chair with side cresting. RIGHT. One of the many variants of the Victorian rococo mahogany side chair. (*Both, The Henry Ford Museum*)

makes elegant sofas, tête-à-têtes, divans, arm and rocking chairs suitable for the southern and western market, together with "new style French lolling couches (chaise-longue) of elegant design constructed so they can be boxed in parts." Smallwood's furniture was made of mahogany, black walnut, and rosewood, and upholstered in Plush, Damask, and Brocatelle. W. & J. Allen of Philadelphia also advertised similar furniture in an atlas of 1856.

However, the best-known name associated with American Rococo furniture was John Henry Belter. Belter set up his shop in New York in 1844 about the time that Duncan Phyfe went out of business, and Belter soon took Phyfe's place as New York's most fashionable cabinet-maker. Belter's furniture was made of six to eight laminated layers of thin rosewood. The wood of the outside layer runs vertically. The backs of his chairs were made from a single concave panel and were almost completely covered with carving. Crestings on sofas, mirrors and

LEFT, TOP AND BOTTOM. Rosewood carved-back parlor chairs. John Belter. (*The Metropolitan Museum of Art*)

BELOW, LEFT. Rosewood carved rococo side chair attributed to Belter. (*The Henry Ford Museum*) RIGHT. Rosewood parlor chair attributed to Belter. (*Carren Limited*)

aprons of tables are also intricately carved with grapes, leaves, roses and scrolls of interlacing foliage. Belter's furniture combines delicacy and strength. In the beginning some chair backs were covered with interlacing scrolls. The carving was elaborate and finely executed. The scroll-back chair had an arched cresting. A simple side chair had an upholstered back with smooth flowing scrolls and a small carved cresting at the top of the back.

The chairs most often associated with Belter have balloon-shaped backs framed by a scroll that is arched and topped by a carved crest. The scrolled medallion in the center of the back has a carving of leaves and a center bunch of grapes enclosed in the scrolls. The seat has a bow-front with a carved flower at the center. The front legs are cabriole and the back legs plain and tapering. Some side chairs have taller backs and the carving includes several bunches of grapes and leaves, with a cresting of roses at the top of the chair back and roses at the knees of the scrolled cabriole legs. Sometimes the side chair has an upholstered oval in the back which is surrounded by scrolls enclosing wide borders of elaborate rose or grape carving. There are also armchairs with intricate scrolls of grape and leaf carving set around a center medallion of upholstery and crested with a large carved rose.

Rosewood rococo sofa pierced and carved with flower, cornucopia and acorn design. (*The Metropolitan Museum of Art*)

There were also lady chairs without arms, but with high balloon-shaped or oval backs surrounded by carving. Belter sofas were made with triple-arch backs of one-piece construction with a continuous band of naturalistic carving enclosed in "C" scrolls, with crests at each end and in the center. There are also carved bosses or roses on the knees of the short cabriole legs and at the center of the front seat rail. Some sofas have a graduated asymmetrical arched back, tall at one end and lower at the other end. There are also couches with one end left backless.

Belter tables had an oval or cartouche-shaped top usually covered with marble. This was upheld by four cabriole legs which were supported by a carved X-shaped stretcher holding a center urn-shaped vase of carved flowers. The apron of the table was of openwork carving

Laminated carved rosewood table with marble top. John Belter. Stuffed birds under glass dome. (*The Henry Ford Museum*)

Rosewood card table made by Charles A. Baudouine. (*Munson-Williams-Proctor Institute*)

of roses, grapes, and foliage. Toward the end, Belter's carving became more naturalistic and on such pieces as the rosewood bed in the Brooklyn Museum the carving is made up of leaves and connecting vines. The legs on later furniture became heavier and straighter. Belter's furniture was covered by patents but few pieces were signed.

George Henkels of Philadelphia and Charles A. Baudouine of New York also made laminated rosewood furniture as well as the more common, less expensive type of French carved furniture. The furniture in President Lincoln's bedroom at the White House is of Belter type. The oval table has a wide apron of grape carving and the tall head-board of the bed is crested with elaborate openwork carving. The maker of this furniture is not known. French rococo furniture was made in many parts of America by many cabinetmakers and manufacturers. Some was well made and hand-carved, but much of it was cheaply made by machine.

The typical Louis XV rococo chair of the period was balloon-backed with plain finger-molding and with or without a carved crest at the top of the back or on the serpentine splat in the open back. The carving was of grapes, a pear or plum, with leafage; or on more elaborate chairs, a rose. These chairs have cabriole front legs. They are usually made of black walnut, but some are also made in rosewood. There is also an upholstered balloon-back side chair and gentlemen's and ladies' balloon-back upholstered armchairs. Open-arm upholstered chairs have a rectangular back topped with a bit of flower or fruit carving and there is also a similar chair with rockers. These were made in walnut, mahogany, or rosewood and were originally upholstered in black haircloth. The heavy Sleepy Hollow lounge chair was completely upholstered within a finger-molded mahogany frame.

The rococo sofa was made in various forms. The one with a serpentine back and enclosed arms is the most common. It is made

LEFT. Mahogany rocker with black haircloth seat. BELOW, LEFT. Rococo walnut side chair with balloon back and paired "C" scroll splat. RIGHT: Balloon-back mahogany side chair with finger-grooved carving and foliated tendrils. (*The Henry Ford Museum*)

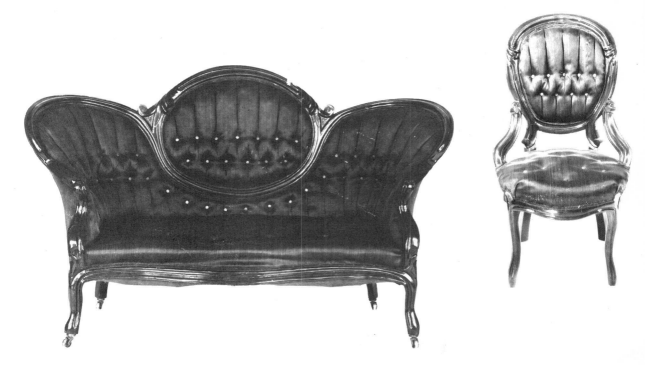

Common-type mahogany settee with carved foliated tendrils and haircloth upholstery. Similar sofas made in walnut. Matching mahogany side chair. (*The Henry Ford Museum*)

with finger-molding, in walnut, and in mahogany and rosewood with carved cresting at top sides and center. Similar sofas were also made with open arms. There were also serpentine-back sofas with an oval medallion of upholstery in their back and some have triple-backs resembling three oval-backed chairs attached together. There were also side chairs and armchairs with upholstered oval backs, and all had cabriole legs. Along with these rococo chairs and sofas there would be an oval table with cabriole legs and a center vase stretcher, or an oval table with scalloped apron and a center pedestal supported by four legs, an elaborately carved étagère, or a tall pier glass with a low elaborately carved table at its base. This would be set between windows whose cornices were often carved to match the pier glass and its table. Closely connected with the popular Louis XV rococo was the heavier straight line Louis XIV style with its broken pediments and baroque cartouche crests on tall rectangular-backed chairs. The Louis XVI style was also copied, but where it was a light delicate style in France, in America it became heavy and bawdy.

Renaissance Revival parlor sofa and chairs. Meeks' Cabinet and Furniture Warehouse. (*Harper's Weekly,* November 14, 1863)

The Renaissance Revival Style

THE Renaissance Revival style with its heavy straight lines and architectural ornament such as pediments, cartouches, and applied medallions of carved decoration came into prominence at the Crystal Palace exhibitions. At the New York Crystal Palace Exhibition in 1853 Thomas Brooks of Brooklyn exhibited a large carved rosewood buffet; a carved sideboard of Renaissance design with carved panels of game and fish was also exhibited by Rochefort. A similar sideboard has a center panel scene of dogs and game and side panels of fish and lobster, while a hunter with bow and arrow stands within the broken pediment at the top of the sideboard. This was made by E. W. Hutchins of New York. Alexander Roux also exhibited a carved walnut sideboard and table. A sideboard of more restrained design by Daniel Pabst of Philadelphia was made c. 1870 and is now in the Philadelphia Museum of Art. A beautiful cabinet of rosewood with tulip and ebony inlay panels within

32

its heavy Renaissance architectural structure lines is in the Newark Museum. It was made by Leon Marcotte of New York in the 1870's.

A great deal of Renaissance Revival furniture was also made at Grand Rapids at about this date. The heavy sideboards have panelled bases with rounding ends which have doors and drawers which conform to the rounded shape, and each panel has a spray of carved fruit. This is surmounted by one or more shelves with pediment and carving. These large sideboards were usually made of black walnut or mahogany in quality furniture factories such as Berkey & Gay in the 1870's. Large round extension tables with center ornate pedestal were made to match. There were also smaller round Renaissance marble-topped tables with a pedestal consisting of a turned column and four scroll legs. A smaller marble-topped table with similar column support and scroll legs was used as a lamp or vase stand. There was also a rectangular

Walnut Sideboard, Renaissance style, Daniel Pabst, 1869. (*Philadelphia Museum of Art*)

Renaissance Revival walnut side chairs with burl walnut panels. (*The Henry Ford Museum*)

Renaissance Revival armchair with incised and carved ornament from Congress Hotel, Saratoga Springs. (*Carren, Ltd.*)

table supported by scrolled trestles and a turned stretcher. It has carved flower and leaf medallions on the drawer and table ends. This table was factory-made in black walnut. A Renaissance Revival drop-leaf table with trestle end supports was also made in black walnut. The upholstered Renaissance Revival armchair has heavy turned legs or legs accented with round medallions, fluted columns, and was often decorated with black enamel and gilt. There is a matching side chair. The Renaissance Revival bed was made of black walnut with panels of burl veneer. The headboard is tall and massive. It is divided into architectural panels and topped with a pediment centered by a large cartouche. The footboard is one of similar design with curved ends. The matching bureau has three drawers with leaf-carved wooden handles or tear-drop pulls, a marble top, and a mirror with bracket shelves and a pedimented scroll top. Sometimes there are small drawers at the base of the mirror, and sometimes the top drawer becomes two side drawers and there is an open space in the center and the huge

Renaissance Revival table with Corinthian column legs and vase on stretcher. Leon Marcotte. (*The Metropolitan Museum of Art*)

ABOVE. Renaissance Revival walnut chest with foliated handles and split urn applied decoration. Mass produced. RIGHT. Renaissance Revival walnut bureau. BELOW. Renaissance Revival bed, oak with walnut trim and burl maple panel. (*The Henry Ford Museum*)

mirror extends to this level. A simpler version is made with four drawers and a curved top mirror supported by scrolls. A heavy tall black walnut secretary of rectangular construction with glass doors above a lower desk is seldom carved except for rosette details on the lower doors and at the top of the glass doors. Renaissance Revival furniture is so large and heavy that there is no place for it except in the old high-ceiling mansion, few of which exist today. However, where such articles as the bed and chests of drawers are well constructed and can be bought cheaply, they may be cut down to smaller pieces of furniture.

Renaissance Revival walnut secretary desk with broken pediment and foliated carving. 1865–1875. (*The Henry Ford Museum*)

Milligan Study from Saratoga. Gothic Revival chairs and Gothic influence in corner étagère, panels on secretary-bookcase, and details of lamp base. (*Brooklyn Museum*)

Victorian Gothic (1840–1865)

GOTHIC style furniture was favored by Andrew Jackson Downing. In his *Architecture of Country Houses* he includes a lengthy discussion of Gothic, and gives the characteristic details and illustrations of the Gothic furniture available in America in 1850. An antique settle for a

38

large hall in country style is made of oak or walnut with a leather cushion. A hall stand and cottage chairs with rush bottoms or haircloth seats, armchairs with Gothic arches and pieced work, and book cases with Gothic panels in their glass doors all show taste and simplicity. Similar chairs with a combination of classic outline and Gothic detail are illustrated in Edgar G. Miller's *American Antique Furniture* and there is a similar chair made of mahogany with pointed arches and trefoil in the Brooklyn Museum. Downing also illustrates more elaborate Gothic furniture—armchairs with twisted turnings, partly Elizabethan; a day bed, a round center table and dining room sideboard. All these are made of oak and are ornate and heavy with elaborate carving of pointed arches, crockets, and trefoil piercing. These were made by Roux of New York and in a footnote Downing says: "The most correct Gothic furniture that we have yet seen executed in this country is by Burns and Tranque, Broadway, New York. Some excellent specimens may also be seen at Roux's." Gothic details were also used in the country furniture made by Hennessey of Boston, and by John Jelliff of Newark, New Jersey.

Although Gothic furniture has been thought of as church furniture a great deal of it was made for private houses. Just how much exists today is questionable since it was long ago relegated to the attic or the bonfire. In addition to that made in quantity by furniture manufacturers, individual pieces and sets were made by such architects as William Strickland, Charles Notman, Thomas U. Walter, and A. J. Davis in the 1830–40's. Some of this furniture exists today, especially in the old houses in and near Burlington, New Jersey, and in St. Mary's Episcopal School in Burlington; in several old New York churches and parsonages; and undoubtedly there is much undocumented Victorian Gothic scattered throughout America since many old furniture ads picture Gothic chairs.

A. J. Davis was probably the most active designer of Gothic furniture and his diaries show that he was sketching and designing furniture as early as 1828. He not only designed chairs, tables, pulpits and organs for churches, but for the many houses which he built along the Hudson and in upper New York State and Connecticut. Although the Davis designs were original he studied Loudon's *Encyclopedia of Architecture* and Pugin's *Gothic Furniture,* which were among the books in his library.

In 1836–38 Davis was designing a Gothic house for Nathan Warren at Mt. Ida, Troy, New York. At the suggestion of the client, Davis drew sketches. According to notes left by Davis' son, two Gothic armchairs, a library sofa and an organ case were designed by Davis and made for Nathan Warren.

In the 1840's Davis also designed the furniture for the J. Angier Gothic cottage in Medford, Mass., and for the Joel Rathbone mansion, Kenwood, near Albany. On May 31, 1844, the entry in his *Diary* at the New York Public Library reads: "Mr. Rathbone here. Designed a table for him." He also designed a "Gate lodge and furniture," and in 1846 "Rathbone Details Bookcase." The sketch of the drawing room at Kenwood in Downing's *Country Houses* shows a Gothic mantel and Gothic chairs, settee and tables, and also an Elizabethan armchair.

A bill to J. J. Herrick dated September, 1853, indicates that Davis had the following Gothic furniture made for Herrick:

8 small armchairs with crockets and back, Gothic
8 lady chairs to match
1 table for dining room extension and round

Victorian Gothic washstand, cottage type. Mahogany veneer on pine. (*The Henry Ford Museum*)

In 1838 Davis began work on a Gothic mansion for the Pauldings in Tarrytown. In the *Diaries* there are many references to this house, which, with its Davis-designed furnishings, stands today as a monument to Davis' ability and an example of the best work of the era. Between June and September, 1841, Davis sketched "50 designs for furniture for Paulding—$50.00 # (*Diary*, Metropolitan Museum of Art). In the *Diary* in the New York Public Library is this item of September I, 1841: "At Tarrytown 6 days and sketching for furniture (Paulding). October 5, 1841: "Designing furniture for Paulding. Oct. 5, 6, 7, 8—Nov. 6. Returned to Pauldings. Designs for furniture." *Diary*, Metropolitan Museum of Art, page 364: "Met P. at Dobbs Ferry. Rode to Wrights', Astounding furniture." In a note added to the *Diary* in the New York

ABOVE. Walnut side chair with carved back showing rococo and Gothic influence. (*The Henry Ford Museum*)

RIGHT. Rosewood chair with open quatrefoil and carved crocket finial. John Jelliff. (*Newark Museum*)

Public Library we are told: "Richard Byrnes of White Plains made with Wright cabinet work at Pauldings."

The opening of Lyndhurst, which was originally the Paulding house in Tarrytown, New York, and the discovery of many pieces of Davis furniture stored there for many years, brings our attention to Davis as a furniture designer. The chair from Davis' own home, probably Kerri cottage, is simple in design and the workmanship is excellent. It is made of rosewood and was given by Davis' son to the Museum of the City of New York.

Picture gallery at Lyndhurst, showing Gothic paneling and Gothic side chairs designed by A. J. Davis. (*Collection, Avery Library, Columbia University*)

Country couple sitting in fancy chairs; table, painted wood graining. Water color by Joseph H. Davis. (*The New-York Historical Society*)

Victorian Country Furniture (1840–1900)

FROM the standpoint of the collector today, Victorian Country Furniture is the most important of all Victorian designs because it fits into the present-day house and is available and inexpensive. In the vocabulary of this writer, Country Furniture includes all furniture of simple design made of less expensive woods such as pine, hickory, maple, chestnut, walnut and other native woods. Country Furniture is often reminiscent of older styles. Actual pieces include Windsor, Hitchcock, and other fancy chairs, spool furniture and cottage furniture. Country Furniture is not a separate style, but a simpler presentation of other styles. It reflects the more sophisticated furniture which was being made at the same time. What we now call Country Furniture was originally called Cottage Furniture, and included spool furniture and cottage French style. At first it reflected the Empire style, later it became related to Louis XV, and some Country Furniture goes back to early American inspiration.

Generally, however, Country Furniture was based on the needs and requirements of middle class customers in the rural districts rather than those of people in the large cities. Practicality was the keynote for Country Furniture. There were no ornate sideboards or heavy-headed beds or large padded chairs. Instead there were essential pieces of furniture such as dry sinks, washstands, light side chairs, and sturdy but small beds, tables, and chests of drawers. There is little carving or decoration and the furniture was usually painted instead of oiled or varnished. This furniture was made in large quantities by rural furniture makers and carpenters, and later mass-produced in factories throughout America. There are great quantities of it today and it can be found in all parts of the country at reasonable prices.

Country-style washstand and bureau. Pine, painted and grained. (*The Henry Ford Museum*)

Early Country Furniture varied with the locality. Thus the Country Furniture of New England, the furniture of the Shakers, and the Pennsylvania Dutch furniture, as well as that made in the Middle West, all had their own distinguishing characteristics, but by the time we reach the middle of the nineteenth century there were factories turning out Country Furniture and shipping it to all parts of America and the regional differences disappeared in the mass production. Early ladder-back chairs and small hickory rockers with rush seats, trestle and tavern tables or drop-leaf tables of maple or ash originally made for the kitchen are all popular country pieces today. The cherry

LEFT, TOP AND BOTTOM. Walnut chest of drawers with towel rack. Country piece with Renaissance Revival influence. Country-type pine washstand. 1850–1880.
(*The Henry Ford Museum*)

BELOW. Kitchen table. Walnut frame stained dark brown. Top unfinished ash boards. c. 1850.
(*The Index of American Design*)

cupboard on a table with turned legs, the storekeeper's desk, the schoolteacher's slant-top desk and even the pupils' desk supported by cast iron, are dear to the heart of the Country Furniture enthusiast. Maple commodes with marble tops and carved-leaf drawer handles were made after 1850. There are also Eastlake walnut commodes with brown marble tops and metal drawer pulls. These were made in the 1880's, but today they are stripped of varnish and sold as *Country Furniture*. Washstands, kitchen safes and dry sinks, kitchen tables, and even the dentist's golden oak cabinet are other pieces that are now collected.

In writing about Victorian Country Furniture it is a mistake to omit slat-back, banister-back and Windsor chairs, or Hitchcock and fancy chairs, for although they were originally made in the eighteenth

Late nineteenth century dry sink and cabinet, pine, with Gothic panels in doors. Pennsylvania. (*The Index of American Design*)

century, they continued to be made with slight variations in the Victorian nineteenth century. Late types of these chairs are found in the average shop today and are our earliest pieces of nineteenth century Victorian Country Furniture. Early chair makers advertised themselves as "Fancy and Windsor Chairmakers." By 1825 almost every town had such a chairmaker. Besides their use in private homes fancy chairs were used on steamboats, and in hotel lobbies. As late as the 1840's fancy chairs were used in great numbers in Castle Garden, New York, and in 1850 Windsor settees were made for church pews and for use in schools.

Windsor chairs were made in factories from 1850. The Windsor chair is an all-wood chair. Its back is made of spindles joined to a conforming saddle seat. The legs are turned with vase or bamboo turnings. Various woods are used: poplar for the seats, hickory for spindles and arms, and hickory, ash, maple, or other light woods for legs and stretchers. Old Windsors were always painted, mostly green but also red, black, yellow, or white. Windsor chairs are classified according to the shape of their backs. There are the fan-back, loop-back, sack-back and comb-back. There was also the low-back or horseshoe Windsor armchair of which the Captain's Chair is a variant. Victorian Windsor types were made as late as 1870 and 1890. These include hoop-backs, square-back Windsor side chairs, and a variety of Windsor loop-back which were made in factories and sold as kitchen chairs. There was also a low-back Windsor with caned seat and carving and a hand-hole in the center of the back which was made of oak or ash for use as a dining room chair. An office chair similar to a Captain's Chair was mass-produced in hickory and oak. These are the Windsors seen today in shops all over the country.

Hitchcock started the making of fancy chairs in quantity and the same type chairs were made at many factories throughout New England in the middle of the nineteenth century. The Hitchcock factory closed in 1852, but in 1949 reproductions of Hitchcock chairs began to be made at the old factory in Riverton, Connecticut. The typical Hitchcock chair was a combination of Directoire and Sheraton. It had a rectangular back with one or more horizontal splats, a turned top rail, with a center pillow, slender turned legs, and a rush or cane seat. Later seats were made of wood. The chairs were painted red-brown or black to imitate wood. Stencil decoration of gold was applied to the legs and splats and the top rail was stenciled with a design of fruit or flowers in a bowl, basket or cornucopia. Designs of roses, shells, a lyre or an eagle were less common. The chairs that concern the collector of Victorian furniture would be made after 1840. If they are marked they would be stenciled "Lambert Hitchcock, Unionville, Conn.," but few of them are found marked. The chairs of late Hitchcock type are usually made by other makers. Some have rush or cane seats and others have wooden seats and the back slats may be horizontal or upright arrow-shaped. Sometimes the chairs are painted yellow instead of reddish-brown and often late stenciling is of a landscape, or a scene showing a country seat may be hand-painted as on the Maryland type fancy chair. There were good stencil painters of the old type working in Maine and Massachusetts until the end of the century and any chairs stenciled by them would be well done. A late fancy chair has a crested balloon-back with three turned spindles, a cane seat, and

LEFT. Painted pine comb-back Windsor chair, 1870. (*The Index of American Design*) CENTER. Painted and grained maple side chair with caned seat, 1860–1875. (*The Henry Ford Museum*) RIGHT. Maple side chair with turned legs and caned seat, 1860–1875. (*The Henry Ford Museum*)

turned legs. Fancy chairs were usually made for the dining room but were also used in the living room, bedroom, and on the veranda. Fancy and painted chairs were popular until the 1890's and many late ones that were made for kitchens are collected for the drawing rooms of today.

The Country Furniture of the nineteenth century was known as Cottage Furniture. *Godey's Lady's Book* was illustrating this Cottage Furniture from 1849 and Downing in his *Architecture of Country Houses,* 1850, recommends Hennessey of Boston, who made Cottage Furniture and supplied orders from various parts of the Union and West Indies. Downing describes it thus: "This furniture is remarkable for its combination of lightness and strength. It is very highly finished and is usually painted drab, white, gray, a delicate lilac, or a fine blue—the surface polished and hard, like enamel. Some of the better sets have groups of flowers or other designs painted upon them." The illustrations of bedroom sets include sleigh beds and bureaus, washstands and a wardrobe which show the influence of French Empire, but the tables, chairs, and towel racks have spool turnings. These sets could be pur-

LEFT. Hitchcock chair painted black with stencil design in gold and colors, 1832–1840. (*The Index of American Design*) CENTER. Hickory rawhide-bottom ladderback country chair. Witte Memorial Museum. (*The Index of American Design*) RIGHT. Late Windsor armchair. Pine and maple, painted green with red line trim. "Firehouse" type. (*The Henry Ford Museum*)

chased with or without "gilt lines" or marble tops. Horace Farrington of New York (1848–1860) illustrated more elaborate cottage furniture —"French style, enameled and grained." At the New York Crystal Palace Exhibition in 1853 enamelled and ornamental Cottage Furniture was exhibited by Gillies & Byrne of New York and by Hart, Ware & Co., of Philadelphia. By 1856 Joseph Meeks was advertising Cottage Furniture, and an interesting letter now in the New-York Historical Society, written in 1859 by the furniture manufacturer J. W. Mason of New York, to his client in Danbury gives added information about Cottage Furniture. He says: 'The seats are made of white wood, arms like Boston Rockers in imitation Rosewood, Black Walnut, Oak, Maple and drab or green color, the price being the same for either color. Drab color we think the best for halls unless it is desirable to match some other color on account of the walls of the house."

This type of furniture continued to be made in Massachusetts, Vermont, Maine, Ohio, and by the Sheboygan Chair Co. in 1890.

Spool furniture forms another group of Country Furniture. Spool furniture is turned on a lathe. It was made in small shops at the beginning of the nineteenth century and later mass produced in factories. The turnings were in various forms; spool, button, knob, sausage, bobbin, vase and ring. Spool furniture represents a resurgence of

Jenny Lind type cherry spool-turned bed, 1850–1870. (*The Henry Ford Museum*)

the turned Flemish furniture of the seventeenth century. However, Victorian spool furniture which was made from 1840 was influenced by the Elizabethan according to Downing, who illustrates two of Hennessey of Boston's bedroom sets made for the bracketed cottage. The simplest set shows a spool bed with vertical spindles in the head- and footboard and a washstand, dressing table, oval mirror and a side chair, all with some form of twisted or spool-turned leg. They were made of black walnut, maple, or birch. The more elaborate set has heavier ball turnings and could be had in dark wood or painted drab "enriched by well-executed vignettes in the panels." There were also spool beds with posts and head and foot boards made of plain wood instead of spindles. Sometimes a pediment topped the row of spindles.

The later style of spool bed had curved corners, and was called a Jenny Lind bed. There are also high-posted spool beds and spool cribs and cradles. There were Pembroke and oval drop-leaf tables with spool-turned legs. Small rectangular side tables and serving tables, washstands and dressing tables also had spool-turned legs. They were made of black walnut in the factory, or of maple, poplar, or cherry stained or painted. There were also towel racks and tall shaving stands, stools and chairs made with twisted or spool legs. Split spindles were applied to the sides of chests of drawers and the frames of mirrors. Spool furniture was the first factory mass-produced furniture. It was simple in design and inexpensive in price.

LEFT. Cherry spool-turned table, 1850–1865. (*The Henry Ford Museum*) RIGHT. Walnut towel rack, 1860–1880. (*The Henry Ford Museum*)

Today the various types of spool beds are easily found. Those of natural wood are more expensive because of the job of removing the sometimes many layers of paint. Towel racks and small tables are also inexpensive, but washstands are more in demand and thus more expensive. The most sought after piece is the small sewing or bedside table, especially when made of maple, cherry, or mahogany.

Another type of Country Furniture which is in demand today and therefore expensive, is the simple *Shaker furniture*. The restraint and

LEFT: Mahogany dressing mirror with twisted supports; Elizabethan style. BELOW LEFT. Walnut side chair with twisted supports and turned legs; Elizabethan style. (*The Henry Ford Museum*) RIGHT. Carved oak settee; Elizabethan-medieval style. (*Mr. and Mrs. William Crawford*)

integrity of their religious life is reflected in stark simplicity and purity of form of this furniture. The severe beauty is due to fine proportions of line and mass and a harmonious relationship between the parts, which result in artistic unity. Shaker furniture has no decoration and little turning. The legs of chairs and tables are thin and tapering and the chair backs have simple slats; one or two on the low dining room chairs and three on side chairs, while the backs of the rocking chairs had three or four slats and often a narrow rod across the top. Armchairs had mushroom knobs at the end of the arms. There were arm rockers and small armless sewing chairs. The seats of the early chairs were made of rush, later seats were of woven tape. Much of the Shaker furniture

Group of Shaker furniture made before 1850. Round stand, pine with curved molded maple feet. Small spool stand. Wall rack with Shaker bonnet hanging. Shaker rocker with scrolled arms and turned pointed finials. (*Celeste and Edward Koster*)

Early nineteenth century Shaker drop-leaf table and side chair. Hancock Museum, Massachusetts. (*Celeste and Edward Koster*)

was made of pine, but apple, cherry, maple, and pear woods were also used. The early furniture was painted or stained red.

The Shakers made several different types of tables. A long trestle table had square or rectangular supports with flat or curved shoes. There were pine ironing tables with crossed braces and horizontal stretchers. Drop-leaf tables were made with a drawer and with or without a rectangular stretcher supporting base. There were also small oval tables, sewing tables, and round and square tripod stands. The long kitchen table had two drawers, a shelf beneath and end supports. A bread-cutting table had a rim around three sides of its top and a drawer. It stood on four tapered legs.

Pennsylvania Dutch painted chair with one
arrow splat in back, c. 1850.
(*The Index of American Design*)

Early Shaker chest showing Chippendale influence in the base and top moulding.
(*Celeste and Edward Koster*)

The Shaker case-furniture included chests, blanket chests, chests of
drawers, high chests with many drawers, cupboards, washstands, and
writing desks. Beds were made of maple and pine with a low-posted
head and footboard. The narrow cots were painted green. Both beds
and cots were set on rollers. In 1874 and 1876 the Shakers of New
Lebanon, Columbia County, New York, issued illustrated catalogues of
chairs, foot benches, etc. R. W. Wagan & Co. also issued a catalogue.
The later commercial Shaker furniture can be recognized by the changes
in design and workmanship.

The Rocking Chair

THE rocking chair is an American invention and an American institution. It was a particular favorite of the Victorian furniture makers. Slat-back, banister-back, ladder-back and Windsor rocking chairs with rush seats go back to the middle of the eighteenth century, but the majority of the existing antique rocking chairs have rockers that were added. Chairs were not made with rockers until 1800 and the rocking chair did not really become popular until after 1840. Windsor rocking chairs were made both with oval and square backs and there are comb-back and fan-back Windsor rockers. Some early rocking chairs show Empire influence in the shape of their top rails and the center vase-like splat in their backs. With the advent of the fancy chair the rocker gained in popularity and both Windsor and Sheraton fancy chairs were made with rockers.

The famous Boston rocker developed from the Windsor rocker. Both the Windsor rocker and the Boston rocker have a solid wooden

LEFT. Mahogany rocker with rococo carving and black haircloth upholstery, 1860–1875. (*The Henry Ford Museum*) RIGHT. Curly maple rocker with birdseye maple crested rail and cane back and seat, 1850–1860. (*The Henry Ford Museum*)

seat and thin spindles in the back and a top rail, but where the top rail of the Windsor rocker is usually more delicate and has a narrow fan or a comb-back top rail, the Boston rocker has a large top rail and the pine wooden seat curves up at the back and down in the front. These curved sections are separate pieces attached to the seat. The legs and arms were usually made of maple, the spokes and rockers of ash and the top rails of pine. The Boston rocker is more decorative than the Windsor. The designs include not only fruit and flowers, but the Boston rocker is often decorated with painted seascapes or landscape scenes. Sometimes the scene is historic, such as the Harrison Log Cabin and Cider Scene which was painted on the rocker during the campaign of 1840. Boston rockers were made in many forms and many variations. There were small rockers made without arms and there were children's rockers. William Eaton of Boston decorated rockers until the end of the century and often labeled them "Boston Rockers—W. P. Eaton." Some rockers are also marked "M. L. Gates, Boston."

The Pennsylvania Dutch rocker had a back splat instead of spindles

LEFT. Boston rocker with painted and stencilled decoration and typical rolling crest and curved seat. (*The Henry Ford Museum*) RIGHT. Shaker rocker with tape back and seat, mushroom knobs at ends of arms and turned finials. (*The New-York Historical Society*)

and both the top piece and the splat were painted with typical Pennsylvania Dutch designs of bright red and yellow tulips, daisies, or birds. It was made of maple and other hard woods. The Shaker rocking chairs have tall backs with three slats and a woven, shaved wood seat. The spindle supports of the chair are simple with no decorative turning. A Windsor rocker of maple with pine seat is called a "Burlington" or "Shelburne" rocker. This type was later painted black with floral decoration on the top splat.

There are many other types of later country rockers with rectangular or oval backs framed in maple, and with backs and seats of cane. These rockers are found both with and without arms. They often have a carved flower or fruit motif or a spray of hand-painted flowers. They are made of walnut, maple, or birch. In 1853 the Oswego Chair Factory manufactured "Grecian cane rockers" as well as Boston rockers, and in 1859 a Reception Rocking Chair, that stood on casters and rocked, was patented by Terry & Wills of New York. There were also Eastlake rockers on platforms, and small folding rockers upholstered in carpet tapestry were made late in the century.

LEFT. Late nineteenth century maple Shaker rocker made at Mt. Morris, New York. (*The New-York Historical Society*) RIGHT. Late Victorian rocking chair with turned construction. Maple painted black with yellow trim. Berlin work upholstery. (*The Henry Ford Museum*)

Eastlake (1870–90)

ONE wonders what would have been the result and what type of furniture we would be collecting today had Whistler's beautiful Peacock Room, which he decorated in 1872, been exhibited at the Centennial instead of Eastlake's cabinets. But Eastlake's book, *Hints on Household Taste,* had reached America in 1872 and, instead of Whistler's Peacock Room, examples of Eastlake's sturdy oak furniture were exhibited at the Centennial in Philadelphia in 1876. The book had already created the market for this furniture and there was an immediate demand for Eastlake. Grand Rapids complied with the public's desire. In his book, Eastlake championed honest craftsmanship and a close alliance between the materials of which an object was made and its design. He wrote: "The natural grain of such woods as oak, rosewood, and walnut, etc., is in itself an ornamental feature. But where an effect of greater richness is aimed at, two legitimate modes of decoration are available for wood, viz. carving and marquetry or inlaid work." Fine examples of furniture are shown as illustrations in the book, but the Grand Rapids interpretation relied on the mass production of machines rather than the personal expression of the craftsman.

The fundamental outlines of the furniture which Eastlake advocated were complied with, and the furniture was made with a straight line rectangular structure, but the quality of workmanship was shoddy and the design motifs of machine incised and veneer panels which were glued on obliterated the simple rectangular structure, and Eastlake's original ideas were completely misinterpreted.

Eastlake furniture was made of many different woods, but that which we see is mostly oak or walnut. It was decorated with machine scroll carving and burl walnut veneer panels. The carving consisted of jigsaw scrolls and rosettes and incised lines of geometric design. Sometimes the furniture was painted black with gold linings. Tables and chests had marble tops and the hardware escutcheons and handles were oxidized or plated brass. The marble for the tops of Eastlake furniture was imported and there were many kinds available, including Carrara, Siena, Egyptian, Brocatelle, Levante, Pyrenees, Bardella and Lisbon.

The typical Eastlake side chair is of straight line construction. It has turned tapering front legs and front stretchers with ring turning. The seat is caned and the open back has three horizontal crossbars divided by turned spindles, two on the lower tiers and a row of from four to six at the top. Sometimes the top rail has a panel of burl veneer. Another style of Eastlake side chair has a machine-cut vase splat in its back. The back and seat are joined together by machine-scroll arms and the seat is caned. These chairs were sold in sets and included a small rocking chair of similar design with a caned seat and back. Eastlake office chairs had the same spindle decoration in their backs. They were set on a steel screw which allowed the chair to tilt back and forth. This was upheld by four bracket feet. An Eastlake chair with upholstered seat and back was set on a similar center screw with four leg supports and was used as a desk chair or a piano stool. There were also rectangular upholstered piano stools without backs.

Eastlake chairs, custom-made of exotic wood. Carved panel designs show Renaissance influence. (*Mr. and Mrs. William Crawford*)

The typical Eastlake parlor chair has a back and seat upholstered in black horsehair. The frame is oak or walnut with applied panels of burl veneer and there is a rosette in the center of the back rail. Three of these chair backs were joined to form a settee. An armchair of ebonized wood made for the Rockefeller House at 4 West 54th Street, New York, in 1885, is now in the Brooklyn Museum. Although it shows Turkish influence in its elaborate embroidered and fringed upholstery, the panel in its back contains a row of spindles similar to those in the panel at the top of the cheap Eastlake side chairs.

The Eastlake platform rocker was a rectangular upholstered chair with arm rests and open arms. It sat on a platform of jigsaw scrolls and the chair and base were connected by springs which allowed the chair to rock. These chairs were made of walnut or oak and were sometimes a part of the parlor set. They were called Queen Anne Patent Rockers. They were also made with a bamboo-turned frame. An Eastlake Windsor was advertised in 1870. This was an armchair with a finger

Eastlake sofa, walnut, with Renaissance vase in center of back. (*The Henry Ford Museum*)

hole in the back rail and these chairs were for offices, hotels, and public institutions. But the bête noir of all Eastlake chairs was the folding chair with carpet seat and back. It was trimmed with wide fringe which hung down over the front of the seat. These chairs were advertised by Heywood Bros. of Gardiner, Massachusetts, in 1883–84. The *tête-à-tête* or conversation chair which had first been made earlier in the century was also in popular favor now. It was built on an "O G" structure holding two chairs with upholstered seats and backs made up of spindles. The padded top rail was hung with long fringe. These chairs were often placed in the center of a room.

Eastlake tables were rectangular or square with marble tops and aprons decorated with typical applied rectangular panels of burl veneer, and machine-carved rosettes. Some table tops were upheld by bracket legs and a center stretcher, others had four legs or tripod supports. There were several types of *desks* and *secretaries* made for both women and men in Eastlake style. The Eastlake ladies' desk has small drawers in the side of its tall base, a flap-top writing compartment and a shelf upheld by spindles and topped with a row of spindles and a pediment. It is made of oak with burl walnut veneer panels. A hanging wall desk has side shelves for bric-a-brac and opens to reveal a desk with drawers, pigeonholes and a fold-down flap for writing. This desk was patented in 1887. There is also a tall Eastlake bookcase secretary with cabinets below the slant-top desk with a glass-doored cabinet above for books. This is topped by an oval fan pediment of machine carving or by a panel of burl-veneer. Similar secretaries and smaller desks were also made with cylinder fronts. The Eastlake sideboard was made of walnut or a combination of walnut and maple. It is much taller than it is wide. The lower chest of drawers is topped with several shelves backed by mirrors and upheld by scroll-cut brackets and surmounted by a rectangular pediment. Similar shelves to hold bric-a-brac were built around the mirror above the mantel. Sometimes this mantel, shelf, and mirror construction was sold in one piece—"ash mantel and mirror." There is also a tall Eastlake bookcase with a set of drawers below the double glass doors. It has an overhanging top with a gallery of scrolled brackets.

The *Eastlake panelled bed* was usually made of oak or walnut. Less expensive beds were of lighter woods such as birch, maple, or ash. Eastlake bedroom sets were advertised in the following combinations: "Silver maple and mahogany, bamboo and maple, whitewood ornamented and ash." Beds five feet wide were advertised for southern trade. The tall headboard and the lower footboard were divided into rectangular panels of burl veneer or incised line decoration. They had an overhanging cornice or the headboard may have had a rectangular, triangular, or fan-shaped pediment. The bedroom set also included a

LEFT. Eastlake fall-front desk, walnut with burl walnut panels. c. 1880. (*Grand Rapids Public Museum*) RIGHT. Eastlake hall stand with inlaid panels, gouged carving and row of spindles in cresting. (*Grand Rapids Public Museum*)

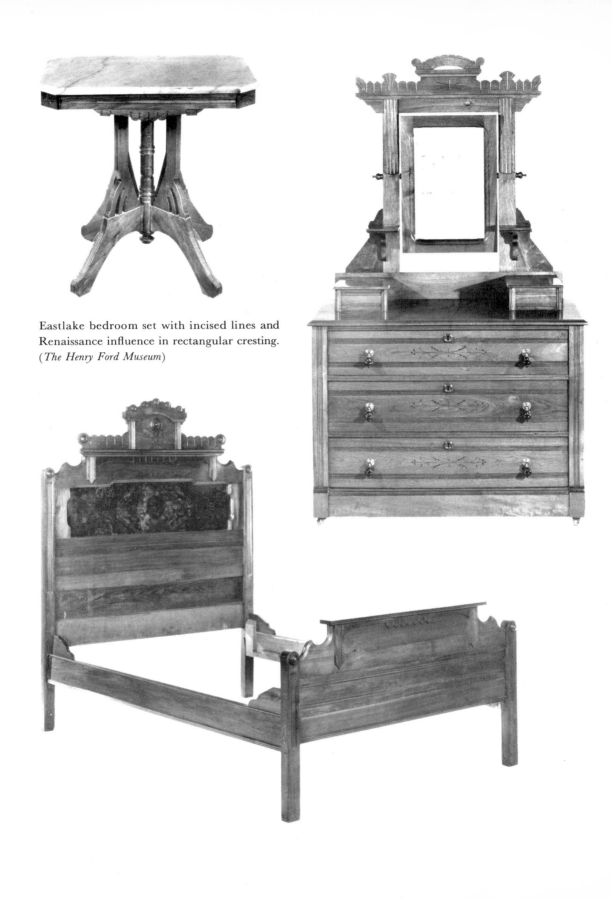

Eastlake bedroom set with incised lines and
Renaissance influence in rectangular cresting.
(*The Henry Ford Museum*)

tall *wardrobe,* and a *bureau* or chest with three ample drawers and a large rectangular mirror surmounted by a pediment of scrolls and machine-cut brackets. The mirror is also fastened to the chest with brackets. The top of the bureau is covered with marble and sometimes there are small drawers at either end. There are also tall sets of drawers for gentlemen, which have five or six drawers. These are decorated with incised line designs and have a gallery of turned spindles at the top. There are tall *Eastlake mirrors* and *pier glasses* with oak or walnut frames decorated with panels of veneer or ebony gilded with geometric line patterns. They are crested with a rectangular pediment. Corner whatnots, hanging shelves and wall brackets of jigsaw oak or

Eastlake pump organ with gouged carving, inlaid panel and rows of spindles. Esty Organ Co.; c. 1900. (*Grand Rapids Public Museum*)

walnut scroll work added to the maze of scroll and jigsaw and incised line machine decoration that characterizes the Eastlake period.

When one recalls the beautiful William Morris designs for chintz and wallpaper and some of the rooms in England which were decorated by Morris and also by Eastlake it seems a sacrilege to call this American factory furniture "Eastlake." Yet Eastlake it is and for lack of anything better people are buying it today not as collector's pieces, but for use. Bad as this furniture is, it is not any worse than some of the hybrid designs still being manufactured and foisted off on the average American housewife who has little feeling for good design. Eastlake is strong if not well made and the pieces found in second-hand shops are usually in good condition, cheap in price, and need little repair.

Other Types

At the same time that America was furnishing with Eastlake there were several other types of furniture which came into being. There was an increased interest in *overstuffed* furniture probably due not only to the American's love of comfort, but to the international attention which was directed toward Turkey and things Eastern. Every house had its *Turkish cozy corner,* piled high with sofa cushions, and the *ottoman* and over-stuffed chairs reached a zenith of popularity.

Overstuffed chair, Turkish influence. Tip-top papier mâché table inlaid with mother-of-pearl. (*The Henry Ford Museum*)

Victorian fancy chair with bamboo turnings.
1840–1880. (*Index of American Design*)

ABOVE. Bamboo-turned screen with Berlin
work tapestry. Brass standing lamp. 1890.
(*The Henry Ford Museum*)

LEFT. Maple table painted black, marble top.
Eastlake with Oriental influence in carved
panels. (*The Henry Ford Museum*)

BELOW. Walnut tête-à-tête, Turkish influence.
1880–1900. (*The Henry Ford Museum*)

Whatnots, Étagères and Hanging Shelves

No Victorian parlor was considered properly furnished unless it had a whatnot or étagère for the display of bric-a-brac and curiosities. All the collected odd pieces of china, shells, coral, bits of carved ivory, and family pictures on fancy standing frames found a resting place on the shelves of the whatnot or étagère. The simple whatnot is really a country piece and thousands of these were made, while the étagère, derived from the French, is a larger, more sophisticated piece of furniture designed for the parlor of the more affluent citizen. The whatnot usually had five shelves of graduating size—small toward the top. The shelves were joined and supported by spool-turned posts of various patterns or by machine-cut bracket supports. There were usually fancy openwork

LEFT. Victorian walnut étagère with Renaissance Revival cresting. Gothic and Rococo influence in mirror framework. (*The Henry Ford Museum*) CENTER. Victorian walnut five-shelf corner whatnot. (*The Henry Ford Museum*) RIGHT. Eastlake étagère. Mahogany with typical fan and ball motifs and grooved line carving. (*Carren, Ltd.*)

galleries at the back of the shelves and the fronts of the shelves were serpentined or cyma-curved. There were corner whatnots with triangular shelves and rectangular and square whatnots to set flat against the wall. Whatnots were usually factory-made of black walnut. Finer examples were made in mahogany or rosewood, and cheaper ones were of assorted woods stained to look like walnut. Some whatnots were made with drawers or with a cupboard base below the shelves. These were also usually made of walnut, but were made by cabinetmakers as well as in factories and are less numerous and more expensive than the ordinary corner or rectangular wall whatnots.

The étagère was really a glorified whatnot. However, it was not made as a corner piece but as a wall piece—for parlor or hall. The shelves of the étagère were usually built at the sides of a mirror. The base or stand with two shelves surmounted by a mirror had tiers of small shelves on either side and a carved crested top, varying with the style of furniture it was made to match. Thus the Louis XV étagère has a carving of flowers or grapes while the Renaissance style étagère has an architectural pediment with vase or cartouche, and the Eastlake étagère has a fan or square-crested pediment. The tall pier-glass étagère was surrounded by tiers of shelves and attached to a low marble-topped table. These were, of course, more expensive pieces and were made of rosewood as well as black walnut with veneer trim. An étagère with a cupboard base had open shelves in its curved sides and a mirror with rows of shelves on either side and a heavy crested pediment. There was also a late Eastlake hanging étagère form with center rectangular mirror and intricate flower and bird carving interspersed with shelves.

Small hanging shelves with scroll-cut brackets were made by novelty manufacturers who also made wall pockets, picture frames, and towel racks. These were called jigsaw or Sorrento carving and were cut out of thin wood by machine and decorated with cut-out leaves, birds, and heads of animals such as fox or deer. There were also small corner shelf brackets of carved leaves and branches. These were made in three parts, the back pieces hinged and folded and the triangular shelf fitted between and hooked to one side piece to hold it

LEFT. Hanging corner wall shelf, cherry. 1860–1880. RIGHT: Hanging walnut wall shelf, scroll-cut design. (*The Henry Ford Museum*)

in place. Many of these small hanging shelves were made by home craftsmen. Information and designs had been available since the Centennial where a demonstration booth had given impetus to this kind of handiwork. Sometimes the wall pockets had Berlin work or beaded pockets.

Various Materials

THE Victorian Age was also noted for the use of materials other than wood. Iron, brass, and later, wire furniture was used in conservatories and as porch and garden furniture. Iron furniture was introduced in the middle of the century but it gained its popularity in the 1870's. Iron furniture was made for use in both house and garden. American iron furniture was cast in parts and assembled. For indoors there were plant stands, cabriole-legged tables, mirror frames, hall racks and umbrella stands and beds. Pieces for indoors were painted black with gilding or

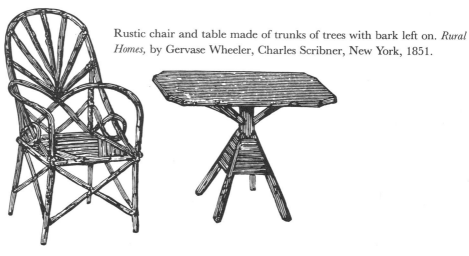

Rustic chair and table made of trunks of trees with bark left on. *Rural Homes,* by Gervase Wheeler, Charles Scribner, New York, 1851.

in colors imitating wood. They were rococo in form and decoration. The round center table usually had a marble top, a scrolled and pierced skirt and an ornate pedestal leg or ornately scrolled cabriole legs braced with a stretcher. The cast iron bed had a foot- and headboard of ornate scrolls and leaves. There were also cast iron washstands and towel racks. In 1853 the Rochester Novelty Company put out a catalogue advertising japanned and bronzed iron piano stools, umbrella stands, foot scrapers, and store stools, and in 1856 the Berlin Iron Company advertised tables, chairs, beds, washstands, hall racks, stools, umbrella stands, sewing baskets and frames. Dozens of other iron companies throughout America were making iron furniture, mirror frames, and iron cases for clocks. The mirrors had small rectangular frames of flower and leaf scrolls, or an eagle design, or had supports of crinolined ladies with cupids above and a flag attached to the center stand. These were made for ladies' dressing tables and the latter type were called Jenny Lind mirrors. Iron furniture for the garden included settees, benches, tables and chairs. These were made in designs of grapes and leaves, ferns, lily of the valley, and all-over scroll pattern. The grape design with a scrolled leaf cabriole leg was the most common and these have been reproduced today. Some of this furniture was also made in a rustic design of tree branches. Furniture of rustic wood had been made earlier in the century and Downing had advocated its use and described it, first in his book, *Cottage Residences,* and later, in the magazine, *The Horticulturist.* There are also sketches of rustic furniture designed by A. J. Davis.

In the Crystal Palace Exhibition in London in 1851 rustic furniture was exhibited by the Oneida Community, and rustic furniture

BELOW AND ABOVE. Cast iron Gothic settee, marble-top table, hall chair, umbrella rack. *A New Phase in the Iron Manufacture.* New York, 1857. (*The Metropolitan Museum of Art*)

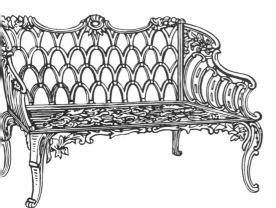

was made by James King in New Haven, Connecticut, in 1860. Wire chairs "for lawns, cottages and piazzas" and wire folding hall, office and rocking chairs were advertised by the New York Wire Railing Co. in their catalogue of 1857. They also picture folding iron beds in "scroll and diamond pattern, high post gothic, lyre, Harp and Union pattern all-over" as well as wire and "swinging gothic cribs." Any of these beds if found today would not only be decorative for use in the present-day house, but valuable as well.

Wicker and bamboo furniture were also popular at the end of the century. The wicker furniture was made in fancy scroll designs and seems to have been related to Eastlake. Gothic designs were also made. The bamboo furniture has an oriental derivation. There were settees, hall racks, tables and bookcases in this stained bamboo which are now coming into the shops. *Bentwood furniture* which originated in Austria was imported from Vienna, but it was also made by several American furniture companies. J. W. Mason advertised Bentwood chairs in 1870 and the Sheboygan Chair Company was making American Bentwood in 1890. This Bentwood furniture was made of birch. *Animal-horn furniture* is another novelty made at the end of the century which has found its way to the antique and secondhand shops and is collected. Chairs and tables had their backs, legs and arms made of steer or buffalo horns

Rattan settee and chair, Chinese design made by Berrian & Co., New York City. c. 1850 *Rural Homes* by Gervase Wheeler, Charles Scribner, 1851.

and the seats were upholstered in leather. In 1889 Robert S. Gould of New York City advertised "Plush and fur hassocks with polished horn legs." The upholstery was of goat or sheep skins or plush and it was trimmed with silk cordings, or a fancy brass apron was tacked on. This horn-legged furniture is considered the height of sophistication with collectors today. Papier mâché furniture which had been made in America and exhibited by American companies at the Crystal Palace in London in 1851 also continued in popularity.

Papier Mâché

ANY discussion of Victorian furniture should include papier mâché, since no parlor of the early Victorian era was complete without at least one table, chair, or writing case of papier mâché.

The French invented papier mâché, but it was also made in England as early as 1772. The base of papier mâché was a damp mixture of vegetable matters, paper, hemp, etc., which was pressed into sheets upon an iron mold. Several such layers were pressed and pasted and finally dried in an oven before being taken from the mold. The article was then waterproofed and the shiny varnish coats applied. Then the piece was ready for the final decoration which was to give it real interest and value. Motifs of decoration included flowers, birds, butterflies, Chinese and English scenes, Gothic architectural scenes and geometric patterns. Methods of decoration, beside regular painting, included bronze put on in powdered form with swabs instead of brushes, mother-of-pearl inlay, and real or artificial gems set in tinsel and arranged in a pattern under glass.

Articles made in papier mâché include trays, fans, screens, tea caddies, writing cases, blotter covers, paper and book racks, bellows, inkstands, jewelry boxes, sewing boxes, snuff boxes, card cases, buttons, tiptop tables, tea tables, chairs and cabinets.

Papier mâché was made at Birmingham, England, by Jennens & Bettridge from 1816 to 1864. Another center was at Wolverhampton where Walton & Company made a specialty of tea trays.

Papier mâché was also made in America by several companies who exhibited at the New York Crystal Palace in 1851. Evans and Millward of New York exhibited a work table and a music stand and Ward & Company also exhibited several small pieces of furniture. In 1853, Bowler, Tileston & Co. of Boston made papier mâché frames, mirrors, work boxes, and cabinet work. But the only company that left any record of making papier mâché was the Litchfield Mfg. Co. (1850–1854), of Litchfield, Conn. The principal output of the Litchfield Mfg. Co. was papier mâché clock cases which they furnished to Jerome & Co. and other Connecticut clock dealers. The most elaborate case was the "Navy, 8 day Timepiece," illustrated in Jerome & Co.'s catalogue of 1852. It was a wall clock in the form of a shield, crested with a spread eagle, flags, and cannon. The Kossuth, an eight-day striking clock, was illustrated in the same catalogue. It also had a papier mâché case. It was decorated with mother-of-pearl inlay and had a center medallion with a picture of Kossuth.

Although the papier mâché clock case was probably the staple which kept the company going, they also made small tip-top tables, standing screens, hand screens, sewing stands, sewing boxes, album covers, and daguerreotype cases.

Papier Mâché sewing stand. Pierced fire screen. Litchfield Manufacturing Co., 1850–1854. Litchfield Museum. (*Shirley S. De Voe*)

Papier mâché snuff boxes were also made with American scenes and portraits of American presidents. In the mid-century there were snuff boxes with engraved portraits of Polk, William Henry Harrison, and Zachary Taylor. However, the boxes themselves were probably made in England.

In choosing papier mâché the collector should select his pieces for aesthetic values, for the painting and decoration determine the worth of the piece. Good pearl inlay is placed so that the grain of each piece in a flower or leaf reflects the same color. Even small snuff boxes often have fine painted portraits or scenes.

From the middle of the century there were also many mechanical inventions which produced furniture that tilted, rocked or reclined to increase the comfort of the occupant. There was also an interest in furniture that folded and converted or was made to serve several purposes. Lindley's Patent Bedstead had been exhibited at the American Institute as early as 1843. In 1848 A. J. Davis records the armchair which was given him by the cabinetmaker Burns. "Mr. Burns presented me with a revolving armchair, carved round back, claw legs, and covered with plush worth $30.00." In the Crystal Palace Exhibition in London in 1851, the American Chair Company of New York exhibited a patented iron-spring chair which attracted considerable attention. A reclining chair that folded out as a bed, Hobe's patented extension table, and a revolving chair patented by M. W. King & Co. of New York were also exhibited. In 1855 M. W. King advertised an Invalid's parlor armchair. This was Louis XV style and was set on four cabriole legs attached to a center pedestal. Also a combination firescreen and desk was made by Victorian cabinetmakers of rosewook or mahogany veneer. It had curved bracket-feet with a turned stretcher between. An armchair which converted into a child's crib, folding beds which could be stored in a small space, and the sofa bed, were all invented and produced in the latter half of the nineteenth century. The advertisement of Nathaniel H. Van Winkle of New York stated that he had the largest variety of combination furniture in the world owning and controlling 30 different patents for sofas and lounge chairs.

Raspberries, Cake and Ice Cream, oil on canvas by C. P. Ream (see Dessert No. IV, page 120) Harnett signature is forged. (*Collection of Oliver E. Jennings*)

II. DECORATIVE
ACCESSORIES

Clocks

A CLOCK consists of two parts—the case and the inward mechanism or works. The age of a clock may be quickly judged by the cabinet work of the case, by its dial, and by the decoration on the glass, but it takes years of study to be familiar with the clock mechanism. For this reason, and since the average clock collector is interested in the appearance rather than the mechanism of a clock, the clock is considered as furniture in this chapter. Indeed, when it is said that a clock was made by a certain clockmaker it is understood that he only made the works. The case was always made by a cabinetmaker, the dial by a dial maker, the hands by a metal worker, the engraving or painting by an engraver or painter. However, the clock works controlled the form and appearance of the clock and the case was usually made to fit the clock. Also, it is the mechanism which is the certain index to the date, and the value of a clock. Names of clockmakers are recorded, but we know little about the cabinetmakers who made the cases or the various other craftsmen employed to finish and decorate a clock.

77

For the antique collector mainly interested in clock cases, there are three classifications determined by the position the clock occupies; namely, the floor or grandfather, the wall, and the shelf clock. Wall clocks included wag-on-the-wall, banjo, and lyre clocks. The majority of floor, tall-case or grandfather clocks were made between 1770 and 1840 and there were not enough made after 1840 to include them here. However, some tall clocks were made, and you can find late tall Victorian clocks with mahogany or walnut cases or in weathered oak mission cases or even fancy wicker cases. The banjo clocks were also early, patented by Simon Willard in 1802. However, a late type banjo was made after 1842 by Howard & Co. of Boston with circular or rectangular bottom and rounded sides.

Lyre clocks which were related to the banjo clock were made by Aaron Willard, Jr., and several other companies in the 1840's and 1850's. The case of the lyre clock was made of mahogany and carved with acanthus leaves; under the face is a door with decorated glass panel. Lyre clocks are rare and expensive. The well-known pillar and scroll mantel clock with its scroll top, pillars, scrolled skirt, bracket feet and painted scene on the glass was first made by Eli Terry in about 1820. The pillar and scroll was also made by other Connecticut, New England, and Pennsylvania clockmakers. Terry style mantel clocks with wooden works were cheap as compared with the more elegant Willard clocks

TOP, LEFT. Mahogany veneer banjo clock, c. 1850. Maker unknown. (*Mr. & Mrs. William Vernon Ashley II*) LEFT. Mahogany veneer clock. H. Welton & Co., c. 1843. CENTER. Black painted and stencilled case with mother-of-pearl inlay. c. 1850. J. C. Brown Manufacturer. RIGHT. OG frame clock with painted tablet. 1859–1861. Burwell & Carter. (*Bristol Clock & Watch Museum*)

and whether made by Eli Terry, Seth Thomas or other makers they were the favorite clocks of the average household until about 1840. Gradually less graceful forms evolved with heavier side columns, less flowing scroll tops, and a flat base with carved animal claw feet, ball feet, or flat bottoms without feet. These are often decorated with a stencil or have a carved and gilded eagle on their tops. Some of these clocks had flat tops and had the appearance of an Empire mirror. Eventually the pillar and scroll clock was replaced by the Looking Glass clock of Chauncey Jerome which had a large looking glass on the face under the dial. Later a third panel with decorations was added and the position of the mirror changed.

In about 1840 the popular OG clock appeared. It was made in six or more sizes. The wave-like OG molding is veneered and is identical with that of the mirrors of the period. The lower part of the glass of these clocks was decorated with such scenes as the Merchants Exchange, Philadelphia, or Monticello, home of Jefferson. Clocks with OG cases were made by Seth Thomas, E. N. Welch, and the New Haven Clock Company down into the 1890's. Now that the case maker no longer had to design the clock case to hold the vertical fall of the weights, he could introduce new designs according to his own whims.

About 1845 the Gothic steeple and the Beehive appeared. The Gothic steeples followed the furniture trend of the day. Some steeples

TOP RIGHT. Mahogany and rosewood sharp Gothic case. c. 1864. E. N. Welch. RIGHT. Double steeple Gothic case. c. 1845. Birge & Fuller. LEFT. Cornice top, columns and scroll supports. c. 1850. Forestville Mfg. Co. CENTER. Round Oriental Gothic ripple case with lyre design on frosted glass panel. c. 1850. Brewster & Ingrahams. (*Bristol Clock & Watch Museum*)

LEFT. Beehive clock case, rosewood veneer. c. 1850. Brewster & Ingrahams. CENTER. Venetian-type rosewood case. c. 1870. E. Ingraham & Co. RIGHT. Black lacquer case with mother-of-pearl inlay. c. 1850. C. Jerome. (*All clocks on page Bristol Clock & Watch Museum*)

were pointed and others had many turnings. The door frames of the better clocks were brass and the door had a brass knob, while the lower part of the glass was either engraved or painted. Some clocks had double steeples and the cases were often ripple-framed. The Gothic case was designed by Elias Ingraham, but this clock was copied by all Connecticut clock makers and remained popular for many years. Rounded top, octagon top, and Beehive were other popular shelf clock styles. These clocks were made in mahogany and rosewood or combinations of the two and often the wood casing is rippled. Another common type of the 1840's–1850's was a plain rectangular veneered wood case with a crudely painted panel below the clock dial.

After 1837 when brass works replaced wooden works the number of clocks increased, and in 1852 the catalogue of Jerome & Co. advertised clocks suitable for Public Buildings, Churches, Banks, Stores, Ships,

LEFT. Cottage case of rosewood veneer. 1831–1855. J. C. Brown.
RIGHT. Cottage-type case with stencil decoration. c. 1850. C. Jerome.

Steamboats, Railroad cars, Parlors, Halls, and Kitchens. Clock cases were also made of many different materials such as marble, bronze, china, glass, zebra wood, iron and papier mâché decorated with pearl inlay, handpainting and stencil. The styles of clocks continued to relate to furniture styles and even the names of clocks reveal the current interests of the times. In the Jerome & Co. catalogue of 1852 the rococo influence is particularly noticeable, not only in the shape of the clock cases, but also in the materials and decoration.

Especially popular were clocks with papier mâché cases. These clock cases were made by the Litchfield Manufacturing Co. and supplied to clock makers, including Jerome & Co. who put in the works. The cases made by the Litchfield Manufacturing Company include a large "Oriental Mantel" with a scene in the cartouche panel below the dial, a Navy eight-day clock with eagle, flags and cannon, a small Tom Thumb, and a Kossuth with a portrait of Kossuth below the dial. The papier mâché cases were decorated with stencils, hand painting, and mother-of-pearl inlay. This was the only firm that made papier mâché cases, but similar cases were made in lacquer and cast iron painted and inlaid with mother-of-pearl by J. C. Brown; Terry, Downs & Co.; E. & A. Ingraham; Bradley Mfg. Company; Otis, Upson Clock Company; and Ansonia. The cases were also made in OG and Cottage shapes as well as the fancy rococo forms. An iron case resembling

LEFT. Cast iron case with gold and mother-of-pearl inlay. c. 1853. E. & A. Ingraham. CENTER. Papier mâché case with gilt and mother of pearl. c. 1855. Litchfield Mfg. Co. RIGHT. Cast iron case with embossed leaves and birds and mother-of-pearl decoration. c. 1860. Bradley Mfg. Co. (*Bristol Clock & Watch Museum*)

a Gothic cathedral with Gothic fretwork painted decoration and two towers was made in several sizes and distributed by the American Clock Company, New York, in the 1860's. These iron clocks were made between 1850 and 1870.

In 1869 Bronze Clock Cases were introduced to compete with the French bronze clocks which were so popular as mantel decoration. The cases were cast in Connecticut and the movements were made by Connecticut clock makers. A design called "Amor" was made up of rococo curves and topped by a cupid with bow and arrow. Other cases had horses, lions, or human figures as crests, and cases showed both Grecian and Egyptian as well as Oriental influence. There were also cases with popular designs such as the sailor with anchor, a baseball clock, and comical Blinking Eye clocks. In 1885 H. H. Tammen of Denver, Colorado, advertised novelty clocks including shapes of an anchor, a cross, a horseshoe, a star, castle, miner's cabin, and artist's palette. These forms were studded with quartz rock crystal and other semi-precious gems. It is not known what company supplied the clock works but William L. Gilbert of Winsted, Connecticut, made clocks in the form of an anchor and a cross in 1879, and George B. Owen made a clock in the form of an artist's easel at about the same date.

In the 1880's carved and scrolled kitchen clocks were made of oak and walnut by E. N. Welch and E. Ingraham. Some of these scroll clock

LEFT. Pressed oak kitchen clock. c. 1900. E. Ingraham Co. CENTER. Carved scrolled kitchen clock. Renaissance influence. c. 1880. E. N. Welch. RIGHT. Black marble case with gold leaf decoration. c. 1890. Waterbury Clock Co. (*Bristol Clock & Watch Museum*)

cases are fantastic beyond description, but others are comparatively interesting. The glass was decorated with a stamped design and often had the company monogram. Jigsaw clock cases with Seth Thomas movements were also sold, complete with movement and pattern for making. Also in the 1890's, black marble mantel clocks with gold leaf decoration and with gilded figures on their tops were popular. These could be purchased with or without the figures. The 1881 catalogue of E. Ingraham & Co. showed clocks of enameled metal with gilt and bronze ornaments and decorated panels. The bronze top and side ornaments could be purchased separately. These included eagles, vases, a seated figure of Ceres, and figures of cavaliers. A toilet table clock had a dial on one side and a mirror on the other. Some clock cases were made of mosaic or marbleized rosewood. Small bedroom or mantel clocks of Dresden, Delft, and Haviland china decorated with painted flowers were also popular in the 1890's. The cases were usually imported, but several American companies, including Willets of New Jersey, made flower-decorated clock cases of Belleek porcelain. Clock cases were also made of pressed glass in the Daisy and Button design, in milk glass and in cut glass.

The value of a clock is determined by the established identity of the maker, either by the printed sheet with his name pasted to the inside of the case or by having the works identified by an expert. The

LEFT. Decorated china clock case. c. 1890. New Haven Clock Co. CENTER. Rosewood veneer case, "Patti", Renaissance design. c. 1895. Welch, Spring & Co. RIGHT. Renaissance Revival design shelf clock. c. 1875. (*Anonymous*). (*Other clocks, American Clock & Watch Museum, Bristol, Conn.*)

age cannot be determined except within the years that the maker was in business and the clocks that he was known to make at a certain period. If the clock is not running be sure to have it checked by a repair man before you buy it. He may also be able to identify the maker. From the standpoint of the average collector who wants a clock as decoration the condition of the case is important. Is the wood in good condition? If veneered, is the veneer chipped? Is the painted glass panel in good condition? Is it original or has it been replaced? Glass panels on old clocks were etched, later they were printed from blocks. Designs include a wreath or heart of leaves, a lyre, eagle, or flowers. Painted panels also vary in workmanship, some are hand-painted and some are stenciled. And finally, which should be firstly, is the clock of pleasing design and does it fit in with your decorative scheme?

Mirrors and Picture Frames

VICTORIAN mirrors and picture frames are given very little attention in most books because they are not fine antiques. In both design and workmanship they are inferior to the mirror frames of earlier periods. Victorian, like other period mirror frames and picture frames, follow the style of furniture in design and general characteristics. There were large ornately carved frames for the more formal Victorian style rooms and rustic frames for the cottage. Many mirrors continued to be made in two sections of glass, but later they were made of one piece of mirror glass. A bevelled edge is a sign of a late date.

Victorian Empire Mirrors, which are the first included within our Victorian boundaries, were larger and heavier than those of the early Empire period. The most popular type still showed the influence of the Sheraton mirror. It was made with two sections of glass and the upper section usually contained a painted emblem such as the eagle or a flower piece or landscape. The most interesting of these had the *Constitution* or the *Guerrière* or "Perry's Victory." These mirrors have cornices under which was a row of balls and there are columns on each side of the glass. On this type of Victorian Empire mirror the delicate

carving has disappeared and the columns are carved in rings. These mirrors are usually gilded, but a popular form had gilded ring sections interspersed with longer sausage-shaped sections of dark stained "ebonized" wood. Sometimes these frames are of walnut or mahogany without the pediment top. These have square corner blocks. A similar mirror with pilasters on all four sides and square corner blocks centered with rosettes is known as a Tabernacle Mirror. Thousands of these were made in the 1840–50's. Mirrors of both of these types were made in three sections for overmantels. These were Victorian copies of earlier mirrors.

Still other mirrors are framed in a wide gold frame with borders of reeding. These mirrors were made by expert craftsmen, by village carpenters, and also manufactured in small looking glass factories. Most of the inexpensive ones were made in rural districts and the workmanship is crude, being cut with carpenter's planes. The painting in the panels is amateurish folk painting. It consisted of village scenes, a church, a landscape or a country couple. Since these mirrors were usually gilded or gilded and painted the wood is not important.

Another type of Victorian Empire mirror had a single panel of glass held in a rectangular "OG" frame of mahogany veneer. Some of these mirrors were pine covered with gesso and gilt, sometimes they were made of light wood or of black lacquer and gilt. Later some were made of oak or walnut. These mirrors were made in several sizes and could be hung either vertically or horizontally. Such mirrors are available in shops today but many have chipped veneer and this is not easily repaired. However, it is possible to remove the veneer and refinish the pine frame for use with Country Furniture. Another type of country mirror had a simple molded rectangular frame with rounded corners. It was pine covered with gesso and painted to imitate wood or enamelled in light colors to match the painted cottage bedroom sets. Later these mirrors were made of black walnut; some carved with tree branches and crested with

TOP. Empire mirror. Black and gilt frame. Painting of cottage scene in upper panel. c. 1840. (*The Henry Ford Museum*) BOTTOM. Pier glass with marble console framed with pilasters and cornice with shell finial. (*The Metropolitan Museum of Art*)

leaves were made in the 1860–70's. There were also octagonal mahogany veneer mirrors originally made to sit between the scroll supports on the mahogany veneer bureaus. Oval mahogany veneer mirrors had rounding narrow frames.

More ornate mirrors were made to accompany more formal Victorian styles. There were oval wall mirrors, large crested overmantel mirrors usually of broad rectangular shape, and tall pier glasses which reached to the ceiling. These frames are usually pine covered with gesso and gold leaf or painted to imitate rosewood. The oval mirror was the popular shape. There were oval mirrors with a simple convex frame, but most of the mirrors had a crested gesso decoration of fruit and flowers. The same manufacturer who made mirrors also made window cornices and picture frames and a whole ensemble could be had to match. In 1840 John Doggett & Co. of New York City advertised looking glasses, and Richards Kingsland advertised matching looking glasses and cornices in 1855. Both square and oval elaborately decorated mirrors are shown in the advertisements of looking glass manufacturers of the 1850's. The gesso carving on these mirrors consisted of leaves, fruit, flowers, and interlacing "C" and "S" rococo curves and pierced borders of round openings. These mirrors and frames relate to the rococo Louis XV furniture. A dressing table ensemble of an oval mirror with a flower-carved crest flanked by figures of naked children holding baskets of fruit with candles was made in about 1855. Pier and console mirrors elaborately decorated with foliage, fruit and birds richly gilded were also made in the 1850–60's. The gilded overmantel mirror has a rectangular frame with an oval crested top heavy with gilded gesso carving of fruit, and flower gilded mirrors are often found with parts of the composition flowers or scrolls broken or missing. Such a frame can be regilded, but the proper job with gold leaf and burnishing and the replacement of composition parts can be quite expensive.

Many of the larger Eastlake mirrors were made of walnut. There were simple rectangular walnut framed mirrors of several sizes and table mirrors with a straight or oval top. The Eastlake pier glass had an architectural flat pedimented top with a center cartouche. The sides and top of the mirror are ornamented with incised geometric line designs and panels of burl veneer. There were also mirrors with cast iron frames made to hang on the wall and small oval dressing table mirrors with ornate flower and scroll designs and sometimes an eagle crest. These were set on stands.

Victorian picture frames are copies of older frames. There was a great variety of nineteenth century frames and they relate to the various styles of furniture and decoration of the Victorian period. Victorian Empire frames were similar to those of the earlier Empire period. They were rectangular in shape with moldings of beading, acanthus leaf, Egyptian papyrus, and lotus leaf carvings. Some pictures in museums are still in their original frames and this is the best place to study picture frames, although reproductions of all period frames are to be had at the picture frame shop today. Since the French Louis XV was the most popular Victorian style there are many large Victorian picture frames of rococo design. These frames were wide and deep. They were

LEFT. Cast iron table mirror with crinoline figures. Patriotic trophy obelisk and flag on base. 1865–1870. (*The Index of American Design*) CENTER. Cast iron mirror frame, rococo design. 1850–1875. (*The Henry Ford Museum*) RIGHT. Cast iron dressing table mirror on stand. Renaissance design influence. 1850–1860. (*The Index of American Design*)

Gilt and gesso frame, leaf scroll border.

Elaborately carved frame. Renaissance design.

Carved and gilt frame, Elizabethan influence in corner motifs.

Rococo carved and gilt frame, acanthus leaf design. (*All frames, Robert D. Bunn*)

made of plaster carved with large flowers, leaves, and foliage borders which were covered with gold leaf. The frames were both oval and rectangular, but often an inner oval held the picture within the wide and heavy rectangular frame. All of the frames in a room were usually of the same design and these often matched the mirror frames and cornices so that there was an effect of dazzling gilt and exaggerated rococo design. Various designs of fluting, guilloche patterns, and criss-cross surface patterns often covered the flat surfaces of the gilt borders and smaller carved borders of grapes, oak, and laurel leaves alternated with the flat surfaces. Some frames were completely covered with a pattern of raised carving and others only had sprays of flowers or heavy cartouches at the corners of the frame.

American nineteenth century primitive paintings were framed in plain wood moldings painted flat black. They had a narrow gold leaf band on the outer edge and on the inner edge next to the picture. Sometimes the frames are marbleized and some frames have silver gilding instead of gold. In the late nineteenth century the frames were made of angular moldings and flat wood veneer or of black walnut with a small border of gilt or with burl veneer decoration. Small oval gilt and black walnut frames were made in the 1860's. They usually contained family photographs and were made of several sizes from 12 to 16 inches in diameter. There were also similar frames made of pine and gesso carved with fruit and flowers, sometimes as a crest at the top of the frame or in four clusters at the top, bottom, and sides or in a twining vine border around the frame. These frames were covered with gold leaf, not paint. Today they are inexpensive, especially the walnut ones containing old photographs which can be removed and mirror glass substituted. There are also many larger rectangular picture frames with heavy gesso leaf or scroll borders covered with gold leaf that will make attractive mirror frames. Late Victorian frames included the rustic tick-tack-toe of oak which have the corners crossed and fastened with a white china button instead of mitered. Carved rustic frames with machine-carved leaves set on their corners were made "for framing mottos." There were also frames of imitation marble, walnut, and ebony with raised white lines "engraved and gilt." Antique bronze,

LEFT. Walnut frame decorated with sliced walnuts. 1885. Made by Henry Ford. RIGHT. Oval pine frame with molded gesso fruit designs. 1850–1870. (*Both, The Henry Ford Museum*) BELOW. Carved rosewood frame made by Ernest Weber. c. 1857. (*The Metropolitan Museum of Art*)

natural wood, and imitation wood and plush-covered frames were also advertised in the 1880's. Walnut frames often had an inside narrow gold leaf molding. This was sometimes stencilled with geometric or vine borders. An unusual fretwork frame with criss-cross corners is made with borders of small hand-carved triangles of soft wood which form a design similar to Flemish 17th century frames. In 1854 *A Complete Guide to Ornamental Leather Work* was published in Boston. It included directions and designs for making mirror frames and other articles out of cut and modeled leatherwork. The frames were usually oval and the designs of leaves, fruit, and flowers heavily massed.

Lamps, Girandoles and Lusters

THE lamp evolved through scientific improvements on its combustive system and the subsequent changes of fuels from grease fat and whale oil to kerosene. The invention of the oil-burning Argand lamp in 1780 marked the real beginning of modern lighting, but the design and development of the lamp as we know it today was made in the nineteenth century. To collectors interested in the development of lighting the various scientific improvements and changes in the mechanical operation and the different fuels used are important, but from the standpoint of the collector of nineteenth century decorative arts the design of the lamp base and shade are the valuable considerations. Early lamp designs were patterned after candleholders. Indeed, it is only since the middle of the nineteenth century that lamps replaced candles. One of the first lamp designs was the brass candelabrum of metal with its tin shade. These were made both with single light sockets and a side standard, and with double and triple lights held by a center bracket. Although they were made as early as 1800 they continued to be made all through the century and are reproduced today.

The Argand lamp had a standard of metal, usually bronze, cast with classic designs including vase forms and acanthus leaves. Argand lamp shades were of frosted glass with cut crystal prisms. These lamps were made with both one and two burners. Although of earlier invention, the Argand lamp was used in America until the middle of the century, together with the Astral or Sinumbra lamps which were a

RIGHT. Argand-type tin sconce with stenciled decoration, 1825–1850. FAR RIGHT. Bronze Argand lamp with cut frosted shade, 1840–1850. (*The Henry Ford Museum*)

Astral lamp with marble base, frosted cut shade with prisms, 1850. Overlay lamps with frosted shades and prisms. Marble base, Sandwich type, 1860, 1875. (*The Henry Ford Museum*)

variation on the Argand lamp. These too were made of metal—brass, bronze or silver—with glass shades. The bases of these lamps followed the various furniture revival designs. They were made with dome and round glass shades.

These lamps and the Carcel lamp, which was similar, were the lamps used in the homes of the well-to-do until the middle of the century. The New England Glass Company advertised Grecian lamps and plain and ground chimneys for Astral lamps, and hanging prisms as early as 1825. In 1850, Archer and Warner of Philadelphia, manufacturers of lamps, girandoles, etc., advertised "Argand, Annular, Parker's Sinumbra, Quarrel's Sinumbra, Quarrel's Albion, Isis, Parker's Hot Oil, Keer's Fountain and Carcel lamps." Such was the wide variety of fine lamps obtainable at the mid-century. Cornelius & Co. of Philadelphia had invented and patented the Solar lamp in 1843 and these lamps are marked with their trade-mark and the patent date. The lamps had round wicks, bulb-like chimneys and globe or flaring white or colored glass shades cut or sand-blasted in floral designs and hung with cut crystal prisms. The standard was brass and the base marble. But lamps were also made of many less expensive materials such as tin, iron, pewter, britannia; and later pottery, china, and glass of all kinds.

One of the most important branches of glass making in the nineteenth century was the manufacture of glass lamp bases. The Victorian lamps made in the greatest quantity were of glass and metal. A great number of lamps were made of blown and pressed glass. Blown lamp bases were plain or mold-blown, overlay, and cut. Some lamps have all types of glass techniques combined. The first glass lamps were blown in spherical or conical shapes. The reservoirs were ornamented with ribbing and panel molding and often cut and engraved. When pressed glass became popular some of the blown glass lamps had bases of lacy pressed glass which was made in a cup-plate mold. These lamps are extremely rare. From 1835 to 1860 pressed glass lamps were heavier

Clear pressed glass table or chamber kerosene lamps, 1875–1900 (*The Henry Ford Museum*)

and their design was influenced by the decorative trends of the period, which included Gothic and Renaissance motifs. Classic columns formed the stems, and the bases were made up of architectural moldings. The dolphin candlesticks and lamp bases in various colors belong to this period. Lamp bases were also made in amber, canary, greens, blues, amethyst, and clear and opaque white, and combinations of color were used on one lamp. These lamps were fitted with whale oil burners of pewter or brass. The glass fonts were conical, cylindrical, or hexagonal with heavy molded panels of simple motifs such as loops, circles, and ellipses. The bases were round, square, hexagonal and octagonal. The early Bigler, Arch, Circle and Ellipse patterns, and Pedal and Loop belong to this period. The Peacock Feather, Argus, Block and Thumbprint, Harp, Bull's Eye, and Fleur de Lys were also early patterns. These lamps were made at the New England Glass Company; Sandwich Glass Company; McKee Brothers; and Bakewell, Pears, and Company, but it is difficult to attribute any lamps to a particular company as designs were not the exclusive property of any one company.

Overlay or cased lamp bases combined one or more colors of glass overlaid on the clear glass, and they were decorated with a bold cut design of circles, ovals, stars, or diamonds. The contrast of the brilliant color of the overlay glass and the clear crystal of the cut design gave an exquisite effect. These lamps were made in the 1850's and 1860's and were never common. They were made mainly at the New England Glass Company and at the Sandwich Glass Company. The majority of those made at the New England Glass Company were ruby on a base of clear glass while those at Sandwich were made in a variety of colors including green, pink, rose, amber, blue and turquoise on clear glass. A Cranberry glass lamp was covered with a white overlay dotted pattern and has a milk glass column and base. A lamp of midnight blue entwined ribbon design has a column and base of pressed milk glass. The majority of these glass bowls were mounted with metal and were set on fluted metal or glass stems and fastened to marble bases. Over-

Kerosene lamp with pressed glass font and cast iron statuary base, 1875–1885 (*The Henry Ford Museum*)

lay lamps are popular and very expensive today, but they have also been reproduced and the collector must be cautious. There were also lamps with translucent colored bowls decorated with a vine design in gold, and lamps with bowls of a Venetian looped pattern of clear and opaque color. These bowls are round, oval or square and are mounted with metal and usually set on a square or round base.

Later lamps, although pleasing in color, were sold in parts and assembled by the lamp manufacturer so that they are not always well proportioned. Shades and prisms were also sold in lots and assembled with lamp bases in the warerooms. Kerosene lamps had large globular fonts blown in molds, the bases were pressed and the parts were connected with brass collars. The square or curved feet were black or white opaque glass. These opaque or translucent colored lamps were made in many varieties and sometimes gilding was added.

The late pressed glass lamps were made to burn kerosene and their fonts were round and larger, and the lamps were taller. Some had cast metal stems with cherubs or other figures. The late pressed glass lamp patterns included Ribbed Ivy, Stedman, Bellflower, Fine Rib, Ribbed Palm, Prism, Sawtooth, Hamilton, Cable, Honeycomb, Sandwich Star, Prism and Flute, and others, although lamps were not made in all pressed glass patterns. In 1876 both standard lamps and squat lamps with handles were made in the Emblem pattern, which had impressed United States flag shields around the lamp font. The metal collars have the inscription: "Pat'd Apr. 19, 1875. M'ch 21, 1876." Many lamp chimneys also have the Emblem design.

The Actress, Three Face, Frosted Leaf, and Lion pattern lamps belong to the 1880's. Pressed glass lamps of various sizes in the coin pattern were made at Wheeling, West Virginia, in about 1892. These were made in both clear and opaque milk glass. There were many other milk glass lamps of all sizes, some with glass bases and others with cast brass or bronze bases. The tall, slender rose bowl lamp is the most attractive. A squat lamp has a panelled poppy design and another

Pattern glass lamp with dark green font and green shading, at top of glass shade. After 1860. (Ruth Little: *Old Lamps and New, Restoring and Decorating*)

small lamp has a pansy panel. Milk glass lamps were made in combinations of clear and colored glass, but seldom in two different colors of milk glass. There were many miniature milk glass lamps, the most common being the little Cosmos design lamp. There were miniature Pansy design and Block and Circle design, which were also common. These lamps were made with pressed milk glass chimneys of the same design and with plain clear glass chimneys.

Miniature lamps were also made in many clear pressed glass patterns. They were designed to be used as night lights in bedrooms but were also used as "sparking" lamps. When the small amount of oil was burned out it was the hour for the suitor to depart. These lamps, which measured from 4½ to 8 inches tall, were made in great quantities at the end of the century. Miniature lamps were also made in various types of fancy glass, such as satin glass. Other types of small lamps include the Acorn lamp made by Hobbs, Brockunier, and the Fairy Lamp. Fairy Lamps were mostly of English make, although the Phoenix Glass Company of Pittsburgh, in the 1880's advertised Art Glassware, Pearl Satin Glass, and "sole manufacturers of Fairy Lamps in U.S." According to Amelia MacSwiggan, author of *Fairy Lamps*, Samuel Clarke manufactured fairy lamps in Newark, N.J., 1884–88 and Houchin Co. in New York City in the 1880's.

There are several types of lamps that came into use after the middle of the nineteenth century, and these old kerosene lamps are the most characteristic Victorian lamps. The earlier peg bowl lamp had been made to fit into a candlestick, but now they were made to fit into glass, metal or marble bases. Small glass hand lamps with a loop finger-hold were made in great numbers. These lamps had a glass chimney but usually did not have a shade. Similar lamps also were made to fit into metal wall brackets. These were designed with fonts of clear glass or in opalescent, cranberry or hobnail glass, and often had ball or fringed petticoat shades to match. The Rayo lamp, a variation of the hand lamp, was made of brass and at first was only equipped with a chimney, but later had a tripod metal holder for a student or Tam O'Shanter shade. The student lamp was another type that was popular late in the century. These were made of metal, with a central stem set on a base and with branches to hold the font and shade on one side and the oil tank on the other. Sometimes the oil tank and font are of glass and recently in a Vermont shop I saw such a lamp with shade and oblong cylinder oil tank painted with the well-known scene of heron and cattails.

ABOVE LEFT. Brass Student Lamp with double burners and green glass shades, 1890–1915. LEFT. Bronze double Student Lamp with green and white overlay glass shades, c. 1900. ABOVE. Brass Student Lamp with green shade, 1890–1900. (*The Henry Ford Museum*)

Hanging lamp with opaque white shade, c. 1875. Hanging lamp with painted glass shade and prisms, 1890–1900. Hanging lamp with hobnail ruby glass shade, c. 1890. (*The Henry Ford Museum*)

The hanging library lamp with glass or metal font, a glass chimney and a glass shade with prisms was set in an adjustable metal frame. A small metal dome hung over the chimney to protect the ceiling. The shades of these lamps were often elaborate and decorative. Some are hand-painted, others are made of hobnail, Rubena Verde, or other colored glass with the border of the frame set with colored stones and prisms. Stem lamps with fonts of pressed or hand-painted glass or china set on a cast brass base were made in the 1880's. These had glass chimneys and ball or Tam O'Shanter shades. The stems were sometimes elongated and cast in the shape of a head, naked child or fluted column. Other stems were cylinders of china decorated with hand-painted flowers. Late in the century a tall brass floor lamp with molded brass bowl and hand-painted ball shade was made. These lamps were sometimes made with tripod legs but more often the lamp rod was set in the center of a small square three-tiered brass table.

Shades on Victorian lamps were of various types and shapes as well as different kinds of glass. There were round ball shades, Tam O'Shanter shades with wide flare and small neck, student shades with rounded flare; and pleated petticoat shades and crimped shades. The shades were plain or tufted and were made of various types of glass including satin, cranberry, opalene, coralene and overlay. Patterns included thumb-print, hobnail and candy stripe. Lamps made in the various types of Victorian Art Glass included a Burmese table lamp made by Mt. Washington Glass Works in 1886. There were also frosted and clear designs and shades with embossed patterns of flowers and all-over designs.

There were many glass companies making shades for lamps, including Gillinder & Sons, who made "etched, cut, sandblast and opal shades and globes." The Novelty Art Metal Company of Brooklyn advertised "Art Bent Glass Globes" in 1897. The Washington Flint Glass Company of Philadelphia made shades decorated with cupids, butterflies, and flowers; and the Murray Flint Glass Works also made colored globes and shades, "Opal Tinted and Windmill Rococo." They also made lamp fonts. Silver etched banquet globes and etched top chimneys were made by F. Horman & Co. The Rochester Lamp Company made lamps decorated with painted scenes, including windmill decorations. Decorated lamps were also made by the Eagle Glass Company, who advertised a Gone-with-the-Wind type of lamp with font and shade decorated with roses. A Venus decorated lamp was made by Thos. Evans of Pittsburgh.

However, the most popular lamp in the 1880's and 1890's was the parlor or so-called Gone-with-the-Wind lamp which had a large globular glass base and a matching globe-shaped shade. The base and shade were usually painted or heavily ornamented with Lalique-like patterns of raised flowers. Glass prisms often hung from the shades. These lamps were also set on rococo stands of openwork cast bronze or

LEFT TO RIGHT. Stem lamp with pattern glass font, pressed Tam O'Shanter shade with prisms. The stem is opaque glass with painted decoration, the base black iron, c. 1880. (*Ruth Little*) "Gone with the Wind" lamp with frosted ruby pressed glass font and shade, 1875–1885. (*The Henry Ford Museum*) Lamp with brass rococo design font and base. Shade frosted pressed glass, 1875–1885. (*Carren Ltd.*) Parlor lamp with painted wild rose decoration on shade and base, 1875–1890. (*The Henry Ford Museum*)

brass. There were also smaller lamps with Dresden china bases, and china lamps for home decorating could be purchased from the Summerville Glass Works and from the Phoenix Glass Company. They also had cream-colored porcelain table and banquet lamp fonts of Limoges and Vienna porcelain available for decorating. E. Aulich of New York, who operated a shop for painting lampshades, was also a teacher of china painting and his design for a globular china shade was illustrated in the *China Decorator*, April, 1900. Some china lamps also had flaring shades. These shades, too, were hand-painted. A familiar small lamp with a tubular base and dome shade had a hand-painted landscape including deer. It was made by the New England Glass Company and the shade was painted by George L. Noyes who was employed to do hand-decorating and who afterwards became a Boston artist of note.

LOWER LEFT. Lamp with cast bronze base with angel heads, Gothic design on font and frosted glass globe. Boston and Sandwich Glass Co., Sandwich, Mass., 1875. (*The Henry Ford Museum*)

Other popular painted lamp base designs included the heron and cattails, Cabin in the Snow, the shepherd scene, Paul and Virginia, bunch of grapes, and wild roses. A rare Burmese lamp has a scene with flying ducks hand-painted on its font and Tam O'Shanter shade. Parlor Lamps with metal bases were also popular and there were also tall banquet lamps with pierced brass and bronze rococo designs, and Renaissance designs with heads in ovals. These tall decorative lamps had a hand-painted or Lalique-like ball shade. Late in the nineteenth century lamp bases and shades were made of cut glass. There is a rare cut glass lamp in the Cobweb pattern, but lamps of Russian, Hob Star, and other deep cut patterns are more common.

Elaborate gold and silver lamp bases were illustrated in the Reed and Barton catalogue of 1885. The designs were a combination of Oriental flower and bird motifs and sculptured Renaissance figures

LEFT TO RIGHT. Brass parlor lamp with hand-painted student shade, c. 1900. (*Ruth Little*) Rochester burner, kerosene lamp with Japanese design bronze base and floral decorated globe, c. 1900 (*The Henry Ford Museum*) Lamp with silver or gold plate in Venetian design. Passion flower design on font and bird and floral decoration on globe. (*Reed & Barton Catalogue, 1885*) ABOVE. Lamp base and globe, cut glass Sunburst pattern, 1900. BELOW. Lamp base and globe, prism pattern 1892. Owens-Illinois Glass Co. (*The Toledo Museum of Art*)

and acanthus leaf scrolls. Globes and shades were purchased separately and the decoration of the shades included birds, butterflies, flowers and landscapes.

Tiffany lamps were first sold in 1895. Some bases were of Favrile glass with mother-of-pearl shades. Others were a combination of bronze and Favrile glass. Among the first designs were the tall-stemmed bronze candelabra in Queen Anne's lace pattern and the dandelion lamps. The earliest of these were made for kerosene and marked with the monogram of the Tiffany Glass and Decorating Company. The same designs were later marked "Tiffany Studios, New York." The Tiffany dandelion lamp and the dragonfly lamp were exhibited in Paris in 1900. The bronze base with leaded glass shade was so popular that it was copied both in America and abroad. The bases as well as the shades varied in design. Among the best known leaded shade designs were the group of flower designs including wisteria, grapes, daffodils, water lilies, peonies, poppies, wood anemones, ivy, pansy,

Tiffany lamps: LEFT. Daffodil, gilded leading and base. CENTER. Dragonfly, shades of amber with vari-color eyes. RIGHT. Twelve Branch Lily. (*The Chrysler Art Museum of Provincetown*)

rose (either red or yellow), leaf, orange petal, geranium, butterfly, tulip, tree, and geometric. Other types included the Scarab, Snail, Turtleback, Mushroom, and Spider and Web. The lamps were marked "Tiffany Studios, New York" on either the top or bottom rim of the shade. There were also candelabra lamps, including the lily-cluster design with morning-glory shades.

The shapes and decoration of the Tiffany pottery also suggested plant and flower forms. The earliest of the pottery bases was deep ivory shaded with brown. Later shades of green were used and some had a mat glaze which gave a crystalline effect. Each piece of pottery was marked "L.C.T." on the base. There were also Tiffany glass shades for hanging lamps and the designs Chestnut, Tyler, and October Night were often copied. Tiffany lamps were never cheap. They ranged in price from $100 to $750 when made. Today, again, they are expensive and in great demand. Copies or similar glass shades are quite common, but not cheap. Lamp shades were also made of Quezal and Carnival glass. Tiffany also fitted shades to pottery lamps made by the Grueby Faience Company of Boston, but after the failure of the Grueby firm, Tiffany Studios began to make pottery bases.

Pottery lamp bases were also made of Rookwood Pottery and since Rookwood was sold at the Tiffany Store undoubtedly some Rookwood pieces were fitted with Tiffany glass shades. The Chesapeake Pottery of Baltimore, Maryland, made parlor and banquet pottery lamps with adaptations of classical designs, and the Pauline Pottery of Edgerton, Wisconsin, made candlesticks and lampstands with hand-painted designs in the Japanese manner. According to Barber, Goodwin Brothers of Connecticut made "fancy lampstands, hand decorated in colored and rustic designs bronzed, silvered, and lustred."

Candelabra lamps with wick burners for camphene or whale oil were set on four to six metal branches ornately decorated with acanthus leaves, grapes, and cupids. There were also many candelabra of bronze and other metals in rococo styles which were made for mantel sets. Sometimes these came in combinations with two candelabra and a matching clock and while many were made abroad there were also such sets made in America. These were advertised in 1853.

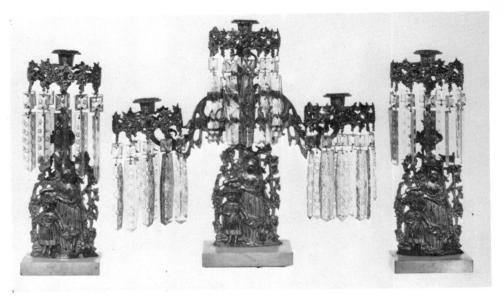

Set of lusters for mantel garniture. Brass stem with Mother and Child in grape arbor set on marble base. Prisms hang from candleholders, 1840–1860. (*The Henry Ford Museum*)

The metal candelabra or girandoles with cut glass prisms which were known as Paul and Virginias were the popular ornament for the Victorian mantel shelf. These gaudy fixtures set on a marble base were made in single and branched forms and also in sets of three pieces. The cast gilt-metal figures included not only Paul and Virginia, but Robinson Crusoe, Columbus, Lancelot, Paul Revere, Robin Hood, Pocahontas, the Crusaders, George and Martha Washington, Joan of Arc, a hound, a vase, a basket of flowers, lovers, Jenny Lind, and a Gothic cathedral. The prisms for these and other lamps and candelabra were mostly made in Brooklyn, New York, and Meriden, Connecticut, but they were also made by T. G. Hawkes Glass Co.; Libby Glass Co.; C. Dorflinger & Sons; L. Straus & Co.; and the Mt. Washington Glass Works. There were also bronze candelabra with Parian figures.

Lusters were also popular mantelpiece garniture. Lusters were made of various kinds of glass, including clear, frosted, and opaque class, enamelled and cut, and were hung with prisms. By inserting a candle the luster became a candlestick. While many lusters were made in France and England they were also made at American glass factories and the prisms too were cut in American shops. Prisms were cut in many shapes. Victorian prisms are long triangular spears with spearhead, arrow, or dumbbell ends.

Collectors of decorative lamps are most interested in miniature lamps, Fairy Lamps, and pressed glass lamps. These lamps are comparatively small, colorful, and give an opportunity to assemble a collection of the various types of glassware and of the many different patterns of pressed glass. Prices of these lamps vary with popular demand. Lamps of any art glass such as Satin, Peachblow, Burmese, Amberina or Mercury glass are rare and expensive. Miniature lamps are usually more expensive than larger lamps because there were fewer of them made and they are in great demand. Collectors of larger lamps are more than likely collecting the lamps for use in the home rather than collecting pieces for a cabinet. The most expensive Victorian lamps that can be adapted for present-day use are the overlay lamps made by the New England Glass Company and the Sandwich Glass Company. These are very expensive. In fact, any lamp known to have been made at any particular company is more expensive than the same type lamp not authenticated. Although Argand, Astral, and Solar lamps are not cheap, there are still bargains to be found and these lamps often have the maker's name. So far they have not been in great demand with collectors. The lamps made late in the century which are truly Victorian in taste and spirit are just beginning to have collectors' attention. When more is known about the makers and decorators these will be more valuable.

Crown Milano lamp base and globe. Soft pink ground decorated with sea gulls, gold scrolls, stars and circles. Mt. Washington Glass Company. (*Flying Horse Antiques*)

Rogers Groups

IN 1859 John Rogers exhibited a small clay group of figures called "Checker Players" which was so well received that he decided to continue sculpture as a profession. Between 1859 and 1892 when his last group was put on the market, Rogers had executed over 80 groups and sold over 100,000 plaster reproductions. The plaster groups of John Rogers expressed the spirit of the American Victorian era. They satisfied the people's love for sentimental story-telling art. Although Rogers was a man of culture he was close to the people in his homey interests, and his artistic ideals were those popular with the majority of the people. Thus thousands of his groups sold and a Rogers Group sat on a table, shelf, or pedestal in every middle-class parlor in America at the end of the century. Rogers is remembered today not because he was a great sculptor but because he pictured in detail the America of his day. His realistic groups depict the costumes, the furniture and the social activities of a century ago. For this reason Rogers Groups are interesting and worth collecting today. The subject matter of Rogers Groups had popular appeal for they were close to the life of the people, the topics and day to day activities of the people.

Many groups were inspired by the Civil War, but even here he chose subjects that were near to the heart of the people rather than scenes of great battles. These groups included "Taking the Oath," "Parting Promise," "The Home Guard," "Camp Life," "Camp Fire," "The Wounded Scout," "The Returned Volunteer," "Sharp Shooters" and "Union Refugees." "The Fugitive's Story" which depicts a Negro slave holding a child telling her tale to the well-known abolitionists Whittier, Henry Ward Beecher, and William Lloyd Garrison; and "Council of War" which includes portraits of Lincoln, General Grant, and Secretary of War Stanton have more monumental subject matter. In fact, this latter group was suggested to Rogers by Stanton in his letters to John Clifford who wrote to Stanton at Roger's request. The scene as suggested by Stanton was the conference after Grant's return from the visit to the Army of the Potomac. After receiving a finished group Stanton wrote to Rogers April 1868: "I think you were especially fortunate in your execution of the figure of President Lincoln. In form and feature it surpasses any effort to embody the expression of that great man which I have seen." When "The Fugitive's Story" was completed in 1869 Garrison ordered copies, but also complained that his face was made "too thin." The poet William Cullen Bryant wrote: "You have succeeded in a higher degree than almost any artist of the age in making sculpture a narrative art."

A number of Rogers' Groups illustrate popular stories of the day such as Rip Van Winkle and Ichabod Crane. Joseph Jefferson, the well-known actor, was the model for the Rip Van Winkle groups and also for "Fighting Bob" of Sheridan's *The Rivals.* There were also scenes from Shakespeare's *King Lear, As You Like It,* and *The Merchant of Venice* and a group of Faust and Marguerite.

Although the Civil War groups have a historical value and the dramatic and literary figures are a commentary on the literary and theatrical interest of the time, it was the homely domestic scenes that were the most popular and more of these groups were sold than any other, and it is for these scenes that Rogers is famous. The people liked the exact detailed story-telling pictures which reflected their own ideas and life. Also, the aim of nineteenth century artists was to tell a story or relate a picturesque incident with realism and this Rogers did with great skill although his work was inspired by higher ideals. He hoped that his figure of "The Landing of Norsemen" would be used "for public parks to inspire patriotism." And writing to Ellen Rogers he says: "I never feel satisfied after I have finished a merely humorous design." There are groups of children such as "We Boys," "Going for the Cows," "School Days," "Playing Doctor," "Hide & Seek,

Fighting Bob, by John Rogers, 1889. (*The New-York Historical Society*)

Whoops!" and "The First Ride." There are also home scenes like "Weighing the Baby," "A Frolic at the Old Homestead" and "The Tap on the Window," and romantic groups like "The Parting Promise," "Neighboring Pews" and "Coming to the Parson."

Rogers also did figures for the lawn including "Hide and Seek" and "Bubbles," and he made several designs of vases for plants. He was also interested in the placing of his figures. For the lawn figures he sold wrought iron pedestals for $10, and for the other groups there were brackets, pedestals and three-tier tables which were obtainable in black walnut, mahogany or ebony. Rogers made several groups in Parian marble and in bronze. In 1900 seven bronze groups including "The Council of War" and a figure of Abraham Lincoln which is now in Manchester, New Hampshire, were exhibited at the Metropolitan Museum of Art. Rogers Groups were also exhibited in other museums, and the National Academy of Design gave Rogers immediate recognition, but in 1955 Rogers Groups formed the center theme of an exhibit at a New York gallery entitled "Bad Taste." Today collections of Rogers Groups are owned by the New-York Historical Society, the Albany Institute of History and Art, and the Essex Institute. The

Weighing the Baby, by John Rogers, 1877.
(*The New-York Historical Society*)

Metropolitan Museum of Art owns two bronzes, a group "Wounded to the Rear or One More Shot," and a figure of George Washington.

Rogers Groups are marked with the date of the patent and "John Rogers, New York" stamped in the plaster. The name of the group was also impressed in the front of the statue base. The plaster is a soft grey color varying from pearl or slate grey to fawn, snuff and cinnamon brown. The color consisted of three coatings of oil wash which protected the surface from chipping. Metal supports were placed inside the plaster to strengthen the group. The average group is from 20 to 24 inches high. Earlier groups made before 1863 were smaller and later groups were larger, some as tall as 47 inches. Rogers Groups were sold in large numbers. Over 100,000 of these groups were made, so they are fairly common today in spite of their perishable material. "Checkers Up at the Farm" and "Coming to the Parson" were especially popular groups and these are not difficult to find today. Other groups like "The Watch on the Santa Maria" and "Fighting Bob" and "The Fairies Whisper" are harder to find. Certain groups are more interesting from the artistic standpoint than others, although generally Rogers' Groups are well composed even though much of the subject matter is

The Tap on the Window, by John Rogers, 1874.
(*The New-York Historical Society*)

trite and the value is thus in the picture of the age rather than any art significance.

Rogers, however, made some excellent portraits such as those of President Lincoln, General Grant, and Secretary of War Stanton in the group "The Council of War;" the portraits of Whittier, Beecher, and William Lloyd Garrison in "The Fugitive's Story" and of the actor Joseph Jefferson in "Fighting Bob." Rogers also made a special study of horses and fine figures of horses are in the groups "Polo," "Fetching the Doctor," "The First Ride," "The Elder's Daughter," "Going for the Cows," "The Peddler at the Fair," and "We Boys." When first made Rogers Groups were advertised from $5 to $25 and in the 1930's when they were beginning to be collected they could be bought for $30 to $40. Now they sell for $100 up. Of course, they should be in good condition, but small chips can be mended although this detracts from the value.

There were several groups by other artists made at the same time as the Rogers Groups were made, and since they were similar they have often been erroneously attributed to Rogers. Several of these groups were made by the Boston dentist Henry Forrest Libby. One of his groups "Conquering Jealousy" is marked H. F. Libby, Boston, Copyrighted. Other groups were made by C. Hennecke & Co., Milwaukee, Wisconsin, a manufacturer of statuary and garden vases. This firm put out a catalogue for "Hennecke's Florentine Statuary" and listed "antique, Roman, Medieval and modern statuary, also 205 busts of celebrated personages." The statuary was made of various materials and included groups such as "Uncle Toby and the Widow," and "Faust and Marguerite" which are similar to Rogers' Groups. The Faust and Marguerite is stamped "C. Hennecke's Copyright" on the base. While these groups are not to be confused with Rogers Groups they themselves are interesting collectors' items. "Tannhauser and Lohengrin," "Minerva" and "Faust and Marguerite" were advertised in the Century Magazine 1886, 1887, and 1889, for $12, and a figure with Mother and Child called "Protection" sold for $8. There was also a figure called "Consolation" and a folksy figure called "Fairy Tales." The description of this figure is a commentary on the age and its attitude toward "Art." " 'Fairy Tales.' 20 inches high. A new group. Price $8.00. Rosy, buxom, and in spite of her years ever young in mind. Grandmother is at her favorite occupation, peeling potatoes. Her two grandchildren cling to her with stormy appeals to 'tell just one more of those beautiful Fairy Tales.' And grandmother smiles with that benign sweetness that is born of a kind heart and tells them for the fiftieth time the well known, old ever new story of Snow-White."

J. J. West of Chicago also made statuary groups. His groups were mainly of children. One group of a boy and girl was called "Getting Mad," another "Making Up." Other groups were "Playing Grandma," "Red Riding Hood," and "The Lost, Found" which was a figure of a girl with a lamb in her arms and a dog standing beside her. It was 20 inches high and sold for $6.00. Each group had its title stamped on the front of the base and "West's Statuary" was stamped on the bottom of the base. West sent out a catalogue and the statuary was sold in shops throughout the country. These groups would be interesting to collect along with the Rogers Groups.

Faust and Marguerite, Casper Hennecke Group, 1886.
(*The New-York Historical Society*)

Currier and Ives, and Other Lithographs

THE lithograph was the most popular type of picture hung on the walls of the average American Victorian home. There were also wood and steel engravings of well known paintings. But the lithograph, and especially those of Currier and Ives, gained the favor of most people, not only because they were cheap, but because their subject matter related to everyday life. Here are recorded the scenes, and contemporary events, and the doings of every day in the life of the average household of the second half of the nineteenth century. These prints have long been collected for their historical and commercial value and today they enjoy a popularity never before known. Nathaniel Currier, who had been apprenticed to several earlier lithographers, started

Spring, 1870, Currier & Ives. (*The Old Print Shop*)

The First Ride, Currier & Ives. (*The Old Print Shop*)

business for himself in New York in 1835. In 1857 he took James Merritt Ives into partnership. After this date until the firm closed in 1907, the prints were marked "Currier & Ives." Lithographs are drawn on stone with a greasy crayon, then transferred to paper by pressure of a press. The Currier & Ives lithographs were printed in black and white and hand-colored until about 1880, when they were generally printed in color from a series of stones. However, some early lithographs were printed or partially printed in color.

Currier & Ives prints offer such a variety of subject matter that there is a group of interest for every collector. There are rural scenes, farm and winter scenes, Mississippi River scenes, railroad, clipper ships and steamships. Sports such as hunting and fishing, baseball, yachting, bicycle racing, trotting and horse racing are other groups. There are scenes of fires and firemen, wrecks and disasters. The series of prints on the Revolution, Civil War, and Mexican War include portraits of Washington and Lincoln. Some of the lesser known prints are the sentimental portraits, pictures for children, kitten prints, name prints, music, and fruit and flower prints. There was also a group of temperance and religious prints, certificates and family registers, and humorous prints.

There are over fifty railroad prints which give an interesting and important record of the development of the American railroad. The earliest print was called "The Express Train." It is a scene on the New York and Erie Railroad and shows an early locomotive without a headlight and logs in the tender which were used for fuel. The pictures of family groups are particularly interesting because they depict Victorian dress and interior furnishings. One print shows the historic Bloomer costume.

Currier never claimed that his prints were works of art, and some of the sentimental and religious prints were crudely drawn. However, some of the best artists of the time worked for Currier and their paintings were reproduced on the prints. The artists included George Durrie, A. F. Tait, Eastman Johnson, George Inness, George Catlin, Thomas Nast, C. H. Moore, J. H. Wright, James Butterworth, Napoleon Sarony, C. Severin, Charles Parsons, W. A. Walker, W. H. Beard, Franklyn

The Great Naval Victory in Mobile Bay, August 5, 1864, Currier & Ives. (*The New-York Historical Society*)

Bassford, Louis Mauer, Thomas Worth, Frances Flora Bond Palmer, and many others, Works of these artists are sought by collectors today and many of their paintings are to be seen in American galleries and museums.

Fanny Palmer produced more subjects than any artist employed by Currier & Ives. She worked on all subjects but horses. Her clipper ship prints are among the finest of the marines and her railroad prints rank among the finest of that group. She also did trout fishing and hunting scenes. "The Happy Family," one of the finest game prints, was her design. But she is best known for the flower print "Landscape, Fruit and Flowers" which was a familiar type of scene dear to the heart of Victorians. George Henry Durrie also supplied some of the most attractive prints. With the exception of "Autumn in New England/ Cider Making" they are all winter scenes. The best known subject was

"Home to Thanksgiving." Durrie's paintings can now be seen at Shelburne Village, Shelburne, Vermont, and in other museums and private collections. Louis Mauer did many of the horse racing and trotting prints, hunting, fishing, and western frontier scenes. John Cameron was also known for his horse racing prints. Many oil paintings of outdoor life by A. F. Tait were also used as subjects for prints. His "Life of a Hunter/A Tight Fix" is one of the most sought after and expensive prints today. Charles Parsons is notable for his clipper ship prints and Thomas Worth specialized in comic prints of white and Negro humorous incidents.

Some years ago a group of experts was asked to choose the best fifty Currier & Ives prints. Although the votes varied on the fifty they were all agreed on the first three. They were "Husking" from a painting by Eastman Johnson, "Maple Sugaring" by Arthur F. Tait, and "Central Park/Skating Pond" by Charles Parsons.

Over 7,000 different subjects were published by Currier & Ives and a total of 10,000,000 copies were sold. Currier & Ives prints sold for 20 cents each and sixty dollars a thousand when new. "The Hunter/A Tight Fix" sold for $3,000 a few years ago. Many prints have been destroyed or mutilated by having their margins trimmed, but hundreds are still in attics or storerooms and the owners are unaware of their value. If you find a print in such places and can buy it cheap, it is a safe bet, but a beginner should always buy from a reputable dealer when paying a high price.

There are certain things that a collector should know. First of all, although all prints are marked, only copyrighted prints are dated, but the various addresses of the firm provide an indication of the date. In the small folio prints which were colored by inexperienced girls, the colors sometimes run over the borders; also there are no tints or gradation of color. The large folios were sent to artists for coloring and more care was taken and tempera or opaque colors were used on the highlights. Prints vary in quality as well as subject, and condition also affects the value of a print. Many prints have been reproduced. Clipper ship and Darktown prints were also printed on the old stones after Currier & Ives were no longer in business. These prints are not reproductions, but they are worth much less than originals. The printing, paper, and coloring is inferior to Currier's work.

The beginning collector would do well to concentrate on children, sentimental name subjects, or moral or religious prints. These subjects are not in so much demand and are therefore less expensive. "Jonny and Bessie" shows two children with a slate, "Pet of the Family" shows a child laden down with Christmas toys. Other subjects with children are "Mother's Joy" and "Early Sorrow." Large head subjects include "Little Manly," "Sailor Boy," "Little Daisy" and the popular "Young America" showing a child with firecrackers. The series of name prints includes individual figures of young girls or men. Temperance prints showing the evils of drink, "The Fruits of Intemperance" and "The Fruits of Temperance" illustrate the contrast between a ragged family and a prosperous family.

There were other American lithographers, some of whose prints are earlier than Currier & Ives, and some are finer. These include Pendleton of Boston; Kellogg of Hartford; Endicott, and Sarony, Major, and Knapp of New York; P. S. Duval of Philadelphia; James S. Baillie; Kimmel & Foster and many others.

Lithographs that had their color printed by a series of blocks instead of being painted by hand were called chrome-lithographs or "chromos." While there were many cheap chromos there were two firms that produced works of quality. In 1854 W. Sharp & Son of

Dorchester, Massachusetts, produced a series of four prints of the water lily known as Victoria Regia. These were large folio size 15 x 21 inches. They are brilliant in color but without the objectionable glossiness of most chromos.

The best known producer of chromolithographic prints was Louis Prang & Co., of Boston, Massachusetts. Prang was a contemporary of Currier & Ives, but he was essentially interested in the reproduction of fine art rather than cheap prints. He, like Currier, employed some of the best artists to make his cards and advertisements and purchased outright the majority of the paintings that he reproduced. Prang is best known for his Christmas cards and sentimental Valentine, Easter, New Year, and birthday cards. These were publicized by competitions for the designs, and exhibitions of the cards were held at the Boston Fine Arts Gallery and the Chicago Art Institute. The Christmas cards have also been exhibited and written about in recent times. While many of these cards were by Mrs. O. E. Whitney, probably a staff artist, artists were selected for the fourth competition and they included such well-known names as J. Alden Weir, Will H. Low, Percy and Thomas Moran and Thomas W. Dewing.

However, the range of Prang chromolithographs was wide and included many types of pictures and subjects. Prang's catalogue, Spring 1876, includes the following headings: Landscapes, Animal Pictures, Figure Pieces, Portraits, Flower Pieces, Dining Room Pictures, Gems

Valentine Card (*New York Historical Society*)

Christmas and New Year Cards, Louis Prang & Co., 1870–1900. (*Hallmark Historical Collection*)

of American Scenery, Bouquets, Children, Imperials and Album pictures, Rewards of Merit, Sunday School Texts, Mottoes and Marriage Certificates. This gives some idea of the scope of Prang's output. Of course, the small cards with sentimental floral greetings included the favorite Victorian flowers such as calla lily, the rose, moss rose, violets, passion flower, pansies and lilac. There were also bouquets with combinations of flowers and small flower or moss crosses covered with roses and lilies, daisies, ferns or autumn leaves. Flower pieces included a series of "Easter morning" by Mrs. James M. Hart and Mrs. O. E. Whitney. There was an interesting "Flowers of Hope" by M. J. Heade, and "Flowers of Memory" by E. Remington. Later there were large prints of flowers including carnations, roses, wisteria, gladioli and many other varieties. There were also fruits in baskets and large branches of fruits such as oranges and plums and a design "Indian Corn and Apples." A series of fifteen chromos of chrysanthemums by the botanical artists James S. Callowell and Alois Lunzer was called "Princess Golden Flower." There was also a series of orchid pictures. Later flower lithographs were also made on satin.

Landscapes in the catalogue included Spring, Summer and Autumn by A. T. Bricher, and a group of New York and New England scenes by J. M. Hart, and California scenes by John R. Key, including "Golden Gate, San Francisco," "Cliff House, San Francisco," "Mt. Diablo," Lake Tahoe, Sacramento Valley, Santa Cruz Mountains, Big Trees and Yosemite. Louis K. Harlow also painted a series of California and New England scenes. There was a series of water colors of western landscapes by Thomas Moran, including Salt Lake and the Yellowstone geysers. Benjamin Champney did a series of New England landscapes, and "Sunset in California." A copy of the now famous Bierstadt painting "Sunset" is available in Prang chromo.

Children included a portrait of "Little Prudy" by Elizabeth Murray. Later, in a list of 1897 "Little Prudy's Brother" is listed. There were also barefoot children, Little Bo Peep, and Young Commodore. There were groups of babies, including Prize Babies by Ida Waugh. Eastman Johnson's paintings, "Whittier's Barefoot Boy," and "Boyhood of Lincoln" were included in a catalogue of 1869, as was George L.

Brown's "Crown of New England," a landscape, the original of which was purchased by the Prince of Wales. Animal pictures included dogs by Alexander Pope, cows by Thaddeus Welch, cats and kittens including a Girl with Kittens by J. Enneking, and chickens, ducks, quail, and deer by A. F. Tait. A picture of a pointer and quail, one of a spaniel and woodcock and one of deer, are marked "A.F.T." Two chromos of inferior sentimental character, "Cluck, Cluck" and "Take Care" are signed "A. F. Tait, N.A. 1891."

However, the most interesting category of chromos listed in the 1876 catalogue were the Dining Room pictures. Included were trout, pickerel, and dead game by George N. Cass, and dessert pictures by R. D. Wilkie, I. Wilms and C. P. Ream. The original of C. P. Ream's Dessert No. IV is now titled "Raspberries and Ice Cream" and, wrongly attributed to Harnett, is owned by Mr. O. B. Jennings of New York City. In 1874 Prang issued a series of twelve chromos of the trades.

Advertisement for Roessle Brewing Company. Lithograph by Prang from painting by Claude Raquet Hirst. (*From book of Prang proofs. New York Public Library*)

These were used as aids in teaching. They show the various American trades such as the Carpenter, Blacksmith, Tinsmith, Baker, Shoemaker, and Tailor. These prints are excellent and are sought for by museums.

In 1889 and 1890 Prang issued calendars with scenes of Boston, New York, Washington, Baltimore and Philadelphia. There were also series of small books of verse and pictures called Prang's Fine Art Books. These included Flower Fancies, Notes from Mendelssohn, The Night Cometh, Haunts of Longfellow, Home of Shakespeare, Golden Milestones, Golden Sunsets, and Autograph Recipes. Another series of pictures were of sentimental subjects, of The Wedding and nuptial felicity.

One of the most ambitious publications by L. Prang & company was a four-volume book, *The Native Flowers & Ferns of the United States*, by Thomas Meehan in 1887-1880. This was illustrated by Alois Lunzer. These botanical prints are decorative and worth framing and hanging separately, but the text of the book is also excellent and if kept "as is" will increase in value. A book on reptiles and one on wild animals was also illustrated by Prang.

Perhaps the finest color work ever done by Prang was the illustration of *The Oriental Ceramic Art Collection of W. T. Walters* published by D. Appleton & Co., 1897. This consists of ten volumes of some of the most beautiful color printing ever done and should once and for all dispel all slighting remarks about Prang & Co.'s chromolithography. In 1897 Prang also made prints of Winslow Homer's "Eastern Shore" and "North Woods" and thus started this artist on his way to fame. The list of other well-known artists employed by Prang and whose pictures were owned

Illustration from 1876 catalogue of Louis Prang & Co. Desserts No. III & No. IV are by C. P. Ream. See page 76 for original painting.

by the company include William M. Chase, Abbott Thayer, Elihu Vedder, Thomas Moran, A. Bierstadt, J. J. Enneking, George E. Brown, J. W. Champney and Benjamin Champney. The pictures were sold at auction in the American Art Association sale in 1892. Prints by these artists are well worth collecting, but perhaps the best buys for present day collectors are the series of Civil War campaign sketches by Winslow Homer and the Civil War scenes of sea and land battles done in 1885 and 1886 by the artists J. O. Davidson and Thure de Thulstrup. These include "Sheridan's Final Charge at Winchester," "Battle of Chattanooga," "Sheridan's Ride," "Battle of Fredericksburg," "Battle of Gettysburg," "Battle of Kenesaw Mountain," "Battle of Allatoona Pass, "Battle of Antietam," "Battle of Spottsylvania," "Battle of Shiloh," "Siege of Atlanta," and "Siege of Vicksburg," all by Thulstrup; and "Monitor & Merrimac," "Battle of New Orleans," "Battle of Mobile Bay," "Kearsage & Alabama," "Battle of Port Hudson," and "Capture of Fort Fisher" by Davidson. Davidson who was primarily a marine

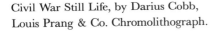

Civil War Still Life, by Darius Cobb,
Louis Prang & Co. Chromolithograph.

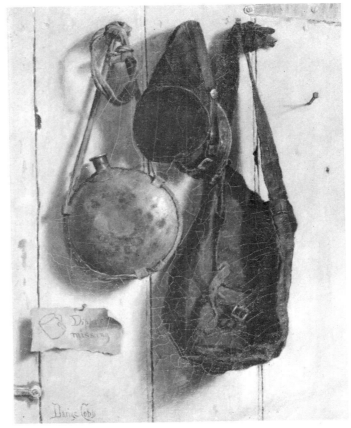

painter also did a series of Yacht Racing pictures for Prang which should be of interest to sports print collectors. The large print which Prang created in 1888 for the Old Army Friends Publishing Company from a painting by Darius Cobb is a trompe l'oeil with a battered soldier's cap, canteen, knapsack hanging against a door and at the lower left a piece of paper with an outline drawing of a tin cup and the inscription, "Dipper Missing." This is a collector's print, as is the still life of book, glasses, pipe, and candle, painted by Claude Raquet Hirst and lithographed by Prang for an advertisement of the Roessle Brewing Company.

In the 1890's Kurz and Allison of Chicago, Illinois, did an attractive series of Civil War prints. There are many of these available today and the prices are reasonable. In fact, at the present writing there is little demand for Civil War prints so if anyone is interested, now is the time to buy.

Colored fashion plates from *Godey's Lady's Book* and other women's magazines of the mid- and late-nineteenth century and flower, bird, and fruit prints whether hand-colored or chromolithographs are attractive when framed and hung in a group.

Fashion plate from Godey's Lady's Book, December, 1839. (*The New-York Historical Society*)

Primitive Painting

ALTHOUGH, contrary to the evaluation of twentieth century critics, there were many good artists in ninteenth century America, relatively few people could afford their paintings. Instead they had portraits, still life scenes, and memorial pictures painted by local artists. Some of them were crude and the best of them flat and somewhat distorted. Included among the primitives were scenes of local industry such as haying, corn husking, quilt making and landscapes, Grandma Moses' style. There were also religious themes such as the "Prodigal Son," "Moses in the Bullrushes," and memorial, allegorical, historical and patriotic pictures. Then there were family group pictures and single portraits. Some of these are large oil paintings and others are small water

Watercolor of family group in Victorian Parlor, c. 1875, Artist Unknown. (*The Henry Ford Museum*)

LEFT. "Lady with a Cat," oil on canvas. Mid-nineteenth century, Artist Unknown. (*Museum of Fine Arts, Springfield, Mass.*) RIGHT. Portrait of a Man with blue coat, water color, c. 1840, Artist Unknown, (*Colby College Art Museum*)

colors. For some years now these pieces have been collected because they have a certain simplicity, vigor, and decorative quality which appeals to present day art standards. At first they were cheap but as the demand has grown even the crudest primitive water color brings a price.

The most numerous of the paintings were the family portraits. Of these the family groups and children with toys are the most popular. These paintings, many done by craftsmen and itinerant artists, give us a picture of the nineteenth century. We see how the people dressed, and how their houses were furnished, what toys the children played with. They teach us American history not through facts and statistics, but at first hand through the faces and surroundings of the simple everyday people. These paintings are an authentic and important part of our national heritage. They are indigenous and perhaps the most truly American of all our art efforts.

Dickens on his visit to America recorded his description of American primitive portraits: "In the best room were two oil portraits of kit-cat size representing the landlord and his infant son, both looking as bold as lions and staring out of the canvas with an intensity that would be cheap at any price." The portraits can usually be identified by their vague stare. Hands if included are poorly painted, but the details of dress such as crimped bonnets, hair style, starched lace collars, and jewelry are painted in detail. Portraits often include books, flowers, chairs, tables, and other furniture as well as colorful carpets; children's portraits usually include toys such as dolls, wagons, pull or squeak toys and live cats or dogs. Still life paintings included a centerpiece with fruit, glasses, a knife, and perhaps a bottle or carafe of wine. All have an appealing period quaintness.

"The New Trick," Oil on canvas, by Charles Osgood. (*Vose Galleries of Boston*)

"Fancy Picture." Fishing, with waterfall, water color, c. 1845, Artist Unknown. (*Colby College Art Museum*)

However, in most cases the portraits are not likenesses but stereotyped blank faces and the painting is decoration, for many of these painters were sign painters and painters of clock fronts and mirror panels. The artist often varied his painting according to the price paid. The majority of the artists were unknown and those whose names are known are not always the best artists. William Prior was one who varied his likenesses with the prices, but today even his high forehead, large-eyed, flat portraits are expensive. Other primitive artists whose paintings are in private collections and museums today are Isaac Augustus Wetherby, Joseph W. Stock, Horace Bundy, Erastus Salisbury Field, Augustus Fuller and Joseph H. Davis and Eunice Pinney. Also each section of the country has its own primitive artists and more named and unnamed are being discovered each year.

Many of the religious and allegorical paintings were done in Female Seminaries. These were usually small water colors of such subjects as The Garden of Eden, Noah's Ark, The Prodigal Son, Moses in the Bull Rushes, or other stories from the Old Testament. The Lady of the Lake was a favorite theme as was the landscape with a Victorian house. There were also stylized landscapes and "Fancy Pictures" with figures fishing, or a shepherd or shepherdess.

The symbolical mourning picture which was often done in needle-work was also a theme for water color paintings. It included a tomb-stone with inscription "sacred to the memory of," a willow tree, and from one to a whole family of mourners. Many of these pictures date from early in the century, but the custom continued into the 1850's.

Any of the above mentioned pictures are expensive, but it is still possible to pick up small primitive water colors. There are water colors of ships and some collectors concentrate on these. Steamship

Victorian Landscape, Oil on canvas, c. 1875–1880, Artist Unknown. (*Colby College Art Museum*)

paintings by J. Bard who worked in New York in the 1860's are expensive, but there are many by unknown artists of the same date that are collectible. Often the name of the ship is given on the painting and the sails and rigging are sometimes reproduced with an authenticity to satisfy any sailor. However, often the painting is so stylized that the only realistic note is the name. Collections of ship paintings are to be seen in the Peabody Museum, Salem, Massachusetts; the Marine Historical Association, Mystic, Connecticut; Mariners Museum, Newport News, Virginia. There are also pen flourish pictures dating from 1850 to 1880's. These were usually done with a quill pen. They included pictures of horses, stags and other animals. There were books of directions and teachers who gave private instructions.

Sometimes primitive paintings were composed with stencils. Directions printed in a magazine of the 1840's gave information for the drawing and coloring which makes them related to our present day number paintings for amateurs.

Flower paintings and genre pictures painted by second rate artists and amateurs of the 1880's and 1890's are also being collected today. Flowers were not only painted on canvas but on silk tapestry, and on shiny black lacquered boards. Roses, violets, lilies, or a mixed bouquet in a Victorian vase were the favorites. Many of the paintings reproduced by Louis Prang and Company were painted by second rate artists who turned out typical sentimental Victorian arrangements of flowers. Some of these pictures were made from studio sketches, others were made from oil paintings, the most of which have disappeared from sight today, but there is still a chance that they will come on the market. For example, there are the "Strawberries and Baskets" and "Cherries and Basket" after Miss V. Cranbery, and the flowers by Ellen T. Fisher, Mrs. James M. Hart, Mrs. O. E. Whitney, Anne C. Nowell, Lisbeth B. Comins, Rosina Emmet, and Maud Stumm. Where is the original of Ida Waugh's "Prize Babies" and "Little Prudy" and "Little Prudy's Brother" by Elizabeth Murray; and where is "Before and After" showing a rooster fight by Leon Moran? These of course would be collected as typical products of the Victorian Age, not as examples of good painting.

Some of these painters although not well known are listed in Fielding and seem to have had a background of art training. Others were pupils of well-known artists or had an artist in the family who recommended them for reproduction work. However, most of their paintings which Prang reproduced were actually "gallery pieces" since many of them were included in the sales of Prang's collection of paintings at the American Art Association in 1892 and at Copley Hall, Boston, in 1899.

There were also pictures of historical significance painted by self-taught primitive artists such as John Lee of Newark who painted the Newark fire in 1845 and whose pictures, ignored by family and public for many years, are now in the Newark Art Museum and the New Jersey Historical Society. Such people as Lee found recreation in their painting as do businessmen, lawyers and doctors today. Their work is seldom better than second rate, but an occasional such painter strikes upon subject matter that has historical significance and paints in a style related to the primitives. Their paintings will be in the collections of tomorrow.

John Lee, Broad Street Fire, Newark, 1845. (*The Newark Museum*)

III. THE VICTORIAN DINING TABLE

DINING in America in Victorian times depended upon your status, your pocketbook and your locale, even as it does today. While there were several levels of dining, the main division was between those who set their tables with pressed glass and electroplate and those who could afford cut glass and silver. Pressed glass and plated ware were used on the tables of most middle class Americans along with gaudy cottage pottery, Willowware or Ironstone china with flowing blue or brown designs or gold decoration such as Wedding Ring, Tea Leaf, or plain Gold Band. Late in the century majolica became popular. Most of this china was made in England, but by the 1870's many factories in Ohio and New Jersey were making sets of ironstone, majolica and also more sophisticated china for the dining table. The sets usually included several sizes of plates, covered serving dishes, cups and saucers, crescent-shaped bone or salad dishes, butter pats, pitchers, and a teapot, sugar, and creamer.

Dining table at Sarah Jordan Boarding House, now in Greenfield Village. Turkey red table cloth, wild rose pattern, Greek key border. Tea leaf ironstone china. Silver plated caster with canary glass bottles. Daisy and Button pressed glass pickle jar in plated holder. Pressed glass goblets "Liberty Bell" pattern, Gillinder & Sons. (*The Henry Ford Museum*)

131

Along with this simple utilitarian china, pieces of pressed glass gave sparkle and variety. Pressed glass was mass-produced and cheap and it caught the popular fancy. Not all items of glass even late in the century were made in all patterns. Some of the patterns made after 1870 which include the largest number of items were Square Fuchsia, Beaded Swirl, Amazon, Art, Henrietta, Westmoreland, and Bar and Diamond. A typical list of items made in these sets included open and covered bowls, butter dishes, celery vases, footed compotes, cruets, creamers, decanters, goblets, pickle dishes, bread plates, salt and pepper shakers (individual salts were made in earlier patterns), sauce dishes, spoon holders, sugar bowls, syrup jugs, pitchers, wine glasses, and a wine set with jug and tray. Typically Victorian pieces were the spoon holder, celery vase, bread plate, pickle caster, and revolving center condiment caster. Knives and forks were of such silver or plated patterns as Fine Thread, or had bone or ebony handles.

In the center of the table stood the revolving caster stand of electroplate with its bottles of clear or canary-colored pressed glass patterns such as Daisy and Button, or thumbprint ovals with chased flower and leaf sprays. All dishes and silver were set on the table. Each place setting consisted of a plate, knife, fork and spoon, cup and saucer, and a napkin in a plated silver napkin ring. Above the plate was the bone dish and butter pat. A covered tureen held the meat or soup, and vegetable dishes were grouped in the center. The spoon holder, celery vase, pickle caster and covered butter dish of glass or electroplate with a cow finial, were placed at the corners of the table. Goblets or glasses were placed at each plate and a milk pitcher was usually on the table, while an ice water pitcher sat on a side table. The bread plate with its inscription "Give Us This Day Our Daily Bread," was a familiar item found on every middle class table. These plates were made in patterns of clear pressed glass and in opaque milk glass.

The simple family table with the above items was set on a turkey-red cotton damask cloth with gay patterns of flowers, fruits, birds and animals with a center medallion and fringed sides. These turkey-red cloths could be bought by the yard at such stores as Sears, Roebuck. Some cloths were also finished with fringe on all sides and ready for use. Most of these cloths were made in Scotland, Ireland, Germany and Austria, but some were also made in America. English designs included hunting scenes similar to but much less elaborate than the cloth illustrating a stag hunt which was used by Queen Victoria in Scotland. Other designs included oak leaves and acorns, cathedral, king's rose, pond lilies, poppies, shamrock, violet, and calla lilies.

Cotton damask table cloth, green and brown, J. Cunningham, New Hartford, Oneida Co., N.Y. 1841. (*The New-York Historical Society*)

A design of wild roses had a lavender border with a gold stripe. A cloth with a spread eagle in the borders was probably American, as were the field daisy, grape, cloverleaf, azalea, cherry, strawberry, nut and fern patterns. There was also a spinning wheel pattern, a wild horse in a tropical forest, and one with Egyptian motifs. A chrysanthemum pattern was also popular. These cloths had medallion centers and Roman Key borders. The colors ranged from turkey-red to soft pink and coral. They were used after the Civil War, and sold at Woolworth's in 1879 and at Sears, Roebuck in 1878.

Of course, the scale of dining graduated between the humble fare set on a turkey-red cloth and the satin damask, silver, and cut glass service supervised by a staff of servants. In between were those who had sets of Canton china or Wedgwood Creamware, heirloom silver and glass. In these homes fruit bowls of china or glass set on a pedestal usually replaced the caster in the center of the table. The compote might be made of clear pressed glass or of lacy-edged milk glass or it might be of imported English or French porcelain. Sometimes there was a mirror centerpiece set with porcelain figures, or for the country, a wooden platform with greens, rocks, and vases of flowers at the corners.

Jacob von Falke in the American edition of *Art in the House* (1879) gives directions for dining room furnishings. He suggests red for the walls, with one light over the table, and portraits, still life, fruit and flower paintings or animal and hunting subjects. The tablecloth should have a broad and rich border. Centerpieces include "flower and fruit

Silver plated fruit dishes. (*Reed & Barton Catalogue, 1885*)

dishes, vases, wine coolers, fountains, temples, statues, or girandolas."
Centerpieces in advertisements of Gorham and other silver manufacturers at this date included sculptured trees with birds and figures of
shepherds, rocky landscapes with deer and hunters, scenes of Paul and
Virginia, oriental temples and seascapes with Neptune and tritons.
A contemporary description of a dinner table in a Fifth Avenue mansion will give a picture of the affluence of the Victorian table of the
wealthy and notation of some of the actual items of silver, china, and
glass.

The following is partially paraphrased from an article in *Jewelers'
Circular* 1874: The centerpiece commanding and unifying the rich
array is a magnificent epergne overtopped with calla lilies bending
from lily chalices, and stems of gold which cluster over the central
basin, and three smaller basins hanging at equal intervals among the
drooping sprays and blossoms are also heaped and overhung with gay
flowers like the center. The surfaces of the four basins are of the soft
lustrous satin finish which the reader must have seen repeatedly to
imagine its beauty, deepened by the flash of narrow burnished bands
and moldings. The stem supporting these gorgeous hanging gardens is
a female figure, fashioned from one of the loveliest of classic models in
massive silver deadened to a pearly tint by oxidation, her feet poised
lightly on the cap of a temple dome that forms a pedestal for the whole.
On the dome is the consummate splendor of shaded and burnished zones
in contrast with sparkling engraved wreaths, glittering cornices, and a
frieze of rich oxidized bas-reliefs around the base, which rests on four
massive feet, as if it floated on the dazzling surface of a silver sea, or
more literally a burnished plateau as it is called, that mirrors back the
beauty. The plateau is oblong and sufficiently extended to float also
two graceful candelabra, one on either side of the epergne, with seven
branches bearing tall wax candles. Spaces for twenty-four guests are
marked off on the white damask by the sparkling cluster of glasses,
spoon, fork, and knife.

"The guests have a moment to admire the beauty of the new style
tureens, and the iridescent oxides and gold on the dainty little butterflies flitting over the edges of the silver salt cellars and the fanciful

forms of the chased pepper bottles and salad casters ranged within reach of every hand—for the old-fashioned omnibus caster is one of the particular vanities now fashionably dispensed with. All at once, at the secret signal of their chief the well-trained and well-dressed attendants appear, and in another moment the silver salvers come floating down before each guest." The bread is handed on plates which have a bas-relief of landscapes of golden grain with Ceres and her reapers, one of the symbolical works of art that hint the special purpose of each vessel. The salmon is served in a nautical dish with a trident fork and a sauce tureen with an enamelled shell spoon. The roast is served on the sideboard. There too stand the wine-coolers, truncated columns of burnished silver twined with the cluster-laden vine and their bases sculptured with the mythology of Bacchus. All the vegetables of the season have their vessels in quadruplicate. The butter bowls with their covers and knives are appropriate silver and gold, crowned with symbols of bucolic fatness. Water pitchers, richly engraved, chased, and embossed with fountains, lakes and oases of palm, flanked by bowls of crushed ice, rimmed with pendant icicles of frosted silver and their bases pitted with rugged Arctic scenery in blocks and bergs and polar bears. The very ice spoon is perforated with an appropriate design. The salad bowl is another combination of lusters and sculptures. The classic olive in appropriate dishes; likewise the pickles with bladed silver forks. The celery vases are tall chalices.

At the pastry and dessert all the foregoing is removed and a fresh array still more elegant arrives. The ice-cream towers on massive silver stands sculptured with Arctic scenery to keep it from melting, with broad mirror trays beneath the knife-edged ice-cream spoon and the cool frost-finished saucers. There are also large vessels for fruit ices, with plates to match. The cakes and bonbons are on low comportiers. Grapes are served on a comportier with a design of fox and grapes and grape scissors are not forgotten. Fruits are on a silver barge. The elegance of the patterns of spoons, knives, and nut picks, and silver knick-knacks is only surpassed by the coffee service which the skillful engraver has used as a picture gallery.

The silver described above was all made by Gorham, but it was typical of the elaborate silver centerpieces and serving dishes also made by Tiffany, Black Starr and Frost, Caldwell, Samuel Kirk and other high class silver manufacturers of the time. Similar pieces were also made in plate by Reed and Barton, Meriden Silver-Plate Company, and Middletown Silver-Plate Company.

Snow white satin-like damask with a Dresden pattern of dancing cupids and garlands of flowers encircling the centerpiece set off the beauty of the silver and cut glass. This same tablecloth could be had in

Silver epergne with symbolic figures of Music, Art, Science, and Commerce. Exhibited at Philadelphia Centennial by Meriden Silver Plate Company. (*The Art Journal, 1876*)

color also. There were also tablecloths with designs taken from Royal Meissen china and tablecloths with colored borders of the Zwiebelmuster or Onion pattern were imported from Germany in the 1870's. There were also damask tablecloths hand-embroidered with monograms or crests in scarlet and blue with traceries of arabesque design. Different china was used with each course. Soup was served in Sèvres, entrées in English china, and fruit and coffee in Chinese or Japanese porcelain. Canton china long a favorite was still used on many tables. Minton china, French enamelled glass, Bohemian glass, Bombay striped glass and Stourbridge glass were also popular.

At the end of the century it became the custom to arrange flowers in the center of the table with small bouquets to detach and give to each guest. The nuts, preserves and bonbons were arranged around the centerpiece in small shell-shaped or basket dishes of silver, cut glass, or porcelain. Constance Cary Harrison in *Woman's Handiwork in Modern Homes* (1881) in her chapter on table decoration also notes that "American finger bowls and ice cream plates in clear blue, red, white, or Venetian thread pattern are $9.00 a dozen at Sandwich." The plateau or table mirror centered the table with china troughs filled with flowers and swans of Royal Worcester and Venetian glass on the mirror. A Dresden centerpiece of Cupid riding a swan was also used.

However, although no writer makes mention of them, there were elaborate centerpieces with branching vases or tiered bowls made at Sandwich in Tree of Life, Millefleur, and combinations of blue and white and yellow and white glass. Clarke and several other American manufacturers made centerpieces combining rose or tulip fairy lamps and tiny hanging vases. Flowers or greenery such as smilax were arranged at their base.

The ceremonious dinner of the 1890's was set on a tablecloth of lace over satin. Cut glass was in its heyday, and wine decanters of cut glass were set on the table and cut glass candlesticks with shades matching the tablecloth were set at each plate with cut glass vases holding violets for each guest. Sometimes there were tall banquet lamps of cut glass. The menus and place cards were of hand-painted silk. Bohemian glass goblets or goblets of harlequin glass, each a different color, were popular. Roman punch was served in the "hearts of a red rose or bosom of a swan or cup of lily or tiny life-saving boat." Tiny wheelbarrows, fans, or some other trinket served as favors. Majolica oyster plates were used, and hand-painted Minton china game plates, dessert plates with orchids and hummingbirds, and botanical fruit plates were popular. Ladies who did china painting painted plates with similar patterns.

The Society of Decorative Art had an influence on table decoration late in the century. Tea cloths and tablecloths with hand-drawn work, Japanese designs, crewel work, sprays of cyclamen, honeysuckle, and forget-me-nots, and cloths made up of squares of plush embroidered in crewel sprays were shown at their exhibitions. Cloths were also embroidered with borders of blue to match the china, and knife handles also matched. These were probably all Meissen Onion pattern. An amber silk table cloth had a design of Eastern embroidery, an old blue

LEFT. Marchian glass epergne with fruit and flowers. RIGHT. Silver Plateau with vase and cornucopias filled with flowers. (*Rustic Ornaments for Homes of Taste* by Shirley Hibberd, 1870)

Chinese bowl held yellow jonquils and roses, and dessert was served on oriental porcelain.

The Victorian dining table offers numerous items for collectors today. In addition to the better known articles of glass, china and silver, there are small objects such as napkin rings, knife rests, and butter pats, and in addition to patterns of nineteenth century silver there are knives and forks with bone handles and decorative and colorful porcelain handles. The blades of knives and serving forks and spoons are also cut and engraved in patterns which make them interesting collectors' items. Many articles can be picked out of junk heaps and forgotten attic trunks, but they can also be found in antique shops, for the dealers have been collecting from nineteenth century waste baskets for some years.

Dessert Molds and Pyramids

For special occasions the table decoration of flowers, crystal, and silver was augmented by centerpieces or pyramids constructed of pulled and spun sugar, nougat, gum paste and almond paste together with molds of various sizes and shapes set on socles or stands of nougat. The artistry for these elaborate concoctions was learned from the French. There were French confectioners in New York in the early nineteenth century. An advertisement of a confectioner gives us information about his products: "A. Lanniuer, Informs the public that he has completed a Monument in Sugar to the memory of the late illustrious, General Washington, which is for sale at his confectionary store in Broadway; in the front is a portrait of General Washington, and on each side the figure of Columbia weeping over his urn, with arms and appropriate trophies . . ."—Mercantile Advertiser, February 24, 1800. Another advertisement describes the "Sugar Delicacies, which are made in a style alto-

LEFT AND RIGHT. Vases of pulled and spun sugar holding sugar flowers

gether new in this country. . . . He has likewise a new assortment of Table Ornaments, such as the Temple of Jedaus, and others, of an elegance superior to anything that has ever appeared in America; and in sufficient quantity to decorate a table of 500 covers. "Mercantile Advertiser," January 3, 1804. Ice cream was molded and sent out in various shapes by G. Chenelette & Co. according to their advertisement: Commercial Advertiser, May 9, 1801. These confectionary decorations were an accompaniment to formal dining in nineteenth century America and by the end of the century there were cook books giving directions for making elaborate and fanciful centerpieces. Full directions for the construction of centerpieces of many types is illustrated in *The Epicurean* by Charles Ranhofer of Delmonico's which was first published in 1894. In the chapter on Centerpieces or Pyramids, Ranhofer states that center-pieces were placed on the table to replace cold pieces in the third service of the French, and placed on the table at the beginning and at dessert for Russian style table service. The long list of subjects suitable for center-pieces includes Swiss cottages, temples, pavilions, towers, pagodas, mosques, fortresses, hermitages, belvederes, cabins, cascades, fountains, ruins, rotundas, tents, lyres, harps, helmets, boats, vases, cornucopias, baskets, beehives, trophies, and other military musical and agricultural subjects as well as trees, animals, flowers, and figures of famous persons. He then goes on to list suitable subjects from mythology such as "Cupid on a shell with swans;" "Neptune with tritons and Naiads;" "Venus teaching Cupid dancing;" "Apollo playing the flute, Jupiter watching." Biblical subjects such as Noah and the Ark are also suggested. Other suitable subjects included Normandy peasants dancing, a Tyrolian mountain climber, American Indian, and a Tartar on horseback.

Detailed directions for making some of the less pretentious pieces such as swans of various kinds of ice cream placed in a setting of pulled sugar, rushes and reeds and set on a socle or stand of nougat are included. The Helmet was a pudding made in a tin mold and decorated with ice

and set on stands of nougat. (*The Epicurean*, by Charles Ranhofer, 1894)

UPPER LEFT. Three-tiered molds filled with game mousse, set on a rustic stand made of nougats and topped by a stearine figure of Diana. UPPER RIGHT. "The Helmet", made of ice cream in a tin mold. The feather is of spun sugar. LOWER LEFT. Ice and ice cream molded in a swan mold and set on a base of reeds and rushes made of pistachio nougat. LOWER RIGHT. Dessert topped with stearine figure of Bacchus, intended for decorating the sideboard or as a centerpiece on the table. (*The Epicurean,* by Charles Ranhofer)

cream and pistachios while the helmet feather was made of spun sugar. There are directions for making a wheelbarrow filled with flowers which is constructed of various kinds of nougat, pulled sugar, fancy ices and glazed fruit. A windmill and a lighthouse are also both edible and decorative. Vases made of pulled and spun sugar holding sugar flowers and set on stands or socles of nougat and sugar were for table decoration only. Tiers of bonbons were also used as table decoration.

There were all manner of tin and copper molds available including melon molds, basket molds, horns of plenty, swans and a Bacchus on the barrel. The stands or socles were constructed by the chef, but there were stearine figures of birds, cupids, Diana, the Goddess of Liberty and other patriotic and mythological figures that could be purchased. Many fish, game and meat dishes were also constructed to be used as table decoration.

One of the interesting features of these centerpieces is their close resemblance to the decorative motifs of the era as seen on the silver, glass, and other accessories of the time. The themes also reflect the spirit and romantic ideas of the Gay Nineties. Although the molds and other cooking utensils used in making these fabulous contrivances were late nineteenth century factory items, they are nevertheless worth collecting. A few of them might still exist in the pantry of an old mansion and could possibly come up for auction. Also stearine figures although perishable may have been treasured and thus might be available to collectors.

Picturesque, story-telling food, a Victorian chef's masterpiece for serving pheasant. (*The Epicurean,* by Charles Ranhofer)

Blown glass birds, flowers and ships on cotton and tinsel rope under glass dome, c. 1875.
(*The Henry Ford Museum*)

IV. GLASS

Pressed Glass

PRESSED glass was made to imitate expensive cut glass. The diamonds, prisms, thumbprint, round lozenge and sawtooth cuttings of cut glass were all imitated and used in patterns of the cheaper pressed glass. Pressed glass was first made in the 1820's, and by 1840 factories for making pressed glass were springing up all over America. In the beginning, only necessary articles of tableware were made, but such was the popularity and demand for pressed glass that sets which included a great variety of pieces were made by 1850. The earliest pressed glass was made of lead flint glass, but after the Civil War pressed glass tableware was made of lime glass. Pressed glass was made in clear glass, but also in opaque white, black, and other opaque colors as well as marble glass, opalescent, and vaseline glass. The early pressed glass has a bell-like ring and is heavy and brilliant. The later lime glass does not have the ring. Also, early pressed glass is clear while much of the later glass is colored.

Almost all of the patterns of American Victorian pressed glass were made at the New England Glass Company in Cambridge, Massachusetts, and at the Boston & Sandwich Glass Company, but pressed glass was also made at several smaller New England glass houses, such as

145

the Portland Glass Company in Portland, Maine. In Philadelphia, James Gillinder & Sons made pressed glass, and in Pittsburgh there were several important manufacturers of pressed glass, including Bakewell, Pears & Co.; M'Kee Bros.; Bryce Bros.; Adams & Co.; George Duncan & Sons; and after 1891, United States Glass Company. The glass manufacturing center in Wheeling, West Virginia, included Hobbs, Brockunier, and Central Glass Company. There were also several companies in Tarentum, Pennsylvania; and in Ohio there were many glass companies, including Lancaster Glass Company, Bellaire Goblet Company; Nickel Plate Glass Company; A. J. Beatty & Co.; and Crystal Glass Company.

Most of the pressed glass made after 1850 belongs in the category of pattern glass which was made in matching sets for the dining table. A table set consisted of matching sugar bowl and creamer, butter dish and spoon holder. Later sets were made for a complete table service, with goblets and wine glasses, and many sets included such specialized dishes as salts, egg cups, celery vases, pickle dishes, jam jars and honey dishes, and the bread plate inscribed, "Give Us This Day Our Daily Bread." There were also cake plates on stands, caster bottles, footed compotes, cordial glasses, sauce dishes, champagnes and decanters in some of the popular patterns such as Bellflower.

In a book such as this, which covers many subjects, we can give only an outline of the glass patterns available and some of the characteristics of their design. Since the serious collector of pressed glass will want to own Ruth Webb Lee's book, *Early American Pressed Glass,* it seems best to follow her classifications. Mrs. Lee divides the various patterns into groups according to the similarity of their designs.

The first pressed glass patterns were the heavy simple designs which have more emphasis on form than surface pattern. These were made during the 1840's, but many of them continued to be made as late as the 1880's. Mrs. Lee calls this group Colonial. The glass is thick and the outlines bulky. There is a similarity between many of the patterns, which are made up of heavy panels, loops, ovals, and thumbprint motifs. However, there are differences even among the same patterns since they were made at several factories, and thus not only the design but the quality of the glass varies in brilliancy and weight. The Colonial group includes 17 patterns of which the following are the most popular: Ashburton, Argus, Excelsior, Petal and Loop, Diamond Thumbprint, Huber, and Washington. There are several patterns in this group such as the Sandwich Star, Four Petal, Sunburst, Waffle, and Thumbprint which are more decorative, and these patterns seem closer related to cut glass. Pressed glass was not marked, but must be identified by the quality of the glass and by acquiring familiarity with the various firms that made it and the patterns that they made. For example, the early Ashburton pattern was made at the New England

Diamond Thumbprint pattern pressed glass. TOP ROW, LEFT TO RIGHT. Rare pint decanter; rare expanded bowl on low foot with scallop & point rim; spooner with scalloped top & broad foot; compote with scalloped edge on low standard; water tumbler; rare whiskey tumbler; footed master salt. BOTTOM ROW, LEFT TO RIGHT. Decanter with stopper; compote with scalloped edge on high standard; celery vase. W. M. Guthrie Collection, Conestoga Auction Co. (*The Spinning Wheel,* April, 1966)

LEFT. Pressed glass celery glass, Bellflower pattern. RIGHT. Pressed glass goblet, Pineapple pattern. (*The Corning Museum of Glass*)

Glass Company in 1849 and at Bakewell, Pears & Co. Fragments of Ashburton have also been excavated from the site of the Boston & Sandwich Glass Company. Ashburton was made in twenty-two different articles, including bitters bottles, champagnes, clarets, cordial glasses and decanters.

The ribbed patterns also form an early pressed glass group. The simplest pattern, the Fine Rib, consists of fine vertical ribs which cover the surface of the glass, leaving plain stems on the glasses, compotes, and other footed pieces. Ribbed patterns with vine designs on the ribbed background are more decorative. These include the popular Bellflower, Ivy, Acorn, Grape, and the heavier, baroque Ribbed Palm and Inverted Fern. Bellflower was made in more pieces than any of the other patterns. It includes a rare cake plate, compotes, caster sets, butter dishes, pitchers, decanters, creamers, sugar bowls, salts, spoon

ABOVE. Pressed glass footed bowl, Horn of Plenty pattern. BELOW. Pressed glass bowl, Ivy pattern. (*The Corning Museum of Glass*)

Pressed glass, footed bowl, Lincoln Drape pattern. (*The Corning Museum of Glass*)

Blue Lincoln Drape syrup jug with applied handle and tin lid. Black glass plate, Gothic openwork edge. Rare electric blue covered sugar bowl, Four Petal pattern. (*The Henry Ford Museum*)

holders, plates, goblets and tumblers. There was also a variety of Fine Ribbed pieces and these plain ribbed articles could be combined to good effect with any of the other rib patterns. As with all pressed glass patterns the plates, wines and tumblers are the hardest pieces to find.

Other early patterns include the many variations of the Sawtooth. The earliest were heavy and coarse with points. Later there was a pattern with smaller points known as the Diamond Point, and still later the points were flattened, and this pattern was known as the Flattened Sawtooth. These patterns were made by many factories over a period of forty years. The early Sawtooth covered sugar bowl and compotes are especially graceful pieces. A toy set was made by Gillinder & Sons of Philadelphia for the Centennial.

The Bull's Eye and certain related patterns such as the Horn of Plenty, Comet, and New England Pineapple, were made in the 1850's–1860's. They are characterized by the large bull's eye circles which form the basis of the designs. These patterns are heavy in weight and bold in design and the glass is brilliant. The most popular of this group is the Horn of Plenty. A great variety of pieces were made in this pattern by the Boston & Sandwich Company and by M'Kee Bros. and others in Pittsburgh. There were several variations of Bull's Eye; Bull's Eye with Diamond Point, or Bull's Eye with Fleur de Lys. These more elaborate designs would be effective used together with the plainer Bull's Eye.

There are several patterns which were first made in the 1860's that are not only attractive patterns, but they are also interesting for their connection with historical events or happenings in the American scene. Gothic architecture and decorations were in style in America at about this date and the Gothic Pattern suggests the pointed arches of a Gothic church, while the pointed ribbings of the Hamilton pattern also suggest the Gothic motif. After the death of President Lincoln in 1865, the tableware pattern known as Lincoln Drape was made at the Boston & Sandwich Glass Company. It was made with a plain drape and also with a tassel, the tassel form being the rarer pattern. Another pattern, the Cable, was made in the 1860's to commemorate the laying of the Atlantic Cable. It is a plain simple pattern with a panel and borders of diagonal ribbing representing a cable. The Cable is a better design than the variant Cable with Ring although the plates in both patterns are attractive. These patterns are all of heavy brilliant glass and have a clear ring. There were also many varieties of Thumbprint and Honeycomb made in the 1860's. These are simple heavy patterns that relate to the Colonial group.

Between 1870 and 1880 a group of grape patterns was made. While the grape and grape leaf have always been a favorite motif with glass makers, it is interesting to note that these grape patterns were made at a time when naturalistic design was especially popular in

Westward Ho footed bowl and covered butter dish, Gillinder & Sons, c. 1870's. Goblet, Frosted Deer and Dog pattern. (*The Henry Ford Museum*)

America. There were grape designs in wrought iron and on the carved wood chairs, sofas, tables and beds of Belter and his followers.

Stippling and frosting was used from time to time to give variety to the clear glass. The charm of the group of ribbon patterns is due to this contrast of clear and frosted surfaces. Ribbon patterns were stripe patterns with alternating frosted and clear glass. These patterns were first made by Bakewell, Pears & Company after 1850. Compotes are particularly attractive and available in the ribbon patterns. These patterns are related to the later frosted group, but the frosted surface on the earlier patterns is rough to the touch, while that on the later Lion, Westward Ho, Three Face, Jumbo, and others is smooth. Gillinder & Sons of Philadelphia produced the Westward Ho, Lion, and Classic patterns soon after the Centennial in 1876, and the majority of the other frosted patterns were made between then and 1885. These patterns are popular with collectors for their interesting shapes, for the decorative finials on the covers of compotes and other dishes, and for the attractive scenes on goblets, plates and other flat surface pieces. The figures on the covers and the bands including the scenes were frosted. The figure of a Kneeling Indian is on the Westward Ho finial and the scenes include a log cabin in the mountains, bison running on the plains and deer. The Lion pattern has finials of a head or figure of a lion and the stems of compotes and vases have lion heads. The platter and bread plate have a panel with a raised scene of one or two lions. Another attractive frosted pattern is the Deer and Dog. The frosted dog stands on the top of the covered dishes and a frosted scene of running deer is shown in panels on the body of the pieces. Westward Ho, Lion, and Three Face are among the most popular pressed glass patterns today so it follows that they are expensive. Other less popular frosted patterns might be a better bet for the beginning collector.

Another large group of pattern glass includes the Dewdrop and Hobnail patterns and their many variations. Dewdrop patterns began to be made in the 1860's. The earliest and one of the most pleasing of the group is the Dewdrop with Star. It is covered with small pointed dots known as dewdrops and in the center of the plates and many other pieces the dewdrops form a star. This pattern is brilliant and decorative and deservedly popular. It is made in many different pieces, but some plates and other pieces have been reproduced. Other variants of the Dewdrop include Panelled Dewdrop, Popcorn, and the later patterns such as Dew and Raindrop, Beaded Dewdrop, Beaded Loop, 101, and many others.

The Hobnail patterns also form a large group. The early Pointed Hobnail is clear and brilliant. One style has a heavy thumbnail base and another has ball feet. Pointed Hobnail was made in amber and blue as well as clear glass and in rare apple and dark green, and yellow. There are attractive footed cake plates and berry bowls with pointed edges and with fan top. The later Hobnail patterns have flattened hobs. There is also a Panelled Hobnail pattern made in yellow, blue, amber, and opaque white as well as clear glass and there are four types of opalescent hobnail in yellow and blue colorings. In the 1860's a group of clear conventional patterns was also made. These included Buckle, Diamond, Chain and Shield, Barley, and Cape Cod.

A group of mythological patterns included Cupid and Venus, Psyche and Cupid, and Minerva. Then there is the well-known Deer and Pine Tree which was made in amber, blue, yellow, and apple green as well as white, and the interesting Hand pattern with a clutching hand on the tops of covered dishes. The Centennial or Liberty Bell was also made at this time. The plates have a bell in their centers and the dates 1776–1876, the patent date September 28, 1875 and the inscription "100 Years Ago." The oval platters have the names of all the signers of the Declaration with a large Liberty Bell in the center. Most of this glass was made by Gillinder & Sons. Needless to say, this pattern is in demand and though available, is not inexpensive.

The flower and fruit groups were favorites in the 1860's and 1880's when they were made and they are some of the best known and most popular with collectors today. The majority of these patterns were partly stippled and were made in colored as well as clear glass. The patterns include many sentimental Victorian flowers such as roses, fuchsias, lilies of the valley, forget-me-nots, and bleeding hearts. Rose in Snow, which is the best known of the various rose patterns, is a favorite with collectors. It is a delightful pattern which is found not only in clear glass, but in blue, amber, and yellow. Some pieces such as plates and goblets have been reproduced. The covered pieces with clear stems and finials are especially attractive and there is a small mug with handles and the inscription, "In Fond Remembrance." Other favorite patterns are Rose Sprig, Wildflower, and Primrose. Among the berry or leaf patterns, Barberry is the most popular and since it was made in great quantities by many factories it is not hard to find. Other attractive patterns in this group are Blackberry, Currant, Strawberry, and the Baltimore Pear. Later stippled patterns include the Princess Feather, Anthemion, Shell and Tassel, Fish Scale, Roman Rosette, and Picket which was made in the 1890's.

Colored pressed glass is especially popular with many collectors and among the most sought-after patterns today is Thousand Eye which was made in yellow, blue, apple green, amber, clear glass and rare opalescent. There were also several red and white glass combina-

Carnival Glass. LEFT. Corn and Husk vase. RIGHT. Thistle design pitcher. (*Rose M. Presznick*)

tions such as Ruby Thumbprint, and Red Block which are late patterns of the '90's. There is also the Ribbed Opal, Emerald Green, a group of Fine Cut patterns, Cane and Basket Weave patterns, which are all made in the colored as well as clear glass. Among the late patterns of the 1880's the best known and most popular was the attractive Daisy and Button with its many variants. These patterns were made in the many articles of tableware, but also in novelties such as hats, shoes, umbrellas, animals, birds, cornucopias and kettles, some of which were for use as match safes and toothpick holders.

This brief outline only suggests a few of the many patterns and articles available to the collector of Victorian Pressed Glass. A few guideposts for collectors might be helpful. In forming a collection of any kind, it is always more interesting to specialize. Also, a collection of any one object or any one pattern of glass is more valuable than odd pieces. A complete table setting of a pressed glass pattern although sometimes difficult to assemble is delightful to own. If the collector is working with a limited budget such pieces as goblets are a good item to collect. Also such articles as toothpick holders, match safes, and other small novelties are comparatively inexpensive and make an interesting display. The most expensive patterns are Westward Ho, Three Faces, and Lion in that order. These are desirable because of their popularity and unique design.

One of the most interesting categories of pressed glass collecting would be plates and platters with American historical significance. Beginning with the Centennial bread plate and platter made by Gillinder & Sons, these commemorative plates with mottos, flags, eagles, portraits and scenery were made down until the time of the World's Columbian Exposition in 1893. They include plates with portraits of Washington, Garfield, Grant, Cleveland and Hendricks, and McKinley. The Washington plates were made by Gillinder & Sons and some had center medallions of Independence Hall, while others depicted Carpenters' Hall where the Continental Congress first assembled. Bread plates or platters, with the Sheaf of Wheat centers, Liberty Bell, or Bunker Hill

Monument, Horseshoe, and a Grape Pattern plate inscribed, "It is Pleasant To Labor For Those We Love," are also interesting collector's pieces. Another commemorative platter is the Railroad platter made by the Bellaire Goblet Company of Findlay, Ohio, to commemorate the opening of the Union Pacific Railroad in 1869. The Knights of Labor platter with steamship and train was made by the United States Glass Company of Pittsburgh. A round tray to hold pitcher and glasses has a center Currier & Ives darky scene and there is a bread plate with grape border and The Last Supper after Leonardo da Vinci in the center. A large attractive tray depicting Niagara Falls was made by Adams & Co. of Pittsburgh in the 1870's. All these pieces are unique and interesting for a historical collection although they are not as attractive as some of the other patterns.

It takes study and experience and familiarity to recognize authentic old pressed glass. The clear ring does not necessarily mean the glass is

Goblets, late bird patterns. LEFT. Hummingbird. CENTER. Flamingo. RIGHT. Cardinal. (*The Bennington Museum, Bennington, Vermont;* PHOTO. *Lloyd Studio*)

nineteenth century. It does mean it is good quality glass. Colored glass will not ring as clear as clear glass, for most colored glass is late glass and not as good quality. However, collectors are not as interested in glass quality as glass pattern, or Daisy and Button, which is not top quality glass, would not be as popular as it is. If you are a beginning collector start your collection with a piece from an authorized glass dealer. Even though you may pay more you can be sure you have a good piece and you can learn much from him before you start to pick up odd pieces at the flea market. So much pressed glass has been reproduced that it is important to watch for copies in certain pieces such as plates, goblets, and sugars and creamers. In reproductions color usually varies and even clear glass may look dull. Also the details of the patterns are often lacking. Although cracked or nicked pieces are sold it is better to have a perfect piece of an unknown pattern than a cracked piece of one of the more popular patterns unless it is a particularly rare item. Also, it is best to start with a pattern that is not too popular such as the late but attractive Herringbone which combines herringbone panels with loops and diamonds filled with dewdrops. Since this design is not too well known it is not in demand and thus the prices are more reasonable, and a clear glass Herringbone covered sugar, footed sugar, and creamer are an attractive addition to any table. The shapes of pieces of pressed glass are a means of dating them, as are the articles made. Early shapes were more graceful while later shapes were bulky and often low-slung in outline. While the sugar and creamer, spoon holder, and butter dish were found in the early sets of pressed glass such pieces as the caster and the syrup jug did not appear until late in the century.

Covered Animal Dishes

ONE of the favorite items with collectors today is the covered pressed glass animal dish. These were made in opaque glass, mostly white, but some were made in blue and combinations of blue and white, and some were made in black glass. Hens and roosters were made in the greatest quantity, but there were also cats, dogs, lambs, fish, horses, bears, rabbits, cows, eagles, lions, elephants, bears, swans, quail and many other animals. There is also a cover with the battleship *Maine* and several with the bust of Admiral Dewey.

Animal dishes were made by many glass factories in the 1880's including M'Kee Bros. of Pittsburgh; Westmoreland Glass Company; Challinor, Taylor & Co.; United States Glass Co.; Central Glass Co.; and Indiana Tumbler & Goblet Co. Many companies advertised farmyard groups which included fish, ducks, swans, hens, roosters and eagles. The farmyard groups of both Challinor, Taylor & Co. and United States Glass Co. were made in opal, turquoise and olive, and were made both with and without glass eyes. There are varying details of bases on the dishes; some have basket bases, others have a pattern of cattails and pond lilies and others have fluted or diamond all-over patterns. The details and workmanship on the Atterbury and M'Kee animal dishes are usually superior to that of other manufacturers. Many of these dishes were patented. The famous Atterbury ducks were patented in 1887 by the Atterbury Company of Pittsburgh, Pennsylvania. They were made in white, blue, black or amethyst, and in many color combinations such as white with a blue head. The ducks had a pressed design of conventional feathers and glass eyes. They are marked on the base with the patent date and are rare. There were other ducks made by Challinor, Taylor & Company and by other glass companies. Also, the Atterbury duck has been reproduced without the patent date.

Hens are the most popular animal dishes because there are more of them available since they were made in vast quantities and distributed as premiums. There were many types of hens, some with heads facing front and others with heads turned. There were also various types of bases: rib pattern, basket weave, and lacy edge. The hens and roosters with basket bases edged with a chain border were shown in the Challinor, Taylor & Company catalogue, and similar large hen and rooster dishes were made by the United States Glass Co. who took over their line. A hen with a base showing small chicks was made by Flaccus Company of Wheeling, West Virginia, who used ornate bases on all of their animal dishes. Hens on ribbed bases were usually made by M'Kee Bros. A hen on a lacy edge base was made by Atterbury as was the rare chick and eggs on a lacy base. Atterbury hens were made in various colors of marble, blue, brown, green and yellow and plain colors with blue, amber and amethyst heads. Lacy edged dishes with fox, lion, fish, hand and dove, cat, and swan were also made by Atterbury. The swan dish has been reproduced by Westmoreland Glass Company. M'Kee made a swan on a ribbed base and other M'Kee animals on ribbed bases include dove, duck, turkey, cow, rabbit, squirrel and lion. These are found marked and unmarked. All of these are rare and scarce. M'Kee dishes are usually found in milk-white glass. Some are marked on the inside of the cover. Later, these dishes were made by the Indiana Tumbler and Goblet Co. in Greentown, Indiana.

Covered Dishes. Opaque white pressed glass fish, dog, cat. Opaque blue rooster. Green clear glass rabbit. (*The Henry Ford Museum*)

Animal dishes were sometimes painted with gold and naturalistic colors. The rare Indiana Tumbler and Goblet Co. robin on a nest is often found with remnants of paint. A similar robin was also made by Vallerystahl and reproduced by Westmoreland Glass Company. The head turns down instead of up and the base is a design of reeds. So many dishes, including the hens and turkey dishes, have been reproduced both by Westmoreland and Vallerystahl in France that one has to be careful when buying these dishes. Also, many dishes are found fitted to bases other than those originally made for them. Sometimes it is easy to spot the wrong base, but if a base fits it may be difficult to know whether or not it is original. Generally speaking, lacy-edge and split rib bases are old, and basket bases have been more often reproduced. The highly decorative story-telling Flaccus bases are particularly interesting although Flaccus dishes are not as good in design and workmanship as those made by Atterbury and M'Kee.

Glass Novelties

THE Victorians loved souvenirs. They bought silver spoons with scenes and names of the cities they visited. They brought back souvenir shells painted or engraved with "Atlantic City"; pitchers inscribed "Niagara Falls," and painted with a scene of the Falls; and red and white glass was marked "Mother," "Father," or "World's Columbian Exposition, Chicago 1893." But some of the most popular souvenirs were the pressed glass novelties made from the 1870's to the end of the century.

The fad probably started at the Philadelphia Centennial where many small pressed glass objects were given away by glass companies at their booths. Other glass souvenirs could be purchased. These souvenirs included such objects as toothpick and match holders, mustard jars, horse radish dishes, and baskets to hold flowers as favors on the dining table. They were made in such shapes as umbrellas, chairs, cradles, wheelbarrows, hands, coal hods, tree trunks and fans, as well as hats, slippers and shoes.

These souvenirs were made by many of the glass companies working in America at this time, but the majority were made by the following companies; Bryce Bros.; King Glass Co.; Gillinder & Sons; Central Glass Co.; Doyle & Co.; Adams & Co.; Bellaire Goblet Co.; Phoenix Glass Co.; and U. S. Glass Co., which later absorbed many of the other companies.

Most of the glass novelties were made in Daisy and Button pattern, some were made in Cube pattern, and others were pressed in wicker or brick patterns. Although some novelties have been found only in clear glass the majority of the pieces were made in amber, blue and crystal, and a few were made in marble glass.

One of the best-known toothpick or match holders was the Kitten on a Cushion with a Daisy and Button cup. It was made in aquamarine blue, amber, and crystal. There was also a dog holding a cornucopia vase, a rooster beside a toothpick holder, a rabbit holding a vase, and a holder with a baby chick. A bird beside a basket was made by Bryce Bros. A rare Daisy and Button cradle was made in clear glass and in amber. A unique corset toothpick holder was made by Bellaire Goblet Co. The clock match safe in Daisy and Button pattern was also made by Bellaire.

Glass novelties in Daisy and Button, Cube, and Wicker patterns. Blue, amber, crystal. (*The New-York Historical Society*)

Glass hats and boots, shoes, and slippers have long been favorite items with collectors. They were also favorites of the glass blowers in the old glass houses who usually made them out of leftover glass for their own amusement. For this reason they were one of a kind pieces and thus rare. Early hats were blown into bottle molds. Some show patterns of thumbprint and ribbing and swirling. There are also hats in all the different types of Victorian Art Glass including Burmese, Spatter, cased glass, and striped glass made by Nicholas Lutz at Sandwich. Needless to say, these are rare and expensive. There were also many souvenir hats made for exhibitions and World's Fairs, and also some hats were made for advertising novelties.

Hats were made in Hobnail and Fine Rib pattern pressed glass. But the hats made late in the nineteenth century in such patterns as Cube, Raindrop, Thousand Eye, Daisy and Star, and Daisy and Button are the ones available to the average collector. The largest variety are to be found in Daisy and Button. Some are made in clear glass with blue or red buttons or hat bands. The Daisy and Button hat toothpick holder was made in clear, blue, amber, canary yellow, amethyst and smoke, with various combinations of colors in the buttons and hat bands. There were also larger hats in Daisy and Button pattern which were designed as spoon holders or celery vases.

Bottles and drinking glasses were blown in the shape of boots. Victorian glass makers were more interested in the ladies' shoe and slipper, and the pressed glass Daisy and Button pattern was made in styles of existing Victorian shoes. There were high button shoes, low laced slippers, and slippers with buckles and bows. These were made as holders for toilet water bottles, pincushions, and salt and pepper shakers. A slipper mounted on a tray was made by Bryce Bros. as an ash tray. It was made in blue, amber, yellow, and crystal. A Daisy and Button slipper on skates was made by United States Glass Co. There is also a Diamond Block pattern slipper on skates. It was made in blue, crystal, and other colors. A slipper in a metal holder is often marked "Gillinder & Sons Centennial Exhibition." It was made in crystal, frosted and milk-white glass in various sizes. A Puss in Boots slipper was made by Bryce Bros. and is a familiar favorite of collectors. It has been reproduced. There were many slippers in Cane and Fine Cut patterns.

Slippers were made in greater quantity than other types of shoes and are therefore more plentiful today. Pressed glass slippers are the easiest to find, but there were also slippers made in milk glass, spatter, marble, and Bristol type as well as other kinds of art glass slippers with painted decorations which were made at Sandwich and New England Glass Company. These are very rare. Shoes of marble glass and black opaque glass are rare and a high glass boot with a spur is also rare. Glass novelties and hats and shoes have been reproduced.

Glass shoes and slipper.
(*The New-York Historical Society*)

Cut Glass

COLLECTORS have been so absorbed in collecting Victorian Pressed Glass and Fancy Art Glass that American cut glass has not only been neglected but scorned, and if one happened to own a piece it was not thought worth keeping. The reason for this scorn and neglect lies partly in the fact that little was known about this glass and the present day popularity of cut glass is to a certain extent due to the information given for collectors in Dorothy Daniel's book, *Cut and Engraved Glass*, the first book in the field. The classification of patterns and glass houses gives the collector definite information on which to start a collection.

There are three periods of American cut glass beginning with the glass cut at Stiegel glassworks in Pennsylvania from 1771. This Early American cut glass continued to be made until 1830 when methods of manufacture changed. The commercial output after this date and especially that of the late Brilliant Period 1880–1905, is the glass which concerns collectors of Victorian cut glass. The glass of the Middle Period is characterized by flute cuttings. Heavy flute-cut compotes, pitchers and decanters with diamond-cut bands, fluted neck rings or panel cutting with heavy steeple or mushroom stoppers were in use on every well-appointed table. This flute-cut glass was made by many glass houses, particularly in Pennsylvania and West Virginia. As the period progressed, more pieces were made and there are flute-cut goblets, champagne glasses, spoon holders, celery vases and bowls made between 1830 and 1845. Attractive celery vases with petal tops and fluted glasses with cutting on their feet were made by Sweeney Glass Company, Wheeling, West Virginia, in the 1840's. Some of these middle period pieces were cut in floral patterns and decorated with engraving. Colored, flashed, and cased glass was also made at this time. The red and crystal glass cut with stars, prisms, and diamonds, as well as blue and green glass made at New England Glass Company and by Dorflinger was especially popular. Other glass with color was made by Hobbs, Barnes & Company of Wheeling, West Virginia, and by Mulvaney and Ledlie

LEFT. Ribbon Star pattern cut glass, Libbey Glass Co., 1890–1893. RIGHT. Butterfly and Primrose plate, intaglio cutting. (*American Cut Glass for the Discriminating Collector* by J. Michael and Dorothy T. Pearson)

at Pittsburgh. The cut glass industry grew profitably until the craze for pressed glass crowded many of the manufacturers of the most expensive blown and cut glass products out of business. But in 1876 the exhibits of cut glass at the Philadelphia Centennial again created a demand for cut glass.

The glass of this later period is distinguished for its fine-line cutting which became known as brilliant cutting. This glass is heavy and crystal clear and is characterized by deep curved miter cuttings called splits, and such design motifs as hob-star, notched prism, and fan. Cut glass could now be bought in table settings, including goblets, wines, champagnes, sherry and claret glasses, plates, ice cream dishes, finger bowls, butter pats, salts and peppers, compotes, bonbon dishes, nappies, pickle and celery dishes, berry bowls, punch cups, flower vases and candlesticks. All of these various cut glass pieces were made in thousands of patterns by all the well-known glass houses of the period. The important glass houses that made cut glass were C. Dorflinger & Sons, White Mills, Pennsylvania; Gillinder & Sons, Philadelphia, Pa.; T. G. Hawkes Glass Company, Corning, New York; the United States Glass Company, Tiffin, Ohio; Libbey Glass Company, Toledo, Ohio; Pairpoint Corporation, New Bedford, Massachusetts; and H. C. Fry Glass Company, Rochester, Pa.

Glass of the Brilliant Period is easily recognized. It is deeper cut than the earlier cut glass and the cuttings are more intricate and elaborate. New cuttings such as Curved Split, Prism, Chair Bottom, and Hob-Star are combined with older simpler motifs such as Hobnail, Fan, Block, Bull's Eye, and Strawberry-Diamond. There are about fifty documented patterns available to the collector today. The earlier patterns such as Russian, Middlesex, Parisian, Strawberry-Diamond and Fan are clearly defined. Later the patterns were more ornate and have several decorative motifs in one pattern such as Star or Pin Wheel with Prism or Bull's Eye motifs so that it is more difficult to recognize the pattern. Also each pattern had many variations. Probably the best-

Cut glass plate, Russian pattern by T. G. Hawkes & Co. (*The Corning Museum of Glass*)

known pattern of Brilliant Period cut glass is the Russian. This pattern
was patented for T. G. Hawkes Glass Company, but was also made by
C. Dorflinger & Sons. Russian pattern was first made for the Russian
Embassy in Washington. It was also made for the American Embassy
in St. Petersburg and for the White House in Washington in 1886. The
Russian pattern is a refinement of the old Star and Hobnail and consists
of borders of various sizes of stars alternating with hobnails and has a
large center star. Another favorite pattern with collectors is the Parisian
pattern. It was made by C. Dorflinger & Sons from 1886. It is a simple
pattern of Curved Splits, Fans, and Strawberry-Diamond crosshatchings.
Pieces have a star bottom. The Middlesex is a pattern made up of the
eight-point star motif. It was made at the New England Glass Company
and is especially attractive and rare. Grecian is another rare pattern
which is of interest to collectors. It has a field of fine star and hobnail
cutting with lozenge-shaped ovals of clear glass.

Strawberry-Diamond and Fan is a fairly common pattern and is

LEFT. Cut glass pitcher, C. Dorflinger & Sons, 1897. (*Brooklyn Museum*) RIGHT. Rose bowl
on standard, Brunswick pattern. (*J. Michael and Dorothy T. Pearson*)

easily recognized and also easy to find today. It was also less expensive and thus more popular when made than the more ornate combinations of stars, although the finest pieces can be identified by a 24 point star in the center. This pattern was made by T. G. Hawkes Glass Company, Libby Glass Company, J. Hoare & Company and many others. It was cut in red, green, and yellow as well as clear glass. Other patterns that are fairly easy to identify and good collectors' items because there were quantities made by the many glass houses, were Princess, a pattern with strawberry-diamond points and fan scallops with hob-star center motif; Harvard, a so-called chair bottom pattern of raised squares with alternate squares crosshatched; and Corinthian which has a 16 point hob-star as its center motif within a Greek cross—decorated by cross-hatching. This pattern was cut by nearly every glass house.

Late in the century cut glass patterns became more intricate and confused. The simple star became a pinwheel or buzz which was a many-pointed swirling star with swirled fan-cuts at the star points. Variations of the pattern were also made. Realistic floral patterns such as Bristol Rose, Lily of the Valley, Cornflower and fruit patterns and combinations of cutting and engraving were made at the end of the period. These patterns were made at the end of the century and the designs are realistic, with none of the old cut glass star or rosette motifs.

Brilliant Period cut glass can be identified by pattern, the weight of the glass, and by trade-mark. However, since the same patterns were made by many glass houses these do not seem good criteria for identification. Many, but certainly not all, pieces of glass were marked with an acid or pressed stamp and this is a definite means of identification, but lack of a mark does not mean that it is not good quality glass. The best way to identify cut glass is to study the finer specimens of the pattern which you choose to collect. Also, it helps to handle pieces. All good cut glass is heavy and the edges should be sharp to the touch. When a piece is held to the light there is refraction. The edges of a motif should appear sharply defined. Every piece should be examined in a bright light. Carry a magnifying glass and look for chips or other flaws in cutting.

Cut glass vase, C. Dorflinger & Sons, 1897. (*Brooklyn Museum*)

Buy only perfect pieces and if your budget is limited collect small pieces. Rose bowls, baskets, finger bowls, candlesticks, water glasses and wine glasses make attractive items for the collector. Also, there are many small articles of cut glass such as cruets, cologne and smelling salts bottles, covered powder boxes, pin trays, salt and pepper shakers, toothpick holders, knife rests and butter pats which should interest the collector of small inexpensive articles.

Cut glass was never cheap but it is the one "antique" which sells for less today than when it was made. Cut glass varies in price according to locality and demand. Generally it is more expensive in city than in country antique shops. Good places to look for cut glass are West Virginia, northeastern Pennsylvania and Ohio, where so many of the glass houses were located. One advantage to collecting cut glass is the fact that it has seldom been reproduced and because of the cost of hand labor and the few glass cutters working today, cut glass probably never will be reproduced.

Paperweights

ALTHOUGH the techniques used in making paperweights go back to ancient craftsmen and to the latticino glass made at the Venetian glass houses in the Renaissance, paperweights as we know them are essentially a product of Victorian times. The first dated weights were made in St. Louis, France, in the 1840's and were introduced to American glasshouses soon afterward by François Pierre and Nicholas Lutz who had been trained in France. However, the most popular period for paperweights was between 1860 and 1875. Although the best American paperweights were made at the New England Glass Company by François Pierre and at the Sandwich Glass Company by Nicholas Lutz, fine paperweights were also made by John L. Gilliland in Brooklyn and at Mount Washington Glass Works in South Boston, and from 1863 to 1912 by Whitall, Tatum & Company at Millville, New Jersey. Some paperweights were made by practically all of the large flint glass houses.

LEFT. Paperweight with canes and latticino background. (*The Corning Museum of Glass*) RIGHT. Paperweight by Ralph Barber, Millville, New Jersey, c. 1900. (*The Henry Ford Museum*)

The techniques of American paperweights followed the French. There were millefiori weights with rods of conventional flower patterns and there were designs which incorporated fruits and flowers. There were also cameos or "sulphides" encrusted in glass. Some weights are further enhanced by cutting and faceting and some are made of overlay or case glass in several colors. Most paperweights are built, not blown. Millefiori weights are made of pieces of glass cane cut into short lengths. These pieces are arranged in patterns face down on a mold. When the design is completed the background of white latticino is put in, then both design and background are encased in the clear glass dome through a process of heating. Then the weight is smoothed and polished. Sulphides and other items are similarly set in place and then encased in the glass dome.

Many millefiori or candy type weights were made at Sandwich Glass Company. They also made fruit and flower designs including the dahlia, pansy, fuchsia, and the well-known Christmas poinsettia. The strawberry weight was created by Nicholas Lutz who specialized in fruit weights that show tiny apples, cherries, or pears with green leaves against a white latticino background. The majority of the paperweights made at the New England Glass Company were also of millefiori glass, but they were best known for the large apples and pears. These were

LEFT. Boston & Sandwich Glass Company. Pink dahlia with green leaves. (C. W. Lyon) RIGHT. Boston & Sandwich Glass Company. Flower with rose stripes. (*The Corning Museum of Glass*)

blown from tubes of glass. When the fruit was blown it was fastened to the glass base by heat. After the Civil War this factory made a weight in the form of a black and white English bulldog, and green glass turtle weights. A late souvenir weight in the form of Plymouth Rock was also made. A rare sulphide of Queen Victoria and Prince Albert was made in the 1850's. John L. Gilliland made fine millefiori weights, some with faceted cutting on the crown and sides which frame the tiny pink, green, and white flowers. The Mount Washington Glass Company is known for a beautiful red aster set on green leaves, and for a frilled pink rose with leaves and two buds.

LEFT. Orange and yellow pear on clear glass base. New England Glass Company. (*The Henry Ford Museum*) RIGHT. Blown glass apple on clear base. New England Glass Company. (*The Corning Museum of Glass*)

The best-known rose, however, was the Millville Rose made by Whitall, Tatum & Company, from 1863. These roses were made in deep rose pink, yellow, and white both with and without stems. The rose is usually upright and rests on a cylinder base or on a baluster stem. This is a late weight made by Ralph Barber between 1905 and 1912. Millville also made a lily weight and one called Devil's Fire. There were also weights showing a hunter and his dog and weights with eagles, horses, sailboats, and flowers in pots. These weights are attributed to Michael Kane and although inferior in craftsmanship are interesting examples of truly American paperweights and are related to American primitive art.

Paperweights were also made by Pairpont Manufacturing Company who made a beautiful red and blue spiral twist set on a pedestal with engraving on top and base; at Dorflinger in Pennsylvania; at the Clyde Glass Works in Clyde, New York; at the Ravenna Glass Works in Ravenna, Ohio; at White Glass Works in Zanesville, Ohio, and at many other midwestern glass houses. About 1890 Ravenna Glass Company made a white lily with bubble leaves. A similar lily, but red, set in a ground of sparkling vari-colored glass is a modern weight made by Ravenna. Crude paper weights of bottle glass were made at Redford Glass Works, Plattsburg, New York, and the Redwood Glass Works, Watertown. Some had an Indian Head cent imbedded in the glass. There were also weights enclosing decals and porcelain plaques.

Late in the century popular sentimental weights were made with inscriptions such as "Remember Me," "Friendship," "From a Friend" and "Home Sweet Home." These were accompanied by floral sprays or clasped hands. There were also paperweights with patriotic symbols and Masonic symbols. The popular Three Little Pigs weight was made at Somerville Glass Company in Massachusetts. The designs in these are usually white against the clear glass. There were also faceted clear cut glass weights. Tiffany made a weight of sea urchins and waves and in the early 1900's he also made a paperweight doorstop in blue and green Favrile glass. It is signed "L. C. Tiffany Favrile." A door knob had cameo busts of Monroe and Harrison encrusted in deep blue glass. Other weights had cameos of Washington and Lincoln. Tiny glass buttons containing roses were made at Sandwich, and footed inkwells with tall pointed stoppers were made at Millville.

Modern paperweights are still being made in America as well as in France, Sweden, Scotland, and Japan. Most of the modern weights, such as the sulphide zodiac series by Baccarat and the Swedish Kosta Glass Works, Hammarskjold weights are original modern weights, but those made in Japan are often copies of nineteenth century millefiori designs and are passed as old by some dealers. The red lily Ravenna weight and the perfume bottle with the pink rose resembling the Millville rose are also sometimes sold as old weights. Modern weights when sold as modern are worth collecting, but because they are being made one must have some criteria for the valuation of old weights. First of all, old weights are heavier. Old paper weights may have smooth bottoms, but they were never frosted. American weights are seldom marked so they must be judged by workmanship, color, and design. It is not difficult to learn the designs of American weights because the most of them are uniquely American, but it is difficult to attribute a certain weight to a definite glass house. For example, all New England glass companies made millefiori weights, and New England Glass Company, Sandwich, and Mount Washington were at one time controlled by the same man; thus both designs and workmen may have been interchangeable. Paperweights made in Japan have harsh chemical coloring. It is, of course, best to buy a paperweight in good condi-

Millville Rose, Whitall, Tatum & Co.
(*C. W. Lyon*)

Paperweight. South Jersey, c. 1900.
(*The Henry Ford Museum*)

tion, but scratches and even chips can be smoothed and polished, and if the weight is authentic it is well worth the price of repair.

Art Glass

IN the last quarter of the nineteenth century American glasshouses began to produce the hand-blown, hand-decorated glass which we call Art Glass. All known techniques were used and many new ones invented by talented men such as Nicholas Lutz, Frederick Carder, and Louis C. Tiffany. The dominant characteristic of Victorian Art Glass is its color, which varied from brilliant clear glass to delicate pastels. Texture was also an interesting feature. It ranged from sandpaper effects such as that of Tree of Life to the satiny smoothness of Satin Glass. Shaded effects were produced by reheating with gold; glass was made to look like silver; and a smooth finish was obtained with a bath of hydrofluoric acid or a sanding process.

Patterns striking or subtle were made by molding, by applied glass decoration, or by enamel painting. Such patterns as hobnails, swirls, and diamond quilt were molded; applied decoration was added by the glass blower after the form was made; and enamel decoration such as flowers, leaves, and Mary Gregory designs were painted after the article was fired. Many of the forms of Art Glass are graceful and dignified, others are frilled, crimped, and fancy. To cover fully the different types of Victorian Art Glass requires a book. In this short résumé the various kinds of glass will be grouped according to their techniques.

In the group of shaded glass, Peachblow was one of the most popular. The Peachblow made by Hobbs, Brockunier & Company at Wheeling is clear and has a milk white lining. In coloring it is a deep red shading to greenish yellow and in its velvety finish it resembles Chinese porcelain. Several different glass houses made Peachblow and the products of each company vary in color and also in trade name. The Peachblow made at Mount Washington and New England Glass Company was a homogeneous opaque glass. That at New England Glass Company shades from ivory to tints of deep rose. It was called

Wild Rose. Agate is a variation of Peachblow with a mottled effect. Mount Washington Peachblow is more delicate and shades from shell-pink to light blue. Burmese was another type of shaded glass. It, however, was made by only one factory, Mount Washington at New Bedford, Massachusetts, in both dull and glossy finish in a variety of forms, including tablewares. The colors range from greenish yellow to delicate pink and the decoration was molded, applied or painted. Molded patterns include hobnail and diamond, and painted designs range from grasses and butterflies of Japanese inspiration to Egyptian motifs.

Amberina was produced at Mount Washington and at the New England Glass Company. Its deep red and yellow colorings are similar to Wheeling Peachblow. Amberina was made in both table and ornamental wares in patterns of thumbprint, ribbing, and expanded diamonds.

Royal Flemish and Crown Milano are also included in the category of shaded glass. Both have colorings of beige and rust and are enamelled with oriental patterns. The designs of Royal Flemish are outlined in gold on the mat ground which varies from beige to russet tones. The flowers and maple leaves of Crown Milano are enameled and gilt on a light creamy ground.

Another type of glass which caught the fancy of the Victorian public was a glass which combined different colors of glass in a confetti-like effect. It went by the general name of spatter or spangle, but certain types such as Tortoise Shell combined browns and tans in a manner which imitated real tortoise shell, and others imitated a moss agate. Spangled glass was a novelty glass which originated at Hobbs, Brockunier & Company in 1883. The finished glass form was rolled in mica and then returned to the furnace. Vasa Murrhina was a variation of Spangled Glass. It was made at Sandwich, and at the Vasa Murrhina Art Glass Company.

Frosted glass was another popular type of Victorian Art Glass. These wares have an interesting textured surface. Pomona glass, which originated at the New England Glass Company, is a delicate clear glass stained with pale amber color and decorated with pale blue flowers and straw-color leaves. Tree of Life is a pressed glass pattern

Wheeling Peachblow vase with tall stem. Small vase, cream with looped design of amber and green. Emil J. Larsen, Vineland, N. J. (*The Henry Ford Museum*)

BELOW. Amberina-Peachblow-Burmese. LEFT TO RIGHT. Amberina trumpet vase, New England Glass Co., Amberina diamond-quilted footed bowl, Sandwich; Amberina toothpick holder, New England Glass Co.; Jack-in-the-Pulpit, "Mt. Washington" Peachblow vase, rose shading to palest blue, Mt. Washington Glass Co.; Satin Burmese Hobnail sugar and creamer, salmon shading to lemon. Mt. Washington Glass Co., New Bedford; fluted bowl, Peachblow, rose shading to cream-white. New England Glass Co., Cambridge, Mass. (*The Chrysler Art Museum of Provincetown*)

first copyrighted by the Portland Glass Company in 1869. It was afterwards made at other companies and is found in both clear and colored tableware, baskets, bottles, and more ornate shapes such as the epergne encircled with a clear red glass snake. Overshot glass is a rough frosted glass covered with bits of crushed glass which were blown into the hot glass. It is sometimes decorated with applied flower decoration. Effects of crackling were produced by blowing the glass into a mold. It was made in several colors.

Pearl wares were made by varying the glass with acid or sand to give it a satiny finish. These pearl wares are of several types, but Mother-of-Pearl and Satin Glass are best known. The majority of the pearl wares have a white lining and a colored coating. Mother-of-Pearl is the most elaborate. It is made up of several layers of glass and distinguished by the patterns of diamonds, swirls, and herringbone. The beauty of this glass is in the beautiful coloring of blues, pinks, oranges and canary yellow. The rarest colors are robin's egg blue, bittersweet, and rainbow.

Plain Satin Glass without decoration or pattern was made in similar colors. It was also made in swirl patterns, with applied decoration such as flowers and leaves, and often glass beads were added. Satin

Group of spatter and spangled glass. LEFT TO RIGHT. "Vasa Murrhina" vase, Boston and Sandwich Glass Co.; "Vasa Murrhina" pitcher, Boston and Sandwich Glass Co.; "Agata" stick vase. New England Glass Co.; Rainbow Spangled vase, Boston and Sandwich Glass Co.; enameled "Tortoise Shell" basket, Sandwich. (*The Chrysler Art Museum of Provincetown*)

Three Sandwich epergnes. LEFT TO RIGHT. Yellow opaque and clear epergne; cranberry and clear epergne; "Tree-of-Life," clear with red snake and gilding. (*The Chrysler Art Museum of Provincetown*)

glass with a bead pattern of coral, seaweed or wheat is called Coralene.

Opalescent glass was made in pressed glass, pattern glass and blown and molded glass. Some pieces are opalescent throughout such as onyx, others have clear or colored glass borders, and some have combination effects such as striped Swirl and Dewdrop. The opalescence is made by manipulation of the various glass mixtures. Spanish Lace and Onyx patterns with their delicate floral patterns and the various Swirl combinations are the most interesting.

Opaque glass was made in pressed tablewares and also in fancy novelty shapes. The best known opaque is white Milk Glass. Opaque glass was made at Sandwich, and at New England Glass Company in the first third of the nineteenth century as lamp bases and candlesticks, vases, and such individual pieces as salts. Later tableware patterns such as Wheat Panel, Ribbed Grape, Blackberry, Almond, Thumbprint, Sawtooth, Flower and Panel, and Lincoln Drape were made in opaque

LEFT TO RIGHT. Overshot vases c. 1875, clear and opaque with applied multicolor decoration of fruit and flowers. Blue overshot; clear pale blue, attached amber rim and feet; white cased with pink, attached bright blue rim and feet; clear cranberry, but opalescent at rim and bottom, attached pale green handle. Boston and Sandwich Glass Co. (*The Chrysler Art Museum of Provincetown*)

LEFT TO RIGHT. Overshot vase. Opaque pink encrusted with clear glass, applied clear glass feet; sapphire blue vase with white enameled Mary Gregory decoration. Boston and Sandwich Glass Co.; Amberina vase with applied handles. (*The Henry Ford Museum*)

pressed glass and also many openwork plates, bowls and compotes intended for dessert were made.

There are a hundred or more patterns of milk glass plates: lacy-edged, flower, bird, historical, children's plates and comic plates as well as geometric designs were made in opaque white, black, blue, amethyst and a rare chartreuse green. Many of the patterns were pressed, but others were painted with bird and flower designs. These plates with their various types of decorative lacy borders are popular with collectors today. They were made down into the twentieth century, as witness the William Jennings Bryan plate.

Milk Glass lamps and candlesticks were made in fewer numbers. The old Sandwich dolphin candlesticks and Loop and Petal are rare, but religious crucifix candlesticks are often found and were not reproduced although they were late products. Syrup jugs and pitchers were made in many patterns. There were also interesting platters including bread platters impressed with "Give us this Day our Daily Bread" and a Liberty Bell platter. There were novelties including hand dishes, and bottles and vases in the shape of animals and national monuments. The small covered milk glass dishes are so popular with collectors today

Shaded opalescent ware, Beaumont Glass Co., Martins Ferry, Ohio—"Spanish Lace" types. LEFT TO RIGHT. Fluted bowl, fluted vase and syrup pitcher, clear with raised opalescent designs; cruet and large pitcher, cranberry with raised opalescence; Barber's Bottle, "Stars and Stripes" red with raised opalescence. (*The Chrysler Art Museum of Provincetown*)

Opaque glass. LEFT TO RIGHT. Candlesticks, fiery opalescent, Sandwich; pitcher, paneled Wheat Pattern, white, Hobbs, Brockunier & Co., Wheeling, W. Va.; stick vase, "Wheeling Peachblow," Hobbs, Brockunier; vase, blue opalene, Sandwich; box, white, "King Charles Spaniel," Sandwich; tumbler, Holly Amber, The Indiana Tumbler & Goblet Co., Greentown, Ind.; "Dolphin" covered dish, Chocolate glass; Holly Amber toothpick holder; "Rabbit" covered dish, Chocolate glass, Indiana Tumbler & Goblet Co. (*The Chrysler Art Museum of Provincetown*)

and are so characteristically Victorian that they require a chapter of their own.

Other types of opaque glass include Caramel Glass, Custard Glass, and rare Maize fashioned in little kernels to represent an ear of corn. This latter was made at the New England Glass Company in 1888. Marble Glass or Purple Slag is popular with collectors, but hard to find and therefore more expensive than other opaque glass. It was never made in such quantities as the opaque white glass and very few complete table settings were ever made. Such pieces as footed compotes, bowls, celery glasses, vases, and match holders and mugs are the articles to be found today.

In 1855 the New England Glass Company secured a patent for a curious Victorian novelty called silver glass. This glass had tremendous popularity in its day. It was first made as curtain pins, door knobs, and globes, but was later made in some tableware pieces such as goblets, wine glasses, salts, sugar bowls and pitchers as well as vases, candlesticks and paperweights. Some of this glass was plain, but other pieces were engraved or painted. Some of the silver glass vases were decorated in brilliant red, blue, and green and on others the designs were painted in opaque white. A few of the vases were gold, blue, or even lavender. Silver glass was made in two layers. The clear glass was first blown, later the nitrate of silver was blown into the hollow space between the layers through a hole in the base. Then the base was sealed. Nitrate of silver came in many colors.

Victorian vases were made in pairs. There are all types of vases from costly overlay to painted and enameled vases and those with applied decoration. There are both clear and opaque vases and those with a satin finish. There is no end of combinations of color. In shape and decoration these pairs of vases are perhaps the most characteristically Victorian of all Victorian glassware. Most of these vases are tall elongated shapes with scalloped and frilled tops or spreading flower lips. Some are made to sit on metal stands. Painted and enamel decoration includes birds and flowers in oriental style and groups of daisies and lilies of the valley. Others are decorated with Mary Gregory children. Colors range from lovely blues, pinks, and yellows of Satin Glass to the glossy tans and caramels and browns. Black glass vases with enameled flower decoration were especially popular. Another group had applied flowers or fruits. Silver glass vases were also made in pairs as were the various colors and sizes of satin glass rose bowls.

Louis C. Tiffany worked in stained glass for some years before he produced his first iridescent glass known as Favrile which was put on the market in 1896 and was made until about 1918. Tiffany glass reproduces the iridescence of ancient glass. Gold, amber, blue, and green were blended to produce a metallic iridescence. Although Tiffany drew on European and Oriental prototypes he also produced many striking and imaginative new forms. He was inspired by natural flower and plant forms—the peacock feather, and the growth and shells at the

bottom of the sea. Waves, clouds, and line effects that suggest the wind decorate some of the more imaginative pieces, but there were also more recognizable motifs such as vines, narcissus, lily of the valley, calla lily, and fish. The lily pad and mushroom were also favorite motifs.

Frederick Carder was another inspired glass designer. He developed Aurene glass in 1904. It has a smooth iridescent surface with ridges, grooves and crimped edges. The colors resemble those of the sunset, and the shapes are often twisted.

Quezal glass was made in imitation of Tiffany and Aurene. The leaf designs are usually green on a light gold ground. Vases and lampshades are the pieces available. Kew Blas made at Somerville, Massachusetts, is an iridescent glass with a smooth opalescent effect.

In about 1910, Carnival glass, an imitation of the finer iridescent glasswares, was made in great quantities to meet the popular demand. Carnival glass was a colored iridescent pressed glass. It was made by companies in Ohio, Pennsylvania and West Virginia, the most important of which were Imperial Glass Company and Northwood Glass Company. Carnival glass was made in a great variety of shapes, including pitchers and tumblers, goblets, cups, berry bowls and dishes, compotes, plates, sugar and creamers, vases, baskets, punch bowls, buttons, lamps and souvenirs. The colors range from shades of gold to red and from yellow green to deep blue or purple. A great many pieces of marigold, blue, purple, and amethyst were made, but comparatively few pieces of red, so that today red is the most expensive color. The patterns

Tiffany "Favrile" glass. TOP. Vases, leaf and full tulip designs. BOTTOM LEFT. Flared vase with peacock decoration. RIGHT. Leaf design vase. (*The Metropolitan Museum of Art*)

include fruit such as grapes and cherries, flowers, birds, butterflies and geometric designs.

Carnival glass is hardly an antique since it was made as late as the 1920's and is being reproduced in quantity today, but it is being collected and will certainly increase in price. However, it is not on the same plane as the other art glassware since it cannot claim artistic workmanship or good design. Nevertheless, like any other category, it can be fun collecting. (See illustration, page 155.)

Mrs. Rose M. Presznick sent me a copy of her *Carnival and Iridescent Glass Book III*. If I were a Carnival glass collector I would take her advice to "get on the old marigold, bronze, pastel, opalware and Imperial Jewels Art Glass wagon while it can be found at reasonable prices." I might add that from an artistic standpoint I consider these colorings the most attractive. Pieces of souvenir Carnival Glass are bound to increase in price because of their historic significance; also, if I were a button collector I would gather Carnival buttons while they can be found.

Iridescent glass. LEFT TO RIGHT. Blue & White, The Imperial Glass Co., Bellaire, Ohio; basket, gold, off-white & green, "Quezal," Quezal Art Glass & Decorating Co., Brooklyn, New York; vase, Jack-in-the-Pulpit style, gold, green and off-white, "Kew-Blas," Union Glass Co., Somerville, Mass.; finger bowl & saucer, gold and green with raised opalescent "jewels," "Aurene," Steuben Glass Works, Corning, N.Y.; fluted, footed vase, green with gold, Steuben. (*The Chrysler Art Museum of Provincetown*)

Silver vase. Designed by J. H. Whitehouse, Tiffany & Co. Presented to William Cullen Bryant, c. 1875. (*The Metropolitan Museum of Art*)

V. SILVER

Flatware

BY 1840 silver was being made by machine, the day of the individual silversmith was ending, and silver companies were being established. However, contrary to common belief, fine silver was made in America throughout the nineteenth century. Spoons and other flatware continued to be made in a variation of the fiddle shape, but with an upturned spatulate handle. The thread design with a ridge outlining the handle was available in patterns called Plain Thread, French Thread, and Oval Thread. One with a shell at the end was a favorite. After 1860 the taste was for heavy ornate designs in high relief. The raised patterns were usually stamped or cast and designs were of various types including naturalistic flowers, conventional, and geometric. In 1871 Tiffany brought out the Japanese pattern in flat silver. It was a design with naturalistic birds, flowers and grasses, and no two pieces were alike. This design reflects the great interest in Japanese art. It is now being made again from the old dies.

The influence of Greek mythology was dominant in the Olympian group of flatware which Tiffany exhibited in Paris in 1878. A description of these pieces will give a good idea of the designs and the elaborateness of the silverware made in America at this date. These

187

descriptions are condensed from the Tiffany folder in the Landauer Collection at the New-York Historical Society.

SOUP LADLE—Jupiter with eagle and sceptre surrounded by gods and goddesses on Mt. Olympus. On the back is Cupid with torch and bow.

OYSTER LADLE—Hebe, cupbearer of gods is watched over by the eagle of Jove. On the back, wine vessel, barley and horn of plenty. On heel, head of Jupiter crowned with olive wreath.

BERRY AND SALAD SPOONS—Paris presenting golden apple to Venus.

TABLESPOON—Venus in shell drawn by dolphins driven by Cupid. On back, emblems of love—myrtle, doves, torches and burning heart.

DESSERT SPOON—Orpheus in search of Eurydice; on back, male and female heads with lyre and laurel.

TEASPOON—Diana and nymphs surprised by Pan. On back, dead stag.

COFFEE SPOON—Bacchantes and infant Bacchus. On back, head of faun, doves.

TABLE FORK. Hercules and Omphale.

DESSERT FORK—Sybil unrolling scrolls of fate.

MEAT CARVER—4th Labor of Hercules.

GAME CARVER—Actaeon devoured by dogs. On back, stag's head and implements of hunting.

DINNER KNIFE—Bacchus feeding the sacred panther.

BREAKFAST KNIFE—Orpheus charming wild animals.

DESSERT KNIFE—Bacchus and Bacchante.

NUT PICKS—2nd labor of Hercules.

MUSTARD SPOON—Sleeping Diana.

SALT SPOON—Satyrs and Sylvanus.

The designs were stamped on these pieces and the work was finished by hand. Gorham also made a heavy ornate pattern called "Raphael," and "King" and "Hindostanee" were the new patterns brought out by them in 1878. In the 1880's and 1890's the designs of American silverware were varied and selected from many sources.

There was a revival of the elaborate old French forms and borrowing from the Orient and the Near East. Gorham put out the "Medici" and "Fontainebleau" patterns in 1882 and the Sheaf of Wheat in 1887. However, these are expensive exhibition pieces and were probably only made to special order. The most of the flat silver available for the average American table in the 1890's was much simpler. It included fine-cut engraved patterns in such designs as "Lily," "Daisy," "Clover," "Wheat," "Windsor" and "Clifton." Other patterns such as "Antique" made by Whiting & Co. of New York had an allover chased pattern with a small panel left for a monogram. Such plain patterns as "Oval Thread," "Plain Thread," "French Thread" and "Plain Tip" continued to be made. Many decorative patterns were made only in teaspoons. Such patterns as "Egyptian," "Persian," "Tuscan," "Athenian" and "Alhambra" reflect the decorative interest of the times. A pattern called "Ivy" had a design of strapwork and a mask which relates it to the Renaissance Revival. Whiting & Co. made a die-pressed spoon in

Silver patterns made by Whiting & Co. in the 1870's, still popular in the 1890's. LEFT TO RIGHT. Oval Thread, Plain Thread, Persian, Plain Tip, Japanese (bamboo), Honeysuckle. (*Jewelers' Circular Keystone*)

Japanese pattern similar to the Japanese design made by Tiffany. The "Honeysuckle" was a related pattern which was made by Whiting & Co. Whiting also made a grape pattern which is Victorian in spirit, and Theodore Starr made a very attractive die-stamped chrysanthemum pattern.

In the 1890's the craze for souvenir spoons promoted the sale of silver and it became fashionable to assemble sets of tea or coffee spoons as souvenirs of different cities and states. These spoons were made of sterling silver and many of the designs are attractive, but their real value is historic since they preserve landmarks no longer in existence such as the old Cliff House in San Francisco and Castle Garden, New York. Souvenir spoon collecting is an interesting and inexpensive hobby related to the American Victorian period.

Almost all of the flat silver patterns are available to collectors today. However, it may take years to assemble a complete set, but many of the patterns such as Tiffany's "Japanese" ("Audubon") and Whiting's "Japanese" ("Bamboo") and "Honeysuckle" are similar and

Group of nineteenth century spoons that reflect the popular design motifs of the era. LEFT TO RIGHT. Ivy, Grape, Egyptian, Alhambra, Italian. (*Jewelers' Circular Keystone*)

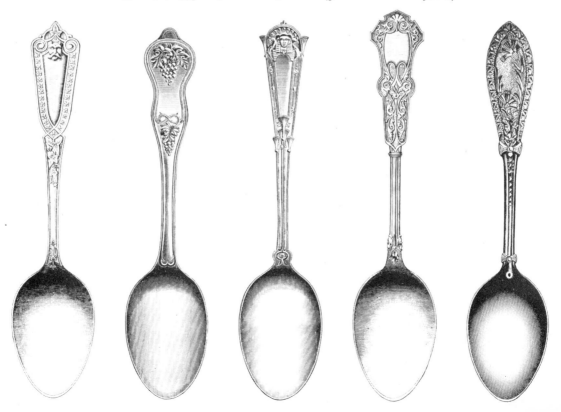

Tiffany Japanese pattern 1871, now called Audubon (*Tiffany & Co.*)

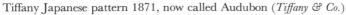

could be used together. There are also many patterns such as "Old King" and "Imperial Queen" which have a shell or anthemion motif which harmonize with each other. When buying old nineteenth century American silver one must remember that the patterns were made in several weights and the heaviness will determine the price as will the scarcity and demand.

In the 1860's the word sterling came into use and silver was marked "Sterling." Also patterns were patented at about this same time and the patent date of the pattern indicates when it was first made. For example, Tiffany's Olympian is marked "Tiffany Sterling Pat. 1878" although it is still being made. Since all of this late American silver is marked it is easy to identify and one can be sure of what one owns. While the prices of these old flat silver pieces are no longer cheap, they are less than the new pieces of the same pattern and a set could thus be assembled with part old and part new pieces at less expense.

Hollow Ware

THE hollow ware reflects the decorative styles of the Victorian period more closely than the flatware. Shapes of Victorian hollow ware changed along with styles and design motifs of the furniture of the period. The characteristics of the Empire style persisted in the silver of the 1840's as they did in furniture and decorative accessories. As the period opens

Silver tea set. Ball, Tompkins & Black, New York, c. 1845. (*The Henry Ford Museum*)

Sterling silver tea and coffee service. Samuel Kirk 1824. This style continued through 1840's.

the classical Empire style with fluted body and pedestal base is characteristic of the tea and coffee service. The gadroon, Greek key, laurel or acanthus decoration was heavy and embossed and shows the influence of the rococo revival. There was also some Etruscan influence and decorative processes included chasing, engraving and pierced work. Some of the companies working in New York at this date were: J. H. Johnston; Wood & Hughes; Ball, Tompkins & Black, and William Gale & Son; in Philadelphia, R. & W. Wilson; Bailey & Kitchen. The bodies of their tea sets were ovoid with incurvate necks and the repoussé decoration abounded in "C" scrolls and moulded grapes. Garlands of oak and acorns, and rustic twig handles and flower finials gave an appearance of abundance.

Samuel Kirk of Baltimore had introduced repoussé decoration as early as 1824 and by the middle of the century the rococo influence was seen in the allover naturalistic repoussé patterns made not only by Samuel Kirk & Son of Baltimore, but by Tiffany & Co. of New York and Gorham Co. of Providence, R.I. The forms of the pieces became wider, deeper, and exaggerated. The bodies were pear-shaped or spherical and handles were covered with leaf ornament. The spout of the teapot and coffee pot often ended in a bird's beak. Grape vines entwined rustic branches on handles, and finials were birds, deer, flowers, or pineapple forms. An ad of 1853 showed a tea set covered with a raised grape pattern and a centerpiece of an oak tree with branches holding glass bowls for fruit. At the base were figures of deer standing on a ground of grasses and fallen leaves. Hexagonal-shaped low-slung forms were covered with engraved patterns of rococo cartouches which sometimes enclosed scenes. In New York Tiffany & Co. sold silver made by Gorham & Co. and Ball, Black & Co. was also a fashionable store. In Philadelphia, P. L. Krider, J. E. Caldwell & Co. and Bailey & Co. were the principal companies.

In the 1860's–70's Elizabethan Renaissance hollow ware shapes were low-slung ovals, or angular with borders of conventional ivy, acanthus, strapwork and other architectural details. The Greek "oenoche" form with hoof-feet was seen in coffee pots. Gradually there was an increased

Silver tea set. William F. Ladd, New York, c. 1850. (*The New-York Historical Society*)

exaggeration of form and elaboration of design. Feet made up of exaggerated scrolls of acanthus leaves took the place of bases. Dulled and matted finishes gave a contrast of texture and an illusion of realism. By the 1870's the machine age produced designs that were a mass of over-elaborate rich decoration. An author writing in 1870 speaks of the after-dinner coffee pot with a long and slender neck made of hand-hammered silver by Kirk, and a coffee pot of niello-work made by Tiffany. Some silver services were made with no two pieces alike. A coffee pot with acorn and oak leaves had a modified Persian shape, and a Grecian-shaped vase with openwork handles made by Gorham had plaques of Thorwaldsen's "Night" and "Morning" with draperies of gold and oxide tints. Aurora and Venus motifs were seen in an elaborate centerpiece. Also, the naturalistic Japanese influence remained popular and etching and niello added richness.

Centerpieces for fruit and flowers were in great demand. These pieces allowed the designer to use his imagination and ingenuity both in the design and workmanship. There were centerpieces of Greek chariots drawn by cupids. These were ornamented with bas reliefs and burnished, and the edges and rims were touched with gold. A silver fruit service designed by Gorham consisted of a tall bowl set on a tripod of Egyptian design fastened to a heavy base. Two smaller matching bowls complete the centerpiece. Another elaborate flower and fruit piece consisted of four matching vases supported by female figures. It was set on a plateau of glass.

A writer in the *Art Journal,* 1875, says: "It was thought that the introduction of electro-plated ware would lessen the demand for solid silver objects but this is not so. The production of the artistic designs of the Meriden Company and other electro-plating corporations appears to have stimulated the taste for the beautiful and our manufactures of solid silverware are not only the equal in gracefulness and originality in the ateliers of England and France, but they are annually rapidly approximating it in value and volume." He mentions Tiffany, Gorham, and Whiting & Co. of New York City and goes on to state: "Machinery is not used to any considerable extent in the manufacture of silver-work if we except certain specialties, such as spoons and forks; and even of

Silver fruit dish. Tiffany & Co. (*The Art Journal*, 1876)

these many are still made by hand though the ornaments on the handle are generally produced by stamping or by letting the object pass between rollers or discs on which the pattern is cut. But in the production of silver design of a high character, machinery performs only a small part."

Through the influence of the Centennial in 1876 and the large plated and silver pieces displayed by such companies as Tiffany, Gorham, Reed and Barton, and Meriden Britannia, the historical and genre influence seen in the painting of the period was reflected in the design of silverware which became literary and story-telling. On the Century Vase exhibited by Gorham we see the story of the progress of American manufactures. There are scenes of pioneer days, Indians, fruits, flowers, and agrarian motifs such as wheat, scythe, plow and beehives which relate to the American scene. Another piece which showed American originality in design motifs was the Bryant Testimonial Vase made by Tiffany. The vase is covered with a meshwork of apple branches, primrose, amaranth and other flowers mentioned in Bryant's poems. The vase is monumental and symbolical in conception, but the design motifs are for the most part original and represent American ideas.

Although American silver designers continued to create new designs, the impact of mechanization had stamped out the craft of the silversmith and his work was mostly taken over by factory processes. Such was the elaborateness of the styles and the demand for large presentation and testimonial pieces, loving cups and trophies, that the large companies such as Gorham, Tiffany, Whiting & Co., Starr & Marcus, and Black Starr & Frost, found it necessary to employ artistic designers and crafts-men to supply their trade. James H. Whitehouse was the top designer at Tiffany. Gorham's head designers were T. J. Pairpont and William Codman, and Charles Osborne was employed by Whiting & Co. These designers worked on the production of testimonials, racing trophies and presentation pieces that were the major products of the silver companies of the late nineteenth century. Extreme style and decorative abandon resulted in flamboyant designs which were a combination of

Silver centerpiece. Gorham Manufacturing Co. (*The Art Journal*, 1876)

naturalistic decoration and heroic subjects from Greek mythology. The popular shapes were vases, bowls and urns. In addition to repoussé and cast reliefs the pieces were chased and engraved, and techniques of matting, frosting, burnishing, oxidation and parcel gilt enriched the surfaces.

The silver which Tiffany exhibited in Paris in 1900 was completely eclectic. There were vases and bowls with ears of corn and jewels in Aztec style, a Zuni Indian basket-shaped bowl, and a bowl in the shape of a Hupa Indian basket with rattlesnake handles. A loving cup illustrated the Indian war dance and had buffalo horn handles. Another was a Sitka Indian design and had Rocky Mountain sheep horns for handles. One coffee pot was in Byzantine style, and another Egyptian. A silver service of 110 pieces in George III style had modeled figures and pierced and chased designs, while a tea set was embossed with a design of American flowers including poppies, buttercups, apple blossoms, dogwood and lily of the valley.

There is not a great deal of American Victorian silver on the market today because there has been so little demand for it that it has not come out of attic hiding. Now and again such pieces come up at auction and there are pieces to be seen in some museums and historical societies. For the most part these pieces were given to the museums, but within the last few years museums have actually been collecting nineteenth century American silver, for example, the Metropolitan Museum of Art to add to the collection of its American Wing. This silver is all marked and the marks are recorded so that there is no difficulty in identifying the maker. There is practically no literature on the subject.

Presentation Silver and Silver Plate

PRESENTATION silver is primarily of historic interest although many pieces are of artistic value and are the work of prominent American silversmiths.

Silversmiths were engaged in making presentation silver almost from the beginning of American history. The first pieces made were given to churches and are to be seen today in such collections as that of Trinity

Church, New York City. Silver presentation pieces were also awarded to college tutors and military men, and there were medals and gorgets given to peace-loving Indians. The most of these pieces are early and they are in museums and historical societies. But there are nineteenth century presentation pieces which have found their way to pawn shops and to second-hand silver shops, and are thus available to collectors to-day. There were pieces which were given as awards to encourage agriculture and business, as well as historical presentation pieces. There were sports trophies for yachting and racing, and cups for best-of-breed dogs and other animals. It is in this field of lesser presentation pieces that the collector will find articles for his collection.

These pieces are interesting because they reflect the shapes and motifs of the American Victorian era. Many show unique and indigenous designs. There are silver vases which have sculptured motifs of American produce such as the Heinz Trophy which was awarded to the district that sold the most Heinz products. The superintendent of the district that won the award for three years was allowed to keep the cup. This vase, with a sculptured group of tomatoes, cucumbers and other vegetables,

Silver Salver showing Brick Church, New York. Made by Ball, Black & Co., 1860. (*The New-York Historical Society*)

should be extant today, and if the owner should need money might come on the market. Many nineteenth century yachting trophies, although made of fine silver, are not always artistic in design, and when the yacht club is no longer in existence they are often disposed of. Then there are the plated trophies and prize cups which have little artistic or intrinsic value but which give a picture of other days and record a forgotten event. There is the plated silver tea set with the inscription, "Given to Mr. and Mrs. Amberson McClinton by the Pastime Social Club," which pictures a way of life no longer in existence.

All of these articles represent the minor side of presentation silver collecting but articles which represent major collecting interests are also available. There are trays and vases with engraved scenes of buildings and ships no longer in existence. One interesting tray has vignette scenes of San Francisco, including Seal Rocks and the old Cliff House. There are also pieces displaying historical sites with appropriate inscriptions and dates.

LEFT. Silver tea kettle made by Wm. Gale & Son. Presented to Commodore Matthew Calbraith Perry, 1855. RIGHT. Silver tea kettle showing Egyptian influence. Tiffany & Co. Presented to yacht "Mallory," 1862. (*The New-York Historical Society*)

Silver trinket box. Gorham Manufacturing Co., c. 1880. Presented to Emma C. Thursby by Gilmore's Band. (*The New-York Historical Society*)

Presentation swords are a major field for collectors. In recent years sword collecting has become a popular hobby in America and the collecting of presentation swords is a specialized category. Washington's swords on display at Mount Vernon were made by European swordsmiths. But American silversmiths were making dress-sword hilts as early as 1770; Paul Revere's books reveal that he made silver sword hilts. There are early sword hilts with lion, dog and eagle-head pommels made by such silversmiths as Jacob Hurd of Boston and William Moulton. Isaac Hutton of Albany, who worked as late as 1855, made stylized eagle-head hilts. The majority of the early presentation swords are in museums and historical societies but some are in private collections. There are presentation swords of the War of 1812, the Mexican War, the Civil War, and the Spanish-American War, as well as World War I, which are available for collectors today.

As time went on the trend toward ornateness in sword hilts increased. Some hilts had a plumed and helmeted head as a pommel motif. The presentation sword of the Civil War was a popular and representative piece of Victorian goldsmith's work. These hilts reflected the ornate

baroque taste of the times. The swords were massive and heavily ornamented, with sculptured mountings of rich metals and precious stones.
The grips had figures of soldiers, sailors, the Goddess of Liberty, classical figures and patriotic insignia. The hilts were made by such well-
known silver companies as Tiffany, Gorham, and Samuel Kirk & Son.
In 1862 Tiffany made presentation swords which were given to the Civil
War heroes, Major General Halleck, Major General Fremont and
Major General Burnside. These were presented by states, cities and
patriotic organizations. After the Civil War officers' swords were simpler,
and the practice of presenting dress swords went out of style after World
War I.

Another piece of presentation silver available to the collector today

LEFT. Hilt of sword presented to Gen. William T. Sherman. Pommel decorated with stars and
mounted with eagle. Goddess Athena in grip niche. RIGHT. Hilt of sword presented to Major
General Winfield Scott Hancock. Ornamented with patriotic symbols. c. 1861. (*Smithsonian
Institution*)

is the silver trumpet. Silver trumpets were the popular trophies given to persons for their heroism at fires or for their work in volunteer fire companies.

The volunteer fire department was an important factor in the political and social life of the American city for several centuries, and it continued to function until the end of the nineteenth century. Today the old fire engines and many of the articles used in early fire fighting, such as hats, leather buckets, signal torches and lanterns, are collector's items. One of the most interesting objects was the fire trumpet. The brass speaking trumpet was used by the foreman of the volunteer fire department to shout directions and to encourage the men fighting the fire. Nineteenth century prints of fires and firemen, such as those by T. W. Strong and Currier and Ives, show the foreman with his trumpet.

In the late nineteenth century it became the custom to present a silver trumpet for heroism at fires and as a recognition of honor for work in a volunteer fire department. These trumpets were ornamented with the symbol of the fire company. The symbols included such motifs as the Beehive, the Eagle, Tiger, Neptune, and other appropriate devices. The trumpets were also engraved with elaborate scroll decoration which might include a picture of the engine, and an inscription which included the name, date, and particular incident of bravery for which the trumpet was presented. They were also hung with bright silk cords. Many of these silver presentation trumpets, including the one belonging to Boss Tweed of New York, are in present-day collections and some are still available for the collector.

Still another presentation piece was the silver trowel. The use of a silver trowel to lay the cornerstone of a public building was a late nineteenth century custom. These trowels were inscribed with the occasion, date and names of the person who laid the stone, the building committee and the architect. A collection of these presentation trowels would not only tell the story of many well-known buildings, but would also include the names of late nineteenth century silversmiths and silver companies.

TOP. Silver Presentation Trumpet, c. 1880's. (*The H. V. Smith Museum of the Home Insurance Co.*)
BOTTOM. Silver trowel. Gorham & Co., 1914. (*The New-York Historical Society*)

There are also yachting trophies and other sports trophies, including baseball, tennis, bicycle racing, horse racing and golf. Many of these are in club collections but others are owned by the individuals who won them. They are often found in pawn shops and second-hand silver shops. The yachting trophies are not only unique in design, with motifs relating to the sea and racing, but they often preserve the pictures of famous boats and give their names, the dates of the races and the names of the persons who presented the trophies. Silver trophies have some artistic and intrinsic value. The plated trophies have value as a picture of popular art of another century. Those including models of old bicycles or golfing figures in knickers and other outdated paraphernalia are amusing as well as possessing a certain historical significance. They also give a picture of the bad taste of much of the silver and plated ware of the late nineteenth century.

One of the most interesting and little known fields of American silversmiths' work was the production of presentation silver for battleships and cruisers of the United States Navy. These were made in the 1890's and they represent the finest design and workmanship of the American silversmith of the late nineteenth century. They are not available for collections.

The most important presentation piece of the Victorian era was the Bryant Testimonial Vase, which was given to the poet William Cullen Bryant and is now in the Metropolitan Museum, New York City. This piece is described here because it gives an excellent picture of American nineteenth century silversmiths' work.

Silver salver with scenes of San Francisco including the Cliff House and Presidio. Made by Vanderslice & Co., and presented to John S. Ellis in 1864. (*The New-York Historical Society*)

As we see the vase today it is covered with a fretwork of apple blossoms and branches designed to express the bloom and wholesome freshness of Bryant's poetry. Beneath the fretwork are primrose and amaranth, and gentian which refers to the poem, "Fringed Gentian." The poems "Water Fowl", "Robert of Lincoln", "The Planting of the Apple Tree", "Forest Hymn" and "Thanatopsis" are all suggested in the design, which includes a beautiful border of Indian corn, water lilies and handles that enclose the bobolink. There are medallions of the poet's bust and scenes from Bryant's life. The vase is typical of the literary silver pieces of the late nineteenth century. The design inspired by a combination of classic and Japanese influence is nevertheless distinctly American in its use of indigenous plants, flowers and subject matter. It was designed by James Whitehouse of Tiffany & Co. The piece cost $5000, but copies were available at $500.

Electroplate

ELECTROPLATE is one of the most characteristic products of the Victorian era. This pseudo-silver provided ostentation and dining table elegance at small cost and immediately captured the popular fancy. Any article, no matter how elaborate, that could be made in silver could be reproduced in electroplate for half the price. Electroplate is made by electrolysis. In a bath of potassium cyanide, silver is decomposed and deposited on a base metal surface such as copper, britannia, white metal, or later, German nickel. John O. Mead of Philadelphia was the earliest electroplater in America. His business, first listed in 1840, never rivalled the larger companies and no pieces have been found with his marks, although in 1859 he had a thriving commercial trade. The companies who are best known in the early electroplate field in America were Reed and Barton, Meriden Britannia, and Rogers Brothers. In the post-Civil War period there were many other important companies making electroplate such as Oneida, Gorham, and Rice.

Electroplate sports trophies. (*Reed & Barton Catalogue, 1885*)

Electroplate centerpiece, The Barge of Venus. Middletown Silverplate Company. (*The Art Journal*, 1875)

America got its first look at electroplate at the Centennial in 1876. The large companies who were makers of electroplate displayed ornate exhibition pieces. Meriden Britannia exhibited a large Neptune epergne with hanging dishes for fruit and bonbons. At the base were figures of Neptune and Earth. They also exhibited a group of figures called Buffalo Hunt. Reed and Barton exhibited their Progress Vase surmounted by the figure of Liberty, which stood on a base with sculptured groups of the landing of Columbus and a group of primitive Aztec Indians on horseback. Middletown Silver Plate Co. exhibited an elaborate plateau centerpiece on which the shell-shaped barge of Venus was drawn by two swans driven by Cupid. Such pieces as these attracted wide attention and created a demand for plated ware. Hotels were soon supplied with huge coffee urns and tea services; every housewife owned an electroplated tea set, and a centerpiece and casters were on every dining table.

Catalogues illustrating electroplate were brought out by the principal companies in the 1860's, 1870's, and 1880's, and these give an idea of the extent of the articles available in electroplate. Tableware was made in the greatest quantities. Pieces included tureens, waiters, vegetable and pudding dishes, candelabra, wine coolers, casters, bread trays, butter dishes, pitchers, fruit stands, berry bowls, cake baskets and tea and coffee sets. The most popular item was the tea set which was usually included among every middle-class bride's wedding gifts. It consisted of from five to seven pieces although early sets before 1850 were usually made in only three pieces. While the designs of tea sets varied from decade to decade, the sets made by the different companies at the same date had little variation in their basic shapes.

The shapes and designs of plated ware are closely related to silver shapes of the same period. The early sets made in the 1850's are large

Silver-plate tea and coffee service. Webster Mfg. Co., Brooklyn, 1859–1873. (*The International Silver Company*)

Floral embossed tea set. Meriden Britannia Co. 1886.
(*The International Silver Co.*)

Silver-plated water pitcher on stand with goblet. Meriden Britannia Co., Patented 1868.
(*The Henry Ford Museum*)

and stand on high pedestal bases. The decoration varies from plain panels to ornate grape patterns, and handles are often made of wood. The urn shape on a pedestal continued into the 1860's, but the handles are of curved metal. The finials in the shape of fruits, birds or flowers are attached with a screw. Instead of embossing, the patterns are formed by chasing, or cutting. Borders are foliated, beaded or gadroon. The chief manufacturers of this period were Meriden Britannia, Reed and Barton, Rogers, and Gorham.

By 1870 the teapot and other pieces are set on legs instead of on a pedestal and the handles are angular. Deep-chased patterns include exotic birds and Egyptian motifs with raised applied bands. In the 1880's the shape changes to a low, broad form set on a rim base instead of legs. The surface was ornamented with ferns, flowers and grasses in bright-cut designs upon a "frosted" background. Later embossed and repoussé allover and hammered designs were popular, and the teapot and coffee pot were smaller in size. Hotel ware was simple in form and decorated with plain fluted or gadroon borders on a pearl-finish body. Trays and hot water kettles usually matched the tea sets.

Ice water pitchers, especially the tilting pitcher, which was set on a tray with matching goblets, is another Victorian electroplate article

Silver-plated tea service. Renaissance Revival, c. 1875. (*The Henry Ford Museum*)

which is collected today. The ice water pitcher dates from a patent of 1854 acquired by the Meriden Britannia Company, but it was also made by several other companies. The earliest ice water pitchers were of simple design, held from two to four quarts and sat on a tray with one goblet. Later the pitchers became larger and more ornate, sometimes decorated with a snow scene. Many pitchers were mounted on tilting racks, with two goblets. In 1886 Meriden Britannia offered 57 different designs of ice water pitchers. By the 1890's the water pitcher is smaller and is usually set on a matching tray with a set of goblets. Elaborate covered punch bowls set on a tray or plateau with a set of twelve "glasses" were probably made as presentation pieces or for special groups. These are rare and were expensive when made and are seldom on the market today. Covered tureens, vegetable dishes, and other serving dishes were made in quantity.

The revolving caster was one of the most widely used pieces of electroplate. According to directions for setting the table given in cookbooks of the period, the caster should sit in the center of the table. Casters had been used on the table early in the nineteenth century, but the early type of casters set on a footed tray with center handle were

Silver-plated casters. Meriden Britannia Company, 1870's. (*The International Silver Company*)

not made in electroplate. The earliest electroplate caster has a wide pierced band which serves as a holder for the bottles. There are usually six bottles and sometimes small salt dips. The base is set on four feet and the bottom is often wood. An ornate handle is in the center. Casters of 1860 are more elaborate and the bottles are of pressed glass patterns. Pressed glass caster bottles were made in the following patterns: Bellflower, Daisy & Button, Beaded Dewdrop, Beaded Grape, Medallion Bull's Eye, Fine Cut, Fine Rib, Gothic, Hamilton, Ivy, Honeycomb, Palmette, Powder & Shot, Thumbprint, Roman Rosette and Eugenia. Caster bottles were also made in many cut glass patterns. The rotary caster was patented in 1862. The bottles fitted into holes on a circular platform which stood on a tall cone-type base and the center handle was often decorated with elaborate openwork design. In the 1870's heavy grape and beaded borders were added. Later, the low caster came back into vogue and colored pressed glass containers with Daisy and Button pattern or milk opalescent or cased glass were popular and the silver frame was reduced to a few wires. There were also pickle and salad casters. The most interesting feature of these late casters was the container. In addition to pressed glass of blue, canary or crystal, they were made of Pomona art glass, opalene twist, imported, decorated ruby glass and cut crystal. The glass containers had a fancy plated cover and decorated tongs were fastened to the stand.

Silver-plated pickle casters. TOP RIGHT. Container Pomona Glass. Meriden Britannia Company, 1870's. (*The International Silver Company*)

Silver centerpiece, "Hiawatha's Canoe." Gorham Manufacturing Company. (*The Art Journal,* 1875)

Trays of all sizes—oval, round, and rectangular—were made with gadroon or fluted borders in plain or satin finish. They were also made with repoussé borders and fancy corners, including Egyptian heads. Etched or chased designs of flowers, birds, and grasses as well as scenes decorated the centers of some trays. Cake baskets with handles stood on legs or center standards.

The most interesting and also one of the expensive electroplated items is the Victorian fruit, berry dish, or centerpiece. This piece is of special interest to collectors because of the glass dish which is set in the frame. Many of these dishes have been taken out of the electroplate framework and sold separately, but now the collector is searching for the complete piece. This, when found, is expensive. The catalogue price was about a tenth of the present asking price. However, many of the stands with their ruffled bowls of various types of American and European Victorian glassware are decorative. Practically every American glass manufacturer made glass containers for these electroplate stands. Pressed glass from the various Pittsburgh factories and clear, colored, and Mary Gregory glass from Sandwich and New England Glass Company were the most common varieties. But there were also containers of hob nail, Satin glass, Wheeling Peachblow, Pomona, Amberina and Burmese glass. Some of the finest pieces have containers of frosted glass with etched designs and some had cut-glass bowls. Parker and Casper & Co. of W. Meriden, Connecticut, in an ad of 1869, stated: "Cutting of glassware used by us in caster, wine, and pickle frames, berry dishes, gives an advantage over other manufacturers." Bohemian, Venetian, Bristol, and Nailsea glass containers were also used.

LEFT. Fruit dish with figure of Cupid, herringbone Satin glass bowl on silver-plated stand by Wilcox Silver Plate Co. CENTER. Plated stand with bowl of pink Satin glass. RIGHT. Bowl, Amberina glass, New England Glass Co. (*The Corning Museum of Glass*)

The centerpiece usually consisted of a tall fruit dish on a metal stand with two lower matching dishes. There were also centerpieces set on a glass plateau. One by Reed and Barton consists of a peacock drawing a chariot which holds a glass container for flowers. Another centerpiece is a rowboat holding children, while Meriden Britannia made a delicate sailboat set on a plateau. A bowl for fruit is set on a pedestal from which springs a decorative vine-entwined arm holding a cornucopia-shaped glass vase for flowers. These were illustrated in advertisements of 1879. Gorham's fruit and flower services had Grecian figures, festoons, and gilded bas reliefs. Many small tablewares such as spoon racks on stands, syrup pitchers, butter dishes, toothpick holders, knife rests, bells, napkin rings and children's mugs are available for the collector with a small purse. Such articles as napkin rings, toothpick holders or children's mugs can form an amusing collection and these small items

LEFT. Satin glass, herringbone design bowl, plated stand, Derby Silver Co., c. 1885. CENTER. Bowl, Peachblow, New England Glass Co.; stand, Simpson, Hall, Miller & Co. RIGHT. Bowl, Satin glass with enamel decoration; stand, Meriden Britannia Co. (*Corning Museum of Glass*)

Silver-plated epergne. Simpson, Hall, Miller Co. Bowls decorated Burmese glass. Mt. Washington Glass Co. (*The Corning Museum of Glass*)

probably tell us more about late Victorian electroplate than almost any other articles.

The popularity of electroplate lasted until late in the century. The falling price of silver then made it possible for those who wanted silver to buy sterling. Although electroplate was first developed in England, American electroplate is superior to the English product, but great quantities of both were made and are available for collectors today. Electroplate is usually marked. Before 1860 the marks were on discs soldered to the bottom of the piece, afterwards the marks were cut directly into the bottom of the piece. The mark included the maker's name and trademark and often the word "triple," "quadruple," or "quadruple plate." Any numbers under the name refer to the pattern. From year to year maker's marks often vary. Electroplate was made in sets and it is not difficult to assemble matching pieces of a tea set or goblets to match a tipping-pitcher. Early electroplate is hard to find and of course more valuable. Some of the early pieces are not marked with the maker's name. The base metal on which the silver is plated partly determines the value. Gorham always produced high class electroplate and together with Reed and Barton used a heavy nickel silver base where many other companies used a lightweight white metal or Britannia. Meriden also used a Britannia base in the 1870's.

The condition of a piece of electroplate is not as important as it might seem, since no matter how battered or worn the scars and scratches can be repaired and the piece can be replated. Since electroplate can be dipped and polished with little time and effort, the collector would first of all do well to buy pieces by well-known makers such as Gorham or Reed and Barton, and also have a reputable shop do the repair job. Gorham is the highest grade electroplate, and is indistinguishable from pure silver in both style and appearance. Since Gorham made electroplate for only a few years, pieces of their plate are not plentiful.

Small Plated Tablewares

IN the search to find inexpensive American Victorian antiques for the collector, small articles of electroplate stand out as a comparatively unexplored field. Small objects were made for the desk, such as inkwells; there were match safes for the gentlemen and chatelaine purses, vinaigrette and hairpin holders for the ladies, but the small accessories for use on the dining table are especially interesting and available. There are numerous small articles such as napkin rings, knife rests, mugs, goblets, toothpick holders, trays and small candlesticks which have been neglected by collectors. These things were all made from the 1870's to the end of the century.

Napkin rings are the most interesting category because of their various forms and the unique, typically Victorian designs. The first patent for napkin rings was taken out in 1869 although they were illustrated in catalogues a few years earlier. There are plain napkin rings with chased initials, names, or floral designs in satin finish; scroll embossed patterns, and rings decorated with hammering. Some rings had contrasting shiny beaded, fluted or plain borders and some had borders of open work. The subject matter of many of these designs on napkin rings is fascinating. Sculptured fruit such as cherries and gooseberries, flowers including lilies and roses, a snail and shell, a frog and lily pad, a dog house with a dog at the door, butterflies and fans, are only a few of the Victorian fancies available to the collector of napkin rings.

However, the figure designs are the most interesting. These have standing figures of people, usually cupids or boys and girls. There are quaint children in Kate Greenaway costume—a little girl is dressed in coat, bonnet and muff, and a boy is in coveralls with a frilled collar. Other children are shown with pets or playing games, such as the children climbing a ladder. There were many napkin rings with animals, and birds. The goat was a favorite, as were the rabbit, squirrel, dog and kitten. There were also hens, roosters, birds, ducks and a cow and

Group of silver-plated napkin rings. (*The International Silver Company*)

camel. The figure usually stands beside the ring and is soldered to it, but some are set on platforms. A combination of a figure of a cupid or butterfly holding a small vase for flowers is rare and thus expensive. Figures of dogs, goats, ponies, or children drawing a two-wheeled cart on which the napkin ring is placed are also rare. A clumsy combination of salt, pepper, butter plate and napkin ring set on a stand with a handle is also hard to find.

In addition to rarity of subject matter the collector should look for the markings. Besides the maker's name or trade mark, the piece was often marked "Triple" or "Quadruple" plate which gives a clue as to quality.

Plated knife rests are also amusing to collect. There are rests upheld by squirrels, chicks, dogs and other animals. The same animals and Victorian children hold barrel toothpick holders set on a stand. A porcupine with holes for the toothpicks is rare.

In the Reed & Barton catalogue of 1885, trays, or waiters as they were called, were made with chased designs in various types of finishes—pearl finish, Persian finish, and Oriental. The designs for the most part are of Oriental inspiration including birds, butterflies or dragonflies, and sprays of bamboo and oriental blossoms. Other designs include groups of naturalistic spring flowers or a spray of geraniums, while still other trays have scenes with cupids or draped figures. There are trays with center designs of a chased dog or cat head with a raised

Silver-plated trays. (*Reed & Barton Catalogue 1885*)

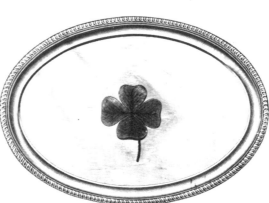
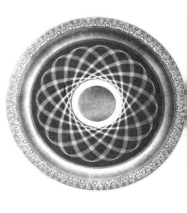

border of birds and flowers. A plain waiter has a geometric pattern or a four-leaf clover in its center, and there are hotel waiters in all sizes with plain, fluted or gadroon edges. Small card plates had similar designs. The crumb tray and scraper was etched with a floral design or a romantic scene of figures and wooded scenery.

Plated candlesticks of the various pedestal types were made in pairs. There were also saucer types, and later four- and five-branch candelabra were made. While there were plain sticks with round and square bases decorated with fluting and beaded bands, the fanciful decorated type seems to have been more popular. In Reed & Barton's catalogue of 1884, in addition to pedestal candlesticks with and without etched wind glasses, there are many small low candlesticks with griffin handles. These were variations of the saucer type and include a grape design socket set on a leaf saucer, a socket with lily pad saucer, and a socket set on a resting camel's back. A candlestick for the horseman includes a horse's head, stirrup and strap. A Victorian pedestal vase also held a candle socket. These candlesticks are marked with the maker's name. The ones marked "Rogers 1847" were made after 1900. The plain candlesticks and candelabra are in demand as substitutes for more expensive Sheffield Plate, but the fancy types when found should be less expensive and amusing to own.

Silver-plated candlesticks. (*Reed & Barton Catalogue 1885*)

Shell and Seaweed patterns of majolica from the collection of Mr. and Mrs. Ellis E. Stern.

VI. POTTERY AND PORCELAIN

AMERICAN ceramics of the Victorian Period not only followed the rococo and neo-classical styles of European ceramics but modelers and decorators from English potteries came as émigrés to America and their influence dominated the ceramic industry in the United States in the nineteenth century. Stoneware, various kinds of earthenware, including the sgraffito ware of Pennsylvania, and even porcelain had been manufactured in various parts of America before 1840 and these wares continued to be made all through Victorian times, but certain other wares such as Parian, Majolica and Belleek, were first made in the nineteenth century and are distinctly Victorian not only because of their material, but because of their shapes and naturalistic and romantic designs which followed the trend of the decorative art of the period. As the period progresses we see exotic influences of Japan and Egypt. Persian and Moorish shapes and Renaissance designs also dominate certain ceramics.

In this period American ceramic manufacturers not only supplied the utilitarian needs of the people, but also began to compete with the European potteries in making the finest porcelains and art wares. As the Victorian period opened in about 1840, the American Pottery

221

Company in Jersey City made blue transfer-printed wares similar to Staffordshire. A water pitcher and mugs with printed portraits of William Henry Harrison, a log cabin, an eagle, and the inscription "The Ohio Farmer" printed in black, were made for the presidential campaign of 1840. The best-known products of the American Pottery Company were the Rockingham hound-handled pitchers which were made after English models by Daniel Greatbach who joined the company in 1839. Stoneware pitchers with hunting scenes and an Apostle pitcher were also made here. These were marked "American Pottery, Jersey City" or "D. & J. Henderson, Jersey City," impressed in a circle. The name of the firm was changed to the Jersey City Pottery in 1845. Later, although the wares were of high quality, they were never marked but were sold to the trade for decorating. It is some of this ware that was decorated by the Lycetts and thus it has value today, but it is very scarce and very expensive.

Another important pottery at this time was operated by Charles Cartlidge, an English potter, at Greenpoint, New York. They made porcelain buttons, door plates and door knobs, candlesticks, and biscuit porcelain busts of Daniel Webster, Zachary Taylor, Chief Justice Marshall and Archbishop Hughes, modeled by Josiah Jones. This factory closed in 1856, but the work was carried on under the name Union Porcelain Works, and porcelain tableware and decorative pieces were manufactured. Karl Müller, a sculptor, designed the famous Century Vase with historical American scenes which was exhibited at the

Group of New Jersey pitchers. LEFT TO RIGHT. Relief steamship and fire engine, both Salamander Works, Woodbridge, N.J. c. 1838–1845; white pitcher with relief grapevine, Swan Hill Pottery, South Amboy, N.J. 1860–1867; brown pitcher with grape pattern, Congress Pottery, South Amboy, N.J. 1849–1854. (*The Henry Ford Museum*)

Centennial. He also designed a Liberty cup and a vase to illustrate Longfellow's poem, "Keramos." A series of statuettes, pitchers and busts of famous Americans were also designed by Müller. The well-known artist J. M. Falconer was also employed as a decorator of plates and plaques at the Union Porcelain Works. Since many of the pieces, including the Centennial Vase, have been found both decorated and undecorated, it would seem that the decorated vase was the work of the two men, both sculptor and decorator. A charming trillium flower-form vase upheld by a frog was also made at the Union Porcelain Works and a tea set with heads of an Indian and a Negro as finials

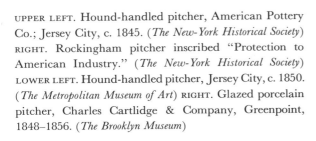

UPPER LEFT. Hound-handled pitcher, American Pottery Co.; Jersey City, c. 1845. (*The New-York Historical Society*) RIGHT. Rockingham pitcher inscribed "Protection to American Industry." (*The New-York Historical Society*) LOWER LEFT. Hound-handled pitcher, Jersey City, c. 1850. (*The Metropolitan Museum of Art*) RIGHT. Glazed porcelain pitcher, Charles Cartlidge & Company, Greenpoint, 1848–1856. (*The Brooklyn Museum*)

and squirrels and goats' heads as handles, was decorated with a rococo floral pattern and panels of birds and flowers. There were also vases with embossed gold and jewel work and grotesque lizards climbing up their sides. These are rare pieces, but since the works continued to the turn of the twentieth century many less important articles must be available. The factory used several marks, including an eagle's head grasping an "S" with "U.P.W." above, and "Union Porcelain Works, N.Y." impressed.

Fine porcelain was also made before 1900 by Kurlbaum and Schwartz of Philadelphia; Greenwood Company, Trenton, New Jersey; Bennett, New York; Lenox; Knowles, Taylor, and Knowles in East Liverpool, Ohio; and the United States Pottery Company in Bennington, Vermont.

The United States Pottery Company produced a great variety of wares—both pottery and porcelain, utilitarian and decorative. In fact, from 1847 to 1858 this pottery produced a vast output of wares. Under the direction of Daniel Greatbach, who had earlier worked at the Jersey City Pottery, such Rockingham ware designs as hound-handled jugs with grape designs and hunting scenes as well as with molded diamond and Gothic patterns were made. The six-sided brown pitcher with raised floral designs on the panels was made in at least four different sizes. The designs on the panels and the handle shapes

LEFT. Two pieces of toilet set of white graniteware decorated in blue and gold. RIGHT. Graniteware presentation pitcher decorated in gold and inscribed "U.S. Pottery Co/Bennington, Vt." (*The Henry Ford Museum*)

vary. These pitchers are marked "Norton & Fenton." Similar Rocking-ham ware pitchers were made by Ballard Brothers, and Nichols and Alford, in Burlington, Vermont, and by J. B. Caire & Co., Po'keepsie, New York, as well as in Ohio potteries.

Since most pitchers of Bennington Rockingham Pottery are scarce and expensive, it is best for the beginning collector to start with small utilitarian articles which are less in demand and therefore less expensive. There are mugs, tea and coffee pots, sugar bowls, pie plates, soap dishes, cuspidors, door-knobs, flowerpots, and picture frames. Of these articles, the most typically Victorian are the cuspidors and the picture frames. Bennington cuspidors were made in different sizes, shapes, and designs. The most common ones are those molded in panels with or without a diamond pattern. The flatter cuspidor with a clam shell design was also made in quantity. The rarer cuspidors are those with panelled columns or acanthus design. Some of the cuspidors are marked with the various 1849 stamps which include the date. Oval, round, square, and rectangular Rockingham picture frames with heavy moldings were made in many sizes at Bennington. They also made an elaborate rococo leaf pattern frame. These were not made at other factories. They are certainly distinctly Victorian, and are similar in design to the heavy walnut frames of the period.

Norton and Fenton paneled Rockingham pitchers with floral designs, 1845–1847 (*Bennington Museum*)

Besides the Parian ware which will be treated elsewhere, the molded pitchers with relief designs are the most characteristic Victorian forms. For the most part the designs and forms of these pitchers followed English leadership and many were exact reproductions of designs by Copeland, Minton, and other English potters. The "Cherub and Grapes" jug was copied from a Wedgwood design, and the "Good Samaritan," "Love and War" and "Pond Lily" jugs were also copies. "Bird and Nest," "Babes in the Woods," "Paul and Virginia" were also English adaptations. The only distinctly original American designs were the "Cascade" and "Corn" patterns. These elaborate relief designs are typically Victorian. They were molded in soft-paste porcelain, Parian and various other materials and cover almost every aspect of Victorian design. The jug or pitcher was on every middle-class Victorian table for use as a water or milk pitcher or as a jug for ale or beer, thus a great many of them were made. While a few of these patterns such as the Corn Husk are extremely rare, and any Bennington jug is rare, there are many small porcelain jugs from other American potteries which are available at less expensive prices.

Parian Ware

PARIAN is one of the most popular Victorian wares. It was first made by Copeland in England in 1842. Parian is a hard-paste unglazed porcelain that was designed for making cheap miniature reproductions of famous pieces of sculpture or portrait busts of celebrities, and was commonly called statuary ware or statuary porcelain. In texture and appearance Parian was a close approximation to Parian marble. Later, many pitchers, vases, boxes, and other small articles were made in Parian ware. English Parian is made mostly in the form of small statues. Statues and portrait busts were also made in American potteries, but the most collectible item is the Parian pitcher or vase.

Parian was made by Morrison & Carr in New York City and by the Southern Porcelain Company, Kaolin, South Carolina, whose products included a jug with an impressed wheat design and rustic

Group of Bennington Parian ware. TOP. Pitcher, Wild Rose pattern; blue and white vase, portrait medallion; water lily pitcher. BOTTOM. Eagle vase; figure of girl lacing shoe; rare blue and white pitcher, Cherub and Grape pattern. (*The Henry Ford Museum*)

handle. Ott & Brewer of Trenton, New Jersey, exhibited Parian vases and statues modeled by Isaac Broome, the sculptor, at the Centennial in 1876. In 1885 Parian wares were made at the Chesapeake Pottery. These included heads, flowers and medallions of Thorwaldsen's "Seasons" as well as original cattle-head plaques modeled by the sculptor James Priestman.

The first, and perhaps the best Parian ware produced in America was that made by the United States Pottery in Bennington. John Harrison, a modeler from Copeland, England, came to the United States Pottery to assist. At first, copies of English statuettes were made and it is difficult to distinguish similar pieces made by Copeland, Minton, Alcock, or other English potters from the American. Parian pitchers were made in the following designs; "Cascade," "Corn Husk," "Cherub and Grapes," "Cupid & Psyche," "Daffodil," "Good Samaritan," "Love & War," "Grapevine," "Pond Lily," "Snow Drop," "Tulip & Sunflower," "Wild Rose," "Bird & Nest," as well as a great many geometric, arabesque and vine designs. Tea sets, syrup jugs, mustard pots, and other tablewares were also made in Parian. This ware was also made in blue and white. The blue was painted on afterwards at most potteries but at Bennington it was mixed with the slip and baked.

Parian vases and fancy articles were not only molded with a design, but modeled decoration such as grapes, flowers, and rustic handles were added. Tall vases had portrait panels with grape and leaf decoration. There were also vases with panelled leaf designs and rare fancy cottage vases with panels of figures and applied molded handles of wheat, grapes or convolvulus. The "Ear of Corn" vase was a strictly American design and was made in various sizes. There were also vases

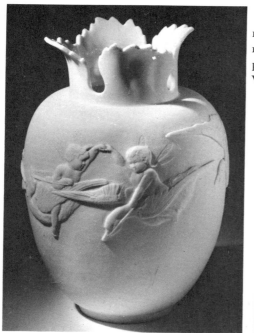

LEFT. Parian vase. Ceramic Art Company, Trenton, New Jersey, 1891. BELOW, LEFT. Parian pitcher, "Tulip and Sunflower." RIGHT. "Cascade" pattern, porcelain. Both pitchers made at U.S. Pottery, Bennington, Vermont. (*Bennington Museum*)

Parian vases with applied grape decoration. Hand, holding vase with molded fern design. (*Bennington Museum*)

with standing Victorian figures of a man or woman, cherub or small animal.

Perhaps the most popular vases with the collector today are the typically Victorian Hand vases. The hand is usually upright with a ruffled cuff and the vase a flower, leaf or shell form. These were made in several sizes. There were also vases in the form of flowers such as crocus or calla lilies and vases in the form of several kinds of shells. Another decorative Parian piece was the cologne bottle. These were made in rounded and square vase forms with molded panelled and fluted designs, and applied flowers and grapes. Covered jars and trinket boxes were also made in great quantities. These were made with molded decoration and applied flowers, grapes or molded cherubs, draped figures, dogs, ducks or lambs. The trinket box with the sleeping cherub is one of the most interesting.

There were also Parian busts and statuettes. Statuettes included the rare "Autumn," the "Greek Slave," after the sculptor Hiram Powers, and figures reminiscent of English Staffordshire cottage statues. There were also typically sentimental figures of children including the

ABOVE AND BELOW. Parian trinket boxes with molded and applied decoration. (*The Metropolitan Museum of Art*)

"Praying Child," the "Tight Shoe," and "Red Riding Hood." The rare poodle carrying a basket was made in several sizes. Baskets and jewelry with applied flowers are also rare. For the collector of miniatures there were small vases, pitchers and toy tea sets. These, however, are rare.

The collector of American Parian Ware will want to own *Bennington Pottery and Porcelain* by Richard Carter Barret. Not only is it a guide to Bennington wares, but its photographs are a guide to types of Victorian pottery and porcelain produced in America in the last half of the nineteenth century and it gives a picture of the forms and designs which dominated the arts of the Victorian Age. How do you identify Parian? By its lack of glaze, by its form, and by its design. Few pieces are marked and it is almost impossible to differentiate between the American and English Parian.

Majolica

MAJOLICA was one of the most popular wares of Victorian times and it is also popular with collectors today. The majolica of the nineteenth century is a crude earthenware with molded relief designs. It is decorated with brilliant and often gaudy color by applying colors mixed with the glaze, green being a favorite. It was Minton in England who really started the craze for Victorian majolica when they exhibited their majolica at the London Exhibition in 1851 and in Paris in 1853. American potteries were quick to imitate the ware. They copied the earlier cauliflower and pineapple teapots and molded leaf plates of Wedgwood, but they also copied the jardinières and plates with fans, kittens and wickerwork made by Minton. Majolica, as no other ceramic, reflected the ornate, gaudy, bad taste of the last half of the nineteenth century.

Typical majolica designs included rustic patterns of basketry and wooden-bound buckets. There were bamboo, corn, pineapple, and cauliflower tea and coffee pots with handles of rustic tree branches or rose stems with thorns. Popular patterns included the wild rose, lily pad and herons, cattails and cabbage leaves, begonia and fern leaves, all of which were molded on plates. There were also plates with raised designs of strawberries and grapes, molded fish, and shells. Syrup jugs, cuspidors, jardinières, mugs, covered boxes, cake baskets and celery vases, sardine boxes, butter dishes with cow finials and beehive honey dishes were among the many articles made. Majolica tea services and a large variety of ornamental pitchers, vases, compotes, centerpieces, and sardine boxes with fish finials on their covers were made by Carr and Morrison in New York City.

The majolica made by E. & W. Bennett of Baltimore includes the famous large fish pitcher with a light blue glaze and molded design of fish, lobsters and shells. Vases with grapevine designs and lizard handles, large pitchers, coffee pots and other pieces with blue, brown and olive mottled glazes, and large jardinières set on griffon legs were also made at this pottery. In 1850 they produced a majolica bust of George

ABOVE. Etruscan majolica platter, Sea Shell pattern. BELOW. Leaf dish, Griffin Smith & Hill, Phoenixville, Pa., 1881–1892. (*The Henry Ford Museum*)

Washington. These pieces were usually marked "E. & W. Bennett/ Canton Avenue/Baltimore, Md." Griffen, Smith & Hill of Phoenixville, Pennsylvania, became widely known for their Etruscan majolica. Compotes with dolphin supports, flower, shell, and jewel cups, as well as the popular design of coral and seashells in delicate pinks, gray and green, and leaf and fern designs were made at this pottery. A catalogue of the pottery shows several types of leaf dishes which were produced in autumn colors, plates with wicker borders, and fluted borders with molded flowers. A wicker vase has a molded spray of oak leaves and a leaf tray has sections to hold a sugar and creamer. The well-known seaweed pattern was available in many different shapes including a tea set, plates, and a berry bowl. Etruscan majolica is light in weight and thin compared to other majolica. The mark was an impressed monogram "G.S.H." sometimes surrounded by a band with the words "Etruscan Majolica." The monogram alone is also used and sometimes "Etruscan Majolica" impressed in a horizontal line.

The Chesapeake Pottery in Baltimore made majolica which is called Clifton Ware and marked "Clifton Decor B" on crossed crescents with the monogram "D.F.H." in the center. Other makers of American majolica include Odell & Booth at Tarrytown, New York; the Hampshire Pottery at Keene, N.H.;

Majolica pitcher, Morley & Co., Wellsville, Ohio, 1879–1885. (*The Brooklyn Museum*) and the Faience Manufacturing Company at Greenpoint, L.I. The majolica of the latter company has no impressed pattern, but is dipped in colored glazes and has a streaked or marbled appearance. Majolica was also made at Evansville, Indiana; by Morley & Co., Wellsville, Ohio, in 1879; and at the Arsenal Pottery in Trenton, New Jersey. Majolica toby jugs from the Arsenal Pottery were exhibited at the Chicago Fair in 1893.

There is a great quantity of majolica on the market today and it is cheap. Even the majolica stand with its matching jardinière, a real Victorian horror, is again offered to the public. However, the majority of the pieces in the shops today are of English make. American-made majolica if marked, and especially the lovely seaweed pattern of Etruscan majolica, is much higher in price and harder to find.

Belleek

ONE of the most unique Victorian ceramics was the thin iridescent porcelain called Belleek. It was first made in Belleek, Ireland, and was manufactured in America by Ott and Brewer at the Etruria Pottery in Trenton, New Jersey, in the 1880's, under the direction of William Bromley Sr. from the Belleek factory in Ireland. Belleek porcelain has a translucent pearly glaze, and is almost as thin as paper. It was made in both useful and ornamental wares, many in shell and flower forms with delicate fluted surfaces with crimpled edges on bowls and vases. The larger vases are simpler in outline, but often have pierced necks, handles and feet, and elaborate covers. Some are decorated in enamels and gold. Ott & Brewer Belleek is usually decorated in delicate blue, pink, and green, combined with gold and sometimes silver. The mark on Ott & Brewer Belleek is a crown pierced by a sword with Belleek above and "O&B" below. This is printed in red on top of the glaze. Another mark was a crescent with "Trenton" and "O&B" with "Belleek" above and "N.J." below. This was printed in red or brown over the glaze.

William Bromley also supervised the making of Belleek at the Willets Manufacturing Company. Many of Willets' forms were reproductions of the shell and coral forms of Irish Belleek, but some were decorated with delicate floral Dresden patterns. Small picture frames with molded flowers and porcelain clock cases were also made. One of the most beautiful pieces was the shell and cupid jug. This piece was also made at Ott & Brewer. The mark on Willets Belleek is a snake coiled to form a "W" with "Belleek" above and "Willets" below. It is printed in red on top of the glaze. In 1889 the Ceramic Art Company was founded by Jonathan Coxon Sr. and Walter S. Lenox, who had learned the process of manufacturing Belleek when employed at Ott & Brewer. In addition to table pieces such as the lily-shaped "Engagement" cup and saucer, they made vases with carved designs and a delicate swan dish. The mark on their Belleek is a graceful "C.A.C." within a circle, with an artist's palette and brushes above at the left, and the word "Belleek" printed in red below this stamp over the glaze. The Belleek swan dish is still made by Lenox. Other companies in New Jersey that manufactured Belleek were the American Art China Works of Rittenhouse, Evans & Co.; and Morris and Willmore.

Belleek dessert set, Ott & Brewer, Trenton, New Jersey, c. 1880. (*The Newark Museum*)

Lotus ware bowl. Knowles, Taylor & Knowles, Co. East Liverpool, Ohio, 1891–1898.

Oval ribbed dish, Willets Manufacturing Co., Trenton, New Jersey, c. 1890.

Cups and saucers, Belleek porcelain, Ott and Brewer, c. 1882–1894. (*The Henry Ford Museum*)

The latter marked their Belleek with a shield enclosing the interlaced letters "MW" with "Belleek" above and "Trenton, N.J." below. A small quantity of Belleek was also made by E. & W. Bennett and Belleek was also made at Bennington.

A considerable amount of Belleek china was made at Knowles, Taylor and Knowles in East Liverpool, Ohio, in the 1880's. Later they developed a similar ware known as "Lotus Ware." This was decorated in dainty colors and had openwork effects and raised gold borders in Renaissance style. The shapes were often oriental, but the decoration favored was cupids and butterflies. Each piece was an individual design. "Lotus Ware" was probably the finest porcelain made in America. The mark was "Knowles, Taylor and Knowles" in a circle surrounding a star and crescent and "Lotus Ware" beneath the circle. Another mark on their art ware was the initials of the company above the word "China." Lotus Ware is very expensive and is sought by museums, so there is little for the collector. The Belleek of the New Jersey potteries is available and the Lenox swans, salts and other

Belleek cup and saucer, Mercer Pottery Co., Trenton, New Jersey, c. 1876. (*The Brooklyn Museum*)

Belleek pitcher made by Walter Scott Lenox, 1887. This cupid design was also available for amateur hand-painters at Willets Manufacturing Company. (*The Newark Museum*)

BELOW LEFT. Lotus ware vase. Knowles, Taylor & Knowles. (*The Brooklyn Museum*) RIGHT. Lotus ware vase with hand-painted decoration. (*The Henry Ford Museum*)

delicate pieces are still being made as is Irish Belleek with green sham-rock designs. Belleek baskets with roses on the rim are also still being made. Since both the Irish Belleek factory and Lenox continue making Belleek, this new Belleek is available, but pieces of old Belleek are diffi-cult to find.

Art Pottery

ANOTHER phase of ceramics which developed in the Eighties was that made by the artist-potter who created original designs and returned to hand production. Through the influence of William Morris, Lewis Day and Walter Crane in England new forms and new methods were intro-duced. The most famous American pottery that was an outgrowth of this movement was the Rookwood Pottery in Cincinnati. The interest started in a class of china painters and developed mainly through the unique artistry of M. Louise McLaughlin who was not only a china painter but also a ceramist. Her famous Losanti Ware, a hard-paste porcelain, was exhibited in Paris at the Exposition Universelle in 1879 and a short time afterwards she organized the Pottery Club of Cincinnati. A wealthy and influential member of this club, Mrs. Maria Longworth Nichols (Storer), founded her own pottery and named it Rookwood. The first kiln was fired in 1880. In the beginning, the pottery specialized in breakfast and dinner services and other useful articles in cream color or underglazed printed decoration of birds, fish and animal subjects. These printed wares were gradually superseded by more artistic forms in the Japanese manner and original work took the place of copying. The shape of the vases and the naturalistic motifs, however, are distinctly oriental in feeling. The vases were modeled on a potter's wheel, then the unbaked piece was painted with colored slip, then fired. The vase was then decorated, dipped and fired again.

There are several types of Rookwood which are distinguished by their color and glaze. The regular or standard ware has an orange and green glaze of which the corn design mug is an example. The mahogany was a red and brown glaze. The sea green glaze was used with designs of fish while the Iris glaze in soft blues and greens with suggestions of pink and green was used on Poppy, Rose, and Iris vases. There was also a mat glaze without gloss and the beauty of this type is in its texture. However, the Tiger's eye and gold stone, in which gold glistens through the dark glaze, is the highest achievement of the Rookwood pottery. According to Barber, the distinguishing feature of all of the varieties of Rookwood is the tinting and blending of the grounds beneath the heavy transparent colored glazes, which produces the effect of rich tones of black, yellow, red, olive, green, brown, and amber of great brilliancy, mellowness, depth, and strength.

The designs on Rookwood vases include White Lilac, Water Lilies, Goldenrod, Trailing Arbutus, Snowberry (orange), Maple, Spanish Chestnut, Chrysanthemum, Primula (red), Lily of the Valley, Poppies, Clover, Orchids, White Roses, Thistles, Pine Cone and Mushrooms. There were also designs with fish, geese, sea gulls, grasshoppers, eagles, dragon, and white storks. The Rookwood decorations are under the glaze. A 1904 catalogue illustrates many vases in color and quotes prices. The

Rockwood pottery. Dark vases mahogany glaze. Center vase chrysanthemum pattern. (*Dr. and Mrs. Robert Koch*)

Group of Rookwood pottery vases. LOWER CENTER. Dogwood design. RIGHT. Lily leaves. (*Dr. and Mrs. Robert Koch*)

Iris glaze designs of Poppy, Rose, Orchid and Iris were priced at $100.00 each, while the White Storks, Dragon and Geese designs were $100.00 to $250.00, according to size. Lamps with Tiffany glass shades were priced at $100.00. However, no two pieces were alike. Early designers besides Mrs. Maria Longworth Nichols (Storer) were E. P. Cranch, William McDonald, Matt A. Daly, Albert R. Valentien, Artus Van Briggle and Kataro Shirayamadani. An eagle vase decorated by A. R. Valentien and a dragon vase by Shirayamadani are among the early pieces and are in the Philadelphia Museum of Art. The Hollyhock design is also by Valentien. An Indian head design is by Van Briggle and a Standing Indian is by Grace Young. All Rookwood vases are marked, dated, and numbered for shape; lettered for size and color, and monogrammed by the decorator. The marks are as follows: 1880–82—"Rookwood Pottery Ohio" painted under the glaze. Also a rare "Rooks & Kiln" mark. 1882–86—"Rookwood" and year in rectangle—Impressed. 1886 —"R.P." monogram with symbol for date. 1887—"R P" with one flame. One flame is added each year. This mark is still in use and a limited amount of the pottery is still being made. Rookwood Pottery is not an antique, but it will soon be, and such is the beauty of design and workmanship that it is well worth collecting. Since it was never produced in great quantities and since every piece is unique and signed, its value is bound to increase. Indeed, it was never cheap and continues expensive today.

Other art potteries of the nineteenth century which produced similar wares were the Newcomb Art Pottery at Biloxi, Mississippi; the Weller Pottery in Zanesville, Ohio; the Pauline Pottery of Edgerton, Wisconsin; and the Lonhuda Pottery Co. in Steubenville, Ohio. Among the decorators of Lonhuda Pottery was Miss Laura A. Fry of Cincinnati. The ware was marked "Lonhuda" with the monogram of the company and sometimes an impressed Indian head.

The Dedham Pottery which started as the Chelsea Ceramic Art Works, founded by Alexander Robertson in 1866, was another art

Dedham pottery plate, Crab design—crackle glaze. Stamped on bottom in blue square enclosing rabbit below, Dedham/Pottery.
(*The Henry Ford Museum*)

pottery. Through the years they made a variety of wares from reproductions of Greek vases and sculptured vases and plaques with illustrations of La Fontaine's Fables to experiments with Chinese sang de boeuf. This latter ware was the most successful, but the product that finally caught the response of the public was the gray crackle ware which was made after the works were moved to Dedham in 1896 where the business was carried on by Hugh Robertson. Dedham Ware has a porcelain body of hard fine quality with a soft grey crackle which is decorated with patterns of in-glaze blue. It is made completely by hand so that the pieces are often uneven. It is fired at a heat of 2,000 to 2,500 which gives it a softness of line and quality of color and makes the delicate tracery of the crackle which is suggestive of Chinese and Japanese pottery. At first the forms included vases and fruit and salad plates, but as the demand grew more pieces were added. The designs are conventionalized and look like stencils. Patterns include flowers such as hawthorn, fleur-de-lis, thistle, azalea, clover, horse chestnut, iris, and water lilies. Animals include rabbits, swan, owls, lion, turkey, ducks, turtles, elephant and polar bear. Other patterns were lobster, crab, dolphin, butterflies and a rare Birds in Orange Tree. These patterns were made in tableware including plates and tea sets. They also made flower holders, knife rests, coasters, boots and a bunny paperweight. Several well-known artists as well as students from the Art Museum School made the designs. The most popular pattern is the rabbit. The elephant is one of the rarest patterns. The marks changed every few years. The familiar mark was a rabbit with the words Dedham Pottery above.

Tea cup and saucer, Rabbit pattern. Stamped Dedham/Pottery with rabbit. (*The Henry Ford Museum*)

Another art pottery was made by Grueby Faience Company which was established in Boston in 1897. The pottery was a hard semi-porcelain, smooth and satiny, and had an opaque, lusterless enamel mat glaze. The colors were green, yellow and blue-purple, the decoration in low relief, Egyptian-inspired in plant forms of a slender plantain leaf and bud on a long stem. These were modeled by women artists who signed their monograms in addition to the impressed mark of the pottery which was "Grueby;" "Grueby Pottery, Boston, U.S.A.;" or "Grueby, Boston, Mass." This pottery was sold at Tiffany and Tiffany glass shades were first fitted on Grueby Pottery lamps. When the Grueby works closed Tiffany began to make his own pottery lamps.

Tiles

THE present-day destruction of many old nineteenth century mansions brings to the antique market various articles used in the decoration of these houses such as ironwork, carved mantelpieces, newel posts and stairways, and old tiles used on floorways, wainscoting and around fireplaces. Decorators have been collecting old ironwork and carved marble mantels, and museums are collecting architectural columns, figures and decorative panels, but old tiles have generally been neglected. The majority of the tiles were made commercially and the shiny majolica ones particularly are looked upon with scorn, but as our collecting outlook gradually broadens to take in the whole of the nineteenth century, no item, however small or unimportant, should be neglected.

Tiles were a popular type of decoration in the late nineteenth century. It was the influence of Eastlake and the exhibits of tiles at the Centennial that brought the production and use of tiles to the fore in both commercial and household decoration in America. Eastlake recommended the use of tiles not only around the fireplace and mantel, but as wainscoting and decorative insets on furniture. Minton produced a set of fireplace tiles with woodland plants and also furnished blank tiles for decorators in the 1880's. The *Art Amateur* illustrated several complete sets of fireplace tiles with designs of flowers springing from vases and gave complete directions for their painting.

The painting of single tiles was usually the first lesson in china painting for amateurs. In books of handiwork for ladies many uses for hand-painted tiles were suggested, including framing tiles to hang or use as teapot rests, tile screens, and fireplace tiles. In the last chapter of *Pottery and Porcelain of the United States* (1893 edition), Barber writes about tiles for decorative effect and he suggests framing art tiles and illustrates tiles with elaborately carved frames. He also suggests attaching tiles to the woodwork of the mantel, vertical tiles on each side and a horizontal tile across the top.

There were many well-known artists and potters who made tiles. In 1877 the famous Tile Club was organized by a group of New York artists. They met at each other's studios for food and recreation, but they also each decorated a tile. The tiles were cream-colored glazed Spanish tiles, eight inches square, and the decoration was usually in "Victorian blue" monochrome. A tile by Winslow Homer, one of the members, is still in existence. Tiles were also made by several of the so-called art potteries. E. P. Cranch decorated several sets of mantel tiles for Rookwood. One set illustrated the ballad of Isaac Abbott and another that of Giles Scroggins' Ghost. Rookwood also made other decorative tiles with floral decoration in the oriental manner. Tiles were also made of Dedham Pottery. Tiffany made glass tiles and used them for fireplace decoration. None of these tiles was made commercially and up into the 1880's the interest in tiles was mainly among artists.

However, the Low Art Tile Works in Chelsea, Mass. had been making tiles since 1877 and in 1883 under the title of J.G. & J.F. Low they produced tiles commercially for mantel facings, panels and stoves. The talented artist Arthur Osborne originated the designs which included heads, mythological subjects and animal, bird, and floral studies. They also made calendar tiles and tiles for place cards for the Papyrus Club in Boston, and the Decennial Dinner of the Lotus Club in New York. These latter were 4 inch tiles with a green glaze and a relief design of an Egyptian figure and a vase of conventional lotus flowers. In 1884

Low put out a catalogue of their tiles. The designs included flowers, leaves, geometric designs and decorative heads showing Egyptian, Greek and Japanese influence. The separate tiles of the designs were made to fit together to use in plaques, panels or fireplace facings. Flower designs included graceful designs of Japanese quince, apple blossoms, daisies, buttercups, mistletoe and wild roses. There were also designs of birds and bamboo, birds and berries, and marguerites and butterflies. Renaissance heads, dolphins and Greek vases, horses and chariots were classical designs. There was also a pastoral plaque of Pan with pipes, and a series of Seasons with winged cherub and inscriptions. One panel had the words "Tempus Fugit" and a design of cherubs while another pattern was labeled "The Revel." These designs were pressed in the clay, but in the high-relief tiles the undercutting was done by hand after the design had been stamped in the press. In *Century Magazine,* November, 1886, J.G. & J.F. Low advertised a book *Plastic Sketches* which contained a series of 47 bas relief designs. The book was satin covered and sold for $7.50. They also offered a free colored print of Low's Art Tile Stove.

Many commercial tile companies also made art tiles and almost every tile company employed an artist to make their designs. Companies producing encaustic or inlaid floor tiles also made relief tiles. Among these companies were the American Encaustic Tiling Co. of Zanesville, Ohio, who employed the modeler Herman Müller. His designs included pictures and portraits in relief, and panels of women and children in landscape surroundings. Also among his designs was a panel of "Swallows." When the company's enlarged works were dedicated in 1892, 15,000 souvenir tiles were given away. Today these tiles would be collector's items. The United States Encaustic Tile Company in Indianapolis, Indiana, also produced decorative tiles including a series of three mantel tiles, Dawn, Midday and Twilight.

Isaac Broome, well-known for his modeling at several New Jersey potteries, was also a modeler and designer at the Providential Tile Works, the Trent Tile Company in New Jersey, and the Beaver Falls Art Tile Company in Pennsylvania. His tiles included a head of Sappho and a series of panels representing Music, Poetry and Painting. He also did a panel of passion flowers, and portrait heads including one of Washington. The designer at the Cambridge Art Tile Company in Covington, Kentucky, was Ferdinand Mersman, formerly of the Rookwood Pottery.

The well-known artist, Charles Volkmar, was also interested in tile work as well as pottery, and in 1888 was a partner in the Menlo Park Ceramic Company and later the Volkmar Ceramic Company. He made tiles in Romanesque style for the decoration of buildings and private homes. These were made in great quantities, and if found today they are worth collecting for their excellent design and beautiful coloring of old ivory, pale blue and light maroon. Some tiles were also finished in old ivory and gold. There were also tile portraits of such well-known persons as President Benjamin Harrison, Grover Cleveland, and other celebrities, made at the C. Pardee Works in Perth Amboy, N.J. As well as being hand-painted, inlaid and decorated with relief patterns tiles were also printed. Many of these printed tiles were made late in the century as souvenirs of such places as Niagara Falls, Plymouth Rock, and Salem and were printed with local scenes.

BELOW. White earthenware tile with pink glaze showing cupids with musical instruments. Providential Tile Works, Trenton, New Jersey, c. 1895. RIGHT TOP. Tile, olive-green glaze, head of U. S. Grant, Trent Tile Works, c. 1885. BOTTOM. Tile, head of man with beard. J. & J. G. Low Tile Works, 1887–1888. (*The Brooklyn Museum*)

Crazy quilt of pieced blocks with appliqués of animals and figures. Made by member of the Haskins family, Granville, Vermont, c. 1875. (Shelburne Museum)

VII. LADIES' HANDIWORK

THE Victorian lady was continually busy with "art recreations," the name given to all sorts of Victorian fancywork. Every article of the household was considered worthy of decoration with gilt, paint, or needlework. Shell work, feather work, moss and wax work, and even taxidermy occupied the leisure of the Victorian lady. There were general books on handiwork including Mrs. Pullan's *Lady's Manual of Fancy Work; Ladies' Handiwork of Fancy and Ornamental Work* by Florence Hartley; *Art Recreations* by Levina Urbino; and *Woman's Handiwork in Modern Homes* by Constance Cary Harrison. There were also directions and patterns in the issues of *Godey's Lady's Book*, and there were separate books devoted to each type of handiwork. Mrs. Urbino lists some of the types of handiwork in *Art Recreations*. Included is shellwork, conework, potichomania, transparencies, leaf impressions, wax work, leather work, moss work, feather work, hair work, and taxidermy. Mrs. Pullan lists the following articles of handiwork as "suitable for presents": antimacassars, bags, book marks, suspenders, bracelets of crochet or bead work, cigar cases embroidered or crocheted, cushions, doilies, foot muffs, lambrequins, music cases, ottomans, and foot stools of Berlin Work, transparent illuminated painting or enamelling on glass; decorated

249

chessboards, screens, panels for doors or furniture. Indeed, the aim seemed to be to leave no article of domestic use undecorated.

Needlework

TODAY quantities of these ornamental articles have been taken out of the attic and are popular with present-day collectors and museums. Fine needlework has been an occupation of women for many centuries. Until the 19th century worsted work was an aristocratic pastime. The designs were conventionalized forms and the results depended upon the individual's artistic ability. When this work was taken up by a growing number of people, many without taste, patterns had to be devised as aids, and these were produced by a Berlin print seller. The patterns were at first engraved and hand-painted on paper, later they were stamped in color on canvas. The resulting work done in wool stitches was called Berlin Work. The patterns included flowers, fruit, parrots, deer, horses, leopards, dogs, cats, and other animals. The favorite Victorian dogs—the spaniel, Newfoundland, pug, and greyhound and the tabby cat were motifs for cushions and footstools.

Berlin Work carpet bag.
(*Museum of the City of New York*)

Berlin Work. Cat with border of grape leaves. (*The Index of American Design*)

In addition to the articles of household usage personal articles such as railroad bags, tobacco bags, glass cases, suspenders, and pincushions were made. Book marks and mottoes were also made in great quantities. Large mottoes framed in rustic walnut frames hung in every household. The inscriptions read: "Welcome," "Home Sweet Home," "What is Home without Mother;" "The Old Oaken Bucket;" "Simply to Thy Cross I Cling;" "Peace Be Unto You," and other such religious and homey sentiments.

One of the most interesting branches of this handiwork was the needlework picture. Copies of landscape, Biblical scenes and portraits as well as sentimental pictures of children and animals were popular subjects in Berlin wool work pictures of the mid-nineteenth century. Favorite pictures included "Mary Queen of Scots," "Washington Crossing the Delaware," "Scottish Chieftain," "The Sicilian Maid," "Byron at the Seashore," "Laertes and Ophelia," and portraits of Benjamin Franklin, Queen Victoria, George Washington and Napoleon.

LEFT. Beaded cushion with eagle and flags, c. 1870. (*The Index of American Design*) RIGHT. Beaded wall pocket, shoe shape. (*The Henry Ford Museum*)

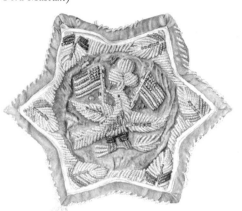

Wool embroidery on hair cloth. Walnut frame with gilt liner, 1875-1900. (*The Henry Ford Museum*)

Godey's, Peterson's, and Graham's magazines also illustrated patterns for beadwork wall pockets, watch cases, needle books, pen wipers, and pincushions. A piece of flannel was cut in the desired shape and the design cut in paper. The beads were strung and then sewed onto the paper pattern. Then this was sewed to the flannel. Designs included a flower spray, a leaf or a bird. Similar beadwork articles were made by the Tuscarora Indians and sold as souvenirs at Niagara Falls in the 1890's. The Indian work is usually backed with shiny cotton cambric, while the homemade articles utilized left-over materials from the scrap bag. Also, since Godey's and other magazines were printing directions in 1859, the ladies' work was older than that made by the Indians. A close examination and comparison would also show a difference in the quality of the beads. Other ladies made Berlin beadwork lambrequins, cushions and pincushions embroidered with chenille and pearls.

Lambrequins and antimacassars were also made of knotted twine called macramé, as well as in crochet or crazy-quilt work. Embroidered draperies and portières for doorways were made of intricate stitchery

Needlework scene New York from Weehawken, by Ann Stebbins, age 10, 1830–40. (*Collection of author*)

and elaborate floral designs. Patterns for these were illustrated in the *Art Amateur*, and exhibitions included a class of this type of needlework. Women also did a great deal of ecclesiastical needlework. Silk and gold thread geometrical and floral symbols were embroidered on the Burse and Veil, the Lectern hanging, and the minister's stole.

Shell, Feather and Wax Work

SHELL work was another fashionable occupation. The shells could be picked up at the seashore, or purchased at a store with directions for their use. Shell work bouquets, some of them charming, were made to

White feather wreath on black velvet ground. Walnut frame with gilt liner, 1850–1875. (*The Henry Ford Museum*)

fit into ornamental vases and set under glass domes for mantel garnitures. Others were made into pictures and framed. Feathers, cut into the shapes of flower petals and leaves, painted or dyed, were also made into bouquets and wreaths. Similar arrangements were made of beadwork, spun glass, and even mosses, dried leaves, pine cones, rice, beans and seeds. Small trinket boxes of shell were made in many whimsical forms. These were fastened to a cardboard foundation with plaster of Paris. These shell miniatures include such forms as slippers, cottages, tiny bureaus, boxes, and stars. There were also shell frames for pictures and clocks, and shell work animals.

In 1850 wax work, which had been popular in the eighteenth century, was revived, but instead of portraits and figures, arrangements

Wreath of seeds. Pine frame covered with gesso. 1865–1885. (*The Henry Ford Museum*)

of wax flowers and fruits were made. The *Handbook for Modelling Wax Flowers* furnished patterns and directions for modelling the fruit and flowers. Molds were available for larger pieces such as animals and birds. The fruit was usually arranged in a plaster of Paris basket and framed or set under a glass dome. Favorite flowers for wreaths or vases were orange blossoms, passion flowers, lilies, convolvulus, and fuchsias. In the Great Exhibition of 1851 a whole section was devoted to wax flowers which were considered not merely a craft but an important art form.

Painting on Various Materials

FLOWER painting on paper, canvas or silk was another popular recreation. It was taught in the schools and became a necessary accomplishment of every young lady of standing. Those who could not draw were taught with theorems or stencils. Painting on silk and velvet by means of stencils began early in the nineteenth century. It was applied to

Hand-painted silk fan. Tiffany & Co., 1873. (*The Newark Museum*)

velvet pictures, fire screens, chair cushions, and bell pulls. Painting was also done on linen, tapestry, canvas and mirrors. Later, flowers were painted on satin fans and fan painting became popular in the 1880's. Designs and directions for silk fan painting appeared in the *Art Amateur* in 1887 and 1889. Fans were painted on satin, silk, paper and vellum.

TOP. Painting on velvet, c. 1840. (*The Index of American Design*) BOTTOM. Landscape with woman. Painting on velvet, c. 1840. (*The New-York Historical Society*)

Basket of fruit. Painting or stencil on velvet, c. 1840. (*The New-York Historical Society*)

Black satin was painted in grisaille or monochrome in black, grey, and white. Designs included garlands of roses, violets, convolvulus, cyclamen, orange blossoms, jasmine and lilac. Pastoral scenes from Watteau, temple ruins, cupids and amorini from Boucher were also popular, as were oriental-inspired designs of birds, birds' nests, flowers and butterflies. Flowers were also painted on glass and the background filled in with opaque paint and crushed tin foil. These are collected as primitive

Towel-rack with hand-painted wild roses on tin, c. 1880. (*The Henry Ford Museum*)

paintings as are the paintings on velvet. Many of the paintings on velvet and plush were made in the 1880's when women were also painting plush picture frames. They also painted scraps of pieced work for crazy quilts. Hand-painted flowers also decorated black lacquer plaques, wall pockets, letter racks, and card trays.

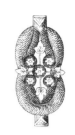

Hair Work

MEMORIAL rings and medallions were made by artists and jewellers of the eighteenth century, but hair work for the amateur did not become the fashion until the mid-nineteenth century. In 1840, *The Jeweller's Book of Patterns in Hairwork* was published in London and in 1859 Godey's *Lady's Book* printed directions for hair work. In 1864 *Peterson's Magazine* included more instructions and the craze for hair work was launched and became fashionable until the end of the century. Bracelets, earrings, necklaces, pins, cuff links and shirt studs were made at home and taken to a jeweller for mounting. The interest in hair work began as an attempt to preserve a sentimental treasure. Brooches and lockets and woven chains contained the hair of a departed relative or friend and were worn as a sentimental memento or as mourning jewelry. Other articles were made by braiding and interlacing hair over hollow forms which included hearts, crosses, flowers, fruit and birds. Small charms for bracelets included fish, bird cages, horseshoes, chairs, teapots and other trinkets similar to those worn on charm bracelets today. Hair wreaths, bouquets and pictures were also made and framed to hang on the wall and hair was used in embroidery work. There were hair albums containing locks of hair of relatives and friends, and hair genealogical family trees set under glass domes were high fashion in the 1860's and 1870's.

Memorials of a tombstone, weeping willow and a mourning figure had been popular since the early nineteenth century and these continued to be painted, embroidered or cut in paper until the end of the century.

Hairwork jewelry from catalogue of A. Bernhard & Co., 1870.

Wood Carving and Fretwork

WOOD carving, which has been neglected by both writers and collectors of Victorian antiques, was considered one of the important art recreations in the last half of the nineteenth century. There were manuals of wood carving and articles giving patterns and instructions ran in several magazines including the *Art Amateur* in the 1880's and 1890's. The important promoters of wood carving were Charles G. Leland, Director of the Public Industrial Art School in Philadelphia, and author of *A Manual of Wood Carving*, and Benn Pitman of the Cincinnati School of Design. William H. Fry also conducted a carving school in Cincinnati. While the average wood worker carved small boxes, trays, plaques, and wall brackets, the pupils of Benn Pitman worked on more ambitious projects. There were 100 women in the first wood carving class organized by Benn Pitman in 1873 and among the articles carved were cabinets, chairs, church lecterns, screens, tables, doors and mantels.

Few of the smaller objects can be identified today but there are examples of mantels preserved in several houses in Cincinnati, chairs and church benches, and Benn Pitman's own house, which includes carved stairways, doors, mantels and a bed, is also preserved. Pitman's class of women, together with Mr. Fry, carved the panels of the organ in the Cincinnati Music Hall. They also carved an oak leaf frame for the portrait of Mrs. Hayes which once hung in the White House.

With a little search smaller items of wood carving such as flowers or portrait plaques, frames, wall brackets, boxes, trays, platters, bread trays, bellows, knife handles, and tankards should be found, especially in such cities as Cincinnati and Philadelphia where schools of wood carving were known to exist. The woods used included oak, walnut, cherry, maple, ash, white holly, and ebony. Designs for plaques included Spring, Summer, Autumn and Winter, portraits of women in peasant dress, animals such as birds, rabbits, dogs, cats and deer, and the favorite

Fretwork patterns for shelves and a hanging cabinet by A. H. Pomeroy, Hartford, Connecticut. (*The Century Magazine*, 1884)

Victorian flowers, wild rose, passion flowers, marigold, lilies, convolvulus and horse chestnut, grapes, oak and acanthus leaves. A favorite motif for the carved wall bracket was a stag's head with antlers, a dog's head, or dead game. Picture frames had a design of carved acanthus, ivy or oak leaves.

Fretwork, Sorrento carvings, or jigsaw work, was closely allied to wood carving and for those with less talent and perseverance, it presented an easier occupation. *Fret Cutting and Perforated Carving* by W. Bemrose Jr., was published in 1869. It gave patterns and directions for such articles as book rests, brackets, table mats, mirrors, card baskets, letter racks, envelope boxes, picture and mirror frames, table easels, hanging bookshelves, cupboards, corner brackets, bread platters, and finger plates for doors. Designs of ivy and oak leaves were combined with fretwork which was cut out with a small scroll saw. Sometimes the fretwork wall pockets and towel racks had panels of Berlin work em-

Designs for carved wood wall pocket and mirror frame by Benn Pitman. (*The Art Amateur,* 1888)

broidery. Fretwork was demonstrated in a booth at the Centennial and later commercial companies furnished designs. A. H. Pomeroy of Hartford, Connecticut, put out a catalogue of designs including a "Curfew" bracket showing a cut-out design of a woman ringing a bell, a card receiver with heron and cattail design, a grape design, and a shelf design of a farm scene with horses and chickens. A wall cabinet had an oriental design. Among the 500 designs offered for $2.00 by Adams & Bishop of New York was a cut-out portrait of President Garfield. Other designs included leaves, scrolls, birds, flowers, and deer.

Charles G. Leland in articles in the *Art Journal* of 1886–1887 mentions other home arts such as gesso painting, shell and horn cutting on nautilus and oyster shells, mosaic powder-work, and pyrography or wood-roasting. Some of these articles are to be found in shops today. Although they are in bad taste, they are bought by decorators who use them to add a bizarre note to a room. They are collected by museums as part of the picture of another age. You, too, can collect them for the same reasons. They are found in second-hand shops, flea markets, and at country auctions.

Pieced, Appliqué and Crazy Quilts

QUILTING is centuries old. In Europe it thrived as a folk art among the peasants and country folk, but it also flourished in the castle as well as the cottage. Materials for quilts varied in different countries. In France, Italy and Spain silks, damasks, brocades, and velvets were used, while in England and the Low Countries the early quilts were of hand-woven linen or East India chintz. Quilting reached its height of popularity in Britain and the Low Countries in the seventeenth century when the English, Dutch, Swedes and French started their migrations to America. Here the art of quilting changed, acquired new vigor, and adjusted to the needs of the pioneer settlers. However, the national characteristics of each group remained imprinted on their quilts and today the quilts of New England differ from those of the Pennsylvania Germans or the Southern Mountaineers.

American quilts are a record of American life. The early Crazy Quilts depict the hardships of pioneer America and the struggle of the wives of early settlers. We get a picture of the social life in the simple recreation of the quilting bee. The materials of the quilts show us the fabrics and patterns of the clothing and the development of the American textile industry, beginning with the homespuns of the Colonies and later the cotton products of the mills in the South and in New England. Early quilts show the Far Eastern-inspired printed floral patterns of England or the French Toile de Jouy and later the small calico sprig designs of American manufacture. Above all else the quilt was a family record. There was a bit of grandmother's wedding dress, a piece of the dress Aunt Julia wore when crossing the plains, the printed cotton that

Appliqué coverlet showing blocks of various patterns. Mid-nineteenth century. (*The Metropolitan Museum of Art*)

Mother wore on the picnic when Father proposed and a piece of Baby's christening bonnet. The different periods of American history are also reflected in the quilt designs. Colonial quilts resemble those made in Europe, and Revolutionary quilts took on a French accent, but in the pioneer period when the West was being settled, quilts became distinctly American in design, material, and workmanship.

The Crazy Quilt is an American product. It was first made in colonial days when new materials were not available or were too expensive, thus the old quilt was patched with whatever material was at hand. It was usually an odd piece left over from a dress. These pieces were also saved to make a new quilt. In the pieced crazy quilt there was no planned pattern or color. Each piece was fitted together as in a picture puzzle. Pieces of wool were put together with linen or calico regardless of size or color. The "Hit or Miss" was the next step in quilt making. Pieces were cut in uniform size and shape, but were pieced together without regard for color or material. Next, colors were sorted and arranged in rows to make the "Roman Stripe" with alternating stripes of light and dark. Alternating squares of dark and light produced the "Brick Wall." Another one-piece design was the Honeycomb. Real design began with the use of the triangle, when the pieces were carefully cut out and pieced together according to a plan of color and design.

The simplest patterns were made up of different arrangements of the four-patch block. One of the simplest designs used in the nineteenth century was the nine-patch Checkerboard. The nine squares of varicolored materials were set on their points and alternated with squares of white muslin. When put together with small blocks the Nine-Patch Chain was made. There were many other variations of this simple square design and oblong patches were set together to form the Zig-Zag. Squares, circles, and triangles were the foundation of many other designs which were given such imaginative names as "Windmill," "Fox and Geese," "Pincushion," "Sunburst," "Star of the East," "Morning Star," and "Flying Birds." Another typical American nineteenth century design was the "Log Cabin." Narrow "logs" were fitted together about a center square. This design was especially popular after the Civil War. There were many geometric variations of this pattern such as "Courthouse Steps" and "Windmill Blades." These quilts usually had turkey-red center squares.

Other popular pieced-work quilt patterns were "Le Moyne Star," "Boxes," and the intricate "Star of Bethlehem" and "Wheel of Fortune." There are also a group of religious quilt patterns among the pieced quilt designs. These include the "Christian Cross," "Star and Cross," "Jacob's Ladder," "Job's Tears," "King David's Crown," "Crown of Thorns," "Garden of Eden," "Golden Gates" and "World Without End."

Sometimes pieced work was combined with appliqué. Appliqué quilts demand more expert workmanship, however, for the design must

Foundation Rose and Pine Tree, red calico with yellow and green. Third quarter 19th century. (*Shelburne Museum*)

first be cut, then turned and hemmed before the final process of appliqué. Although there are geometrical design appliqué quilts, the most popular designs were floral, and of all flowers the rose had top priority. There is the beautiful "Rose of Sharon" made of red and pink calico with green

Patchwork "crazy quilt" of velvet put together with various embroidery stitches. 1890–1900. (*The Henry Ford Museum*)

leaves and stems, " The Rose Wreath," "Cactus Rose," "Rose Tree," "Rose of Dixie," "Wild Rose," and dozens more. Other flower designs included the "Aster," "Bleeding Hearts," "Cockscomb," "Dahlia," "Daisy," "Poppy," "Lily," "Prairie Flower," "Sunflowers," and "Tulip." There were "Autumn Leaf," "Oak Leaf," and "Laurel Leaf" designs and "Christmas Tree," "Charter Oak," "Cherry Tree and Birds," and "Tree of Life." There were also many kinds of fruit designs and designs with birds and animals—some naturalistic and some geometric or symbolic. The basket group includes some of the most popular and decorative designs. There were "Basket of Daisies," "Basket of Oranges," "Rose Basket," "Tulip Basket" and "Grandmother's Basket."

Many quilts were named after people. These patterns include "Cleopatra's Puzzle," "Fanny's Fan," "Martha Washington Star," "Mrs. Cleveland's Choice," and "Peeny Pen's Cottage." Designs were also named after games and puzzles such as "Jack-in-the-Box," "Merry-Go-Round," "Puss-in-the-Corner" and "Tic-Tac-Toe." Especially interesting to the collector is the group of quilts made for special occasions such as the "Bridal Wreath" quilt which had hearts set in the well-known wreath design. "Wedding Ring," "Bridal Stairway" and "Game of Hearts" were other nuptial patterns. Usually these quilts were sewn at quilting parties held to announce the engagement of a happy pair.

Other quilts made by a group were the Friendship. Presentation, Autograph and Album quilts. They were made by exchanging quilt blocks among a group of friends. As the name indicated, they expressed admiration or friendship for a particular person and the presentation took place at a gathering where each block was presented, then assembled and stitched. Many of the blocks were signed with names embroidered, cross-stitched or written in indelible ink. Each block was different in design and no set pattern was followed.

Historical or political quilts are among the most interesting and valuable quilts for collectors. These included flag quilts with star and eagle emblems. These quilts can usually be dated by the number of stars. Such patterns as "Cleveland Tulips," "Garfield's Monument," "Harrison Rose," "Kansas Sunflower," "Peary's Expedition," "Tippecanoe and Tyler Too," "Union Star," and "Confederate Rose" have political implications. It is also possible to trace the pioneer trail westward by the various quilt names. "Road to California," "Prairie Lily," and "Log Cabin" tell the history of settlement. The westward move from state to state is also recorded in the names of quilt patterns. There was "Boston Beauty," "New Jersey Rose," "Ohio Beauty," "Indiana Rose," "Kansas Sunflower," "Kentucky Peony," "Missouri Star," "St. Louis Star," "Star of Texas," and "California Star." Many of these names are variations of the original star and rose patterns. Elizabeth Wells Robinson lists over a hundred star patterns and almost fifty rose pattern variations.

Two unique historical quilts made in the third quarter of the nineteenth century are in the collection of the Shelburne Museum. One is the Civil War counterpane which is a combination of pieced work and appliqué with figures of cavalry and foot soldiers, animals, and a figure cut from the ad of Baker's Chocolate. The Abraham Lincoln spread includes a block with a seated figure of Lincoln and a block showing the Lincoln-Douglas debate. There are also blocks with animals, flowers, a clock, a Bible open to Psalms 103 and 104 and a vase of flowers on a table. The quilt is signed and dated February 10, 1865.

Late in the nineteenth century the lowly crazy quilt was revived, but velvets and silks were used instead of cotton and wool and the quilt was used as a throw for the couch or a cover for the parlor table. The various shaped pieces of the quilt were fastened together with a variety of feather stitches in silk floss and even the centers of the patches were ornamented with fanciful embroidery flower sprays, fruits, hearts, horseshoes, fans, and hand-painted designs on plush. Although these silk crazy quilts took endless hours of work and some of them contain intricate stitchery, many have been relegated to the scrap bag, the Good Will or the Salvation Army. Today, however, they are being collected again and even displayed and used. If you have one, keep it.

After the designs were pieced or appliquéd the actual quilting was done. The purpose of the quilting is to hold the pieced or appliquéd quilt top to its back and lining. The simplest quilting consisted of vertical, horizontal, or diagonal lines. When diagonal lines crossed they formed a diamond pattern. Leaves, vines, and interlacing squares, diamonds, and circles are used as borders, and plain blocks and borders are filled with geometric squares and circles. Sometimes the design of the appliqué square such as a basket is repeated in the background quilted square. Quilting designs include shells, feathers, wreaths, harps, stars, birds, peacock feathers, doves, eagles and rosettes. Religious motifs such as crosses and patriotic symbols such as anchors, flags and Liberty Bells often appear in quilted backgrounds.

Collecting quilts can be a fascinating hobby, whether you are

Civil War quilt, chintz, Scotch gingham, calicoes on homespun linen backing. Colors brown, cream, blue, rose and dull reds. Third quarter 19th century. (*Shelburne Museum*)

looking for a few as covers for your antique beds or whether you are form-ing a collection. Quilts of the American Victorian period are a distinct form of American folk art. The majority of the patterns were originated by the American needlewoman, for the European influence had disap-peared by the mid-nineteenth century. You can collect quilts for pat-tern, for color, or for beautiful handwork. Be sure the quilt is in perfect condition, unless it happens to be a historical quilt, where some wear and fading is permissible. Quilts that are signed or dated are also rare, as are friendship and autograph quilts. Appliqué quilts with intricate patterns of flowers or long slender lines such as the Mariner's Compass should be noted for good needlework. Quilts with elaborate quilted backgrounds are rare and expensive. Color as well as pattern is an im-portant consideration in quilt collecting. Some quilts have such beautiful color combinations that the maker must certainly have been an accom-plished artist working with the needle instead of the brush. You can find quilts in country antique shops and at country auctions. Quilts are still being made in rural districts and exhibited at county and state fairs so if you want a quilt and not necessarily an antique one, go to the fair!

Hand-Painted China

CHINA painting was among the accomplishments of the fashionable Victorian lady and if we are to judge from the literature on the subject, china painting had priority over such other fashionable handicrafts as hair work, needlework or leather work. The craze for china painting which was popular in England and the Continent from the middle of the nineteenth century did not become the vogue in America until some years later.

The first china painting classes in America were those taught by Edward Lycett, formerly of Staffordshire, England. He came to America and established a china decorating business in New York in 1861, where he employed thirty or forty people painting and gilding imported and some American porcelain wares. His first classes in china painting were organized in New York after the Civil War. Later Lycett taught classes at the St. Louis School of Design and in Cincinnati. He decorated some stoneware for a company in East Liverpool, Ohio, in 1879. He also decorated vases for the Jersey City Pottery. In 1884 Lycett joined the Faience Manufacturing Company of Greenpoint, Long Island, and assumed direction of the factory. He designed new shapes with richly embellished ornamentation and embossed and perforated work on the handles and foot. The shapes showed Persian and Moorish influence. Lycett's three sons were also china decorators at the factory and for many years were actively engaged in teaching china painting as well— William Lycett in Atlanta, Georgia; F. Lycett in Bridgeport, Connecticut; and Joseph Lycett in Brooklyn. An original vase by Edward Lycett is in the Henry Ford Museum, and a plate with game decoration is in the New-York Historical Society.

The second step in the development of china painting in America was taken in Cincinnati, Ohio, in 1875. Benn Pitman, the Director of the Cincinnati School of Design, organized a class in china painting which was taught by Miss Eggers, a German lady who had studied at Dresden. There were many talented women in this class, including M. Louise McLaughlin, whose pottery, when exhibited at the Centennial in Philadelphia and in Paris, won special recognition. From this successful class the interest in pottery and china painting spread rapidly and in a short time there were china painting classes in all big cities throughout the country. Young ladies' seminaries and art schools included china painting in their curricula, china painting was taught at Chautauqua, and by 1900 there were courses in china painting at the International Correspondence School. China painting clubs also sprang up all over the country. Indeed, china painting, which has been looked upon as perhaps the worst Victorian horror, was the most stylish attainment of the ladies of the gay nineties. Also, although china painting was an amateur accomplishment, it was treated with esteem and given serious approval, and even in the art world its acclaim was world wide. Exhibits of china painting were held in London (The First Annual Exhibition of China Painting in 1875); at the Centennial Exposition in Philadelphia in 1876; at the National Academy of Design in New York in 1878; at the Exposition Universelle at Paris in 1879; and at the Brussels Exposition in 1881.

RIGHT. Plate decorated with panels of game by Edward Lycett, c. 1877. (*The New-York Historical Society*) LEFT. Vase made for Edwin A. Barber by Joseph Lycett at Faience Manufacturing Co., Greenpoint, New York, 1889. (*The Henry Ford Museum*)

The first annual exhibition of china or mineral painting in America was held in Chicago in June, 1888.

China painting had thus not only become the craze but was also an accepted branch of decorative art. At least a dozen books on china painting were published in America and many more published in England were available in American shops from 1875 down into the twentieth century. The best-known books were by M. Louise McLaughlin of Cincinnati whose *China Painting: a Practical Manual* was published in 1878. Camille Piton, the Principal of the National Art Training School, also published *A Practical Treatise on China Painting in America* in 1878, and in 1888, A. H. Osgood, the Director of Osgood's Art School, published *How to Apply Royal Worcester, Matt, Bronze, La Croix and Dresden Colors to China*. The advertisement of the Osgood Art School which appeared in *The China Decorator* in 1888 gives considerable information about china painting in America at this time. Instruction was $1.00 for a three-hour lesson, six lessons for $5.00. The ad read as follows: "Mineral painting upon china—heads, figures, landscape, flowers. Royal Worcester, Doulton, Dresden methods. Fruit, fish, game. Pupils are supplied with original designs to copy from. (China fired daily. 5 kilns.) French and English china, also American Faience. Hand-colored Royal Worcester and Doulton decoration suitable for lamps, vases, plaques. Royal Worcester, Matt and Bronze colors. La Croix colors. Royal Dresden colors. Special directions for Fish. Twelve different designs." Mrs. Osgood also gives a few notes on the different kinds of china available for paintings. She recommends Berlin porcelain for figure painting and French porcelain for its general excellence. "Of English ware Copeland's (Spode) has a blue-white glaze. Minton's has a gray tone and Doulton is creamy—good for pinks and gold. American ware is beautiful and unique in forms for table and art pieces. Trenton Ware has a creamy glaze and delicate finish." Mustache cups and rose jars of Teplitz Ware from Germany were also available to amateur china painters.

The Book of the China Painter by L. Vance-Phillips, the teacher at Chautauqua, was published in 1896. In addition to the many books, *The China Decorator,* a magazine devoted to china painting, was published from 1887 to the end of the century and the *Art Amateur* (1879–91) also contained a section devoted to china painting.

In the 1870's the National League of Mineral Painters held competitions for designs for a government table service for state dinners. It would seem that this competition did not produce the desired designs, but it did create interest, for in 1879 Mrs. Hayes, wife of President Hayes, retained the New Jersey artist Theodore R. Davis to design shapes and water color studies for a complete set of china for the White House. These designs were of American flora and fauna, including corn, goldenrod, buffalo, wild turkey, a scene of Indians, Harvest Moon, Clam Bake and Clam Chowder, and a scene of the artist's studio in Asbury Park, New Jersey. An effort was made to have this china made at a New Jersey pottery, but when this could not be done in the time alloted, the china was made by Haviland in Limoges, France. A year later this china was reproduced by Haviland and sold in New York by Davis, Collamore.

Haviland china plates painted by Nellie Bonham Foreman of Charlotte, Michigan, c. 1891. (*The Henry Ford Museum*)

Any of these pieces are collector's items today. Mrs. Harrison, the wife of a later President, was herself an active china painter. Some of her original designs of corn and goldenrod were used on Limoges plates for the White House.

In general the shapes and designs of hand-painted china were typical of the era and had a definite Victorian flavor. Tops of bowls and lips of vases were crimped. Handles and feet of many vases were in the form of lion's heads and feet, grotesque masques or cupids, and many vases had handles and bases of ornate perforated work. Designs included cupids, veiled figures, and flowers in the Japanese manner. Persian, Moorish and Renaissance influences were also seen in both forms and decoration. Although patterns of Royal Worcester, Doulton, Wedgwood, Royal Vienna and Dresden were copied, many of these designs were beyond the talents of the average amateur, so that simpler designs of flowers, butterflies, birds and fruits were used. Violets, pansies, chrysanthemums, poppies, morning-glory, passion flower, cactus, wild roses, clematis and periwinkle were favorite flowers; cherries, grapes, peaches, currants, blackberries and gooseberries were popular fruits.

Sets of fish, game, fruit, and nut plates had appropriate designs. The fish set usually included various kinds of fish amid grasses, seaweed, shells and rocks. Fishing rods, creels and flies often completed the scene.

Salmon were reserved for the platter. The game set included different species of game,—redhead ducks, peacocks, wild geese, mallard ducks, clover pheasants, canvasbacks, woodcocks, partridge, snipe, teal, prairie chickens, with wild turkeys on the platter. Fruit plates would have various kinds of fruit in their centers. Sprays of leaves and nuts decorated nut plates, while the ice cream dishes were painted with winter scenes. The punch bowl usually was decorated with grapes and leaves. The bread plate had sprays of wheat, and for oatmeal there was a bowl and saucer decorated with oak leaves and acorns. *The Art Amateur*, 1889, contained an article on cupid designs after Boucher, and Amelia G. Austin in her series of articles in *Ladies' Home Journal* says: "No branch of mineral painting is more fascinating than the painting of cupids and tiny heads."

China painting is scorned today and rightly so, since pieces available are generally of the worst amateur variety. However, many of the teachers and designers were artists of ability who were recognized in the art world of their time. One of these was Charles Volkmar who had studied in Paris

LEFT. Porcelain vase, Knowles, Taylor & Knowles, painted by Harry R. Thompson, 1891–1898. (*The Henry Ford Museum*) CENTER. Vase with designs of landscape and cattle painted by Charles Volkmar, c. 1881. (*The Brooklyn Museum*) RIGHT. Covered pitcher with grotesque dragon handle and chrysanthemum decoration attributed to Joseph Lycett, Faience Manufacturing Co., c. 1890. (*The Henry Ford Museum*)

under Harpignies and others, and was known for his paintings of landscape and cattle. While in Paris, Volkmar became interested in the Limoges method of underglaze painting. He worked in one of the potteries to learn the secrets of the process. When he came back to America in 1879 he built a kiln in Greenpoint, Long Island, and manufactured vases and tiles. These were marked "Ⅴ." In 1895 Volkmar established the Volkmar Keramic Company. These products are decorated with underglaze blue designs of historical buildings and American portraits. They are marked "Volkmar" with raised letters. Later together with Kate Cory, Volkmar opened a pottery at Corona, New York, and the mark here was "Volkmar and Cory Crown Point Ware" impressed. Vases with plain green glazes were marked "V" in 1896. Later Volkmar was engaged in architectural work in the William Rockefeller Mansion in Tarrytown, New York, in the Boston Public Library, and also many other residences of prominent people.

In 1903 Volkmar established a works at Metuchen, New Jersey, and made tiles, lamps and umbrella stands. The patterns were made by the running of the glaze. There were sprays of foliage and decorative patterns on white grounds with glazed orange linings in the bowls. Tile designs included ducks, also tiles with designs of Dutch Windmills by Volkmar are shown in the *Book of the China Painter* by L. Vance-Phillips, and there are designs for a game service and for a fish service also by Charles Volkmar. These designs would surely be beyond the ability of the average amateur and if any such plates were found today they would undoubtedly be well executed and worth collecting. Since each design was signed perhaps they were engravings of actual pieces which Volkmar himself decorated.

Another artist of ability who taught china painting and furnished designs for amateurs was Camille Piton, the Principal of the National Art Training School. Some of Piton's designs together with directions for painting are included in the *Art Amateur* as supplements. These included the following plate designs: Morning-glories; Blackberries; Pink Azalea; Pyrus Japonica; Wild Roses and Wheat; Poppies, Daisies and Wild Asparagus; Horse Chestnuts and Dogwood; and Vesuvius in Eruption seen from the Amalfi Drive. Piton also furnished the designs for hand-painted plaques including the following subjects: Fair Yseult, Sarah Bernhardt, Le Bel Ysambeau, Fleur de Pommier, a Lady and Gentleman of the XVI century, and In the Greenwood. Especially interesting is the plate design of Corn and Squash. Original designs for plates and plaques by Georges Wagner were also illustrated. These included Chicks and Mushrooms, Bird and Willow, and Mouse and Wheat.

George Theophilus Collins was another china painter and teacher in New York, who had studied in both Meissen and Sèvres potteries. Collins' designs for vases, bowls, cups and saucers and chocolate pots were illustrated in *The China Decorator*. These designs included a bowl with raspberry design, a wisteria vase, poppy vase, chestnut, wheat and daisies, ferns, sweet peas, heliotrope, pussy willow and Easter lilies. A teapot with animal handle and spout and bird finial has a design of flowers and rococo shells and scrolls. E. Aulich, another New York china painting teacher who operated a shop for decorating lamp globes, also furnished designs illustrated in *The China Decorator*. In the 1900 issue a color supplement of his familiar design of white roses on a round lamp globe was included. A design for corn and wheat on a simple pottery jug was by H. W. Staradin who also furnished many other designs for *The China Decorator*. Louis Prang & Co. also made many colored chromos of plate designs for hand painting.

There were 20,000 professional china painters and probably twice that many amateurs in 1905. *The China Decorator* lists Franz A. Bischoff, a well-known artist of Detroit, together with Aulich, Marshall Fry, Miss Mason, Mrs. Leonard and Mrs. Robineau (Adelaide Alsop Robineau, who later became famous for her own pottery, started as a china painter) as the best china painters of the 1880's. Marshall Fry was a well-known New York decorator and W. A. Mason was an instructor at the Pennsylvania Museum School. A china painting design of holly by Mrs. Mason was illustrated in the *Art Amateur* January, 1887. Mrs. Leonard was from Cincinnati.

There are several different methods of china painting. The majority of the pieces of amateur china painting are done by the overglaze technique, that is, the painting is applied to the glazed surface that has previously been fired. The colors are then refired at a low temperature. Underglaze painting is done on the biscuit china before it is glazed. Colors are then applied and the surface fired with high heat. Underglaze is the oil painting of the ceramic artist.

The women of the Cincinnati Pottery Club used both overglaze and underglaze methods. Miss McLaughlin worked and taught the Limoges or pâte-sur-pâte method of painting the surfaces of unbaked pieces with colored slips. The colors mixed with clay and water were applied to the damp clay and water surface.

By far the largest American pottery which catered to the amateur china painter was the Willets Manufacturing Co. of Trenton, New Jersey. Under the title of "The Celebrated Willets' Art Porcelain For Amateur Decoration" many pages of illustrations of the various articles and shapes appeared in *The China Decorator* between 1887 and 1889. These included tea cups, after dinner coffee cups, bowls with crinkled edges, and vases with perforated handles, covers, and bases. There are also vases and bowls with rustic handles and stands and bowls and bottles of wicker design. A rustic tree trunk with acorns holds a cornucopia vase and another tree trunk vase has a basket and jug at its base. There are also interesting bamboo jugs and a bamboo teapot, sugar and creamer. A squat jug or pitcher has a fancy handle and a masque spout.

Vase made by Willets Manufacturing Co., c. 1880. Overglaze decoration by amateur china painter. (*The New-York Historical Society*)

However, the finest designs are those of shell or flower forms. There is a delicate three-inch water lily vase and a lily cup on its lily-pad saucer. A fluted shell compote stands on a rustic base decorated with small shells and there is a small 2½ inch shell vase on a stand and a larger 7½ inch shell jug with coral handle. The most graceful and important piece is the shell and cupid jug. This jug was illustrated as the colored supplement of *The China Decorator* in March, 1888, with a description of its color—pink, white, pale green and gold. The jug (9½" x 9½") in blank Belleek porcelian for decorating could be purchased for $12.00. A duplicate jug in the Newark Museum is marked "W.S.L. 1887" and is said to have been designed by Walter Lenox when he was working at Ott & Brewer. However, the jug was never copyrighted and must have been the property of several New Jersey potters. In comparison with the prices of other blanks for decorating, which ranged from a few cents to several dollars, twelve dollars was expensive. Probably few of these jugs were decorated by amateurs and those which were decorated must have been highly prized.

Although the majority of the pieces of hand-painted china available to the collector are poor in both design and painting, there was a great deal of excellent amateur china painting and good pieces must eventually come on the market. The collector should first of all look for good design and good painting. Any designs which can be traced to a known designer are interesting for a collection. Also, signed pieces even if they are not by any of the well-known painters add interest to a collection. Pieces by such men as Lycett are especially valuable as are articles marked with the name of an American manufacturer of blanks such as Ott & Brewer or Willets. Many factors enter into collecting. A piece of pottery or china may possess a shape, color, or quality of glaze which will make it attractive regardless of any attribution to a particular decorator or potter and thus, aside from its esthetic or ceramic value, some collector will be attracted to it. On the other hand many ugly pieces are collected because they are marked and thus valuable.

Although the bulk of undecorated china for amateur decorators came from abroad there were many companies in America which provided china in the plain biscuit state. Among the first was A. H. Hews and Company of Cambridge, Massachusetts. In addition to machine-made flower pots this company made a specialty of art pottery reproductions of antique Grecian, Roman, Etruscan, Phoenician and Cypriote models. They also furnished ware in the plain biscuit for decorators which was known as Albert and Albertine Ware. One of the first books published in America which included a reference to amateur pottery decoration was *Art Recreations: A Guide to Decorative Art* published by S. W. Tilton, Boston, 1877. This book includes designs and instructions for decorating Albert Ware using Flaxman's designs and Tilton's colors. This, however, was pottery, not porcelain, and never gained the popularity of china painting on porcelain. Another type of china painting which was popular with the unskilled amateur was the tinting of plaques. In 1880 Juliano Ware by Gyula de Festetics was manufactured for this purpose. It consisted of modelled plaques of lightly baked or unbaked biscuit clay which could be tinted with watercolor. The designs illustrated in the *Art Amateur*, May 1880, included Daisies, Water Lily, and Birds and Fruit Blossoms. This was not real china painting but an art recreation.

Many American pottery manufacturers furnished blanks for the serious china painter. Between 1884 and 1892 the Jersey City Pottery furnished glazed ivory white ware for decorators, including the "Worcester" vase which was a reproduction of an old pattern produced at the Worcester Works in England. Another style was called the "King" vase. These forms decorated by Edward Lycett and his son William Lycett are illustrated by Edwin Atlee Barber in *Pottery and Porcelain of the United States*. In 1887 Bawo and Dotter, dealers in chinaware in New York City, offered a price list and illustrations of over 200 items of chinaware decorated and undecorated. They sold Haviland Limoges, "Worcester and Royal Vienna for copying." Blanks included cups and saucers of various shapes, vases, creams, sugar baskets, plates, leaf and cake plates, also bone dishes, cheese dishes, and rose jars. Willets "Art Ware" for decorating included a bowl with rustic stand, wicker and shell designs. Also "Ott and Brewer Belleek to decorate beautifully." Another pottery which sold white china for decorating was the American Art China Works of Trenton, New Jersey, established in 1891. Their ware was thin, translucent and strong and resembled Belleek. Also in 1891 The Ceramic Art Company (Coxon and Lenox) advertised: "Fine Porcelains for high class decoration. Original and exclusive designs and shapes. Belleek. Pretty conceits in tableware, trays, after dinner coffees all in egg-shell china. White ware for amateur decoration." On a back page of the 1893 edition of Barber's *Pottery and Porcelain of the United States* the Knowles, Taylor & Knowles Co., East Liverpool, Ohio, advertised Lotus Ware and added this paragraph. "This ware is adapted to the requirements of amateur or professional decorators, and may be obtained usually through first-class crockery dealers. It is of a variety peculiar to itself; very pure and translucent in character, having a beautiful, soft, transparent glaze. It is made in artistic shapes designed for practical utility." Lotus Ware decorated at the pottery was marked "K.T.K. Co., Lotus Ware" with the date and initial of the decorator. The Kezonta ware of the Cincinnati Art pottery was a deep blue and white pottery made for decorators. The forms are modifications of Greek and Roman shapes and many ladies painted these for the market. The mark was "KEZ-ONTA" impressed.

Punch bowl and cups, Limoges china. Painted by George Leykauf, Detroit, Michigan. Awarded bronze medal at Columbian Exposition, 1893. (*The Henry Ford Museum*)

BOOKS FOR FURTHER READING

FURNITURE IN GENERAL

ANDREWS, EDWARD DEEMING AND FAITH, *Shaker Furniture.* Dover Publications, New York, 1937.
BAIRD, HENRY CAREY, *Cabinet Maker's Album of Furniture.* Philadelphia, 1868.
COMSTOCK, HELEN, *American Furniture.* (Studio) Viking. New York, 1962.
CONNER, ROBERT, *Cabinet Maker's Assistant.* New York, 1842.
DOWNING, ANDREW J. *Architecture of Country Houses.* New York, 1850.
EASTWOOD, CHARLES LOCKE, *Hints on Household Taste.* New York, 1872.
HALL, JOHN, *The Cabinet Maker's Assistant.* Baltimore, 1840.
KOVEL, RALPH AND TERRY, *American Country Furniture.* Crown Publishers, New York, 1965.
LEA, ZILLA RIDER, *The Ornamental Chair.* Charles E. Tuttle Co., Rutland, Vt.
MILLER, EDGAR A., JR. *American Antique Furniture* (2 vols.). (Studio) Viking. M. Barrows & Co.,
    New York, 1937.
OTTO, CELIA JACKSON, *American Furniture of the Nineteenth Century.* The Viking Press, 1965.
ROBACHER, EARL F. *Touch of the Dutchland.* A. S. Barnes & Co., Inc., 1965.
SCHWARTZ, MARVIN D., *Victoriana,* Catalogue of Loan Exhibition. Brooklyn Museum, Brooklyn, N.Y. 1960.
SMITH, WALTER, *The Masterpieces of the Centennial International Exhibition,* Vol. II, Industrial Art.
    Philadelphia, 1876.

COTTAGE FURNITURE

ANDREW J. DOWNING, *Architecture of Country Houses.* New York, 1850.
ANDREW J. DOWNING, *Cottage Residences.* New York, 1844.
Godey's Lady's Magazine, 1849 pp, 60, 132, 276.

PAPIER MÂCHÉ

Antiques Magazine, August, 1960.
McCLINTON, KATHARINE MORRISON, *Handbook of Popular Antiques.* Random House, 1945 Bonanza, 1963.

DECORATIVE ACCESSORIES

DREPPERD, CARL W., *American Clocks & Clockmakers.* Branford.
HEYDENRYK, HENRY, *Art and History of Frames.* Jas. H. Heineman, Inc., New York, 1963.
McCLINTON, KATHARINE MORRISON, *Antique Collecting for Everyone.* McGraw Hill, New York, 1951.
Bonanza, 1964.
PALMER, BROOKS, *American Clocks.* The Macmillan Co., New York, 1950.

ROGERS GROUPS

Rogers Groups in The New-York Historical Society by Dorothy C. Barck, *Quarterly Bulletin,* October, 1932.
Rogers Letters, Notebook, and Clippings, (7 boxes) The New-York Historical Society.

CURRIER & IVES AND OTHER LITHOGRAPHERS

PETERS, HARRY T. *Currier & Ives, Print makers to the American People,* Vols. I and II. Doubleday, Doran & Co.
PRANG, LOUIS & Co. *Catalogue,* 1876.
PRANG, LOUIS & Co. Publishers' Proofs, Vols. 1-15.

PRIMITIVE PAINTING

Boston Museum of Fine Arts, Maxim Karlick Collection.
FORD, ALICE, *Pictorial Folk Art New England to California.*
LIPMAN, JEAN, *American Primitive Painting.* Oxford Univ. Press. 1942.
Studio Publications, 1949.

THE VICTORIAN DINING ROOM

HARRISON, CONSTANCE GARY, *Woman's Handiwork in Modern Homes*. Charles Scribner's Sons, New York, 1881.
HIBBERD, SHIRLEY, *Rustic Ornaments for Homes of Taste*. London, 1856.
SHERMAN, ELLEN EWING, *Practical Cooking and Dinner Giving*. 1876.
SHERWOOD, MRS. JOHN, *Manners and Social Uses*. Harpers, New York, 1884.
VON FALKE, JACOB, *Art in the House*. L. Prang & Co. Boston, 1879.

GLASS

BELKNAP, E. MCCAMLY, *Milk Glass*, Crown Publishers, New York.
BERGSTROM, L. R., *Old Glass Paper Weights*. Crown Publishers.
DANIEL, DOROTHY E., *Cut and Engraved Glass*. Barrows, 1950.
KOCH, ROBERT, *Louis C. Tiffany, Rebel in Glass*. Crown Publishers, New York, 1964.
LEE, RUTH WEBB. *Early American Pressed Glass*. Lee Publishers.
MCCLINTON, KATHARINE MORRISON, *American Glass*. World Publishing Co., 1950.
MCCLINTON, KATHARINE MORRISON, *Handbook of Popular Antiques*. Random House, 1945.
MCKEARIN, GEORGE S. AND HELEN, *American Glass*. Crown Publishers, 1948.
PEARSON, J. M. AND D. T., *American Cut Glass for the Discriminating Collector*. Vantage Press, 1965.
PRESZNICK, ROSE M., *Carnival Glass Books*.
REVI, A. CHRISTIAN, *Nineteenth Century Glass*. Thos. Nelson, 1959.
REVI, A. CHRISTIAN, *American Cut and Engraved Glass*. Nelson, 1965.

SILVER AND SILVER PLATE

Art Journal, 1875, 1876
Catalogues: Reed & Barton, 1885; Meriden Britannia; James W. Tufts; Gorham & Co. (All 19th Century) Whiting & Co. Catalogue, 1895.
FREEMAN, LARRY AND BEAUMONT, JANE, *Early American Plated Silver*. Century House, Watkins Glenn, 1949.
Jewelers' Circular, 1885.
KOVEL, RALPH M. AND TERRY, *A Directory of American Silver Pewter & Silver Plate*. Crown Publishers, New York, 1961.
MCCLINTON, KATHARINE MORRISON, *The Complete Book of Small Antique Collecting*. Coward-McCann, 1965.

POTTERY AND PORCELAIN

BARBER, EDWIN ATLEE, *The Pottery and Porcelain of the United States*. G. P. Putnam, New York (1893, 1902, 1909.)
BARRET, RICHARD CARTER, *Bennington Pottery and Porcelain*. Crown Publishers, New York, 1958.
KOCH, ROBERT, *Rockwood Pottery. Antiques Magazine*, March, 1960. Rockwood Catalogue, 1904.

LADIES' HANDIWORK

CARLISLE, LILLIAN BAKER, *Pieced and Appliqué Quilts at Shelburne Museum*. Shelburne Museum.
FINLEY, RUTH, *Old Patchwork Quilts*. Lippincott, Philadelphia, 1929.
HARTLEY, FLORENCE, *Ladies' Handbook of Fancy and Ornamental Work*.
LELAND, CHARLES G., *A Manual of Wood Carving. Art Amateur*. New York, 1879–1891.
MRS. PULLAN, *Ladies' Manual of Fancy Work*. New York, 1859.
PETO, FLORENCE, *American Quilts and Coverlets*. Chanticleer Press, New York, 1949.
ROBERTSON, ELIZABETH WELLS, *American Quilts*. Studio Publications, New York, 1948.
URBINO, LEVINA, *Art Recreations*. J. F. Tilton, Boston, 1859.

CHINA PAINTING

LITTLE, RUTH, *Painting China for Pleasure and Profit*. Little, Lubbock, Texas.
MCLAUGHLIN, LOUISE, *China Painting, A Practical Manual*. New York, 1878.
PHILLIPS, L. VANCE, *Book of the China Painter*. 1896.
PITON, C., *Practical Treatise on China Painting in America*. J. Wiley & Sons, 1878.
The China Painter. New York, 1887–1900.

INDEX